# BOOKS BY JEROME WEIDMAN

### NOVELS

I CAN GET IT FOR YOU WHOLESALE
WHAT'S IN IT FOR ME?
I'LL NEVER GO THERE ANY MORE
THE LIGHTS AROUND THE SHORE
TOO EARLY TO TELL
THE PRICE IS RIGHT
THE HAND OF THE HUNTER
GIVE ME YOUR LOVE
THE THIRD ANGEL
YOUR DAUGHTER IRIS
THE ENEMY CAMP
BEFORE YOU GO
THE SOUND OF BOW BELLS
WORD OF MOUTH

### SHORT STORIES

THE HORSE THAT COULD WHISTLE "DIXIE"
THE CAPTAIN'S TIGER
A DIME A THROW
MY FATHER SITS IN THE DARK
NINE STORIES
THE DEATH OF DICKIE DRAPER
 *and Nine Other Stories*

### ESSAYS AND TRAVEL

LETTER OF CREDIT
TRAVELER'S CHEQUE
BACK TALK

### MUSICAL PLAYS

FIORELLO! *
TENDERLOIN *
I CAN GET IT FOR YOU WHOLESALE †

* *with George Abbott, Jerry Bock, and Sheldon Harnick*
† *with Harold Rome*

# THE DEATH OF DICKIE DRAPER

*and Nine Other Stories*

# JEROME WEIDMAN

# THE DEATH OF DICKIE DRAPER
## and Nine Other Stories

 *Random House   New York*

FOR

*Bennett*

AND

*Phyllis*

# CONTENTS

# THE
# DEATH
# OF
# DICKIE
# DRAPER

ntil a few
minutes before noon, Breedon had no idea what he looked
like.

This was odd. Almost incredible. Because several times
during the morning Breedon had examined himself carefully in a
number of mirrors. He could remember doing it.

First, in the small glass on the wall of Mr. Kinsey's office,
where the warden himself had presented Breedon with the
double-breasted blue suit and, smiling encouragingly, had
helped him try on the coat. Then, in the oval-shaped mirror in
Mrs. Kinsey's living room, while Breedon was saying goodbye to
the warden's wife. And finally, in the cracked square of glass
over the chewing gum machine on the Jutger's Junction station
platform, while Breedon was waiting for the eleven o'clock train
to Manitaw City.

It was a three-hour run from the small prison town, in the
northeastern corner of the state near the Canadian border, to the
nation's fourth largest city on the western shore of Lake Michigan. Or so the timetable said, and Breedon had been content to
take the timetable's word for it. During that first hour, anyway,
when his mind had been a pleasant mixture of reverie and
anticipation.

Then, all at once, he had become restless. Breedon didn't
know why.

The fact that the train was almost empty may have had
something to do with it. He had lived for too many years as a
numbered member of a large interdependent group to accept so
quickly the fact that he was now completely on his own. And
Breedon did not doubt that the fog rolling in off the Great Lakes
contributed to his restlessness. Even after all those years in
Jutger's Junction, Breedon had not learned to live with that
fog.

Whatever the cause of his restlessness, it had driven Breedon from his seat in the coach. Moving down the swaying aisle, not quite sure where he was going, Breedon had felt a sudden desire to see what he looked like. It was as though, unexpectedly, he had forgotten who he was.

Breedon stepped quickly into the washroom at the end of the car, and he stared into the mirror over the basin. At once, the restlessness fell away. Breedon's sense of identity returned. He knew who he was. He saw clearly what he looked like.

And Breedon was pleased by what he saw: the lean, strong, finely chiseled face of an attractive, intelligent man in his early fifties; a man to whom the years had brought, not only a touch of white at the temples and a network of wrinkles around the alert, brown, sensitive eyes, but also a quality of relaxed maturity. It was the face of a man who, in the race with life, had neither beaten it nor been outdistanced; the face of a man who had kept pace, learning as he went; a man ready to draw on his large store of useful knowledge for the benefit of others as well as himself.

It was, in short, the face of a decent, adult, responsible citizen.

"Who will need his second shave of the day by the time this train gets to his old home town," Breedon said cheerfully into the mirror as he rubbed the faint stubble along the edge of his jaw. "If he wants to look his best."

Breedon did. He wanted to look his very best.

It was strange, he thought as he moved back up the aisle of the swaying train, how some things were impervious to the shock of events and the flow of time. A man's beard, for example. It never changed. No matter what happened to the man, his beard remained the same. Breedon's beard had always been tough. Much too tough for his tender skin. Even as a boy, a prodigy in knickerbockers who had entered the University of Manitaw at fourteen, he had already started to shave. Three years later, the youngest student ever to be admitted to the University's Law School, Breedon had already discovered that, if he had a date at night and wanted to look his best, he had to shave a second time before he went out.

That second shave was a refinement he had not indulged for a long, long time. For almost thirty years, in fact. Today, however, he would indulge it. And Breedon knew where, too.

In Binaggio's Barber Shop, on Gary Street, off Michigan Avenue, just around the corner from the Manitaw, Chicago & Western Railroad Terminal.

Binaggio's had been the only place in the great city that was Breedon's home town where they knew, where they *really* knew, how to shave a man whose beard was too tough for his skin. They knew a lot of things in Binaggio's. Things you would expect to encounter only in the barber shops of Paris and Rome. In Breedon's opinion, it was places like Binaggio's that had raised Manitaw above the level of a huge, reeking stockyard and given it the right to be called, along with Chicago and New York and San Francisco, a truly cosmopolitan American city. Even Ted Bier had shared Breedon's passion for Binaggio's, and Ted Bier had never had a beard at all.

On the day he died, slashed to bloody ribbons in the prison shower room a week after his thirtieth birthday, Ted Bier had still been as round-faced, pink-cheeked, and free of beard stubble as he had been on the day in 1920 when, at the age of fourteen, Breedon had watched the new neighbors, a family named Bier with a boy named Ted, move into the house next door on Lake Superior Road.

Poor Ted. He would never again know the thrill of easing himself back into one of Binaggio's chairs. Well, Arthur Breedon would enjoy that particular thrill for him. He was sure Ted wouldn't mind. On the contrary. Ted would be pleased. If Ted were alive, his generous nature would be delighted by the knowledge that he was the cause of somebody else's pleasure. Especially if that somebody else was Arthur Breedon.

That was one thing the defense had overlooked. Ted Bier's generosity. Even Elmer Haywood, in the great twelve-hour summation that had held the courtroom spellbound and had gone down into the law textbooks, even Elmer Haywood had overlooked Ted Bier's generosity. Of course, neither Elmer Haywood nor the rest of the defense counsel had really known their clients. Not even the psychiatrists employed by the defense had really known the deepest truths about the boys they had tried to explain to the court and save from the gallows. So how could Elmer Haywood possibly have known about Ted's generosity? But Breedon had known. He stopped short.

"Oh," he said. "Excuse me."

A sailor had taken the other half of Breedon's seat. The boy in uniform looked up from the newspaper, saw Breedon, and leaped to his feet.

"Sorry," he said, and he held out the newspaper. "This yours, sir?"

"Yes, but go right ahead," Breedon said. "I'm finished with it."

"You sure, sir?"

"Positive."

"Thank you, sir."

The young sailor waited politely until Breedon had slipped into the seat against the window. Then the boy dropped back into the aisle seat, and he bent forward again over the newspaper. For several moments, Breedon stared out the train window, pretending to be absorbed by the fog. Finally, when he could stand it no longer, Breedon turned and glanced at the newspaper in the boy's hand. His heart leaped with excitement. The paper was still folded back to page three. Exactly as Breedon had left it when his curious restlessness had driven him down the aisle to the washroom. The young sailor was absorbed by the page dominated by the headline:

SOLE SURVIVOR OF FAMED BIER-BREEDON CASE

PAROLED TODAY

Breedon leaned across and tapped the paper with his forefinger. The young sailor looked up.

"Interesting story, that," Breedon said casually. "I happen to know something about it."

He could hear, and was a little amused by, the faint but unmistakable touch of pride in his own voice. Breedon doubted, however, that the boy heard it. The young sailor was too astonished. At any rate, he was staring at Breedon in obvious amazement. Breedon smiled and nodded.

"That's a fact," he said pleasantly. "I happen to know a good deal about it. More than the reporter who wrote that story, anyway. He says Bier and Breedon were sentenced to life imprisonment on September 10, 1924, and were sent up to the Jutger's Junction penitentiary at once, which is true enough, but the reporter omits the fact that there was an additional sentence of ninety-nine years on the second indictment, the indictment for kidnapping, and that's the whole point. The whole point of the parole, I mean."

Breedon paused, and he chuckled slightly. The expression on the young sailor's face may have been a bit ludicrous, but it was also flattering. He was staring at Breedon as though he could not quite believe what he was hearing.

"You see," Breedon said, "in 1945, after he had been in prison more than twenty years, Breedon volunteered as a human guinea pig in a medical experiment. He was inoculated with malaria germs, and he almost died. But almosts don't count, and three years later, in 1948, when he made an application for executive clemency, Breedon not only got it, but a year after that, on June 22, 1949, his ninety-nine year sentence on the kidnapping charge was commuted by the governor to eighty-five years. Under the laws of this state, that made Breedon eligible for a definite sentence parole in December of 1952." Breedon chuckled again as he tapped the dateline at the top of the newspaper in the sailor's hands. "That's why you're reading this story in today's paper, in December 1952."

"What story, sir?"

The puzzlement in the boy's voice caused Breedon to blink.

"Why," Breedon said, and then, as he tapped the headline, his voice became sharp. "*This* story!"

The sailor looked down at the paper.

"Oh," he said, and then he blushed with obvious embarrassment. "I'm sorry, sir," the boy said. "I wasn't reading that, sir." He pointed to a box below the Bier-Breedon story. "I was reading that, sir," the sailor said. "The daily horoscope." He looked at Breedon and apparently gathered, from the expression on the older man's face, that he had hurt Breedon's feelings. "I'm sorry, sir," the boy said, and he added helpfully, "I guess it's a pretty important story. Is that what you mean, sir? That they were big shots or something?"

It was Breedon's turn to stare in astonishment. But the boy seemed quite serious.

"Do you mean to say you never heard of Theodore Bier and Arthur Breedon?" The sailor shook his head. Slowly, on a note of mounting incredulity, Breedon repeated, "You never heard of Theodore Bier and Arthur Breedon?"

The sailor shook his head again.

"No, sir," he said. "Should I have heard of them?"

Breedon drew a deep breath. He was struggling with a sense of shock. It didn't seem possible. It just didn't seem possible.

"The Bier-Breedon Case was the most sensational criminal trial of this century," Breedon said, trying to keep the sudden anger out of his voice. "Twenty-eight years ago, when they were defended by Elmer Haywood, who at that time was the most famous criminal lawyer in the world, they were more widely known than—" Breedon paused, and he looked sharply at the boy. "How old are you?"

"Nineteen, sir."

"Oh," Breedon said, and the anger disappeared from his voice. "I see."

But Breedon didn't really see. It was true that this boy had been born nine years after Ted Bier and Arthur Breedon had been locked away in Jutger's Junction. But how many years had *he* been born after Napoleon had been locked away on St. Helena? Was that any excuse for not knowing an important historical fact? The young sailor seemed to realize that, in some way, he had offended the older man. The boy made an obvious effort to repair the damage by a display of interest.

"What was it all about, sir?" he said politely. He nodded

toward the newspaper. "I mean these two men, this Bier and Breedon," the boy said. "What did they do?"

Breedon hesitated. The sense of excitement and anticipation with which he had lived all morning, the feeling of eagerness with which he had turned toward the young sailor, all that was suddenly gone. The strange restlessness was descending on him again.

"They didn't do anything that would interest you," Breedon said shortly. He stood up. "Besides, it's pretty hard to explain."

It shouldn't have been. Few cases had ever been spread before the eyes of the world in such exhaustive detail. No man knew those details better than Arthur Breedon. And yet, as he stood on the train platform and stared out into the slowly vanishing fog, Breedon found that his reply to the young sailor was absolutely true.

For some puzzling reason, a reason that seemed in an even more puzzling way connected with his strange restlessness, Breedon suddenly found himself incapable of explaining what had happened thirty years ago.

With a sense of panic, as though he could feel his identity slipping away from him again, Breedon turned and hurried back to the washroom. As soon as he saw himself in the mirror over the basin, however, everything was all right. The sensitive, intelligent face in the glass knew nothing of panic. The decent, adult, responsible citizen who stared back at Breedon from the mirror was as reassuring as a vote of confidence. It told Breedon that what had happened thirty years ago, the things he was suddenly incapable of explaining, did not matter.

"The past is dead," said the face in the mirror to the man looking into it. "It is only the future that matters."

And the future, as Breedon had known ever since the governor had commuted his sentence, would begin at two o'clock this afternoon, when the train from Jutger's Junction pulled into Manitaw City.

It pulled in on time.

Swinging down from the iron step with his small bag,

Breedon suddenly understood the meaning of a phrase he had read and heard all his life but had never before thought about: his heart, almost literally, was in his mouth!

Breedon swallowed hard, and he grinned ruefully at his own excitement. It was difficult to believe that he was a man of fifty. Why, he felt like a schoolboy coming home for the holidays!

Unlike a schoolboy, however, Breedon's first thoughts were for that second shave. He wished all at once that he had not accepted by mail Ben Tuttle's offer to meet him at the train. If he were not being met, Breedon could have gone directly around the corner, to Binaggio's. It would have been much more pleasant to face Ben Tuttle, and his briefcase full of legal documents, after a wonderfully luxurious hour in one of Binaggio's chairs. On the other hand, nothing in the world, not even an hour of the full treatment at Binaggio's, could ever make a meeting with Ben Tuttle really pleasant. The sooner he got rid of him, Breedon decided, the better.

He came across the marble floor of the huge vaulted railroad station, and paused near the Information Desk, where Ben Tuttle had said in his letter he would be waiting. Breedon set down his bag and looked around. There was no sign of Ben. This was odd. Breedon's father used to say that the main reason why he had chosen the firm of Digby, Tuttle, Yavner & Moody to handle his legal affairs was that Ben Tuttle, the senior partner, shared his passion for promptness.

Old Mr. Breedon really believed that he had risen to the senior vice-presidency of the country's largest mail order house, and had accumulated a personal fortune of several million dollars, merely because he had never in his life been late for an appointment. As beliefs went, it was harmless enough. Staring about him with the beginnings of irritation, however, Breedon wished his father's lawyer had chosen some other day to demonstrate that he, too, could be late. Standing around like this was taking the edge off Breedon's excitement.

He glanced at his wrist watch and compared it with the marble clock on the Information Desk. Six minutes after two. Breedon wondered all at once if he had read Ben Tuttle's letter correctly. Maybe Ben Tuttle had not said two o'clock. Breedon put his hand into his breast pocket and pulled out the letter.

"I beg your pardon?"

Breedon looked up from the piece of thick, engraved stationery. A young man wearing a snap-brim felt hat was regarding him anxiously.

"Yes?" Breedon said.

"You wouldn't happen to be Arthur Breedon, sir, would you?"

"I would," Breedon said. "Why?"

The young man shifted his grip on his briefcase, pulled a card from his pocket, and handed it over. In the lower left-hand corner appeared the names: "Digby, Tuttle, Yavner & Moody." In the center of the card, engraved in somewhat larger type, was the name, "Benjamin Tuttle, Jr." Breedon looked up.

"I didn't know Ben Tuttle had a son."

"He didn't, sir, when you—"

The young man paused and blushed.

"When I went up to Jutger's Junction?"

"I'm sorry, Mr. Breedon. I didn't mean to—"

"You didn't," Breedon said cheerfully, and then he laughed. "Unless my arithmetic has abandoned me completely during my long stay as a guest of the state, you must be under twenty-eight?"

"Twenty-six, sir," said Benjamin Tuttle, Jr., looking at Breedon in surprise. He couldn't seem to believe that the older man could actually be amused. "I've been with the firm for two years."

"I'm sure that's to the credit of the firm," Breedon said with a small, gracious bow. Who would have thought that Ben Tuttle, thin-lipped, sour-faced, and dyspeptic, would sire a son as attractive as this young man? Breedon said, "How is your father?"

"Fair, Mr. Breedon, all things considered."

"What sort of things?"

"Why, just age, I guess, Mr. Breedon. He's all right, Dad is, nothing actually wrong physically, but he just can't seem to get used to the fact that he's seventy-one. He keeps going as though he were still a young man, and every now and then he just sort of folds up, as he did last night. That's why I came down to meet you today, Mr. Breedon. I'm substituting for Dad."

"I'm glad you are," Breedon said. "And I hope you won't consider that a reflection on your father. It's just that old Ben Tuttle never quite approved of me—" Breedon paused, and then he smiled again as he added dryly, "All things considered, if I may borrow your phrase, there was a rather good reason why he shouldn't. In fact, there were several million people who shared your father's disapproval." Breedon paused again. The young man was staring at him with a curious expression. Breedon said, "What's the matter?"

"Nothing," Benjamin Tuttle, Jr., said hastily. "Nothing at all."

"Surely you wouldn't stare at me like that if it was nothing at all?"

"Well, I was just surprised by the way you looked, sir."

"How did you expect me to look?" Breedon said quietly. "Like a monster?"

The young man's face went white, and then, swiftly, he blushed again.

"No, sir," he said quickly. "No, of course not. It's just that—" He hesitated, as though he were struggling to find the right words. "It's just that the only pictures I ever saw of you were taken around the time of the trial. I mean I looked up the clipping file in the office. The newspaper and magazine pictures. They all showed, I mean the pictures all looked like—"

"Like the pictures of a young man of nineteen?"

Benjamin Tuttle, Jr., nodded.

"Yes, sir," he said hastily. "That's *exactly* what I mean, Mr. Breedon."

It wasn't, of course. Breedon knew what Benjamin Tuttle, Jr., meant. What Benjamin Tuttle, Jr., meant was that the newspaper photographs of that young man of nineteen gave no hint of the intelligent, decent, responsible man of fifty by whom Benjamin Tuttle, Jr., was now faced. But Breedon saw no point in explaining to this embarrassed young man what he really meant.

"If I look so different from what you expected," Breedon said, "I wonder how you recognized me?"

"I didn't," Benjamin Tuttle, Jr., said. "I've been walking around this Information Desk since ten minutes to two, looking for someone who would answer the description Dad gave me, but it was no soap until you pulled out that letter." He nodded to the piece of Digby, Tuttle, Yavner & Moody stationery in Breedon's hand. "As soon as I saw one of the firm's letterheads, I figured it must be a letter you got from Dad, so I figured you must be the man I'd come to meet."

"That's pretty good figuring," Breedon said. "Now that you've met me, what do we do?"

"Why, Dad thought it would be best—" Benjamin Tuttle, Jr., paused and blushed again. "I mean to say, if you haven't yet had your lunch, how would it be if we went somewhere and—?"

"I had a sandwich on the train," Breedon said. "But if you postponed your lunch on my account, I'd be glad to join you."

"No, no, I'm not hungry," Benjamin Tuttle, Jr., said. "Dad merely thought—I mean we *all* thought, all of us at the office, we thought a restaurant, a place with a lot of people around, would be less conspicuous for you. Less *embarrassing* for you, I mean."

He looked around the large waiting room, as though he were hunting for a place where he could set down his briefcase, and then it occurred to Breedon that this was precisely what young Tuttle *was* doing.

"Look," Breedon said. "Are you trying to tell me that it isn't necessary for us to go back to your office?"

"Not unless you insist, Mr. Breedon," the young man said. "Dad thought, everybody at the office thought that you might prefer it if we transacted our business in some place where people wouldn't stare at—where people didn't know who you—" Benjamin Tuttle, Jr., shook his head a little desperately. "I mean, sir—"

"I know exactly what you mean," Breedon said. "And not

only do I prefer it, but I'm also very grateful to you and your father for being so thoughtful. Since neither of us seems to be interested in food, why don't we just sit down on one of these benches?"

They chose one in the far corner of the waiting room, near the battery of cigarette vending machines. Young Tuttle placed the briefcase on his knees. It was a beautiful briefcase, stitched by hand and finished with silver mountings. A disinterested passer-by might have assumed it was because the briefcase was so beautiful that young Tuttle kept staring at it as he talked. Breedon was not a disinterested passer-by. He knew why young Tuttle kept his eyes on the briefcase. Breedon kept his eyes on young Tuttle.

"The first thing Dad wanted me to make clear, Mr. Breedon, is the financial situation," he said. "When your father died, eleven years ago, his will contained a great many bequests, to friends, relatives, servants, charitable institutions, and so on. The bulk of the estate, however, was placed in trust for you, his only child." Young Tuttle drew a sheet of paper from his briefcase. "It's quite a substantial amount—"

"I know the amount," Breedon said. "Your father mentioned it in one of his last letters."

"I suppose he also mentioned that he is the trustee?"

"He did."

"Please understand, Mr. Breedon, that everything I say is a direct quotation from the trustee, namely, my father."

"I understand that completely."

"At the time your father drew this will," young Tuttle said to the briefcase on his knees, "it was not contemplated that you would ever be released from prison. For this reason, even though the residue of the estate was placed in trust for you, Mr. Breedon, the act was no more than a gesture. The terms of the will place the actual disposition of the money within the complete discretion of the trustee. I don't know if that's clear, Mr. Breedon?"

"Thirty years ago I was the youngest student who ever

matriculated at Manitaw Law School," Breedon said quietly. "It is perfectly clear. What you are trying to tell me is that I am a very rich man, provided I do nothing to offend the trustee, who is your father. If I do offend him, Mr. Tuttle is in a position to cut me off without a penny. Is that the size of it?"

"Yes, sir," young Tuttle said to the briefcase through a worried scowl. "That's precisely the size of it, Mr. Breedon."

"What do I have to do?" Breedon said. "In order to get my inheritance without offending your father?"

The worried scowl on young Tuttle's face grew deeper. He cleared his throat uncomfortably.

"Stay away from Manitaw City," he said. "Permanently."

There was a moment of silence. Breedon broke it by clearing his own throat.

"Why?" he said.

"My father feels it's best for all concerned," young Tuttle said to the beautiful briefcase. "The Bier-Breedon Case has been pretty much forgotten by the general public. Contemporaries remember it, of course. But only, my father feels, if they are reminded of it. Thirty years have gone by. A whole new generation has grown up. To most people, young people who have been born since 1924, the names of Theodore Bier and Arthur Breedon are meaningless. Even I, who studied the case in law school and once knew much of Elmer Haywood's famous summation by heart, even I had to go to the clipping files this morning to refresh my recollection about your appearance and read up on the other details before I felt equipped to come and meet you here at the train. If you leave aside my special interests, not only as a lawyer, but as a member of the firm that handles your affairs, Mr. Breedon, I think you'd have a fairly representative example of the average young person's knowledge of the Bier-Breedon Case. I'm sure you agree, Mr. Breedon, that most young people today know very little or nothing about it."

Breedon thought of the nineteen-year-old sailor on the train. He nodded slowly.

"Yes," Breedon said. "I agree."

"So much for the public," young Tuttle said, still staring relentlessly at the briefcase on his knees. "Now for the parties of interest. First, the Biers. Soon after the trial, as you know, several members of the family moved away from Manitaw City. Since then, others have died, and the rest have been dispersed in one way or another. When Ted Bier was slashed to death by that fellow convict in the shower room at Jutger's Junction in 1936, the last member of the immediate family was gone. There are a few collateral relatives living in various parts of the country, but the main point is this: there are no more Biers living in Manitaw City." Young Tuttle coughed nervously. "The same is true of—" He paused, swallowed hard, and tried again. "The same is true of—" The name seemed to stick in his throat. Young Tuttle cleared it and, in a rush of words, said, "The same is true of the family of the victim. They're all gone from Manitaw City. That leaves only—"

"Me?" Breedon said.

"Precisely," young Tuttle said to the briefcase. "The Breedons have disappeared even more thoroughly. Eleven years ago, when your father died and my father filed the will for probate, he tracked down all the Breedons. Not only those who were legatees, but *all* of them. Like the Biers, there are collateral relatives in different parts of the country, but none in Manitaw City. And, of course, as you know, Elmer Haywood has been dead for twenty years. In other words, until you stepped off that train at two o'clock, Mr. Breedon, there was no longer living in this city anybody who was in a position, by his mere presence, to remind the people of Manitaw City about the Bier-Breedon Case." Benjamin Tuttle, Jr., drew a deep breath. He lifted his glance from the briefcase. "Father wants to keep it that way."

"Is that why he had his convenient collapse last night and sent you to meet me instead of coming himself?" Breedon said quietly. "Is that why he thought it better not to have me come to your office?"

Young Tuttle blushed again, and he hesitated. Then he shrugged and scowled down at the briefcase.

"Yes, sir," he said. "You may have seen the morning paper. There was a story on page three about the last survivor of the Bier-Breedon Case being paroled today."

"Yes," Breedon said. "I saw it."

"Ever since the parole went through, Father has been trying to keep it as quiet as possible. He's even been in touch with the warden up at Jutger's Junction. Mr. Kinsey agreed that a lot of publicity wouldn't do anybody any good. But it's impossible to maintain a complete news blackout, of course, and the story got into this morning's paper. Since then, we've had a lot of calls from reporters, asking if you were coming back to Manitaw City, and if so, when. Luckily, Mr. Kinsey up in Jutger's Junction has been referring all such requests for information to Father. And Father has been telling the press that he doesn't know when you'll show up in Manitaw City, because your plans are still indefinite."

"They're not very indefinite so far as your father is concerned," Breedon said slowly. "Are they?"

"No, sir," young Tuttle said. "Father is very definite. He wanted me to make that absolutely clear."

"Go ahead," Breedon said. "I'm listening."

"Father feels that no useful purpose can be served by your coming back to live in Manitaw City," young Tuttle said. "For the older people, contemporaries of the Bier-Breedon Case, your coming back can only revive a painful memory. For younger people, who will learn about the Bier-Breedon Case only because of the publicity connected with your coming back to live in the city where you—where you and Ted Bier—where it *happened*, for those younger people, Father feels you will be introducing them to an unpleasant chapter out of the past that he thinks can only do them harm to know about. From your own standpoint, well, Father feels certain you'll agree that it's best for you, too, not to come back to Manitaw City."

"I'm sorry," Breedon said. "I'm afraid I don't share your father's certainty on that point."

Young Tuttle's glance came up from the briefcase. He stared

at Breedon as though he wanted to make sure what he had heard was not intended as a joke. Apparently satisfied that Breedon had spoken in all seriousness, young Tuttle scowled.

"Father feels that you'll be much happier living in some place where you're not known. A foreign country, perhaps."

"Under an assumed name?"

Young Tuttle's face went red again.

"Well, that did come up in the discussion," he said. "But that part of it is entirely up to you."

"The rest of it, however, isn't," Breedon said. "Is that correct?"

Young Tuttle hesitated, and then he shrugged.

"Yes, sir," he said through his uncomfortable scowl. "Father wanted me to make it plain that, if you insisted on coming back here to Manitaw City to live, he would turn over every penny of your estate to charity." The young man paused, and he looked at Breedon with an expression of such intense puzzlement that he seemed to be in actual physical pain. "If you don't mind my saying so, sir," he said, "I don't understand why you would *want* to come back here. You're a rich man. You can go anywhere. Wouldn't you be happier living in some place where they didn't know anything about you? Wouldn't you be better off in some place where you could start life all over again?"

"I might be better off," Breedon said. "But I wouldn't be happier."

Young Tuttle shook his head.

"I don't understand."

"You said you studied the Bier-Breedon Case in law school," Breedon said. "You said you once knew chunks of Elmer Haywood's great summation by heart."

"Yes, sir," young Tuttle said. "I did, but I'm afraid I've forgotten most of it."

"I haven't," Breedon said, and he added dryly, "Perhaps because the reasons for my remembering it are stronger than yours. At any rate, I'm sure you remember that Bier and Breedon both pleaded guilty, and that all of Elmer Haywood's efforts were directed, not toward having them acquitted, but merely toward keeping them from the gallows. All Haywood wanted to do was save their necks."

"Yes, sir," young Tuttle said. "I remember that."

"Do you also remember this passage from the last part of the summation?" Breedon said, and then, very softly, he began to quote: " 'Nobody knows more clearly than I, your Honor, that these boys I have been defending are not fit to be at large, to move freely in the company of other human beings. These boys are dangerous. They are detestable. They are vile. In spite of their vileness, however, they, too, are human. And all human life is worth saving. Even if what is saved is a mere fragment. I cannot say to this court how much salvage there is in these two boys. I can say only that whatever there is, however small it may be, the attempt must be made. Despicable and sick though they are today, it is possible that some day these boys may become healthy. Living as they have up to now in the shadowy darkness of abnormality, it is possible that some day they may achieve the right to hold up their heads in the bright sunlight of decency. It may never happen. Or it may take a long time. They may not achieve this right until they are men of, let us say, fifty. But these boys must, merely because like you and me, your Honor, they are human, they must be given the right to reach that age.' "

Breedon paused, and he drew a deep breath, and he smiled at young Tuttle.

"Last week, at Jutger's Junction, I celebrated my fiftieth birthday," Breedon said in a low voice. "I could take the money, and I could go to another country, and I could change my name. I could do all that, all the things your father wants me to do, and I would never know."

"Know what?" young Tuttle said.

"Whether Elmer Haywood was right," Breedon said. "Whether I was worth saving from the gallows. Whether I have achieved the right to hold up my head in the bright sunlight of decency. There's only one place where I can find out." Breedon stood up. "The same place where the world once learned that I was dangerous, and detestable, and vile. Right here," Breedon said. "In Manitaw City."

Young Tuttle stood up.

"Mr. Breedon," he said, still addressing the beautiful briefcase. "May I suggest something?"

"Of course."

"Don't make your decision now. Give yourself a little time to think it over."

"I've been thinking it over for thirty years."

"Then surely a few more hours won't make any difference," the young man said. "Dad thought it only fair to give you those few hours. Why don't you take them? I'll tell Dad you'll call him at home later in the day. In the meantime, sir, Dad thought you might want some cash for, oh, you know, sprucing up a bit." He held out an envelope. Breedon took it. "I really wish you wouldn't do anything rash," Benjamin Tuttle, Jr., said quietly. "It's an awful lot of money, sir, and every penny of it will go to charity. It really will. My father is quite serious."

"So am I," Breedon said, even more quietly. "Dead serious."

But the mood of seriousness did not last long. As soon as the tall young man in the snap-brim hat disappeared with his beautiful briefcase into the crowd at the far side of the station, Breedon remembered what he had been looking forward to ever since he had climbed aboard the train at Jutger's Junction. He turned and he moved across the station in the opposite direction, toward the Michigan Avenue entrance. Brushing past the men and women hurrying to and from trains, Breedon recalled something Mr. Kinsey had told him the day the news from the governor had come through.

"Most people on the outside," the warden of Jutger's Junction had said, "have completely erroneous impressions about the attitudes of parolees. They take it for granted that because a man has been in prison for a long time, for ten, twenty, or more years, he has lost touch completely with the world outside his prison walls. They think, when such a prisoner is released, he stares with disbelief at the clothes people wear on the outside, in astonishment at the shape of automobiles, and rubs his eyes in amazement at the design of new buildings, and so on. Such people are basing their notions about long-term prisoners on romantic recollections of Edmond Dantes in *The Count of Monte Cristo*, or on the way Rip Van Winkle acted when he woke up from his twenty-year snooze. People on the outside forget that all the efforts of modern penology have been directed toward doing just the opposite, namely, keeping the prisoner in *touch* with the outside world: through movies, books, newspapers, radio, magazines, television, lectures, and all sorts of carefully planned recreational and educational programs. No prisoner who is paroled today, no matter how many years he has spent in prison, is going to be astonished by the clothes people on the outside are wearing, or by the fact that, let us say, William McKinley or Warren G. Harding is no longer President. I'm sure, Arthur, that you won't be, either."

The warden of Jutger's Junction had paused and smiled at the prisoner in whom he and his wife had taken a special interest from the very beginning and toward whom they had felt, for many years now, a special sense of friendship.

"The biggest problem the released prisoner faces is not the change in the world outside, but the change inside himself," Mr. Kinsey had said. "When he enters prison he is one sort of person. When he gets out he is a completely different sort of person. This may seem a simple enough concept to grasp. Few prisoners, however, grasp it. I want you to be one of those few, Arthur."

"Yes, sir," Breedon had said, not quite sure that he knew what the warden was talking about. "I think I know what you mean, sir."

"I'd feel a lot better if you were *certain* you knew," Mr. Kinsey said. "In the thirty years you have spent here, Arthur, you have changed, not only from a boy of nineteen to a man of fifty. You have changed from a criminal into a decent citizen. If you don't grasp that completely, if you don't really understand

and believe that this change took place inside you and is now a fundamental, basic, and integral part of the man the world outside will see and deal with, your first contacts with the world outside may be unhappy. You may be expecting the members of that world outside to eye you with suspicion, to regard you with contempt. They may do just that, if you approach them apologetically, with a sense of guilt, because you have not grasped the fact that you have changed, that you are a new person. If you *do* grasp the fact that you have changed, you will accept the fact that the world outside is dealing with a new man, a decent citizen, the Arthur Breedon of today. And the Arthur Breedon of today, if I may say so, will have no difficulties with the world outside."

"Thank you, sir."

"What are your plans?"

"Well, sir, I used to be quite a good amateur ornithologist, and I've kept up my studies while I've been here. I gather from Mr. Tuttle's letters that I won't have any financial problem, so I thought I'd find an apartment, and then, when I'm settled in it, I thought I'd place an ad in the Manitaw City papers, offering to give private lessons in ornithology for reasonable fees."

"I think that's an excellent idea," the warden said. "Ornithology instructors are not very common. You won't be bucking trades or professions that are crowded. May I make a suggestion, Arthur?"

"Of course."

"Don't find that apartment on the North Side of Manitaw City. As long as you're determined to return, I think it would be best if you settled in a part of town that holds no strong past associations for you. Just being in Manitaw City is going to be difficult enough. Seeking out actual places you once knew intimately may prove to be a grave mistake. Don't you agree?"

"Absolutely, sir."

To this emphatic agreement, Breedon had made only one mental reservation: Binaggio's. He wasn't altogether sure why the old barber shop had taken such a firm hold on his imagination. Breedon knew only that, from the moment he had learned he was going to be released from Jutger's Junction, he had spent some part of each day imagining what it would be like to lie back in one of Binaggio's chairs.

Coming out of the station now, into the afternoon sunlight of Michigan Avenue, Breedon was aware of a sense of imminent fulfillment. He didn't care to examine it too closely. He wanted only to translate the anticipation into reality. Moving down Michigan Avenue toward the Gary Street corner, Breedon had to restrain himself from breaking into a trot. Even so, he made the turn so quickly that he was some ten or twenty feet down Gary Street before he realized he was heading directly into an ornamental fountain in the center of which a stone dolphin was spouting through its open mouth a long, fine stream of water high in the air.

Breedon stopped and stared. Then he turned and stared at the blue and white metal sign fastened to the lamppost on the corner. It said Gary Street, all right. Breedon turned back. But what had happened to the rest of Gary Street? Instead of the two rows of old office buildings that once had stretched all the way down to Lakeland Drive, there was nothing.

Nothing, that is, except a colorful park, full of bright green benches, roller skating children, women with baby carriages, and a policeman on horseback. Breedon walked up to him and tapped his stirrup. The policeman looked down.

"Say, Officer, I wonder if you could tell me what happened to Binaggio's?"

The policeman's face creased in a frown.

"What's that, mister?"

"Binaggio's," Breedon said impatiently, and he pointed to the north side of what had once been Gary Street. "A barber shop. It used to be over there, in the lobby of the Winetka Building."

"The *Winetka* Building? Listen, mister, the WPA tore that down during Roosevelt's first term. Where you been all this time?"

"Away," Breedon said slowly, and then, because the policeman's frown was beginning to take on a note of suspicion, he added quickly, "Far away."

Not in terms of miles, of course. Jutger's Junction was, after all, a mere three hours by train from Manitaw City. Yet all at once, as Breedon turned from the mounted policeman and headed back toward Michigan Avenue, it seemed to him that Jutger's Junction was further away than any place in the world that his suddenly uneasy brain could think of.

Moving along slowly, without plan or even interest in a destination, Breedon wondered why he *should* feel so uneasy. After all, nothing very terrible had happened. A barber shop of which he had once been fond had been torn down. What was so extraordinary or terrible about that? Why, in thirty years, *hundreds* of buildings he had once known must have been torn down. Was the discovery of each one going to have this effect on him? If so, then perhaps he would be wise to adopt old Ben Tuttle's suggestion and go to another city, or even another country, to live.

Breedon shook his head angrily. The discovery of other missing buildings couldn't possibly have this effect on him. Then why should he feel this way just because he had discovered that Binaggio's was gone? Breedon didn't know.

All at once, it seemed to Breedon that he didn't know anything. How long he had walked, or how far he had come, or even who he was. It was like those two terrible moments on the train, before and after meeting the young sailor, when it had suddenly seemed to Breedon that he had lost his sense of identity. Again, as on the train, feeling the sudden compulsion to see what he looked like, Breedon stopped and turned, hunting for a mirror.

He saw that he was standing on a quiet tree-shaded street. Both sides were lined with large houses, set well back from the sidewalk, each in its own expensive nest of beautifully land-scaped grounds. There was something so familiar about the street that Breedon found himself holding his breath. He looked up, quickly, at the huge house in front of which he had stopped, and his heart turned over with the shock of recognition. Breedon knew where he was.

He was in Harworth, on the North Side of town. He was in the most fashionable residential section in Manitaw City. He was standing on Lake Superior Road, the most desirable street in Harworth, in front of the largest and most expensive house on the street. There had been a time when Breedon had known to the last penny what that house had cost. He had heard his father mention the amount often enough. Old Mr. Breedon, who had not been so old when he built it, had been proud of that house. His only child had been born in it. A son.

Old Mr. Breedon's only child, now a man of fifty, turned and started slowly up the circular driveway. Just as Breedon passed the copper beech, a boy on a bicycle came racing down the driveway. He jammed on his brake. The bicycle screeched to a halt.

"Hi," the boy said. He seemed to be about fourteen. "What do you want?"

Breedon was too astonished to reply. The boy was a stranger! A total stranger!

"What's the matter?" the boy said insolently. "Can't you talk?"

For several moments, Breedon couldn't. Not aloud, anyway. He was too busy talking to himself, telling himself angrily that, *naturally* this boy was a stranger. He *had* to be. Ben Tuttle had written long ago, in one of his letters to Jutger's Junction, that the house had been sold soon after old Mr. Breedon's death. And yet there was something about the boy that made Breedon feel he was not a stranger at all. Breedon couldn't think what it was. He couldn't really think about anything. The strange uneasiness had descended on him again.

"Don't just stand there like a moron," the boy said. "Didn't you hear me ask a question? What do you want?"

Breedon wanted a mirror. The way he had wanted one on the train. To see what he looked like. To establish his own identity. But how could he tell that to this insolent boy?

"Nothing," Breedon said. "I don't want anything." He turned and started back to the street. "I made a mistake."

But he hadn't. By the time he reached the bottom of the

driveway, Breedon knew what it was about the boy that had seemed familiar. Breedon knew why he had turned into the driveway. Breedon had found his mirror. He turned, at the foot of the driveway, for another look.

He was disturbed by what he saw.

Staring back at him, from the seat of that bicycle, was the boy Breedon himself had been at fourteen. Not in appearance, of course. This boy was tall and blond and well built. Breedon had been dark and undersized and round-shouldered. But the boy he was looking at, and the boy Breedon remembered, both had that same insolent look, the look of the viciously spoiled child.

Breedon turned and walked away, swiftly, down Lake Superior Road. But there was no way to walk away from the voice of Elmer Haywood. All at once, after thirty years, Breedon could hear again the voice of the great lawyer as he pleaded for the court's mercy.

"Not because, in view of his crime, Arthur Breedon deserves your Honor's mercy," Elmer Haywood had said. "But because, your Honor, of what was done to Arthur Breedon as a child. For this he is blameless, and for this he deserves our pity. Even though he was not an orphan, Arthur Breedon never knew a father's or a mother's loving care. This function, which to most men and women is an almost sacred trust, was turned over by Arthur Breedon's parents to a series of hirelings, nurses and governesses whose affection could be bought and paid for. This notion, the belief that everything in the world could be bought and paid for, was planted in the boy early. His every whim, provided it cost money, was indulged. He was trained to believe that the rich are different, a special and privileged group, set apart from the rules and even the emotions that guide the less fortunate. No attempt was ever made to instill in the boy any sort of religious or moral convictions. Aside from the father's pride in the brilliant record his son was making in school, nobody bothered to inquire what Arthur Breedon was really learning. Everybody knew of his precocity, the astounding fact that at thirteen he had already mastered several languages, and possessed through intensive reading a frame of reference in the sciences that was an embarrassment to his teachers on the faculty of Manitaw University. Nobody, however, knew what was going on inside the boy, in his heart, in his soul, in his mind. Nobody knew that one of his governesses, a sexual pervert, had corrupted Arthur Breedon when he was fourteen and had introduced him to practices so loathsome that I shrink from recounting them in this courtroom. Nobody knew that the brilliant but distorted boy had fallen under the spell of Nietzsche's philosophy. Nobody knew that he had come to believe with his whole heart and soul that, for superior beings like himself, there was no such thing as right and wrong. Nobody knew that this child of fifteen had retreated from the world of reality into a world of fantasy, seeing himself as the abject and willing slave of a superman, a Nietzschian figure of colossal proportions mentally, a superman he could worship and obey without hesitation or question. In this sick, distorted, abnormal world that was the daily climate of his existence, it never occurred to Arthur Breedon that, when his superman appeared, he would take the form of a fourteen-year-old boy moving into the house next door."

Breedon stopped in his tracks, and he cocked his head, in the attitude of a man straining to hear more. But there was no more. The voice, the moving, low-pitched, powerful voice of Elmer Haywood had ceased. It was as though a telephone wire, reaching back thirty years into the past, had been cut.

Panting slightly, Breedon made an effort to readjust to the present. He had been so anxious to escape from the boy on the bicycle, to get away from the living mirror of a time that thirty years in Jutger's Junction had almost obliterated from his consciousness, that he had moved without thought, walking quickly, almost running, concerned only with the desire to cover distance.

Now, as he looked around him to get his bearings, Breedon's heart seemed to stop beating. He must have been moving in a circle. He was back where he had started from. Or almost where he had started from. On Lake Superior Road. In front of what had been known, when he was a little child, as the house next door but, during Breedon's fifteenth year, had become forever identified in his mind as Ted's house.

Breedon did not repeat the mistake he had made a short time before in front of his father's house. Breedon did not turn into this second driveway. Benjamin Tuttle, Jr., had told him, on a bench in the railroad station, that there were no more Biers left in Manitaw City. Besides, the only Bier he had ever cared about was dead. Breedon had seen his mutilated body, sixteen years ago, after Ted had been slashed to death in the Jutger's Junction shower room.

Disturbed by this encounter with recollections he would have preferred, on this first day of his freedom, to do without, Breedon turned away, toward the late afternoon sun, and he moved west. Walking quickly, trying to disregard the strange uneasiness that once again had him in its grip, Breedon became aware all at once that he was listening intently. It was as though the telephone line that went back thirty years into the past had been repaired. Once again Breedon could hear the moving, low-pitched, powerful voice of Elmer Haywood addressing the court.

"To understand what happened to Arthur Breedon, your Honor, one must know something of the only human being he ever loved: Theodore Bier. He, too, was the son of wealth. And, like Arthur Breedon, whatever loving care Ted Bier received as a child came from people who were paid to give it to him: nurses and governesses. They gave him too much—of the wrong kind! For, unlike Arthur Breedon, Ted Bier was physically attractive, a good-looking boy, tall, well built, and altogether charming. The fact that he stuttered, and had a nervous tic in the muscles of his face, and had a tendency to fall without warning into fainting spells, aroused in those hired to care for him nothing but the desire to give him everything he asked for. Ted Bier asked for a lot. Under similar circumstances, any average child would.

But Ted Bier was not an average child. He was almost ab-
normally brilliant. He soon tired of the game of asking for the
moon and being presented with the nearest equivalent that
doting servants, with limitless funds at their disposal, could
provide. Ted Bier stopped asking for entertainment. He decided
to entertain himself. At fourteen he began to drink. He began to
invent ingenious and elaborate lies, to test his own intelligence
against that of people around him. The people around him
always came off second best. He began to steal, to test his nerve
as well as his skill. He was never caught. He embarked on a
series of acts of vandalism, breaking plate glass windows,
cutting up tires of parked cars, spilling acid on theatre seats.
None of these acts was ever traced to Ted Bier. He lost himself
in an orgy of secret reading about crime and criminals. He began
to shadow people on the street to test his ability. Like Arthur
Breedon, he too retreated from the world of reality into a world
of fantasy. There was this difference, however. In Ted Bier's
fantasies he played the role of a master criminal, a superman
capable of any exploit. In this sick, distorted, abnormal world,
Ted Bier began to toy with the idea of planning and carrying out
the perfect crime. The broad outlines of the crime had begun to
take shape in his mind, and he had just come to the conclusion
that what he needed was a willing accomplice, when the Bier
family moved to Harworth, the most fashionable residential
section in Manitaw City."

With a short, sharp gesture, as though he were dropping a
phone back into its cradle to cut off a distasteful conversation,
Breedon stopped walking. He did not want to hear any more. He
yielded to no man in his admiration for the memory of Elmer
Haywood. Breedon, at fifty, even agreed with a good deal of
what the great lawyer had said thirty years ago about the Arthur
Breedon of nineteen. But Breedon, even if he lived to be a
hundred, was damned if he would listen to any of that kind of
talk about the early days of his friendship with Ted Bier.

"The psychiatrists talked a lot of the same sort of mumbo
jumbo about abnormality and the sick, distorted world of fan-

tasy," Breedon said sharply. "But there's one thing they never talked about, and the great Elmer Haywood didn't, either, because none of them knew anything about it, and that was—"

Breedon stopped again. He had not realized he was speaking aloud. He saw now, with considerable embarrassment, that a number of people on the busy street had stopped to stare at him. Feeling his face grow hot, Breedon turned quickly and moved on.

What Elmer Haywood and the psychiatrists had never talked about, because they had not known, was the sweetness of those early days. One thing Haywood had said was true enough: Ted Bier was the only human being Arthur Breedon had ever loved. He had loved Ted with all his heart, so fiercely, so completely, that he had even been jealous of the food Ted ate and the water he drank because these became a part of his being. They could take all their mumbo jumbo about abnormality, and they could take all their pious talk about practices too loathsome to be recounted in a courtroom, but there was one thing they could never take away from Arthur Breedon: the memory of his love.

"What's the matter, bud? You cockeyed?"

"Sorry," Breedon muttered to the man into whom he had stumbled. "I was thinking about—"

"Try thinking about where you're going, or you'll find yourself under a truck or something."

"Sorry," Breedon said again. "I was just going in here."

He did, and found himself in a diner. At once, Breedon realized that he was hungry. He had eaten nothing since the sandwich on the train from Jutger's Junction. Breedon slipped onto one of the stools at the counter. A girl in a green and white apron came down from the far end near the coffee urn.

"What'll it be?"

"Two on a raft and burn one."

Not until he saw the girl staring at him, open-mouthed, did Breedon realize what he had said.

"Come again?" the girl managed to say.

Breedon chuckled.

"When I was a kid that was soda jerk slang for a couple of fried eggs on toast and a chocolate malted," he said. "But I guess that's all changed now."

The girl looked at him curiously.

"You *guess?*" she said. "Don't tell me you haven't ordered a couple of fried eggs on toast and a chocolate malted since you were a kid, mister."

"As a matter of fact, I haven't," Breedon said, and he chuckled again. "Not in Manitaw City, anyway. I've been away."

"Welcome home," the girl said dryly. "And let's start again. What'll it be?"

"Two on a raft and burn one," Breedon said and, as he smiled at the girl, he added, "If you don't mind?"

"You like that," the girl said, smiling back at him. "Don't you?"

"Yes," Breedon said quietly. "I like it very much."

"Then I don't mind," the girl said. "Two on a raft and burn one it'll be, mister." She gave him a shrewd glance as she moved away. "I hope those words bring back pleasant memories."

They did, but Breedon doubted that she would share his feeling that the memory was pleasant. Those words had been the secret password invented by Ted Bier to indicate the day when the plan was to be put in operation.

Almost thirty years later, seated on a stool at this lunch counter, Breedon could still hear the ringing of the phone on that fateful morning of May 21, 1924. He turned over in bed and took the receiver from the hook.

"Hello?" he said sleepily.

"Arthur?"

Breedon sat up in bed.

"Yes, Ted?" he said tensely.

*"Two on a raft and burn one!"*

Arthur Breedon's heart leaped with excitement.

"I'll be there!"

He got out of bed and dressed slowly. Not because he felt like dressing slowly, but because Ted had ordered him to dress slowly.

The first phase of the plan had consisted of a careful analysis, by Ted Bier, of the personalities of the accomplices themselves. As a precaution, Ted had said, it was of primary importance. A study of the records indicated that almost every so-called "perfect crime" had failed, Ted Bier said, not because of some unforeseen circumstance that cropped up unexpectedly at a crucial moment and upset all the meticulous preparations. In a really good plan, Ted said, there were no unforeseen circumstances. A really good plan provided enough alternatives for each phase of its execution to overcome any contingency.

Ted Bier had learned, from his study of what the world so stupidly called its "perfect crimes," that they had all failed because the criminals, while they made it a point to learn everything possible about their victims, never bothered to learn anything about themselves. As a result, they did not know how they would act in moments of crisis. When the crises came, being unprepared, their own actions surprised them. And a man who is surprised at any phase of his own plan, Ted said, has lost control of it.

"We are going to be different," Ted Bier had said slowly, and the glance from his beautiful, dark, fiery eyes seemed to sear its way down, through Arthur Breedon's skin and flesh and bones, to his very marrow. "Because our plan is not going to fail," Ted Bier said in the soft, throaty voice that never failed to set Arthur Breedon's pulses racing. "Is that clear?"

"Yes, Ted."

"Our problem, one that we must face, is your tendency to get excited, *too* excited, in anticipation of critical events. You're all right once the events are set in motion. But thinking about them in advance gets you all steamed up. So we'll have to guard against it. Is that clear?"

"Yes, Ted."

"On Execution Day, when you get the phone call from me with the password *Two on a raft and burn one*, I want you to make a deliberate effort to dress slowly. As slowly as you can. There will be plenty of time. I'll see to that. And it will help keep you calm. Is that clear?"

"Yes, Ted."

It would no more have occurred to Arthur Breedon to disobey Ted Bier than it would have occurred to old Mr. Breedon to suspect what his son, and the son of his neighbor, had planned for that day. So Arthur Breedon dressed slowly, managing in this way to keep the seething excitement within him from overflowing.

He was lacing his shoes when the big limousine, in which his father was driven to the office every day, pulled away from the front of the house. Without looking at his watch, Arthur Breedon knew it was ten o'clock. His father was as dependable as the huge clock on the tower of The Manitaw Tribune Building downtown. Arthur straightened up, tiptoed to his bedroom window, and watched the big car roll down the curve of the driveway, past the copper beech.

"You boob," he whispered cheerfully. "You poor dumb sap," he said through a small, uncontrolled giggle, addressing his father's disappearing figure. "You think this is just another day, don't you?"

The limousine rolled out of the driveway and disappeared. Arthur suppressed his giggle and turned from the window. He went to his desk and picked up the briefcase in which he carried his textbooks and notebooks to Manitaw Law School every day. He paused, holding the briefcase, his head tipped to one side, listening for sounds from the hall.

There were six servants in the Breedon house. None of them had ever come into young Arthur's room without knocking. But it was a possibility, of course. In the first two or three drafts of the plan, Arthur had suggested, therefore, that he lock his bedroom door. But Ted Bier had overruled him.

"If one of the maids should try to come in, and find the door locked, she'll remember that," Ted had said. "It's safer to leave the door unlocked. You must be absolutely certain, however, that you hear no sounds from the hall before you begin to pack the briefcase."

When he was absolutely certain that he could hear nothing from the hall, Arthur began to pack the briefcase.

From the bottom drawer of his desk, where they were hidden behind two volumes of *Williston On Contracts*, he drew the cold chisel and the length of rope he and Ted had bought the day before in the hardware store on Cottage Grove Avenue. From the medicine cabinet in his own bathroom, where it stood innocently on the shelf between his tube of toothpaste and his jar of shaving cream, Arthur took the bottle of hydrochloric acid that had come from the drug store on 43rd Street. He tested the wrapping of adhesive tape he and Ted had put around the chisel to form a handle. It provided a good, firm grip. Arthur put the chisel, the rope, and the bottle of acid into the briefcase.

Then, from between the pages of his thick copy of *Black's Law Dictionary*, he took the ransom note that he and Ted had composed the day before. It had been typed on paper especially purchased for the purpose, using the Underwood typewriter he and Ted had stolen in Ann Arbor five months before, when the final details of the plan had begun to fall into place.

Arthur put the note into his pocket, then walked to the center of his bedroom, and closed his eyes.

Carefully, slowly, fighting the excitement churning inside him, he forced himself to go over each step, exactly as Ted Bier had ordered him to do. After several moments, Arthur Breedon nodded and opened his eyes. He had omitted nothing. He picked up the briefcase and left his bedroom.

In the hall downstairs he paused, as he did every morning, to choose a coat from the closet. And, as he did every morning, when the butler appeared, Arthur Breedon shook his head.

"No, thanks, Curtis," he said. "No breakfast. I'm late for class."

Swinging the briefcase casually, he left the house, walked down the driveway, and turned into Lake Superior Road. As he reached the Bier driveway, a car stopped on its way to the street.

"Hi," Ted Bier called from behind the wheel. "Going my way?"

The timing was so perfect, exactly as planned, that for a moment Arthur Breedon couldn't answer. All he could do was giggle. Then he saw the smile begin to fade from Ted's face, and he saw the nervous tic begin to tug and thrust at the skin under Ted's left eye. With a stab of fear for Ted's disapproval, Arthur pulled himself together.

"I don't know," Arthur said, reciting the exact words of the plan. "Depends on what's your way."

"The University," Ted Bier said. "I have an eleven o'clock class."

"So have I," Arthur said. He walked over, opened the car door, and slid onto the front seat beside Ted. "Thanks for the lift."

Ted did not reply. A reply was not necessary. According to the plan, by the time Arthur Breedon finished saying "Thanks for the lift," the car would be out in the stream of traffic and it would no longer be possible for anybody to hear what they said to each other. Ted Bier waited until he had made two turns before he spoke.

"Got everything?"

Arthur nodded. He tapped the briefcase. Then he turned to glance into the rear of the car. The things that the plan designated as Ted's responsibility were all there: the hip boots, the lap robe, and the small pile of rags that would be needed for gags. The giggle, bubbling up in Arthur Breedon like champagne, began to shake his body.

"*Quit that!*"

Arthur's body froze. He turned back. Ted's face was grim. Arthur couldn't see his eyes, because Ted's glance was fixed on the traffic around them, but Arthur knew what Ted's eyes looked like. During the four years that had gone by since Ted Bier had moved into the house next door, Arthur Breedon had come to know every aspect of the younger boy's uncontrollable rages. They made Arthur Breedon feel sick at heart. He could stand anything except Ted Bier's anger.

"I'm sorry."

"Don't be sorry," Ted snarled. "Use your head before it becomes necessary to be sorry. Stop that stupid idiotic moronic dumb giggling. We've got a job to do. You hear?"

"Yes, yes, yes, I hear," Arthur Breedon said sullenly. All the excitement, all the fun of this day toward which their thoughts had been turned so eagerly for months, all of that wonderful feeling was suddenly gone. You would think, on this one day, on this one day that meant so much to both of them, Ted wouldn't pick a quarrel. Pouting, Arthur said, "I told you I'm sorry."

"Now I'll tell *you* something," Ted Bier said through his teeth. "This is the biggest day of my life. This plan means everything to me. This is the moment I've lived for. If anything goes wrong because of your damn stupid silly giggling, if we miss on anything because you lose control—" Ted Bier paused, and then he said in a low, deliberate voice, "I'll kill you. You hear? *I'll kill you!*"

Arthur Breedon didn't answer. He kept his glance down, on his hands, which were clasped on the briefcase in his lap. He didn't want Ted to see that he was crying. There was a long silence. Ted broke it.

"Arthur."

Breedon's head came up. He gasped. Ted was smiling at him!

"Forget it," Ted said softly. Arthur Breedon's heart leaped with happiness. Ted was forgiving him! He brushed away the tears. He smiled back at Ted. "We've got a job to do," Ted said, and he reached across to touch Arthur's arm. Lightly, affectionately, a gentle caress. The tears came back into Arthur Breedon's eyes, but now they were tears of joy. Ted was no longer angry with him! Ted said, "Let's go do it."

Neither boy spoke during the rest of the drive downtown. It wasn't necessary. People who love each other don't need words.

At 16th Street and Michigan Avenue, Ted brought the car to the curb and parked. The boys got out, walked around the corner, and entered the office of the Rent-a-Car station. As the door closed behind them, Arthur Breedon glanced at the clock over the counter. It showed eleven o'clock, sharp. They were exactly on time.

"Good morning, gentlemen," the clerk said. "What can we do for you?"

Ted told him. Five minutes later, Ted Bier and Arthur Breedon rolled out of the Rent-a-Car parking space in a light blue Willys-Knight roadster. On the clerk's records, the car had been rented by a Mr. Morton D. Ballard who, several months ago, had established his credit with the Rent-a-Car concern. Ted drove the Willys-Knight around the corner and parked it behind his own car.

"All right," he said quietly.

Arthur got out of the car. Moving casually, managing by the expenditure of every ounce of his self-control to give no outward sign of the sudden resurgence of inner excitement, he went to Ted's car, opened the door, and began to transfer the lap robe, the boots, the rags, and the briefcase to the rented car. When he was finished, Arthur got back into the rented car.

"Well done," Ted said in a low voice, and once again he gave Arthur's arm the small tap of approval that was a caress. "Next step."

Ted pulled the rented car away from the curb and headed back toward the North Side. Arthur Breedon glanced at his watch.

"A quarter to twelve," Ted said, without glancing at his own watch. "Right?"

Arthur nodded. He couldn't speak. Ted gave him a short glance.

"We're getting close," Ted said. "How do you feel?"

"I—I—" Arthur paused. There was no way to describe the way he felt. No pleasure he had ever before experienced even approximated the climax toward which he could feel himself mounting. "I feel—I feel like—"

He shook his head. Ted Bier reached across and touched his knee, soothingly.

"I know," Ted said quietly. "Take it easy."

Arthur nodded, mute with gratitude and happiness. Was there ever before anybody like Ted? Anybody in the whole wide world? Who understood so much? Who knew so clearly how—?

The car stopped with a jerk. Arthur twisted sharply on the seat, his heart pounding with sudden fear.

"What's the matter?"

Ted nodded to the side of the street. A house was being built on the lot to their right.

"Those cement blocks," Ted said. His voice sounded strange. "Get six or seven."

"Why?" Arthur said. "What for?"

"What the hell do you think for? To weight the body, you moron! We forgot something to weight the body!"

Arthur could scarcely believe it. It had taken them months to work out the plan. They had gone over it hundreds of times, examining every conceivable detail for gaps and omissions. They had the lap robe for wrapping the body. They had the hip boots for carrying it out into the middle of the swamp. But they had forgotten the weights that would sink it! It was incredible. It didn't seem possible. Not after the care they had given to each step. How could they have forgotten a thing like—?

"Hurry up!" Ted said harshly. "We're falling behind schedule!"

Arthur leaped from the car. Luckily, the lot on which the house was being built was deserted. He ran to the pile of cinder blocks. They were awkward to carry. Arthur could manage only one at a time. He made five trips. When he put the fifth block into the rear of the car, Ted reached over and seized his collar.

"Come on," Ted rasped. "Get in!"

"I've only got five," Arthur said. "You said six or seven."

"Damn you, get in! Get in! Get in, you dumb, stupid—!"

Ted Bier's voice ended in a strangled jumble of incoherence as, with a frenzied jerk, he hauled Arthur Breedon into the car. Arthur pulled the door shut. The car leaped forward.

"I didn't do anything," Arthur said with a sob. "You told me to get the blocks. You said to get six or seven. You said—"

"*Shut up!*"

Arthur Breedon shivered, and he shut up. He had never heard Ted sound like that. Frightened, Arthur turned. Ted was hunched over the wheel. The twitching under his left eye had started again. The car was doing sixty. Arthur shivered again. An important part of the plan had called for performing every phase of it in the most inconspicuous manner possible. If they were picked up for speeding, it would mean—

"Ted! Ted, don't! Please, Ted, please!"

The car shuddered. The brakes screeched crazily. Arthur was flung forward. When he thrust himself back, away from the dashboard, the car had made the turn and was rolling smoothly past the brick and sandstone front of the Cambridge School for Boys. Arthur looked at Ted in astonishment. All the rage and the desperation seemed to have flowed out of him. The skin under his eye had stopped twitching. Ted looked as cool and calm as he had looked when they had walked into the Rent-a-Car office.

"We picked up two minutes," he said quietly. "We're only three minutes late. Maybe four, but no more than that. We may still be on time."

But they weren't. By the time they had passed the football field, and Ted had turned the car into Ontario Street, the boys of the Fourth Form had already dispersed. Arthur could see the group beginning to break up at the end of the block, the individual boys spreading out toward their various homes where their lunches were waiting for them. Arthur could even see the Wentworth boy, legging it up the hill toward his house.

"There he is!" Arthur said, and he started to get out of the car. "There he—!"

His words stopped. Ted had hauled him back into the car.

"Don't be so damn stupid," Ted rasped. "We can't chase him. Anybody looking out of a school window would see us."

"Oh," Arthur said.

"Yes, oh," Ted said bitterly, and he kicked the rubber

matting on the floor of the car. "Eight months' work shot to hell."

He sounded so dejected that Arthur wanted to take him in his arms and comfort him. But he didn't dare. It was the last thing in the world Ted would stand for when he was depressed. Trying to think of some other way to ease his disappointment, Arthur heard voices behind him. He turned.

The Third Form exit door had opened. A double line of boys was streaming out into the street. Arthur suddenly remembered that, just before he graduated from the Cambridge School, there had been some talk about a staggered dismissal system. Apparently it had been put into effect.

"Listen!" Arthur said with sudden excitement. "Why does it have to be the Wentworth boy? Why don't we—?"

"I don't know why the hell we don't!" Ted cried exultantly. He had already put the car into gear. Nobody could catch onto a new idea more quickly than Ted! Nobody! Absolutely nobody! "Everything may still be all right!" he said. "We may still pull it off!"

He swung the car out into Ontario Street, backed it around, and headed in the opposite direction, away from the double line of Third Formers streaming out of the school.

"They start breaking up at the corner," Ted said, speaking in a low, flat, calm voice. "By the time they do, we'll be at the top of MacDougal Street."

They were. By making three right turns, Ted had circled the school completely and reached the slight rise of MacDougal Street, a block above the school. He pulled the car against the curb.

As Ted cut the ignition, Arthur could see the Third Formers reach the foot of the street in a group. He found himself holding his breath. Ted leaned toward him. Together they peered through the windshield. Ted's lips were an inch or two from Arthur's ear.

"We'll take the first one that comes along," Ted said softly. "Everything else in the plan remains the same. Is that clear?"

Arthur nodded. Ted put his hand on Arthur's knee. "Take it easy," Ted whispered. "Just stick to the plan." Arthur nodded. He couldn't speak. All the excitement and anticipation of the past eight months seemed to have settled in a single lump in his throat. He could scarcely breathe. "Remember," Ted whispered. "The first one that comes along."

For several agonizing moments it looked as though none of them would come along. The boys at the bottom of the street were spreading out in all directions. Some went left, into Ellis Avenue. Others turned right, up the elbow of Ontario Street. A few went down MacDougal. But none, not a single one, turned up MacDougal, toward—

Ted Bier's fingers tightened on Arthur Breedon's knee. A boy had turned up MacDougal! He was coming toward the car! Arthur Breedon tried to swallow. He couldn't. He fought to control himself. He couldn't do that, either. His whole body began to shake. Ted Bier's fingers dug deeper into his knee.

"Don't!" Ted hissed savagely. "Not now! Damn you, don't ruin everything by—!" Ted's voice stopped. He drew a deep breath. His lips brushed Arthur Breedon's ear. "If you hold on, if you make it," he whispered fiercely, "I'll take you to Binaggio's right away! The minute he's in the car! Before we even go out to the swamp! I'll drive you down to Binaggio's, and we'll both have the full treatment! All right?"

Arthur nodded. He didn't even try to speak. The approaching climax, and the full treatment at Binaggio's—the combination was beyond his powers of expression. He couldn't put it into words. Even to himself. All he could do was *feel* it. He could feel the saliva begin to gather at the corners of his mouth. He could feel his breath coming in short, hard pants. He could feel the points of heat gathering in his head, behind his eyeballs. He could just manage to make out the boy ambling along up the street, coming closer and closer.

"Well, I'll be damned!" Ted said in a whisper.

"Huh?"

"It's the Draper boy!" Ted said. "Little Dickie Draper!"

Arthur peered, and then he nodded. They both knew the Draper family. Arnold Draper was in Arthur Breedon's class at the Manitaw Law School. All the Draper children knew Ted Bier and Arthur Breedon. What a piece of luck! After losing the Wentworth boy, what a fantastically lucky break to get Dickie Draper! By sheer accident! Why, it couldn't have been better if they had planned it that way! Ted eased the door of the car open.

"Hi, Dickie," he said.

The boy stopped and stared. Then he recognized Ted and Arthur.

"Hi," Dickie said. "What are you two guys doing around here?"

"Arthur just bought a brand-new tennis racket, and we thought we'd come over and try it out on the school court," Ted Bier said. "Like to see it?"

"Sure," Dickie Draper said.

"Go ahead," Ted Bier said to Arthur Breedon. "Show Dickie your new tennis racket."

Arthur got out of the car. He was certain the small boy could hear the pounding of his heart, but Arthur Breedon no longer cared. The exquisite moment of climax was drawing closer and closer. He cared about nothing.

"Here, Dickie," he said. "Step in."

He opened the rear door. The boy climbed into the car. Arthur Breedon climbed in after him. The moment the door slammed shut, Ted Bier started the motor.

"Hey!" Dickie Draper said in a surprised voice. "What do you two guys think you're—?"

The boy did not finish his question, and Dickie Draper never got a chance to ask another. Arthur Breedon had seized him from behind. His fingers dug into the small, soft throat. The boy made a gurgling sound. The car swung around the corner, into Ellis Avenue. Arthur Breedon's body swung with it. The struggling boy fell. Arthur Breedon landed on top of him.

Holding down the slender, squirming body with both knees

and one hand, Arthur Breedon reached into his pocket. His fingers found the taped handle of the cold chisel. He pulled it out, moved his suddenly sweating fingers into a better grip, and lifted the chisel over his head.

"All right," Ted Bier said quietly, without turning, from the front seat. "Now!"

He gunned the motor to drown out the screams.

"*Yes!*" Arthur Breedon gasped. "*Yes, now!*"

Even before the chisel came down in the long, hard, vicious lunge, he could already feel himself sliding back into a chair at Binaggio's. The climactic ecstasy of fulfillment shook his body like a reed in a high wind. Arthur Breedon closed his eyes with a sob of pleasure such as he had never known.

For a long moment, after he opened his eyes, Arthur Breedon did not know where he was. Astonished, he saw that he was sitting at the counter in a diner. Even more astonished, he saw the waitress in the green and white apron.

"Two on a raft and burn one," she said cheerfully. She set down the fried eggs on toast and the chocolate malted. "For a minute, there, mister, from the sounds you were making, I thought you were—"

The words stopped in her throat. Her hands went up to her cheeks. A look of horror washed across her face. She stepped back, away from the counter, with a small, shocked moan of disgust.

Arthur Breedon, dragged back violently from the past, turned in desperation, unaware of what was happening to him, aware only that he was hunting for something. On the wall behind him, under the row of coat hooks, he found it.

He came to his feet with a lunge. He swung around and dipped down. He stared into the mirror. He moved closer. He peered harder. But it was no use.

He could not find in the mirror the lean, strong, finely-chiseled face of the attractive, intelligent man in his early fifties, the face of the decent, adult, responsible citizen. What Arthur Breedon saw was the face the waitress had seen.

There was a touch of gray at the temples, and there were creases at the corners of the eyes, and the years had left their indelible marks, but the face was the same: the face of a man who, at the age of nineteen, had been described, by the greatest criminal lawyer of his day, as dangerous, and detestable, and vile.

Breedon turned away, unaware of his own gesture of revulsion. Breedon turned away, without hearing from his own lips what he had heard so clearly from the waitress: the small shocked moan of disgust.

Now he knew the meaning of the strange restlessness that had settled down on him that morning, soon after he had boarded the train from Jutger's Junction. Now he knew why, all day long, he had been upset by the feeling that his identity was slipping away from him. Now he knew why, for some puzzling reason, he had been unable to explain to the young sailor on the train what had happened thirty years ago. Now Arthur Breedon knew why his thoughts, and then his footsteps, had been drawn to Binaggio's like iron filings to a magnet.

Thirty years had not cured him. Three decades had not changed him. It merely looked that way. The intelligent face of the responsible citizen was an illusion. It existed only on the surface. And the existence of the illusion depended entirely on the surroundings in which the illusion had been created. As soon as he changed his surroundings, he changed his identity. As soon as he returned to the scenes of his youth, he was in danger of returning to the acts of his youth.

Blindly, without thought, Breedon clawed at the contents of the envelope young Benjamin Tuttle, Jr., had given him a few hours ago in the Manitaw City railroad station. He slapped some money on the counter and hurried out of the diner. In the street, dipping his head down, away from the sight of passers-by, he turned up his coat collar and started to run.

He ran blindly, a man possessed, a man trying to escape the inevitable. He couldn't. Nobody could outrun his own thoughts. They caught up with Arthur Breedon at the corner of Gary

Street and Michigan Avenue. They told him what he had come back to Manitaw City to learn: Elmer Haywood had been wrong; there were people who were not worth saving.

The act that had made a boy of nineteen dangerous, and detestable, and vile, had also made it impossible for him ever again to hold up his head in the bright sunlight of decency. Because the past refused to cooperate. The past never died. It was always there, shaping the future.

A forger might turn his back on it. A bank robber might shrug off the past. Even a murderer, a man who had killed in the heat of passion, might be said in thirty years to have paid his debt to the past. But there were crimes so loathsome, there were acts so obscene, that by their commission a man removed himself from the possibility of repayment. The man who had killed Dickie Draper had by his own act become less than human, and there was no way to buy his way back into the human family.

"Yes, sir?" a voice said. "What do you want?"

For a moment, Breedon didn't know. He looked around him. He saw that he was back in the railroad station. Puzzled, he saw himself standing in front of the ticket window. Then the puzzlement vanished. Breedon knew why he was here. He understood what he wanted. There was only one place where a man who had removed himself from the human family was safe, and where the human family was safe from him. His only chance lay in getting back before he did something for which not even Elmer Haywood, if he were alive, could save him.

"I want a ticket to Jutger's Junction," Arthur Breedon said to the man behind the ticket window, and he added, very quietly, "One way, please."

# THE
# THREE-TWO
# PITCH

I don't think you'd better go in," Ruth Sayre said. "He's tied up." Powell's hand, which was reaching out for the knob of D. J.'s door, stopped moving. He turned back to his boss's secretary.

"Badly tied up?" he said. "Or just . . . you know?"

"I can't tell yet," Ruth said. "There were two calls from Washington before these men came in, one of them from the White House—one of the calls, I mean—and if there's a connection, then God knows. They might be in there for hours."

Harry Powell glanced at his wrist watch. It showed seven minutes after twelve.

"Gosh," he said. "Our lunch date with Doc Hapfel is for twelve-thirty."

"I know," Ruth Sayre said. "Just before these men went in, D. J. told me when you came to pick him up I should tell you to wait."

"Oh, well, then I guess everything is all right," Powell said, and for a moment, hearing the relief in his own voice, he was embarrassed. Then he remembered that it was no longer necessary to be cautious with Ruth Sayre, and he smiled in a way that was intended to indicate exactly how relieved he did feel. "I mean," he said, "even if there *is* a connection between those men in there now and the calls from Washington, D. J. will get rid of them in plenty of time for this date."

"I'm sure of it," she said. "When D. J. wants to get rid of people, he does it so smoothly they don't even know they've been given an intentional walk."

Ruth Sayre's loyalty to her boss was so total that, Harry Powell had noticed, the tone and color of her conversation actually changed with each of her boss's campaigns. Ever since D. J. Crawford had been called in by both major leagues to make an attempt at breaking down public resistance to changing the players' traditional uniform for something more comfortable,

Ruth Sayre's conversation had been studded with baseball phrases. Harry Powell supposed that, if and when D. J. actually landed the huge Hartwell-Koch account for which he was at the moment angling, Ruth would drop the language of the diamond for that of automotive engineering.

"Besides," she said, "you and D. J. are lunching with Doc Hapfel at Pierre's, and that's no more than a sacrifice bunt from here, so there's really no rush. You can walk it in three minutes."

"Pierre's, eh?" Powell said, and Ruth, who was inclined to be fussy about office decorum, especially when she was at her post outside D. J.'s door, forgot herself to the extent of responding with a quick smile.

"Nothing's too good for Doc Hapfel," she said. "You know how D. J. feels about the old boy."

"If I didn't," Powell said, "I'd better go back to Cleveland."

"I don't think that will be necessary," Ruth said.

Powell looked at her quickly, but she was jogging some papers into alignment on a corner of her desk.

"If that last remark means what I think it means," he said, "I guess I'll be calling my father tonight and breaking the news to him about us. Right?"

"If you're right, you'll find it out after hours, when we're having dinner," Ruth said. "This is no place to discuss personal matters." She slipped a clip over the batch of papers and held them out to Powell. "Here," she said. "You might want to take a look at D. J.'s first draft of the proposed Hartwell-Koch campaign. Just in case he should raise the subject while you're walking over to Pierre's."

"Thanks," Powell said and, after a moment of hesitation, he decided to risk the personal note. "That's very nice of you, Ruth," he said.

It was more than that, Powell thought as she nodded and he took the batch of papers and carried them to the couch. It was a sign of how far he had come since he had arrived in New York eleven weeks ago.

Not that there had been anything openly hostile in Ruth Sayre's attitude at the beginning. It was merely that the moment he was introduced to her, Harry Powell sensed at once the truth of what his father had told him in the taxi on the way to the train back in Cleveland.

"I know I'm just an old fogy lawyer in a hick town," Mr. Powell had said, "and you're a bright young genius on your way to take the big city by storm, so I don't expect you to pay any attention to what I say, but I'm going to say it."

"Look, Dad. Do we have to go through that again?"

"No, we don't, and we're not going to. I still think now that you've got your college degree under your belt you should stay here in Cleveland and go to law school and become a member of a profession that has some solidity to it, instead of running off to New York to become another smart aleck trying to get rich on hot air. The least I can do is give you some sound advice.

"I don't know a damn thing about the public relations business, and aside from his tremendous reputation I know even less about this D. J. Crawford you're going to work for, but I know a great deal about offices. At the top in every one of them there is a boss, and every boss has a secretary. I don't know who is the secretary to D. J. Crawford, but my advice to you is to find out the moment you set foot in his office, and then try to work out some kind of a relationship with her."

"Why, Dad, do you mean what I think you mean?"

"No, I don't, but if you had to try that to get along with her, my advice would include the suggestion that you try that, too."

"I don't know why you assume I won't get along with her, whoever she is."

"If you did know, I wouldn't have to give you this piece of advice. Try putting yourself in her shoes for a couple of minutes. She is the confidential secretary to a famous man who has a peculiar quirk. Just because he was born in Cleveland and went to college there, and he is sentimental about both facts, the great D. J. Crawford every year brings into his office to serve as his confidential assistant for three months some young hick honor student from his alma mater's graduating class. It doesn't seem a peculiar quirk to D. J. Crawford, but D. J.'s secretary must hate the guts of these annual visitors, who are threats to her position near the throne. She undoubtedly does everything she can, without being obvious, to see that they fall flat on their faces before their three months in the city are up. If I felt that by falling flat on your face in D. J. Crawford's office you would come to your senses, return home, and enter law school, I might be tempted to withhold this bit of advice. I have not observed you closely for twenty-one years, however, without learning that you are the owner of a stubborn streak wide enough to reach from here to Springfield, and if you fail on this job, you will stay in New York until you prove it was not your fault, a task that may conceivably last forever and will almost certainly take so long that by the time you've completed it you will be too old to enter law school. Believe it or not, I want you to succeed on this job, and in order to do that you will have to work something out with D. J.'s secretary."

What Powell had worked out, much to his own surprise, could be traced more readily to the elementary principles of good manners his mother had taught him at eight than to the advice his father had given him at twenty-one.

Although Ruth Sayre was not an unattractive girl, there was nothing about her merely adequate figure, her pretty but rather sharp features, and her lusterless blond hair that set Harry Powell's pulses racing. On top of that, it was perfectly obvious that there was plenty of justification for the fact that she was heartily disliked by almost everybody on the staff. It was Powell's normal inclination, therefore, to steer clear of her. But Ruth Sayre, whose twenty-eighth birthday had slipped by unnoticed a week before Harry Powell arrived from Cleveland, was what his mother had taught him to think of as An Older Person. As such she was entitled to the respect of her juniors. The fact that she had not always got it may have been responsible for the way she reacted when Harry Powell gave her his.

Apparently astonished by a young man who stood up when

she came into a room, Ruth Sayre seemed to forget that the young man was a potential threat to her position outside D. J.'s door. The small, helpful hints about office routine with which she repaid Powell's completely guileless politeness were gratefully received. Ruth Sayre, unaccustomed to gratitude as well as politeness from D. J.'s junior geniuses, responded in kind. The effect on Harry Powell was to make him think more kindly of Ruth Sayre's figure, see more gold in her hair, and overlook the sharpness of her features. During his third week in New York, when she had helped him move from his expensive and uncomfortable hotel room into a neat little two-and-a-half-room apartment on Bank Street that she had found for him at an astonishingly modest rent, Harry Powell decided that not only was Ruth Sayre's reputation with the D. J. Crawford staff completely unjustified, but she was actually, if you wanted to be fair about it, a damned pretty girl.

By the end of his fifth week in New York, when Powell had repaid Ruth's many kindnesses by taking her to dinner several times, the staff was making jokes about the way D. J.'s dragon had finally succumbed to the grand passion. In fact, a couple of the stories were imaginative little accounts of intimate goings on in Harry's little hideaway on Bank Street.

So far as Harry Powell could see, Ruth didn't mind the jokes. Her indifference to what people said about her at first astonished, and later impressed him. On the other hand, the staff could hardly be blamed for making malicious jokes about him and Ruth, since it was obvious that she had been largely responsible for Powell's success with D. J. Powell was certain that, once his father had a chance to meet Ruth, he would realize the fact that she was seven years older was unimportant. The difference in their ages was, in fact, an advantage. Ruth's longer experience in the business world, especially in the part of it over which D. J. ruled and in which Harry Powell's future now so clearly lay, had already proven of tremendous help to a young hick from Cleveland. How much more helpful that experience would be to a young husband from New York.

It was Ruth, for example, who had pointed out to Powell the

significance of D. J.'s invitation that Harry join his boss for the lunch with Doc Hapfel. And now, instead of just letting Powell cool his heels while he waited for D. J. to shake himself free for that important lunch, Ruth had slipped Harry the first draft of the proposed Hartwell-Koch campaign. She had given him another leg up on the rest of the staff, every member of which had been angling for weeks to find out what D. J. had in mind for snagging the biggest account of his career. Powell appreciated the fact that Ruth, who had already given him so much, had chosen to add this gift on the day when he was already receiving D. J.'s crowning accolade of lunch with Doc Hapfel.

The combination could mean only one thing. In Ruth's eyes the hick from Cleveland had vanished. She had decided Harry Powell was ready. Tonight, when they had dinner, she would give him permission to call his father and break the news about their engagement. Ruth would not do that unless she was certain of their future. For the first time since he had arrived in New York, so was Harry Powell. The box on Ruth's desk buzzed.

"Yes?" she said. She listened for several moments. "All right, yes, sir," she said finally. "I'll tell him." She flipped the key back into place, and said to Powell, "D. J. is stuck. He isn't going to be able to walk those men for a little while yet. He wants you to go over to Pierre's, start lunch with Doc Hapfel, and then, as soon as he gets rid of these people, D. J. will join you."

"How long will that be?"

"Not very," Ruth said. "Fifteen, twenty minutes. What difference does it make?"

"None at all, I guess," Harry Powell said. "It's just that I've never met this Doc Hapfel."

"So what?" Ruth said. "Suppose D. J. told you to go over to Pierre's and start lunch with Coles Hartwell or Bruce Koch? You've never met them, either. If you expect to end up in D. J.'s shoes some day, you'd better get used to the idea of meeting men like Hartwell and Koch. No matter how many automobile plants they own, they're just potential clients, that's all. You can't let yourself be intimidated by their money or their reputations. You have to step up to the plate and take your cut at the old apple as though they were no different from any other pitchers."

Powell raked back quickly through his last words, all innocently spoken, trying to find the ones that had brought the tense look to Ruth's face and that edge into her voice. He found nothing.

"All I meant," he said, "is that I don't know anything about Doc Hapfel."

"All you have to know is that he's D. J.'s old high school teacher from Cleveland and that once a year, no matter how busy he is, D. J. makes it a point to have lunch with him on the old man's birthday." Ruth relaxed her rigid rules about office decorum long enough to give him a friendly laugh. "Quit acting like a hick from Cleveland," she said. "This is the three-two pitch, Harry."

He laughed with her and then, all the way out of the office and down the elevator and walking up Madison Avenue to 52nd Street, Powell kept wondering if he had laughed because no matter how bright they were, women could never quite master the lingo of baseball. Ruth couldn't have meant the three-two pitch. The three-two pitch was behind him. Harry Powell had got his hit. What Ruth had obviously meant to say was that this lunch with Doc Hapfel was Harry Powell's grand slam. Even Pierre, who was standing just inside the restaurant door when Harry came in, seemed to realize that.

"Good afternoon, Mr. Powell," he said. "Your guest is seated."

Harry followed him to a corner table and had a moment of surprise.

"You are Harry Powell," said the old man at the table, smiling shyly as he half rose in his chair and hesitantly extended a not very steady hand. "I'm Doc Hapfel. D. J. has told me a good deal about you. It is a great pleasure to have this opportunity to meet you."

"Thank you," said Harry, wishing as he took the

outstretched hand and slipped into the chair facing D. J.'s old
high school teacher that he could think of some way to put the
little old man at ease. "I've heard a good deal about you, too,
sir."

The old man flushed with pleasure and then shot Powell a
quick, anxious glance.

"Have you?" the old man said, uncertainly but with unmistakable eagerness. "Have you really?"

"I certainly have," Powell said, wondering what was troubling this old man who, according to D. J., was the most
extraordinary human being he had ever known. "Ever since I
joined D. J.'s staff eleven weeks ago," Powell said, "I've been
hearing all about how you taught him all he knew, and encour-
aged him in the early days, and urged him to go into business for
himself when he was still not much more than a kid. D. J. talks
about you all the time, sir."

"Isn't that nice?" the old man said. "Even if he exaggerates
what I did for him, I still think it's nice of D. J. to say things
like that." Doc Hapfel turned toward the hovering Pierre and
said, "I wonder if you would mind bringing me another one of
these, please?" Then, as Pierre bowed and reached for the old
man's glass, Doc Hapfel turned back to Powell and said nervously, "If that's all right with you?"

"Of course it's all right," Powell said quickly.

"Another martini, sir," Pierre said.

"Thank you," Doc Hapfel said and then, with an uneasy side
glance at Harry Powell, "Could you make it a double, please?"

"Certainly, sir," Pierre said. "Another double martini, sir."
He turned to Harry. "Will you have something to drink, sir?"

"Thanks, no," Harry said.

"Won't you really have a drink?" Doc Hapfel said, looking
as distressed as though Powell, who needed it to save his life,
had refused a blood transfusion. "After all, this is something of
an occasion for both of us. My birthday and . . ." He smiled
uncomfortably. "D. J. won't be along for another fifteen minutes."

"Oh," Harry said. "Then Miss Sayre called you?"

"No, no." The old man suddenly sounded frightened. "Not at all. Nobody called me. It's just that I—" He paused and smiled apologetically. "It's just that I know how terribly busy D. J. is, and when I saw you coming across the restaurant by yourself, I assumed he got stuck at the last minute."

"That's exactly what happened," Harry said, smiling back at the old man. "And since you're absolutely right about this being an occasion, while we're waiting for him I think I will have a drink." He turned to Pierre. "Scotch and water, please."

"One double martini, one Scotch and water," Pierre said, setting down two menus. "I recommend the Pintade Rôtie."

"One can hardly blame him, can one, at three dollars and seventy-five cents a serving," Doc Hapfel said in a tone of wonder as Pierre left, and then he added quickly, "Not that it isn't worth it, I'm sure. I mean, an establishment like this, the expenses, the rent, their laundry bills, salaries for cooks and waiters, all that—"

The pointless apology dribbled away into an uneasy silence. Doc Hapfel put his hands up on the table, folded them neatly in a gesture that reminded Harry Powell of a child in school composing himself at a desk, and looked worriedly across the restaurant toward the door.

"He'll be here," Harry said reassuringly. "He just has to get rid of a couple of men who barged in on him unexpectedly."

"Oh, I'm sure of it," the old man said even more quickly. "It's not that," he said, turning back toward the door. "I was only looking to see if—"

His voice trailed away into the same uncomfortable silence, and Harry tried desperately to think of something to say. It was not easy. He suddenly realized that, even though D. J. never seemed to stop talking about his debt to this little old man, he never said anything specific. After leaving Grover Cleveland High at the age of seventeen, D. J. had kept in touch with his old teacher, and when Doc Hapfel reached sixty-five and was automatically retired on a pension, D. J. had urged him to come to

New York. For sixteen years he had been living comfortably in a small apartment on East 48th Street, no more than a five-minute walk, even for a man of eighty-one, from D. J.'s office as well as Pierre's.

"Ah, here we are," Doc Hapfel said with an eager smile, and Powell realized it was not the door the old man had been watching so anxiously. "Thank you very much," he said as the waiter set down the glasses. The waiter nodded and walked away. Doc Hapfel picked up his martini and, with a small, courtly bow, held it out toward Harry. "To your future," he said. "May it be just as bright as D. J.'s."

"Thank you," said Harry. He touched his glass to Doc Hapfel's. "And the same to you, sir."

"What a nice thing to drink to on one's eighty-first birthday," the old man said, bringing his other hand up to the glass to steady it. "Thank you, yes. To both our futures."

The glass shook badly, but he succeeded in getting it to his lips without spilling its contents. Harry wondered nervously whether, as the old man's technical host until D. J. arrived, he should offer Doc Hapfel another drink. He had put down at least one before Harry arrived, and while that may not have had anything to do with the way his hand was shaking, two doubles seemed to Harry to be enough for a man of eighty-one. Doc Hapfel obviously did not agree.

"I wonder if I might have another one of these?" he said anxiously, and then, perhaps because he saw Harry's moment of hesitation, the old man added, "I'm sure it's quite all right with D. J."

"Of course," Harry said, feeling his face grow hot. Turning to order the drinks, he saw another waiter approaching with a telephone.

"For you, sir," he said as he set the phone on the table and plugged it in.

"Thanks," Harry said. "Excuse me," he said to Doc Hapfel, who nodded, and then, into the phone, "Hello?"

"Hello," said Ruth Sayre. "Harry?"

"Yes, hello."

"How are things going?"

"Why, fine," Harry said. "Why do you ask?"

"Well, D. J. just buzzed me. He's still stuck with these two men so he said that you and Doc Hapfel should start to eat. He probably won't be able to join you until you have your coffee, but he'll get there as soon as he can. All right?"

"Sure," Harry said. "Of course. Thanks, Ruth."

He hung up and saw that the anxiety on the little old man's face had turned to disappointment.

"He's still stuck with those men," Doc Hapfel said quietly. "He wants us to start and he'll join us a little later. Is that it?"

"As a matter of fact," Harry began and then, making no effort to conceal his surprise, he said, "How did you know that, sir?"

Whatever reply the old man was about to make was deflected by the arrival of the waiter with the fresh martini. He set it down, unplugged the phone, and carried it away. Doc Hapfel's narrow shoulders moved in a fragmentary shrug of resignation. He released a low, tired sigh, picked up the glass and disposed of the contents.

"I'm his good luck piece," he said.

"I beg your pardon, sir?" Harry said.

"Like a silver dollar," Doc Hapfel said. "Something you carry in your pocket for luck. In this city—" He started to make a gesture clearly intended to take in the room, but his hand was shaking too much, and he allowed it to drop to the tablecloth. "In New York, to be successful in New York you must have a good luck peesh, no, a *piece*, you must have a good luck *piece*. I'm D. J.'s good luck piece. That's why he asked me to come live in New York when I retired. He wanted me near him. Where he could—"

The old man's voice stopped, and he reached out to touch the sleeve of a passing waiter. He missed by several inches, and his slender body, following the movement of his arm, would have toppled forward, perhaps out of the chair, but the waiter, seeing the gesture, had turned, so that the old man's shoulder rammed against the waiter's thigh and stopped the falling motion. With a gentle assist from the waiter, Doc Hapfel leaned back safely in his chair and Harry Powell, dropping back with relief into his, wished to God that D. J. would hurry up and get here. Lunch with his boss's old high school teacher, which Harry had been assured by Ruth was an accolade, was proving a rapidly accelerating embarrassment.

"May I have another one of these?" the old man said to the waiter, tapping the rim of his glass, and this time he did not glance at Harry Powell, apologetically or otherwise, as he added, "A double, please, if you would be show kind?"

"Certainly, sir," the waiter said, taking the glass. He turned to Harry. "You, too, sir?"

"No, thanks," Harry said. He turned to Doc Hapfel. "Don't you think we ought to order?"

"I am not hungry," the old man said. "But do not let—" A small, gastric disturbance interrupted him. He patted his lips, smiled foolishly and said, "But do not allow my lack of appetite to interfere with your own desire to consume this excellent Pintade Rôtie at three dollars and seventy-five shents a sherving."

"Why don't we order?" Harry said. "By the time our food arrives, you'll probably be feeling hungry and—"

"This does not conshern you, young man," Doc Hapfel said politely to the waiter. "If you will be good enough to fetch my drink, I will be mosht grateful."

"Yes, sir," the waiter said and, after a short glance at Harry, moved away. "One double martini, sir."

Doc Hapfel watched the waiter's departure for several moments with complete absorption, then said with ponderous slowness, "If that young man had a good luck peesh like me, he would own this restaurant in a week. But there are not many good luck peeshes like me. That is why D. J. wants me near him all the time, and that's why he always takes me to lunch on my birthday, and that's why I refuse to order this excellent Pintade Rôtie at three dollars and seventy-five shents a sherving, because to do so would be to violate the ritual D. J. established for these lunches many years ago. Am I making myself clear?"

"Well," Harry Powell said, shooting a nervous glance toward the door and wondering why Ruth, who had given him so many helpful hints during the past eleven weeks, had not tipped him off, on this crucial day of his grand slam, about Doc Hapfel and alcohol, "I'm not sure that I follow you, sir."

"You will," the old man said. "I cannot live forever. Shome day D. J. will need a new good luck piece. Peesh? No, piece. And when he does, why not you? Miss Sayre told me on the phone when she called me to invite me to this lunch that D. J. thinks very highly of you, much higher than any of the others, so it is important for you to understand the ritual of these lunches. It is like scarlet fever. Or perhaps I mean pneumonia? I am not sure. One of those diseases where the victim must go through all the stages. He can't skip any, in spite of miracle drugs or anything else. First there is the call from Miss Sayre setting the date of the lunch. Then, on the day of the lunch, D. J. gets stuck just before he has to go to the restaurant. So he asks his confidential assistant to go on ahead and shtart lunch with old Doc Hapfel and he'll be along in fifteen or twenty minutes. In the restaurant, at the table, comes the first call from Miss Sayre. D. J. just buzzed her. He's still tied up with these two men, so he said you and Doc Hapfel should start to eat. He probably won't be able to join you until you have your coffee, but he'll get there as soon as he can. Then, perhaps ten or fifteen minutes later—" The old man paused, lifted his arm with great care, and squinted at his wrist watch. "Yes," he said. "Ten or fifteen minutes later comes the second call. Aah, here we are."

He leaned back, as though the waiter were setting down an enormous platter instead of a martini glass, and then Powell saw that the waiter was also setting down the phone.

"For you, sir," he said. He plugged the phone in.

"Thanks," Harry said. The waiter went away and Harry, picking up the receiver, saw Doc Hapfel pick up his fresh drink. Harry said, "Hello?"

"Hello," Ruth's voice said. "Harry, look, something terrible has happened. You know those long distance calls I told you about? From Washington? One of them from the White House? That came in just before those two men showed up? The men D. J.'s tied up with?"

"Yes," Harry said, watching Doc Hapfel uneasily. "What about them?"

"Well, it turns out that there *is* a connection between those calls and the unexpected visit of the two men, and D. J. just isn't going to be able to get away at all. Will you please convey his apologies to Doc Hapfel? And see that the old man has a very nice lunch? And tell him that D. J. will call him in a day or so, as soon as he's out from under, and make another date for them to get together?"

"Sure," Harry said. "But—"

"I've got to run now. D. J. is buzzing me."

"But Ruth—"

"And don't forget to wish him a happy birthday from me, too."

Harry Powell sat there for several moments, holding the dead phone to his ear, not because he expected Ruth to come back on the wire, but because he felt he should paraphrase the message. He didn't understand why, but it suddenly seemed terribly important to tell it to the old man in his own words, not Ruth's, but Harry Powell never got the chance.

"It turns out there *is* a connection," Doc Hapfel said quietly, "between those calls that came in from Washington just before you left the office and the men who dropped in on D. J. unexpectedly. He isn't going to be able to get away at all. Will you—?" The old man paused. He seemed to have forgotten what he wanted to say. His eyes opened and closed slowly, and he swayed slightly in his chair. He was trying to shake his head, as though to clear it. A look of annoyance crossed his face, as though he was irritated with himself for getting so drunk, and thus impairing his memory at a time when it was important to remember everything. "Oh, yes," he said, and his face cleared.

"Yes, like this. Will you," he said, putting invisible quotation marks around the laboriously uttered words, "convey D. J.'s apologies to me? And see that I have a nice lunch? And tell me D. J. will call me in a day or two, as soon as he's out from under, and make another date?" The old man's face expanded in the foolish smile from which the haze of alcohol could not erase the suddenly vivid smear of pain. Breathing hard, fighting for coherence, the white-haired old man mumbled, "Have I got it right?"

"Yes," Harry said carefully. "Except for one thing."

"Whatsh that, may I ashk?"

"Miss Sayre said—"

Before he could tell Doc Hapfel what Ruth had said, the old man's forehead, dropping forward abruptly like the blade of a jack knife snapping back into its slot, struck the empty glass from which, in two long gulps, he had just taken his fourth, or possibly fifth, double martini. Harry Powell moved quickly, but not quickly enough. By the time he got around to the other side of the table, the slender body had hit the floor. The glasses and silver followed with a splintering crash that stopped the buzz of conversation in the crowded restaurant as though a switch had been pulled. Then Harry Powell saw that Pierre had arrived. He rapped out orders to several waiters and, at the same time, pushed Powell out of the way.

"Stand aside, please," Pierre said sharply. "He is all right. They will carry him into my office. There is a couch in my office."

By the time the waiters had put the old man on the couch in Pierre's office, Powell became aware of the way Doc Hapfel was breathing.

"I think we'd better get an ambulance," Powell said. "He looks—"

"Yes, of course," Pierre said. "At once, sir."

The sarcasm in his voice was so unmistakable that Harry Powell took a good look at Pierre's face. What he saw told Powell clearly, as the small, sick feeling started churning in his stomach, that Ruth's knowledge of baseball lingo was more accurate than he had thought. The lunch with Doc Hapfel, which Powell had considered a grand slam, was not that at all. It was precisely what Ruth had called it, the three-two pitch, and as he listened to Pierre's cold, impatient voice, in which the scarcely controlled anger hummed venomously, telling the hospital attendant at the other end of the phone where to send the ambulance, Harry Powell realized that he hadn't even swung at the pitch. He had struck out looking.

"They will be here in perhaps ten or fifteen minutes," Pierre said as he hung up. "I would now like to go back to reassure and attend to my customers," he said and added sarcastically, "If it is all right to leave you in here alone with him, that is."

Powell could feel his face flush.

"Yes, sure, go right ahead," he said, trying to keep the anger out of his voice. "I'll stay here with him until the ambulance comes."

For several moments after Pierre had gone out and slammed the door, Powell stood motionless beside the desk, looking down at the unconscious Doc Hapfel on the couch, telling himself it was just as foolish to postpone making the call as it was to be angry with this little man of eighty-one whose rasping, irregular breathing filled the small office with sounds that made Powell think of long, rusted spikes being pulled out of a waterlogged plank. The only person with whom Harry Powell was entitled to be angry was Harry Powell. If he was half as bright as D. J. seemed to think he was, if he possessed any of the qualities that Ruth felt were essential to achieving success on the levels she expected the man she married some day to reach, Harry Powell would have met this simple test successfully. He would not have allowed sentimental embarrassment about cutting off An Older Person's flow of liquor to stop him from preventing a public spectacle that D. J. was bound to hear about. In short, if Harry Powell had acted like the experienced New Yorker that Ruth Sayre believed he had become, instead of the hick from Cleveland he so obviously was, he would not now have to walk back to the dugout with his head hanging. There was no point in postponing the humiliating journey. Harry Powell picked up the phone on Pierre's desk and dialed his office number. Then he waited.

"D. J. Crawford Associates, good afternoon."

"Hello, Miss Dunne," Harry Powell said to the switchboard operator. "Could I talk with Miss Sayre, please? This is Harry Powell."

"Just a moment." There was a series of clicks, a long pause, and then Miss Dunne came back on the wire. "Sorry, Mr. Powell. She stepped out for a few minutes. Can I have her call you back?"

"Well, I—" Powell turned with the phone to glance at the inert, white-haired figure on the couch. "Do you have any idea where Miss Sayre is? I mean, did she go out to lunch or something?"

"Oh, no," Miss Dunne said. "She's somewhere around the office. The little girls' room, maybe. I don't really know."

"Then she ought to be back at her desk soon?"

"Oh, yes. In a few minutes, I should think. If you'll give me a number, I'll have her call you?"

Powell drew a deep breath and blew it out slowly. There was nothing to be gained by trying to filter the bad news through a third party, even a sympathetic one like Ruth.

"No, that's all right," Harry Powell said. "Put me through to D. J., will you?"

"D. J.?"

"Yes, I'd like to talk to him right away, Miss Dunne. It's urgent."

"Mr. Powell, are you kidding?"

Powell wished he was.

"I know he's tied up in a meeting, but this is urgent," he said. "If you'll tell him I'm calling from Pierre's, I know he'll take the call."

"But Mr. Powell, D. J. is in Detroit."

"He's where?"

"In Detroit, Mr. Powell. He flew out last night for a conference with Coles Hartwell and Bruce Koch. He's not expected back until late tonight or tomorrow. Didn't you know that?"

Powell scarcely heard the question. He certainly made no effort to answer it. All at once the inside of his head felt like a jigsaw puzzle that had been tossed in the air. He was snatching busily at the slowly floating pieces as though it was tremendously important to fit them all back into place before any of them touched the ground.

"Mr. Powell?"

He brought his mind back to the voice at the other end of the phone.

"Yes?"

"I said do you want me to have Miss Sayre call you when she gets back?"

"Yes, please."

Long after he had read off to Miss Dunne the number on Pierre's telephone, Powell stood there beside the desk, snatching at those scraps of the puzzle. Taking the piece that covered Ruth's insistence that he postpone calling his father in Cleveland with the news of their engagement until after dinner that night; adding it to the piece that covered her neglect to warn him about Doc Hapfel's drinking; fitting them all against one persistent image: Ruth sitting at her desk outside D. J.'s door less than an hour ago, telling him irritably that his not knowing anything about Doc Hapfel was unimportant, answering the call box, going through the elaborate pretense that D. J., who was actually in Detroit, was tied up in a conference behind the door at her back.

"I'm—I'm terribly sorry."

Powell turned. The little old man on the couch had opened his eyes. "I'm—I'm—" Doc Hapfel said again, his voice hoarse and low, the words coming with an effort "—terribly—sorry."

"That's all right," Powell said. "There's nothing to be sorry for."

Not for Doc Hapfel, at any rate. He was not a temporary

employee, with three months in which to make good. He was
D. J.'s good luck piece.

"I didn't mean to get so—so—" The little old man rolled his
head helplessly from side to side, unable to utter the humiliating
word. "It's just that every year, when I come to these lunches on
my birthday, every year I hope that it—" He paused, as though
gathering his strength. "I knew I shouldn't have so much to
drink," he said finally, his eyes still closed. "You see," he said,
"I don't know anybody else in New York. I have no family, and
I'm too old to make new friends. Everybody is so busy. I came
here sixteen years ago because I thought it would be nice to live
near someone who—"

"When did you see D. J. last?" Harry Powell said.

The old man opened his eyes. A look of uneasiness, almost of
fear, washed across his face.

"He can't help it," Doc Hapfel said, speaking too quickly.
"He's a very important man. He's terribly busy. His time is
valuable. He can't—"

"When did you see him last?" Harry Powell repeated.

The old man merely shook his head helplessly. The phone
rang. Harry stepped across to Pierre's desk and picked up the
instrument. "Hello?"

"Harry?"

"Yes," he said to Ruth Sayre.

"I'm sorry I wasn't at my desk when you called. Anything
wrong?"

"No, everything's fine," Harry Powell said, and all at once he
realized that it was. The pieces of the puzzle had fallen into
place. "Doc Hapfel and I were just talking," he said. "And there
was one small point he couldn't seem to remember, so I thought
I'd call the office and check."

"What point?"

"He couldn't seem to remember when he saw D. J. last.
Would you mind putting him on, Ruth?"

There was a pause at the other end of the wire.

"Ruth?"

"Yes?"

"I said would you mind putting him on?"

"Who?"

"D. J."

"I'm sorry," Ruth Sayre said. "He's still tied up with those men who—"

"Put him on, anyway," Harry insisted.

"I can't do that."

"Why not?"

"Now, look, Harry." There was a familiar edge in Ruth's voice. "I never interrupt D. J. when he's in conference, and I'm not going to do it now."

"Even if I insist?"

"What does that remark mean?"

"If you didn't know what it means," Harry Powell said, "I don't think you'd be sitting at that desk right outside of D. J.'s door."

This time the pause at the other end of the wire was so long that a stranger might have thought Ruth Sayre had hung up. But Harry Powell was not a stranger. Not after eleven weeks. He could hear her breathing.

"Harry," she said finally, in the precise, carefully modulated voice that she considered consonant with her notions about office decorum. "I don't know what Doc Hapfel or anybody else has told you, and I'm not interested. I'm very interested, however, in making sure that you don't reach any foolish conclusions about what you've heard. Everything I've done has been for your own good. This is not Cleveland, Harry. I thought after eleven weeks you'd finally got that through your head. In this town the thing that counts—"

"I know," he said. For the first time since she had started to repay his guileless politeness, one of Ruth Sayre's helpful hints was totally unnecessary. Harry Powell did not have to be told what counted. It was merely that away from home, playing in a strange park, he had temporarily forgotten. "Sorry to have bothered you," he said to Ruth Sayre. "It won't happen again."

He hung up and walked back to the couch and looked down on the slender figure fighting for breath. Doc Hapfel didn't look too good, but he would probably be all right as soon as the ambulance arrived. Bending over to loosen the old man's tie, Harry Powell wondered if, after he saw D. J.'s old high school teacher safely to the hospital, he should call his father in Cleveland or just get on a plane and do all his talking when he got home. He preferred the latter, because it would give him time to work out an explanation that might save his face. But, as Harry Powell recalled the schedule, law school started in mid-October, and it was already the last week in September. If he expected to get in on such short notice, it might be wise to ask his father to start pulling strings at once. The old man probably couldn't get a table in Pierre's, but in and around Cleveland, where he had been practicing law for almost thirty years, his name meant something.

# WAIT
# FOR
# ME!

here was no
reason to be annoyed. On the contrary. In view of the way she
had lived for three years, ever since Harry went away, there
should have been every reason for her to be pleased. Even excited. After all, how often was the changeless monotony of her
days brushed by a phone call from a total stranger?

"I'm terribly sorry," said Alice, who was neither pleased nor
excited. "I'm afraid I didn't catch the name?"

This was not surprising. The phone was on the landing,
installed in this strategic location by Mrs. Crager so that it could
be reached with equal ease by what the landlady called her
"upstairsers" and her "downstairsers." As Alice had written to
Harry almost three years ago, soon after she moved into this
rooming house on West 87th Street and she became one of
Mrs. Crager's "upstairsers," there were days when, at eight
o'clock in the morning, Alice considered herself fortunate
if she could catch her breath.

"I said my name is Hodge," the pleasant but somehow
blurred voice at the other end of the wire said. "Can you hear me
now, Mrs. Willett?"

"Yes, I think so," Alice said. "May I ask who—?" The
remainder of her question was drowned out by Mrs. Crager's
two other "upstairsers." Clattering across the landing, in their
morning race for the bathroom at the far end of the hall, the two
girls finished in a dead heat and slammed their way in together.
"Hello?" Alice said in the welcome silence. She hoped she did
not sound as annoyed as she felt, because she knew her annoyance was unreasonable. So far as Mr. Hodge was concerned, at
any rate. Whoever he was, and whatever he wanted, Mr. Hodge
could not be expected to know that, on Monday mornings,
anything that delayed Alice Willett's movements, from the
moment she opened her eyes until the moment she reached the
pile of unsorted mail on Mrs. Crager's table in the hall down-

stairs, was a source of annoyance. "We've had a bit of confusion here, but things have quieted down now," Alice said apologetically. "I'm afraid I didn't hear what you said, Mr. Hodge. It *is* Mr. Hodge, isn't it?"

"'That's right," Mr. Hodge said cheerfully. "All I said, Mrs. Willett, I said I'd just come up from Georgia, and I was wondering—"

"Oh," Alice said. That explained the faintly blurred quality in the pleasant voice. Unfortunately for the special pleasure that Monday mornings brought into the changeless monotony of Alice Willett's strangely happy life, Mr. Hodge's announcement that he came from Georgia also explained why her unreasonable annoyance, sliding away abruptly, was replaced at once by a sudden and completely reasonable tension. "Are you sure you want me?" she said, trying not to sound excessively cautious. "I mean, are you sure you're talking to the right person?"

"Fairly sure," Mr. Hodge said, and his drawling, Southern voice broke in a small friendly chuckle. "That is, if you are married to a man named Harold B. Willett?"

"I am," Alice said, struggling to suppress the unwelcome tension, which she always felt when she heard Harry's name spoken aloud by a stranger. "What can I do for you, Mr. Hodge?"

"You can, if you will, give me a few minutes of your time," Mr. Hodge said. "I'd like very much to see you, Mrs. Willett."

"May I ask about what?"

"Why," Mr. Hodge said in obvious surprise, "about your husband, of course."

"Oh," Alice said again, and now she almost regretted the silence on the landing. Because now Alice Willett could hear her own heartbeats. They were so loud that she had the feeling Mr. Hodge, at the other end of the wire, could hear them, too. This was ridiculous. During the past three years she had grown accustomed to receiving from Harry more than that intensely welcome letter every Monday morning. Every now and then, at intervals of three or four months, there was one of these unex-

pected verbal messages from men who had been with Harry
recently and had come north after getting out. She had learned
long ago that, when the unexpected call came through, she must
not ask questions on the telephone. She had not received one of
these messages for a long time, however, and the hammering of
her own heart drowned out the lessons of caution. "Is he sick?"
Alice heard herself saying. "Mr. Hodge, please tell me. Is
Harry—?"

"Sick? Good Lord, no! I wish I was half as healthy myself!"

"Mr. Hodge, please," Alice said. "What's wrong?"

"Wrong?" The low, friendly chuckle started up again but,
perhaps because he had become suddenly aware of the desperate
intensity in her voice, Mr. Hodge's chuckle stopped short. "Mrs.
Willett," he said, "I assure you that absolutely nothing is
wrong."

"It's nothing bad?" Alice said. "He's not in any trouble?"

"Just the opposite," Mr. Hodge said. "Even though I can't
discuss it on the phone, Mrs. Willett, please believe me that
what I want to talk with you about is something good." There
was a pause. Almost gently, Mr. Hodge said, "Is that better,
Mrs. Willett?"

"Yes, thank you," Alice said, and she closed her eyes for a
moment. "I'm terribly sorry if I sounded—"

"Forget it," Mr. Hodge said. "I know how you feel."

"You're very kind," Alice said, even though Mr. Hodge's
well-intentioned words were so silly that, in spite of her relief
and gratitude, she had to fight back the desire to laugh. They all
said that. Her mother, her sisters, Harry's father. Even Harry
himself, in his letters. They all said they knew how she felt. And
their words always inspired in her that same secret desire to
laugh. Nobody knew how she felt. Neither her mother, nor her
sisters, nor Harry's father, who all thought they knew. Not even
Harry himself, who had better reasons than all the others to
suspect, even if he did not actually know. How could he? How
could Harry, or anybody else, possibly know? Alice said, "When
and where can I see you, Mr. Hodge?"

"Would six o'clock tonight be convenient?"

"But that's so late," Alice said. "Couldn't you make it earlier?"

"I'm afraid not," Mr. Hodge said. "I've got a flock of appointments scheduled that will keep me busy all day."

"Oh, dear," Alice said. "That means—" She paused, and she tried again, more calmly. "I'm sorry," she said. "I'm afraid my impatience is no concern of yours, Mr. Hodge."

"As a matter of fact, it is, Mrs. Willett, but I really can't make it any earlier," Mr. Hodge said. "If six o'clock is all right, may I come to your place at that time?"

"Well," Alice said, and she glanced nervously across her shoulder, toward the bathroom door. Neither Mrs. Crager, nor her "upstairsers" and "downstairsers," knew about Harry. Keeping them from knowing was one of the reasons, although not the major one, of course, why Alice made it a point, on Monday mornings, to reach the table of unsorted mail, in the hall downstairs, before anybody else did. "I don't know that my place is, well, I don't think it's quite right," Alice said in a low voice. "You see, Mr. Hodge, it's a rooming house."

"I do see," Mr. Hodge said. "How about my hotel, then? I'm staying at The Montevideo, on East 53rd. Could you meet me in the bar at six o'clock?"

"I could, and I will," Alice said and then, as the bathroom door, at the far end of the hall, slammed open, she said hurriedly, "Thanks so much, Mr. Hodge. I'll see you at six. I must run now."

It was only because she did run that Alice managed to reach the small table, in the hall downstairs, two steps ahead of the newest of Mrs. Crager's "downstairsers"; a beady-eyed girl with glasses who worked for an essential oils company on lower Broadway and, apparently as a relief from her taxing duties, spent a good deal of her spare time staring at other people's mail.

The long official-looking envelope, with the censor's rubber stamp in the lower corner, was lying on top of the pile. Alice picked it up and, with a swift movement, turned it face down.

"That's a funny-looking envelope," the girl with the glasses said across Alice's shoulder. "I mean, with that rubber stamp in the corner, it's sort of like letters from overseas during the war, isn't it?" Alice, pretending to be absorbed in the hunt for more envelopes marked with her name, merely nodded. The girl with the glasses said, "Do you mind if I take a look at it?"

"It's nothing but a bill," Alice said, keeping the envelope face down as she straightened up. There were never any more envelopes marked with her name. "I guess that's all there is for me."

She hurried back up the stairs, into her own room, for the hat and coat she had been about to put on when Mrs. Crager's shout had summoned her to the phone. Even though all the nerves in her body urged her, as they did every Monday morning at this moment, to tear open the envelope and gulp its contents greedily, Alice resisted the temptation, as she resisted it every Monday morning. This resistance, this postponement of the moment of fulfillment to which she looked forward all week, was part of the changeless routine by which she maintained the high level of secret happiness she drew endlessly—or had been drawing for almost three years—from her strange existence.

In accordance with this routine, she carried the envelope, unopened, from the rooming house to the subway station. She held the envelope tightly in her gloved hand all the way down in the noisy train to 42nd Street. She kept the envelope in her purse until she had entered the cafeteria, in the lobby of the building on Madison Avenue in which she worked, and had seated herself before the glass of orange juice, the cup of coffee, and the two pieces of toast that were her invariable breakfast.

Not until she had taken the first sip of coffee—which, on this Monday morning, as on all the others that had preceded it during the past three years, she did at precisely 8:35—did Alice Willett permit herself to slit the envelope that bore, in the lower left-hand corner, the rubber stamp of the Georgia penitentiary's censor.

Once this was done, she was lost. For twenty minutes, anyway.

The fierce rapture, with which she devoured the closely written page of prison foolscap, rendered her oblivious to the noises and the people around her in the crowded cafeteria. Nothing, however, not even the extraordinary emotion she managed to extract from Harry Willett's neat, meticulous, and completely unemotional handwriting, could make his wife forget, promptly at 8:55, to rise from the cafeteria table.

She was due in Mr. Burnham's office, sixteen floors above the cafeteria, promptly at nine. Mr. Burnham, who was a wealthy friend of her mother's, imported fine bindings and occasional pieces of period furniture, more as a pretext for keeping busy than as a matter of business necessity. Alice knew that he had given her the job, after Harry went away, not so much because Mr. Burnham needed her as because she had pleaded for it so desperately. Once she had the job, which was the cornerstone of the routine by which she had lived for three years, Alice Willett saw to it that she gave Mr. Burnham no occasion for believing anybody else could do the job better. She was never late.

Not even on Monday mornings, when she read for the first time each week the letter that, during the following seven days, she would read over and over again, until every word was seared into her hungry heart. Even if there had been a possibility that one of Harry's letters, which were always long, might have caused her to overlook the moment when the minute hand of the large electric clock on the cafeteria wall jumped to 8:55, that possibility was eliminated on this particular Monday morning. For, on this particular Monday morning, Harry's letter was surprisingly short.

"My own dearest darling," he wrote. "I know you will forgive the fact that this letter is no more than a line or two when I tell you that I am too excited to write because of something I have just heard. It is so extraordinary, and so wonderful, that I dare not put a hex on it by relating the details even to you. All I will say is that, by the time this reaches you, I am certain a gentleman by the name of Hodge will have been in touch with

you. Or perhaps his name is Lodge. I am not sure. Which gives
you some idea about the state of excitement I was in when I
heard the news. But the gentleman's name does not matter. All
that matters is what he will talk to you about. I know I don't
have to urge you to be completely frank with him. About me, as
well as about yourself. But this is so important that I will urge
you just the same. Tell Mr. Hodge, or Lodge, everything he
wants to know. Absolutely everything. And never forget what I
have written to you so often during the past three years and
what, from the bottom of my heart, I will never stop writing to
you: wait for me, darling, wait for me!"

To her very considerable surprise, all the way up in the
elevator Alice was aware of a sudden and small but nagging
sense of fear. It was as unreasonable as the annoyance that had
assailed her, almost exactly an hour ago, when Mrs. Crager had
shouted up that Alice was wanted on the phone. There was no
earthly reason for her to be frightened. Certainly not now, when
she was still warmed by the glow that had swept through her, as
it did every Monday morning, when she had read those expected
but still magical words: wait for me!

How often, during the past three years, had she read them?
How many lonely hours, how many dragging days, how many
empty weeks and dreary months had they quickened into vivid
life for her? Wait for me! When she thought of the thirty years
that had preceded the entrance of those three words into her
consciousness, Alice knew that they were more than a source of
warmth and strength. Wait for me! Those three words had
brought her out of the shadows and into the sun. Wait for me!
They had made her life.

Without them she had been nothing. With them, because of
them, Alice Willett had as much as any woman, including her
three beautiful and happily married sisters, could possibly want
or ever hope to get. They didn't know that, of course. Nobody
knew it. Not even Harry. But that did not matter. Alice knew it.
And she knew that nothing could dim the glow of those words,
or their special meaning in her overflowing heart.

Why, then, should they seem, all at once, less bright? Because the letter, with which those shining words ended, contained a reference to the hint Mr. Hodge had already given her on the phone? That good news was in store for Harry? Why should that cast a shadow over the inner glow by which, and for which, she lived? Why should that arouse in her this small but nagging sense of fear?

"Good morning, my dear," Mr. Burnham said when she opened the door. For a moment, Alice stared at him in astonishment. Mr. Burnham, who sometimes did not come into the office for days, never came in before noon. It was the reason why her job had been created. "Don't look so surprised, my dear," he said cheerfully. "I dined at your mother's house last night, and she asked me if I thought she could possibly have lunch with you today, and I said I saw no reason in the world why she couldn't."

"But I don't want to have lunch with my mother," Alice said. A moment later, when she saw the shocked look on Mr. Burnham's face, Alice added hastily, "I mean, when you gave me this job, it was distinctly understood that I was to have my lunch sent in every day, so that the office would be attended at all hours."

"So it was," Mr. Burnham said affably. "And now it is distinctly understood that today, as a welcome change for both of us, *I* will have my lunch sent in, and *you* will eat yours with your mother. Twelve-thirty, she said, at The Vincennes on 49th Street, and I need hardly caution you to be prompt, since I was horrified to learn yesterday, from her own lips, that she has not seen you for almost three years."

Alice did not blame Mr. Burnham for being horrified. At fifty he was still a bachelor, and so he held all the conventional views about the relationships between parents and their children. But Alice did blame her mother. All morning, as she performed her few duties in the office and struggled in vain to understand the small but nagging fear that had assailed her at breakfast, Alice wished that her mother had not chosen this of all days to violate the truce they had worked out so long ago.

"You are thirty years old, and so it is rather pointless for me

to say that you are of age and free to do as you choose," her
mother had said on that day, almost three and a half years ago,
when Alice had announced her intention to marry Harry Willett.
"You are, however, even at thirty, my own daughter, and so it
is far from pointless for me to say that I think you are acting like
a complete fool."

Alice had turned away from her mother, toward the window
of her bedroom. It looked out on the beautiful lawn that rolled
down, from the large house in which she had been born, toward
the beautiful gray-green of the Hudson in the near distance.
From that window she had watched her three younger sisters
going off to parties she had never attended, with boys who had
never come for her. And from that window she had heard them
discussing—in troubled tones from which they could not keep,
first, their impatience, and then their laughter—why she had
never gone to those parties, and why those boys would never
come for her.

"If what you say is true, and I am acting like a fool, it is
because you are judging by your standards," Alice said. "I am
forced to judge by my own."

"By any standards, this Harry Willett is impossible, and you
know it," her mother said. "He has no career, he has never had a
job, and he is held in complete contempt by those who know him
best. He is thoroughly untrustworthy and completely irresponsible, a cheap, vulgar, and flashy opportunist. He has only one
interest, which is gambling, and he will do anything to get the
money with which to gratify that interest."

"Even marry me?" Alice said. "Is that what you mean?"

Her mother hesitated. Mrs. Colby, who was very handsome,
was also very kind. It was not her fault, and Alice did not
consider it her mother's fault, that Mrs. Colby had found it
difficult to lavish as much of that kindness on her awkward and
unattractive eldest child as she had always been able to give to
her three lovely younger daughters.

"I don't want to hurt your feelings, but that is precisely what
I do mean," Mrs. Colby said finally. "Harry Willett seems to be

under the impression that you have a lot more than you actually do have."

"I've corrected that impression," Alice said. "I've told Harry exactly how much money Father left me."

"And he still wants to marry you?"

"Yes."

"I suppose you will think me cruel if I point out that he must surely be at the end of his rope," Mrs. Colby said, and then her face softened somewhat. "I can understand a man with his predilections marrying anybody because he is hard up, but why in heaven's name are *you* marrying *him?*"

"Because he asked me," Alice said. Watching the amazement spread across her mother's face, Alice added gently, "Nobody else ever did, Mother."

"Good God!" Mrs. Colby said. "That's no reason!"

"It is," Alice said, even more gently, "at my age."

Mrs. Colby's lovely gray eyes narrowed, as though the familiar face of her dowdy daughter had suddenly lost its contours, and she was trying to bring it back into focus.

"Alice," she said finally. "Do you love him?"

Alice turned away. Since she could not answer the question honestly, it seemed wise not to answer it at all.

"Alice," her mother said. "Does Harry Willett love you?"

Alice turned back. She could answer that question.

"He says he does," Alice said, and then she added, very gently, "I don't really care, Mother."

"Well, I do," Mrs. Colby said. "I must tell you, Alice, that if you marry Harry Willett, I shall never allow him to enter this house."

"You won't have to," Alice said. "We've taken an apartment in New York."

"When he has squandered your money, and he chases off after some girl with a fresh supply, you may have a bit of difficulty paying the rent," Mrs. Colby said. "This room will always be waiting."

"Not for me," Alice said. "I'm not coming back, Mother."

"That remains to be seen," Mrs. Colby had said tartly as she stood up. "I give you six months."

She had been wrong by a mere five weeks.

Eight days before Mr. and Mrs. Harold B. Willett's rent was due for the sixth month of their tenancy in the handsome apartment on East 65th Street, just off Fifth Avenue, two members of the police force dropped in to ask Harry some questions. He answered them with his customary charm and frankness, but the two members of the police force seemed to think Harry's replies were inadequate. They asked him to accompany them downtown. He did not come back. Eight days later, as Alice was writing the check for the rent, and wondering if it would clear the bank, her doorbell rang. She went to the door and opened it.

"Hello," her sister Carol said. "May I come in?"

Alice hesitated. Carol was twenty-two, the youngest of Mrs. Colby's four daughters and the prettiest of Alice's three sisters. Alice had been expecting her mother for a week, ever since the story about Harry had broken in the papers. She guessed now that her mother, far too kind to come herself on what would inevitably have to assume the unpleasant overtones of an "I-told-you-so" mission, had chosen Carol as the family's emissary because Carol's husband, Dick Stanton, was an enormously successful lawyer.

"Of course you may come in," Alice said, and she held the door wide for her sister. "How are Dick and the children?"

"They're fine, and having said that, let's both consider the subject closed," Carol said as she sat down. "As you can probably guess, I didn't come all the way down here from Scarsdale to make, or listen to, a lot of irrelevant polite talk. Fair enough?"

"More than fair," Alice said and, in spite of the confused churning of her thoughts, with which she had been living for eight uneasy days, she managed to smile at her youngest sister. She had always liked Carol more than the others. Not so much because of Carol's engaging frankness. Nor even because Carol, being the youngest, had naturally grown up and become popular later than Mary and Susan, and, as a result, had caused Alice to suffer through a shorter period of envy. Alice had always liked Carol more than the others for a much simpler and far more human reason: she had always suspected that Carol liked *her* more than the others did. "I'm not really up to a lot of irrelevant polite talk myself," Alice said as she sat down facing her sister. Hoping she did not sound as weary as she felt, she said, "What does Mother want?"

"She wants you to come back," Carol said. "And Dick says he can get you divorced from Harry Willett without the slightest fuss or bother."

"I'm not coming back," Alice said and, for the first time in eight days, she had a moment of relief. The difficult words, which she had been hoarding in terror against the expected visit from her mother, had at last been uttered. And she had succeeded in uttering them calmly. So they had sounded, anyway, in her own ears. Alice drew a deep breath and said, "And I don't want a divorce."

Carol nodded, as though to indicate that, in these preliminary phases of a painful discussion that involved her oldest sister's pride, the younger girl had expected no less than this categorical refusal.

"Perhaps you'll change your mind when I give you the facts," Carol said. "I happen to have them at my fingertips because Dick knows the district attorney personally, and they've had several talks about Harry's case, and Dick briefed me thoroughly. May I?"

Alice looked at this young girl, who happened to be her sister, with a touch of the envy she had known all of her life and which, when she had become Mrs. Harold B. Willett, Alice had thought she would never experience again. It must be wonderful, she thought as she stared at Carol, to be so young and so self-assured, to know always exactly where you stood in a world where others, like Alice, for example, scarcely knew from moment to moment at what they could grasp next for support.

"You can say anything you like, if it will make you feel better when you report to Mother that you did your best," Alice said. "Aside from that, Carol, you're wasting your time."

"Let me try, anyway," Carol said pleasantly. "You know, of course, what they've got on Harry, don't you?" Alice nodded. "Forgery," Carol said. "On a Georgia bank." Alice nodded again. It was much simpler than making the painful effort to talk. Carol said, "Do you know also that he'll get ten years?"

Alice closed her eyes. Nothing was simple. Just when you were beginning to think you could handle the blows that already struck, new and unforeseen disasters were hurled at you. Alice opened her eyes.

"I retained a lawyer yesterday," she said, making no effort now to conceal the weariness in her voice. "He told me the most Harry could get is five years, and that would be cut down for good behavior."

"I don't know who your lawyer is," Carol said. "All I know is that he obviously doesn't know what you don't know: this is not Harry's first offense." She paused and, for a moment, a look of sympathy crossed her youthful, pretty, and self-assured face. "Look, Sis," Carol said. "I don't suppose Harry ever told you, but the district attorney told Dick: Harry has forged checks before. He'll get ten years."

Alice closed her eyes again. This time, when she spoke, she did not try to open them.

"I don't care," she said. "I'm not coming back." She drew another deep breath. "And I don't want a divorce."

"Alice, listen to me," Carol said. "Dick says the district attorney subpoenaed your joint bank accounts. Dick has examined them. In the last five months, Dick says, Harry Willett has lost at the race track every penny Father left you. That's why he forged checks in the past, and that's why he turned back to forgery again. He's a thoroughly bad apple, and you're broke, Sis. You can't pay that lawyer you retained yesterday. You can't even pay the rent on this apartment. Alice, be sensible. How are you going to live?"

"I don't know," Alice said. She knew only that she felt cheated. She had gambled and she had lost. The price had been high, every penny she had in the world, but that curiously defined yet intensely real sense of certainty, of well-being, of belonging—the thing called happiness, the thing that others, like Carol, had all their lives and received in fuller measure when they married, the thing that Alice had wanted so fiercely—had been denied her. She could not go back to what she had been. She could not go on without it. Somehow, somewhere she must find it. Alice said again, "I don't know how I'm going to live," and she added, with a sort of helpless savagery, "And I don't care."

There was a long moment of silence. When Carol spoke again, there was a note in her voice that Alice had never heard before.

"He must have made you very happy," the young girl said quietly, almost enviously. Alice, taken completely by surprise, opened her eyes. She had been so wretched during the past five months that she had assumed everybody, even the members of her own family whom she had not seen, must have known it. Staring at her sister in astonishment, Alice saw that Carol knew nothing of the sort. Carol, quite clearly, assumed that Harry Willett, thoroughly bad apple though he was, had earned Alice's loyalty by giving her five months of bliss. The young girl's lip quivered. A look of tenderness washed across her lovely face. Sadly, with a tremor of understanding, and clearly with pity, Carol said in a low voice, "Poor Sis, you love him very much, don't you?"

Alice blinked dazedly at her sister. It was the one question that, during the agony of the past five months and the nightmare of the past eight days, she had never even thought about. Thinking about it now, as she stared at Carol, Alice realized with a stab of shock that she preferred not to answer that question.

Three years later, hurrying across town from Mr. Burnham's office to the luncheon date with her mother that she did not want to keep, Alice realized that she still preferred not to answer it. But now, after three years of living in Mrs. Crager's rooming house and working for Mr. Burnham, the preference did not shock her. Because now, after three years of the changeless but wonderful monotony she had built up carefully around Harry Willett's Monday morning letters and the magic words with which they always closed, Alice knew that the answer—to the question her mother had asked before she married Harry, and the question Carol had repeated before Harry went away—did not matter.

Certainly not at the moment. What mattered at the moment was this unexpected and nagging sense of fear that had gripped her three hours ago, when she rose from her breakfast in the cafeteria, the fear that seemed to be pursuing her now, as she pushed through the elegantly curtained doors of The Vincennes.

"Darling," Mrs. Colby said, rising from the settee, just inside the doors, on which she had been waiting for her daughter. "Oh, darling," Mrs. Colby said as she took Alice in her arms, "don't you think it's time, after three long years, that we both stopped being silly?"

Alice did not think she had been silly, and the three years had not seemed long to her, so she refrained from answering this question. But, as they settled themselves at the table Mrs. Colby had reserved and they ordered their lunch, Alice answered all her mother's other questions: about her job with Mr. Burnham, and what living with Mrs. Crager was like, and what she did with herself in her spare time.

"I mend my stockings, or I read a book, and I go to bed early," Alice said and, to the waiter, "No dessert for me, thank you."

"It doesn't sound like much of a life," Mrs. Colby said, and she shook her head at the waiter's inquiring glance about dessert. "Don't you think, Alice, that after three years you've had enough of it?"

"Look, Mother," Alice said quietly. "As I told Carol three

years ago, and as I know she told you, it's my life, and I want to live it my way. If you can't understand that, surely you can understand my wanting to be left alone. I'm grateful to you for having done precisely that for three years. I can't say I'm grateful to you for this lunch, or for the way you arranged it, through Mr. Burnham."

"Who else could I arrange it through?" Mrs. Colby said. "You never call me, or write to me, or come out to see me."

"Because I want to avoid just this sort of pointless wrangling," Alice said. "I don't want to seem rude, Mother, but I can't believe you invited me to lunch for no better reason than to hear me say that again. I assume you have something specific on your mind. Please get to the point and tell me what it is. I must be back in the office by one-thirty."

Mrs. Colby stopped toying with her coffee spoon. She was not only an attractive woman. She was something far more rare: a sensible woman.

"Since you put it that way, Alice, I must confess I do have something on my mind," she said. "Much as I have disapproved, for three long years, of your stubborn refusal to divorce Harry Willett, your determination to wait ten years for his release, and your strange way of life, it has not puzzled me, because I know how you feel." Mrs. Colby paused, and she stared hard at her daughter. "What I have been unable to understand," Mrs. Colby said. "What has puzzled me for three years, Alice, has been why Harry Willett should be willing to wait for *you*."

The small, vague, and nagging sense of fear, which had pursued her since breakfast, seemed all at once to come closer to clarity in Alice's mind. It stabbed at her like a warning.

"I'm terribly sorry," she said carefully. "I don't quite know what you mean, Mother."

"Don't you?" Mrs. Colby said. "Try, then, to look at it from my point of view. I said from the very beginning, three and a half years ago, that Harry Willett was a complete and heartless scoundrel who was marrying you for your money. Events proved me soon enough to be absolutely right. When he went through your money, he also went to prison. Knowing the Harry Willetts of the world a good deal better than you do, my dear, I assumed at the time that he was through with you, that from now on he would plan, against the day when he is released from prison, how to catch another solvent victim. Instead of that, from all I have been able to gather, Harry Willett is planning to return to his bankrupt victim, namely, to you. This is so contrary to everything I know about men like Harry Willett that for three years I have been asking myself: why?"

Mrs. Colby paused again. She looked coolly at her daughter. It cost her a strenuous effort, but Alice managed to meet her mother's glance.

"Is that why you asked me to lunch?" Alice said. "Because you've found your answer?"

"Precisely," Mrs. Colby said. "Only the other day, Alice, the contents of your letters to Harry Willett came to my attention." This time, when Mrs. Colby paused, she apparently expected her daughter to say something, but Alice found it simpler—as she struggled with the vague fear that seemed to be trying so hard to make itself clear to her—to remain silent. "I learned," Mrs. Colby said, "that you have been writing Harry to the effect that the terms of your father's will, by which you inherited the sum Harry Willett has already squandered, call for your receiving another and more substantial bequest seven years from now."

Alice looked at her mother with surprising equanimity. It was as though the troubling fear, having skirted the truth, could not face it and, at the last moment, had shied away.

"Who told you that?" Alice said.

"Does that matter?" Mrs. Colby said.

"Very much," Alice said. "Because it happens to be a lie." Mrs. Colby's eyebrows went up. "All I have written to Harry is that we won't be completely penniless when he gets out," Alice said. "And we won't be. Mr. Burnham pays me quite well. My rent at Mrs. Crager's is not exorbitant, and my other expenses are small. I manage to put a large part of my salary into the bank each week."

Mrs. Colby's handsome face broke in a surprisingly gentle smile.

"I know what Mr. Burnham pays you," she said. "But don't you see that, even if you put your *entire* salary into the bank every week, it still won't add up to Harry Willett's idea of a substantial sum by the time he gets out?"

"I never wrote Harry it would be a substantial sum," Alice said. "I told him it would be enough."

The expression on Mrs. Colby's face changed. It reminded Alice of the expression on the face of her youngest sister, Carol, three years ago. The recollection caused Alice a twinge of irritation. Once again she, who needed it less than anybody she had ever known, was being pitied.

"Is that fair?" Mrs. Colby said gently. "I don't mean to Harry, because I think he is beneath contempt. I'm talking about you."

"I don't understand," Alice said. She was genuinely puzzled. "What about me?"

"Do you think it is fair to yourself, to the love you have in your heart, to sustain it in his with a mere promise of money?"

Alice stared at her mother in astonishment just as, three years ago, she had stared at her sister Carol. Mrs. Colby was, quite clearly, making the same error Carol had made. Mrs. Colby was assuming that there could be only one explanation for Alice's conduct. Like Carol, Mrs. Colby was convinced that the happiness Harry Willett had given his wife during their brief life together had been so remarkable that Alice could not give up the hope of, some day, recapturing it.

"I never noticed, during the first thirty years of my life, that there was anything particularly fair about love," Alice said. "Everybody has to work out his or her own rules." She picked up her purse. "I'm sorry if you don't like mine," she said as she pushed back her chair. "If I had been born beautiful, like you, or attractive and popular, like Carol and my other sisters," Alice said, "I might have learned to play by your rules." She smiled at her mother. "But I wasn't born beautiful, or popular, or even attractive." Alice stood up. "So thanks for lunch, Mother," Alice said, and she shrugged. "I'll just have to continue with the rules I made up for myself three years ago."

Happily, Mr. Burnham was gone for the day when Alice got back to the office. Thus she was at least spared the embarrassing explanations about her lunch with Mrs. Colby that Mr. Burnham would undoubtedly have asked. Unhappily, however, Mr. Burnham's absence left Alice's mind free to return to, and circle endlessly around, the small, vague, and nagging sense of fear that, for a brief moment, in the restaurant with her mother, had seemed about to come into focus. But it had slipped away from her, and it kept slipping away all afternoon so that, when her watch showed five o'clock and it was time to close the office, Alice felt exhausted, as though she had been struggling for hours with a hopeless physical task.

She decided she must shower and change her clothes before she kept her six o'clock appointment in the bar of The Montevideo with Mr. Hodge. Alice would have had ample time to do both, because the trip from her office to the rooming house on 87th Street took only twenty minutes, but Mrs. Crager changed her plans when Alice stepped into the hall.

"There's a gentleman to see you," the landlady said. "He came in a few minutes ago, and I told him you always got home by five-thirty at the latest, so he said he'd wait. He's in the parlor."

"Thanks," Alice said, trying to control her voice. It shook badly with the sudden violence of her heartbeats. She had made it so clear to Mr. Hodge, on the phone in the morning, why she did not think it was wise to see him at her rooming house, that this change in his plans could mean only one thing: something had gone wrong. "Thanks a lot," Alice said to Mrs. Crager, and she hurried across the hall, toward the parlor. "Oh," she said, stopping short on the threshold. The elderly gentleman, rising with a small, courtly bow from the chair near the potted aspidistra, was not Mr. Hodge. "Why, hello," Alice said hesitantly as she closed the door behind her and moved across the room to take the outstretched hand of Harry Willett's father. "This is a pleasant surprise."

"You are very kind to put it that way," the old man said with a smile. "I know I am intruding, but there is something I wanted to say to you, and since it is rather important, I thought I would run the risk of being rude for a few minutes."

"You are not rude at all," Alice said. "Please sit down, Mr. Willett."

She had met him several times, but very briefly, three years ago, outside the courtroom in which Harry had been tried and sentenced. Alice had been so confused at the time that she remembered nothing about the meeting except the pressure of the old man's hand as he had held hers, and the look in his pale blue eyes as he had stared at her, and the sound of his voice as he had murmured that he had no words with which to convey his regrets, since he knew how she felt. He seemed much older now, or perhaps Alice had not noticed then the whiteness of his hair and the extent to which his slender body was bowed, but the look in his eyes was the same: a confused mixture of overwhelming sympathy and painful embarrassment.

"In some quarters, my failure to write or call or come to see you during the past three years may be construed as heartless indifference," Harry Willett's father said awkwardly as he stared down at his long, bony fingers. "I ask you to believe me that this is not so. You have been much in my thoughts, but it seemed to me, in view of the shameful manner in which you have been treated by one member of my family, that you would prefer to be spared the empty sympathy of another."

"I'm sorry you felt that way," Alice said. "I haven't needed or wanted sympathy but if you had brought me yours, I would not have considered it empty."

The old man looked up and, as he stared at her, his pale blue eyes were full of wonder.

"I wish I knew what it is in the human heart that makes a man as worthless as my son worthy of a woman like you," he said. Even if Harry Willett had been worthy of her, which Alice knew he was not, there was almost no answer she could have made to his father's words. Besides, they had been spoken more to himself than to her, so Alice merely glanced at her watch. The old man said at once, "I'm afraid I'm keeping you from an appointment."

"That's quite all right," Alice said, even though it wasn't. She would never get a chance, now, to shower and change her clothes before she had to rush off to keep her appointment with Mr. Hodge. "I don't have to leave for ten or fifteen minutes."

"I will try to be brief," Harry Willett's father said. "The correspondence between Harry and myself has been desultory. This is not surprising. After all these years of trouble, we have very little left to say to each other. I know he pays no attention to my letters, and I seldom find anything worth paying attention to in his. Last week, however, I had a long and boastful communication from Harry that bothered me. I would have disregarded it, since I am accustomed to his boasting, but for one fact. Harry seems to have got the notion, somehow, that you are about to come into a large sum of money and that, when he is released from prison, you will place this sum at his disposal. It is impossible to know when Harry is dealing with fact or fancy but, even if there was only a shred of truth in this particular boast, I felt it was my duty to do something to prevent a recurrence of the tragedy he visited upon you three years ago. Perhaps I should have come to you at once, last week. I decided not to, for the same reason that kept me from coming to see you earlier."

Alice, feeling a new and sharper stab of the nagging fear by which she had been troubled all day, looked quickly at the old man.

"You went to my mother instead?"

"I did," Harry Willett's father said. "I hope you don't mind?"

"No, of course not," Alice said, and she wondered if she was telling the truth. "It's just that I had lunch with Mother today, and she said more or less the same thing, and I thought—"

She stopped. It was a relief to know where her mother had got the information, but it was not as much relief as Alice wanted. That vague, nagging fear was still with her.

"Mrs. Colby was good enough to say she would see what she could do," Harry Willett's father said. "It occurred to me later, however, and I hope you won't mind my putting it this way, that since your mother has been able to do nothing with you for three years, so far as Harry is concerned, I mean, it was my duty to come and see if I could do something myself."

"There is nothing to do," Alice said as calmly as the nagging fear would permit. "I have been working, as you know, and I have been saving part of my salary every week. Since I write to Harry regularly, and tell him everything about myself, he knows this. It seems clear that Harry has apparently got the impression that my savings will amount to a considerable sum by the time he gets out. I can't imagine how Harry got that impression, but—"

"I can."

Again, as the nagging fear stabbed more sharply, Alice looked quickly at Harry Willett's father. The old man was regarding her with a shrewd but kindly smile.

"Can you?" Alice said and, to her intense distress, she found she had to drop her glance. "How?"

"I think you know my son so well that you know the only way to retain his interest is by holding out to him the promise that, when he is released from prison seven years from now, you will have waiting for him a sum of money at least as large as the one he squandered three years ago." The old man paused and, when Alice raised her glance, he said quietly, "Isn't that more or less the truth?"

Alice drew a deep breath. In the strangely complete and happy life she had worked out for herself, there was no more room for truth than there was for sympathy or pity.

"Suppose it is?" she said. "I fail to see how it affects you."

"I am not thinking of myself," Harry Willett's father said. "I am thinking of you."

"I've never asked you to think about me," Alice said. "I don't want you to think about me now."

"I cannot help it," the old man said. "Harry is my son, and I feel responsible. He is thoroughly worthless. He always has been, and he always will be. Harry can bring you nothing but a repetition of misery. He does not deserve your loyalty or your love. You have your own life to consider. Even though I know it is difficult, because I know how you feel, I urge you to cast him out of your heart. It is your only hope. You are still a young woman. Seven years from now, you won't be. If you divorce him now, as you should have done three years ago and as you still have every right and justification for doing, you may yet find happiness."

Alice stared at him in astonishment. Just as, three years ago, she had stared at her sister Carol. Just as, a few hours ago, she had stared at her mother. They all said the same thing: they knew how she felt. And they all inspired in her that same secret desire to laugh. What did they know of hope who had not, like herself, lived without it for thirty years? What did they know of happiness who had not, like herself, been forced to make her own?

"I have all the happiness I want," Alice said. "If I had any more, it would be unbearable."

She stood up. Harry Willett's father rose from the chair near the potted aspidistra. He came slowly across Mrs. Crager's parlor, and he took Alice's hand.

"Then it's true," the old man said and once again there was a touch of wonder in his voice. "Until this moment, I never really believed it."

"Believed what?" Alice said.

"That you really love him," the old man said. "With all your heart. In spite of what he is, and what he has done, and what you know he will do to you as soon as he gets out, in spite of everything you still love him, don't you?"

Alice hesitated. What her mother and her sisters believed was one thing. They were, in a sense, her adversaries: more fortunate and far more powerful than herself. The beliefs of this kindly old man were something else again. He was, in the truest sense, a fellow victim: less fortunate and much weaker than herself. The suffering Harry Willett had caused his wife had lasted a mere five months. The suffering Harry Willett had caused his father would last a lifetime. Her mother and her sisters were not entitled to the truth. This kindly old man was. After three years, however, Alice was no longer certain she knew what the truth was.

"I must hurry," she said. "Or I'll be late."

She wasn't but, as she came breathlessly into the bar of The Montevideo, Alice wished she had risked being late. A quiet pause—a few minutes of rest between her unusually hectic day and this unusual evening appointment—might have stilled the small, vague, and nagging fear that had hung over her since breakfast and which, as she looked nervously about the crowded room, seemed all at once to be standing mockingly at her elbow, as though it were a masked dancer about to reveal his identity at a ball.

"Mrs. Willett?"

Alice turned, and she had a moment of shock. Since she had spoken with him on the phone that morning, Alice had formed unconsciously a mental picture of Mr. Hodge. It was based on her vivid recollections of the released convicts to whom Harry, during the past three years, had entrusted his occasional verbal messages to her. Alice saw now that her mental picture bore no relation whatsoever to this slight, mild, friendly-looking, sandy-haired man who stood smiling at her.

"Yes, I am," Alice said. "Mr. Hodge?"

The sandy hair dipped in a cheerful nod, and Mr. Hodge, after shaking her hand, led Alice to a small table at one side of the room.

"I really must apologize for being so cryptic when we talked on the phone this morning," he said as they sat down and he signaled to a passing waiter. "It's just that we hate to talk about these things on the phone. What will you drink, Mrs. Willett?"

"Nothing for me, thank you," Alice said. "I didn't mind your being cryptic at all, Mr. Hodge, once I knew you were the bearer of good news about Harry."

"It's the only real reward I get out of my work, since the pay is not what my wife calls sensational," Mr. Hodge said with a chuckle, and he turned to order a scotch and soda from the waiter. When he turned back to Alice, Mr. Hodge's friendly face was beaming. "Mrs. Willett," he said, "I wonder how you would like to have your husband back here with you in New York, a free man, by Christmas?"

Three times that day Alice had stared at people in astonishment: at Mr. Burnham, at her mother, and at Harry's father. Staring now at Mr. Hodge, she realized that she was doing it with more than astonishment. She was staring at Mr. Hodge with horror. The small, vague, and nagging fear that had been circling elusively around her all day had come, at last, into the open. Staring at Mr. Hodge, she saw it for what it was: the end of a dream, the collapse of a world, the destruction of an edifice into which every ounce of her energies and every moment of her life for the past three years had been poured.

"But I can't have him back!" she cried, and then, as the words spoken in desperation and terror hurled themselves back, like a savage echo, into her stunned brain, Alice saw the look on Mr. Hodge's face. "I mean, you must be joking," she said quickly. "Harry's sentence has seven more years to run!"

"It has," Mr. Hodge said. "But a number of factors must be taken into consideration. First, your husband has already served three years. Second, he has been a model and useful prisoner. Third, we gather from his letters, which as you know are read before he gets them, that he has a loyal and devoted wife waiting for him outside. And fourth, we conclude from those same letters that, if your husband is released, he is not likely to become a public charge, or be tempted once again into criminal paths, because that devoted and loyal wife is possessed of considerable means. Taking all those factors into consideration, the parole board, whose representative I am, of course, feels that it will be a service to the state, as well as to Harold B. Willett, to return him to the custody of that loyal and devoted wife." Mr. Hodge turned toward the drink the waiter was setting down. Picking it up, Mr. Hodge smiled at Alice and said, "On one condition, of course, and that's what I am here to discuss with you."

While Mr. Hodge took a long and welcome pull at his glass, Alice tried desperately to pull together her scattered thoughts, to shore up the toppling structure of happiness it had taken her three years to build. She couldn't. Not right now. All she could do, in this moment of stunned confusion, was seek more time.

"This one condition," she said hesitantly. "What is it?"

Mr. Hodge set down his glass and smacked his lips gently.

"Your consent," he said. "If you agree to take on what we might call the responsibility of keeping an eye on the prisoner, seeing to it that he stays on the straight and narrow, so to speak, your husband will be a free man by Christmas, Mrs. Willett."

The toppling structure seemed to halt in mid-air, like a motion picture of a demolition scene that is stopped abruptly by some mechanical failure in the projection booth. Seeing, in the unexpected but welcome pause, the way out, seeing her chance to turn the camera backward, to put the toppling structure back on its foundation, intact, unmarred, as solid as it had been this morning, before Mr. Hodge's unexpected phone call and Harry's surprisingly short letter had set in motion the vague rumblings of disaster, Alice saw also, and with bitter clarity, the unfair harshness of her dilemma: she held in her hands seven years of a man's life.

"I don't know what—" she started to say, slowly, painfully, like a victim in a train wreck crawling out of the wreckage. Harry was what her sister had called a bad apple, and what her mother had called a heartless scoundrel, and what his own father had called thoroughly worthless, and her own experience had proved them all to be absolutely right, but Harry Willett was still a human being, and he was still her own husband. "I mean," she said, "it's so sudden that I—"

And then, as her hammering heart moved from the senseless clamor of terror to the slow, rhythmic dirge of defeat, Alice saw something else: Harry Willett held all of *her* life in *his* hands. When he had been able to control what he held, Harry Willett had smashed it ruthlessly. Only the recollection of the terrible emptiness of her first thirty years, plus a blind refusal to go back to it, had kept her from divorcing him three years ago. There must be something, she had told herself fiercely, there *had* to be something. And, in the splinters Harry Willett had left behind him, she had found the raw material for what she had been seeking. Slowly, painfully, she had patched together her substitute for happiness. It could not last forever. And nobody knew better than Alice herself that it was founded on a lie. But it had lasted three years, and she had counted on another seven. It was more than she had owned during her first thirty years, and the memory of it would be enough to sustain her during whatever years might remain after she was forty, after Harry came back and smashed it again. The choice with which Mr. Hodge had unexpectedly faced her was harsh, but it was also simple: she could give those seven years to Harry, or she could keep them for herself.

"I'm terribly sorry," Alice Willett said. "I don't think I can take on that responsibility."

It was Mr. Hodge's turn to look astonished.

"I don't understand," he said. "We gathered from reading your letters to him, and his letters to you—" Mr. Hodge paused, and he stared worriedly at his glass. "Look," he said finally. "Do you really want me to accept that as your answer?"

Alice hesitated. She knew there was no way to answer Mr. Hodge's question without sounding cruel. But she knew a good deal more than Mr. Hodge could possibly know. She knew Harry. And she knew herself. She knew that what Mr. Hodge had read in Harry's letters, those three shining words with which all his letters ended, had been composed, not by Harry Willett, but by his wife. With painstaking care, over a period of time, by the discreet hints in her own letters that had played so shrewdly on Harry's lust for money, she had won back in writing the lie Harry Willett had once spoken when he asked her to marry him, the lie Harry now wrote once a week on a sheet of prison foolscap for the wife who, so long as she did not have to see him, was willing to accept the lie for truth.

"I'm sorry," Alice said with an effort. "It's the only answer I can make."

"Don't you love him?" Mr. Hodge said in perplexity. "Don't you want him back?"

Alice hesitated again. How could she tell the perplexed Mr. Hodge that what she loved was not a man, who had long ago proved he was incapable of loving her, but an illusion of her own creation from which she had drawn for three years, and with luck would continue to draw for another seven, the only love she had ever known?

"No, I don't want him" Alice said and then, as her voice broke, she managed to say through her sobs, "All I want is to wait for him."

# THE
# LOVE
# PHILTRE
# OF
# VITTORIO
# ADAMELLO

**I** had just turned, for a last glance around the hotel room to make sure my wife and I had left nothing behind, when the phone rang.

"Milan calling, sir," the operator said.

"For me?" I said in surprise. I knew nobody in Milan. "Who is it?"

"Vittorio," a voice at the other end said. "Vittorio Adamello."

I blinked at the gleaming blue of Lake Como outside the window of the hotel in which my wife and I had just spent three days. It did not seem possible that I had heard correctly.

"Who?" I said again.

"Vittorio Adamello," the voice said impatiently. "I must see you at once."

I could not quite believe it. I had last seen Vittorio Adamello three weeks before, in the supermarket on the main street of the small Connecticut town in which we both live. He had just learned that my wife and I were going to Italy for a month, and he had wished us both a pleasant holiday in his native land.

"Where are you calling from?" I said.

"The airport outside Milan," he said. "I just flew over from New York. I must see you at once."

"How did you know where we are?"

"My brother Frank gave me your itinerary," Vittorio Adamello said. "There's a bus to Como in about an hour. It gets up there around noon. It is of the utmost importance that I see you."

"We won't be here when you arrive," I said. "We're just leaving. My wife is already downstairs in the car with the luggage. We're driving down to Milan to catch the two o'clock train to Venice. Why don't you stay right there in Milan and meet us in the restaurant at the railroad station for lunch?"

"All right," Vittorio Adamello said. "But please do not fail me. It is very urgent."

I did not doubt it. My wife and I had been worried about the Adamellos for more than a year.

We had met Frank Adamello and his wife Rosa soon after we moved to Connecticut. He was a violinist with the NBC Symphony Orchestra, and they lived in a modernistic house about an eighth of a mile up the road from us. The Adamellos were our closest neighbors. They were also a charming couple, warm, attractive, and gay. There was something about them—a kind of relaxed fitting together, so to speak—that made it impossible to imagine them married to anybody but each other. You never thought of them as individuals. Frank and Rosa Adamello were, as much as any couple I have ever known, a team. Knowing them was a very pleasant experience.

About two years after we became neighbors and friends, Frank Adamello brought his younger brother to this country. The boy, who was not quite twenty-one and named Vittorio, had just graduated with honors from the University of Padova, and he wanted to become a doctor. His brother Frank, who had prospered in America and was now a citizen, felt there were much better medical schools in his adopted country than in Italy, and he wanted Vittorio to have the best.

When young Vittorio arrived, Frank rented a room for him near the medical school in New York. Every now and then the boy came out to Connecticut to spend a week-end with his brother and sister-in-law. He was, however, an industrious student, and he usually spent these Saturdays and Sundays locked away with his medical books in the Adamello guest room.

As a result, during Vittorio's first three years in America, while my wife and I continued to see as much of Frank and Rosa as we ever did, we rarely saw young Vittorio. I was quite surprised, therefore, one Saturday morning when he was in his last year at medical school, to see Vittorio Adamello coming up my driveway.

"Hello," he said shyly when I opened the door for him. "May I come in and talk for a few minutes?"

"Of course," I said. "I'm afraid, though, that the only one you'll be able to talk to is me. My wife just drove into the village with Rosa to do some shopping."

"I know," Vittorio said. "That is why I came now. I wanted to talk to you alone."

I was puzzled. I did not know this tall, awkward young man terribly well.

"What did you want to talk to me about?" I said.

"You know my brother's house, of course," Vittorio Adamello said. "I've been wondering what you think of it?"

I hesitated. It seemed an odd question.

"Why, I think it's a very nice house."

"You do not think there is anything peculiar about it?"

"Well, when you're dealing with modernistic houses," I said cautiously, "I suppose it's all a matter of taste. Personally, I've never been very keen on—"

"I do not mean that."

"Perhaps you'd better tell me what you do mean."

"It is a beautiful house," Vittorio Adamello said. "Everything in it is the most modern and new. And yet it does not have a nursery."

It was a subject my wife and I had discussed many times since we had met Frank and Rosa Adamello. We knew, from the way they treated our two small boys, that they liked children. Rosa, who was not a career girl, had plenty of time on her hands. And the Adamellos could certainly afford to raise a family. We had often wondered why they hadn't.

"Yes, I've noticed that Frank's house doesn't have a nursery," I said. "What about it?"

"That is what I have come to ask you."

"I'm afraid I don't understand."

"Neither do I," Vittorio Adamello said. "In Italy, all our relatives have large families. Italians always have large families. Frank and Rosa have now been married seven years, but they have no children. When they built this house, they made no room in the plans for a nursery. I have been visiting them every week-end for three years, but never once do I hear them talk of children to come." Vittorio Adamello shook his head. "It is very distressing," he said. "I would like to know the reason."

"Why don't you ask Frank?"

"I cannot," he said. "I am the younger brother. It is something one cannot ask an older brother. That is why I have come to you."

For a moment I did not grasp what he meant. When I did, I shook my head in protest.

"Oh, now, look," I said. "I couldn't do a thing like that."

"You are one of my brother Frank's best friends," Vittorio Adamello said. "To whom else can I appeal?"

An hour later, when my wife came home from the village, I told her about Vittorio's visit. And I had my second surprise of the day.

"Good!" she said. "I'm glad you promised him you'd ask Frank."

"You mean to say," I said, "you approve of the way that great big overgrown medical student wormed out of me a promise to poke my nose into his brother's affairs?"

"Of course I do," my wife said. "I've been dying to know for almost five years why the Adamellos don't have any children. Besides, I think they've both been acting a bit peculiar these last few weeks. Go on over right now and ask Frank."

"I'll do nothing of the sort," I said irritably. "And what do you mean they've both been acting a bit peculiar?"

"You know how close they are," my wife said. "We've always remarked, from the moment we met them, that they were a team rather than a couple of individual people. Well, these last few weeks I've sensed a change. All of a sudden, there's a gap, a sort of space between them, if you know what I mean. Both of them, Rosa as well as Frank, seem to be worried about something, and I'm willing to bet it's connected in some way with this visit you've just had from Vittorio. Are you going over?"

"Not now," I said. "I want to think this thing through, and decide on some way to approach him."

By Monday morning, when I ran into Frank Adamello on the 9:14 train to New York, I had decided the most sensible approach was complete honesty.

"Your kid brother Vittorio came over to see me on Saturday," I said after I dropped into the seat beside Frank. "We had a talk."

"Really?" Frank said. "What about?"

I told him. As he listened, I began to understand more clearly what my wife had meant when she said the Adamellos had been acting a bit peculiar. I also began to regret my decision to be completely honest. I could see that my wife was absolutely right. The Adamellos obviously had something troublesome on their minds. As I talked, Frank sat slumped down in the train seat, staring fixedly at the folded newspaper in his lap. Even as I cursed myself inwardly for yielding to young Vittorio's request, and tried to ease the words in which I reported our conversation to his brother, I could see the muscles in the side of Frank Adamello's jaw ripple. He seemed to be holding himself together around some inner pain.

"I suppose I should have told Vittorio it's none of my business and let it go at that," I concluded lamely. "But frankly, since I know how much you and Rosa like children, once Vittorio raised the subject I couldn't help worrying about the same thing he's apparently worried about. Is something wrong, Frank?"

"I don't know," Frank Adamello said, scowling at his newspaper, and he hesitated. I didn't blame him. It is not the sort of thing one man likes to tell another, even when that other man is his friend. "We've been to doctors, of course," he said slowly. "Half a dozen of them. They all say the same thing: there's nothing wrong with either of us so far as having children is concerned, but there's something definitely wrong with Rosa's heart. It would be dangerous for her to become pregnant. So, according to the doctors, nature takes care of it by seeing to it that she doesn't."

I had never heard of such a thing. But there are many things about medicine that are a mystery to me, and this was hardly the moment to discuss my ignorance. I cleared my throat.

"A great many people who want children and can't have them, Frank, solve the problem by adoption."

"We've been all through that," Frank Adamello said. "But Rosa said it wouldn't be the same." He hesitated again, and then Frank Adamello said something that surprised me even more than his account of what the doctors had said. "You can tell Vittorio that Rosa is absolutely firm about wanting children of her own, or none at all."

That night, after I had reported this conversation to my wife, I asked her if, next Saturday, she would do me a favor and convey the gist of it to Vittorio Adamello. I wanted to discharge my promise without getting further involved. My wife shook her head.

"Vittorio came to you as a young man asking the help of an older man," she said. "It would be wrong for a woman to interfere. I think you must keep it on a man-to-man basis. Frank is going to New York on Saturday for a rehearsal, and as soon as Rosa and I drive off to the village to do our shopping, I'm sure Vittorio will hurry down to see you."

My wife was right. Saturday morning, ten minutes after she left the house, I was repeating to Vittorio Adamello in my own living room the upsetting reason why his brother and sister-in-law had not yet raised a family and, according to Frank Adamello, never would.

"The medical aspects of it sound a little strange to me," I said. "But Frank assured me half a dozen doctors had given him and Rosa the same diagnosis, so I suppose it's sound enough. In any event, as a medical student you're in a much better position to know about that than I am."

Vittorio Adamello nodded and scowled at his large, powerful hands. I had the impression that he was struggling with the information I had brought him and, in view of it, trying to reach some sort of decision. The sun, striking him in profile and at an angle, made me suddenly aware of something I had never realized before: Vittorio Adamello was an extremely handsome young man. Finally, with a gesture that seemed to indicate he had reached a decision, he looked up.

"The medical aspects are indeed, as you put it, strange," he said. "If Frank is willing to take a certain amount of risk, however, I think they are not insoluble. Would you tell that to my brother?"

"Why don't you tell him yourself?" I said. "You're staying in the same house with him."

"It is, as I said last week, a subject a younger brother cannot discuss with an older brother," Vittorio Adamello said. "I ask you please, as my brother's friend, to tell him that I said, if he is willing to take a certain amount of risk, the medical aspects of his and Rosa's problem are not, in my opinion, insoluble."

An hour later, when my wife came home and I had told her about Vittorio's request, I asked her if she could figure out what was behind it.

"I don't know what's behind it," my wife said thoughtfully. "But I can tell you, because it seems pretty obvious, what's happening on the surface."

"What's that?"

"The Adamello brothers are trying to say something to one another. They don't want to say it directly. Perhaps they can't. So they are using you as their communications system. It may be puzzling, and even annoying, but it doesn't seem to me to be too much to do for a friend. I think you ought to give Vittorio's message to Frank."

I did, on the 9:14 Monday morning. His reaction to the message was the most peculiar thing that had happened thus far. First he looked delighted. Then he looked frightened. And for a long time he just sat there, chewing his lower lip, staring blindly out the train window, and obviously struggling with the message I had brought him in an effort to reach some sort of decision. I was reminded of a child—whose delight in the receipt of a wonderful present has been shattered by the donor's advice that it might at any moment explode—trying to make up its mind whether to keep or return the alluring but dangerous gift. Just before our train pulled into Grand Central, Frank Adamello seemed to make up his mind.

"Please tell my brother," he said in a low voice, without looking at me, "that in spite of the risk, I give him my permission to make the attempt."

I neither understood nor liked the word risk. I made that perfectly clear the following Saturday, when I conveyed Frank's message to his younger brother, and then I asked for an explanation. Vittorio said he was sorry, but he was not at liberty to enlighten me. My wife did, two days later, when I came home from New York.

"Rosa came down the hill this afternoon for a cup of coffee," she said. "Between sips she dropped the rather startling news that there's a chance she might finally be able to have children."

"But according to the doctors she and Frank consulted, I thought it's impossible for her to become pregnant?"

"That's what Rosa thought, too."

"Why does she think differently now?"

"Because of Vittorio. According to the doctors, what has prevented Rosa from becoming pregnant up to now is her heart condition. Well, Vittorio, who seems to be more than just a brilliant medical student, has made a study of Rosa's heart condition, and he thinks he can cure it."

"How?"

"By changing the chemistry of her blood. It seems to be a matter of putting into Rosa's blood stream certain chemicals that are not there now. Some of these she can take with her food. Others Vittorio will have to inject into her veins. The whole process, according to Vittorio's calculations, should take about three months."

I stared at my wife for several long, silent moments. She is not a woman who is given to talking nonsense, or repeating the nonsense other people talk.

"Look," I said finally. "Do you believe this claptrap?"

"No, and I don't think Rosa does, either. But apparently Vittorio is being very persuasive."

"What about Frank?"

"He seems to be for it."

"I guess that explains the messages I've been carrying back and forth between them."

"Not quite," my wife said. "If what's involved here is this preposterous scheme of Vittorio's, why couldn't he and Frank discuss it face to face?"

"I don't know."

"Neither do I," my wife said. "It seems to me logical to assume, therefore, that this scheme about Rosa's blood stream is only a cover up for something deeper, something Frank and his brother really couldn't discuss face to face. Where are you going?"

"Up the hill," I said. "I want to have a little talk with Rosa."

She was not, however, at home.

"Rosa just drove Vittorio down to the station," Frank said after he opened the door for me. "Vittorio came out for dinner, but he has to get back to New York tonight because he's got an exam in the morning."

I decided not to waste words.

"This crackpot scheme about changing the chemistry of Rosa's blood," I said. "You're not going to let her and Vittorio go through with it, are you?"

"Why not?"

I stared at him. Frank Adamello avoided my glance.

"Why not?" I repeated. "Because medicine is nothing for amateurs to fool around with," I snapped. "Because this is a ridiculous theory invented by an inexperienced boy, and if you allow him to try it out on your wife, it may damn well kill her, that's why not!"

Frank Adamello's jaw twitched, as though a twinge of pain had raced through it.

"Rosa wants children," he said in a low voice. "She's waited seven years for them, ever since we got married. She's not going to wait much longer. If she cannot have children, Rosa says she would rather be dead."

For several stunned moments I didn't know what to say. I felt like a man who volunteers to cash a small check for a friend and finds himself unexpectedly involved in a bank robbery. It had never occurred to me that these two warm, gay, charming people, this man and woman who on the surface appeared to be so close that I had always thought of them not as individuals but as a team, had actually been driven so far apart by a problem that, in the lives of most people, never even arises.

"It seems to me," I said uncomfortably, "the least you can do is check this theory of Vittorio's with a few reputable doctors and hear what they have to say."

Frank Adamello shook his head.

"I don't want to hear what the reputable doctors have to say," he said. "I've got to believe that this scheme of Vittorio's is going to work. If it doesn't—" Frank Adamello paused, and he shrugged helplessly. "If you love someone very much, you don't want her to die," he said. "But you want her to be happy, too." He paused again, and he drew a long, deep, tired breath. "Unless Rosa has a child soon," Frank Adamello said quietly, "there won't be anything left to keep us together."

Two days later Vittorio gave up his room in New York and moved into the Adamello house. Every minute of the day that he could spare from his classes, to which he now commuted, Vittorio Adamello spent with his sister-in-law Rosa. According to my wife, who got her information from Rosa, Vittorio measured out her food, mixed in the various chemicals, forced her to stick to a schedule of mild exercise and prolonged rest periods, gave her the necessary injections, and kept a complete record of the entire process in a set of black leather notebooks which he carried in a locked briefcase.

I found the whole thing a trifle unreal. My emotions alternated between a strange conviction that it was all a hoax, that absolutely nothing was happening in the house on the hill, and the nervous feeling that I should report it to the police. I might have done it, too, if it were not for the fact that one day, about a month after the strange experiment began, my wife made an interesting discovery.

"Rosa rang me up this morning," she said when I came home. "Her car was down at the garage for its regular thousand-mile checkup, and Vittorio had to catch the 11:32 to New York because he had a one-o'clock class, so Rosa asked if I would run him down to the train, and pick him up when he came out again on the 4:10. I managed to get him to the 11:32, but it was a pretty tight squeeze, and in all the rush, Vittorio forgot his briefcase in our car. I didn't notice it until I got back to the house, when the briefcase fell out of the car as I opened the door. It fell with quite a bang. The lock snapped open, and those black leather notebooks tumbled out." My wife paused. "Those notebooks," she said, "are blank."

I didn't bother to express, or even analyze, my astonishment. I could tell from my wife's face that there was more to come.

"By the time I drove down to the 4:10 to pick up Vittorio," she said, "I'd had almost five hours of putting two and two together. As soon as Vittorio stepped off the train, I could see he'd had almost five hours of panic. His first question, as soon as I handed him the briefcase and he saw the lock was snapped, told me clearly that I'd been putting my twos and twos together correctly."

"What was Vittorio's first question?" I said.

"He wanted to know if I'd told Rosa the notebooks were blank."

"Had you?"

"Of course not," my wife said. "It seemed silly to give away a piece of information as valuable as that for free. I wanted to swap."

"For what?"

"Another piece of information," my wife said. "I told Vittorio I'd say nothing to Rosa about my discovery if he'd answer one question."

"Did he?"

"Yes," my wife said. "I now know what it was Frank and Vittorio were really discussing when they were sending all those messages through you." She paused again. "When Frank told you that the doctors said there was nothing wrong with him or Rosa so far as having children is concerned, but there was something definitely wrong with Rosa's heart, Frank was lying. There is nothing wrong with Rosa's heart or, for that matter, all the rest of her. The trouble, according to the doctors, is Frank. Rosa is perfectly capable of bearing children. Frank, unfortunately, is incapable of siring them."

In the sudden silence, it seemed to me I could almost hear the missing pieces of the puzzle falling into place.

"This whole so-called experiment," I said slowly. "This whole silly business of changing the chemical content of Rosa's blood stream—"

"Is nothing but camouflage," my wife said. "Neither Vittorio nor Frank believes in it. It's just a gag, something they invented as a cover for throwing Rosa and Vittorio together."

She had taken the words out of my mouth, and yet I was shocked to hear them spoken aloud.

"Frank told you himself," my wife continued, "that he and Rosa have reached a point in their relationship where he knows that, unless she has a child soon, there will be nothing left to hold them together." My wife shrugged. "Since Frank can't give her a child—"

"He's arranged to throw her into the arms of someone who can do what he can't," I said slowly. "His own brother."

"Precisely," my wife said.

"Do they think they can get away with it?"

"Apparently," my wife said with another shrug. "Or I don't think they would try it. Up to now, at any rate, Rosa seems to have fallen for it. She thinks Vittorio is changing the chemical content of her blood stream so that her heart condition will be cured and she will be able to become pregnant by her husband."

"But sooner or later she's bound to find out this is not so!"

"By that time," my wife said, "I think the conspirators are hoping she will be pregnant by Vittorio."

"Well," I said grimly, "they're wrong."

"How do you know?"

"Because I know Rosa," I said. "And she's not that kind of girl. She may want children desperately enough to risk her life. And she may even be gullible enough to believe this silly business about changing the chemical content of her blood by diet and injections. But at a certain point, if this scheme is going to work, Vittorio will have to abandon the diet and the injections, and resort to the traditional method. It is precisely at this point that Vittorio is going to get his handsome face slapped."

My wife gave me a funny little look.

"I suppose it is precisely for this sort of situation," she said, "that the phrase *wait and see* was invented."

I could have wished, during the three months that followed, for a more efficient invention. We waited, but saw nothing. Nothing new, that is. Rosa and Vittorio were together constantly. Vittorio continued acting out the elaborate pretense of the experiment. And Rosa, so far as my wife and I could see, continued to be completely taken in by it.

The only noticeable change, from the moment my wife and I discovered the experiment was a fraud, took place not in the house on the hill, but in our own. While neither of us had uttered a word to bring the situation into existence, it became perfectly obvious before long that my wife and I were on opposite sides of the fence about Rosa's virtue.

I did not believe Vittorio would be successful. My wife did.

"You men are so much more sentimental about technical fidelity," she said. "You can't seem to get it through your heads that there are situations, and this seems to me to be one of them, when it is a good deal like refusing, for purely sentimental reasons, to take a new road when the old one, to which you've always been accustomed, has been washed out by an act of God."

Acts of God were very much on my mind the Saturday

morning, almost four months after the experiment began, when
Rosa Adamello called up during breakfast to announce in a voice
quivering with excitement that she was going into New York to
be examined by one of the obstetricians who had previously
declared it was impossible for her to have children. I was pleased
to note, when my wife put down the phone, that she seemed
shaken.

"Rosa says that, according to Vittorio's black notebooks, the
process of changing the chemical content of her blood was
completed six weeks ago, so the obstetrician should have some
good news for her today." My wife scowled at me across the
breakfast table. "But you and I know those notebooks are
blank!"

"Vittorio obviously didn't show them to her," I said. "He
merely told Rosa what he wanted her to believe they contain." I
was not surprised to detect a note of smugness in my voice as I
added, "In any case, Rosa is still obviously unaware that the
whole preposterous thing was a fake, so you can guess for
yourself what kind of news the obstetrician will have for her
after he finishes examining her. I'm sorry that Rosa will be
disappointed, but I'm glad that I judged her correctly when I
said she wasn't that kind of girl." I poured myself another cup of
coffee. "Did Rosa have anything else to say?"

"They're coming back on the 2:34," my wife said. "They'll
stop in here on their way home from the station."

"Good," I said. "We'll be waiting."

I think we would have done it with less wear and tear on our
nerves if we had not been completely astonished, shortly after
lunch, by the arrival of Vittorio Adamello.

"What are you doing here?" I said. "I thought you'd gone
into New York with Frank and Rosa?"

"Oh, no," the handsome young medical student said uncomfortably. "I—I couldn't do that." He glanced at his watch, and
compared it with the clock over the fireplace. "I've been waiting
up at the house, but I—I—" He paused, and drew a deep breath.
"Do you mind if I wait here?"

"Of course not," my wife said. "Sit down and be comfortable."

He sat down, but he could not make himself comfortable. All afternoon, when he was not looking at his watch, Vittorio Adamello kept squirming in his chair and staring morosely out the window, while the tension in our living room mounted steadily, like steam pressure in a boiler. Even though I secretly enjoyed his discomfort, because it underscored my conviction that he knew as surely as I did that his plan had failed, I was acutely aware that the knowledge of its failure would come as a terrible blow to Rosa. For almost four months she had so obviously believed completely, with all her heart, in something that we all knew was a hoax. I could not escape the unhappy conviction that the return of Rosa and Frank from New York would be one of the most depressing events I had ever witnessed or participated in.

I cannot remember when I have ever been more completely wrong.

"Good Lord!" my wife said when we finally heard the Adamello car turning into our driveway. "Is that singing I hear?"

It was. And several moments later, as Frank and Rosa leaped from their car, we heard more of it.

"It worked!" Frank shouted jubilantly. "Rosa is pregnant!"

Things became somewhat confused during the next few minutes. I remember clearly, however, in spite of the daze into which my shocked astonishment had flung me, that the excited discussion which followed included endlessly repeated references to the look of amazement on the face of the obstetrician.

"He couldn't believe it!" Rosa cried gleefully. "He kept saying he just couldn't believe it!"

Neither could I. But for different reasons. My confidence in Rosa Adamello, my certainty that in the crucial moment of revelation she would resist Vittorio's advances, had not been based entirely on what I recognized in myself as a perhaps prudish repugnance for a scheme that, no matter how worthy its

ultimate aim, nevertheless called for a man to perform temporarily the marital duties of his own brother. My confidence in
Rosa had been based largely on what I felt about her as a
person.

She was a small girl, with a round, delicately molded face in
which the enormous eyes, because of her great vivacity, seemed
to twinkle like lanterns. And like lanterns, there was a re-
freshing simplicity and directness about the warm glow she shed
on those she allowed to come close to her. For four years, ever
since we had become neighbors and friends, Rosa Adamello had
admitted me and my wife to that small circle. For four years I
had been entranced by her warmth, and delighted with her
simplicity and directness.

I saw now that I had misjudged her. Rosa Adamello's warmth
was only skin deep. Her simplicity and directness were spurious.
At heart, she was obviously as accomplished a cold-blooded
schemer as her husband Frank and her brother-in-law Vittorio.

All three of them knew precisely what had happened. And all
three of them knew that my wife and I knew precisely what had
happened. Yet here they were, in my own living room, acting out
with their enthusiastic congratulations the embarrassing pretense that Rosa was carrying Frank's child because Vittorio, by
means of a brilliant medical experiment, had removed the
barrier that had previously kept husband and wife from fulfillment.

After a while, I began to find the spectacle distasteful. I
walked out to the kitchen, and left the house by the back door.

I did not see Rosa for almost two months. Then one day,
pushing my shopping cart around a rack in the local supermarket, I found myself facing Rosa in front of the dry cereals.
Pregnancy, I had once read, is the time of a woman's greatest
beauty. Looking at Rosa Adamello, I could well believe it. The
child she was carrying had already begun to distort her figure,
but her face had never looked lovelier. The old warmth, the
quality that had captured me from the very beginning, seemed to
surround her like a visible glow. I found it difficult, as I watched

her smile at me with obvious pleasure in the unexpected meeting, to believe what I knew about her.

"You've been avoiding me," she said, and then, with the directness that had always charmed me, she added, "I think I know why, too."

"Yes," I said, "I think you do."

"If you put it that way," Rosa said, "I suppose there's no point in my trying to explain."

"No," I said, "I suppose there isn't."

"I'm sorry about that," she said. "I'd much rather we continued to be friends." She paused, but I could think of nothing to say. "Since that's not possible," she continued, "I'd like to tell you something that I think, because we once were friends, you're entitled to know."

"What's that?" I said.

"No woman can do what I did," Rosa Adamello said quietly, "unless she loves a man more than she loves anything else in the world, including the opinions of her friends."

She turned her cart, moved it around mine, and walked off down the aisle. Watching her go, I was suddenly assailed by so many tangled emotions that I considered myself fortunate to be able to identify one: sympathy for her husband.

Poor Frank. The risk that both he and Vittorio had foreseen from the very beginning, the danger that had lurked just below the surface of their plot from the moment it was hatched, had caught up with him. Rosa was getting at last what she had always wanted more than life itself: a child. In the process of arranging for her to have it, however, Frank had lost her to the man who had helped him: she had fallen in love with Vittorio.

They were all obviously waiting until the baby was born before Rosa divorced Frank and married Vittorio. I did not much enjoy the waiting process. For this reason, almost six months later, when my wife and I were about to leave for our holiday in Italy and Rosa was expecting the baby momentarily, I did not go up the hill but used the telephone to say goodbye to the people with whom I had once been so friendly.

Now, three weeks later, driving down from Lake Como to meet Vittorio Adamello at the railroad station in Milan, I could think of only one reason that would bring the young medical student to Italy so unexpectedly: something had gone wrong with Rosa's pregnancy.

"No, no, nothing has gone wrong," Vittorio said impatiently after we had all exchanged greetings in the restaurant and I, somewhat nervously, had asked the anxious question. "Rosa gave birth two days ago," Vittorio said. "A boy. Six pounds, nine ounces."

"How wonderful!" my wife said. "Congratulations!"

I added my own congratulations, and then asked why, instead of remaining at the mother's side in Connecticut, he had come to Italy.

"I have come to find work in a hospital as an interne, and then I will set up my medical practice here," Vittorio said. "I can no longer remain in America. Rosa says it is impossible."

Somewhat belatedly, it seemed, Rosa was becoming aware of the outrageous aspects of what she had done.

"In other words," I said, "as soon as you've got yourself settled here, and Rosa and the baby are strong enough, they're coming over here to join you. Is that it?"

Vittorio shook his head.

"That is how I thought it would be," he said. "Until two days ago, when the baby was born. Then—" He paused, and he brought his troubled glance from the far corner of the restaurant, and he fixed it on me and my wife. "In the hospital I said to Rosa now we can talk to Frank about a divorce and we will be able to get married, but Rosa looked at me and she said quietly there will be no divorce. Frank has finished helping to put you through medical school, Rosa said. You are now ready to become a doctor. Go to Italy, she said. They need doctors in Italy. But the baby, I said. It is my child. Rosa shook her head. No, she said. It is Frank's child, she said. Frank's and mine. We needed help, she said, and you are a member of the family, so Frank and I let you help us. But now we don't need any more help. Neither do you. We've both graduated, Rosa said to me, go to Italy."

Vittorio's voice stopped, and he shook his head as though to fling away the puzzling recollection. I was no less puzzled, but I could not fling the problem away.

"You told me, when you telephoned this morning to Lake Como," I said, "that it was very urgent for you to see me."

"Yes," Vittorio said. "Rosa suggested it."

"Rosa suggested that you come to see me here in Italy?" I said in astonishment.

The handsome young man nodded.

"I told her in the hospital I did not understand why she was acting this way to me. I thought she loved me. I thought that was why she consented in the first place. Then, when the baby is born, she suddenly says she does not love me! If she does not love me, how could she do what she did?"

"Well," my wife said slowly, "I'm afraid that's going to be a little difficult to explain."

"Not for your husband," Vittorio Adamello said. "Rosa said your husband could explain it to me, because she once explained it to him."

My wife turned from the puzzled young man to stare at me with even greater puzzlement.

"You can?" she said incredulously.

"Why, yes," I said with a sudden smile, because at last I understood. I had not misjudged Rosa Adamello after all. "I'm pretty sure I can explain it."

But I paused for a moment. I did not want to make any mistakes. I wanted to get the words right, exactly as Rosa Adamello had uttered them, in front of the dry cereals in our supermarket, when she had tried to tell me how far a woman will go in order to save her marriage to the man she loves.

# A
# KNIGHT
# LAY
# DYING

The pain itself was not the problem. After all this time he had learned how to handle that. Nor was he bothered by the change in plan. To a man who lived the way for a dozen years Scott had been living, changes in plan were a commonplace.

This, however, was the last plan he would ever have anything to do with. Dr. Benatti, by whom Scott had been examined the day before down in Rome, had left no doubts about that. The problem, therefore, was how to conceal the pain. Unless he did, it might prevent Scott from completing this plan on which everything, including what was left of his life, now depended.

"I'm sorry," he said into the phone. He shook his head, two hard, sharp twists, one to the left and one to the right, and the pain moved back, the way it always did, as though it were an intruder who had been caught and flung away from a door he had no right to enter. "I was lighting a cigarette," Scott said. "I didn't hear you."

"I said hold everything," Tullio said. "There's been a change in plan."

"What kind of change?" Scott said.

"The kind that makes the difference between a nice profit and a big killing," Tullio said. "Have you got the Aphrodite?"

"It's in my bag," Scott said. "I just picked it up at Enzo's a half hour ago. Your phone call caught me in the middle of packing to catch the train back to Rome." He glanced at his wrist watch. "If you don't get off this wire, I'll miss it."

"Never mind that train," Tullio said. "I want you to stay up there in Siena."

"Listen," Scott said.

The pain was coming back slowly, almost imperceptibly, easing up into his head like the incoming tide on a lonely beach. He had to get off the phone before it engulfed him.

"No, you listen," Tullio said. "I haven't got much time. Crager is expecting me in a few minutes. I'm driving him to the train."

"What train?"

"The train to Siena," Tullio said. "They're having dinner with you up there tonight."

"Who is they?"

"Crager and his wife."

Scott closed his eyes. Perhaps the pain, which he had learned to handle, was beginning to handle him. Perhaps it was doing things to his mind. Scott opened his eyes and turned with the phone so that, through the window of his hotel room, he could look down into the Piazza del Campo.

"Tullio," he said into the phone. "When I left Rome yesterday I didn't know anything about a Mrs. Crager."

"Neither did I," said Tullio. "I thought all we had on our hands was a sucker from Ohio who wanted an Aphrodite to take back to his Cleveland living room and you were going to Siena to pick it up and bring it back to him. This morning, when I went over to the Excelsior to have breakfast with him, it turns out he's got a wife, and when Mrs. Crager learned her husband was buying the Aphrodite, she started sounding off about art, and the next thing you know, it turns out she's crazy about cameos."

"Cameos?"

The word seemed to hang in the air, like a puff of smoke from a distant, faintly heard explosion.

"Yeah," Tullio said. "What's the matter with cameos?"

"I don't know," Scott said slowly. Oddly enough, he didn't, and it bothered him. "It seems a funny thing to be crazy about."

"It may be funny to the rest of the world," Tullio said. "To you and me, though, it's an oil well. Or it can be, if we handle it right, so I want you to listen."

Scott did, concentrating hard on the flat, nasal voice that, in spite of the poor long distance connection, came through to him clearly. It was one of the tricks for outwitting the pain that Scott had learned long ago, when he first met Tullio Pazelli. In those days, soon after the war, when Scott had not yet been fully aware of the extent of the damage, his only problem had been how to eat. He hadn't wanted to go back to America, and he had no way of earning a living in Italy. When he met Tullio that problem had been solved. Tullio had been born in Naples and had spent fifteen years on the fringes of New York's underworld before, at the age of thirty, coming back to Italy. The two young men, working together, discovered before too long that there were always enough rich tourists pouring through Rome and Venice and Milan to keep a former art student like Scott and a former thief like Tullio in pasta and wine. When the pain became more persistent, however, and Scott met Dr. Benatti, and he did learn the extent of the damage, Scott also learned the necessity for outwitting it. Concentrating hard on Tullio's flat, nasal voice was one way.

It was also a necessity. The legendary honor that was supposed to exist among thieves existed, Scott soon found, only as a legend. He had no illusions about how he had made his living during the past dozen years. He had even fewer illusions about the man with whom he had worked hand in glove to earn that living. Now that he had come to the end of the road, now that he knew from Dr. Benatti that his share of this Aphrodite deal would probably be the last money he would ever be able to earn, Scott knew also that concentrating hard on every word Tullio uttered had become more than a way to outwit the pain. It was a matter, almost literally, of life and death. The possibility of being double-crossed by Tullio had always existed. Now it could not be allowed to happen.

"That's the plan," Tullio said in conclusion. "How do you like it?"

Scott didn't.

"We have Crager hooked on the Aphrodite," he said. "Why not let it go at that?"

"Because on the Aphrodite all we make ourselves is a profit of two million lira or sixteen hundred bucks apiece," Tullio said impatiently. "What's that?"

It was, at the small place near Bern that Scott had picked out, a year in Switzerland. And from here on in, according to Dr. Benatti, a year was going to be to Scott a lifetime. But Tullio didn't know that, and it was important for him not to know it.

"Sixteen hundred dollars for each of us on one deal looks like nice money to me," Scott said carefully. "Let's not be greedy."

"Let's not be dumb, either," Tullio said. "On top of this sixteen hundred, if you do like I say, we can pick ourselves up another couple of grand, easy. This Crager is loaded and his wife is nuts about cameos. The way I've got them primed, they'll go for practically any amount. All you have to do is follow instructions. What do you say?"

Scott hesitated. Not, as he had said to Tullio, because he didn't want to be greedy. Or because what Tullio proposed didn't make sense. On the contrary. Tullio's change in plan made a good deal of sense. Especially for Scott, to whom fleecing the Cragers was a swan song, and the more fleece he carried away with him to Switzerland, the better. Scott hesitated because the basic problem still remained: he had been able to conceal the pain up to now; he knew he could conceal it long enough to bring the Aphrodite to Rome and pick up his half of the profit; he was not sure he could conceal it long enough to take on this additional work.

"I don't know," Scott said. "I don't like it."

"What's the matter?" Tullio said. "You sick or something?"

There was no change in his voice. But Scott could feel the sudden tension. Tullio Pazelli didn't have to change his voice to indicate that he knew—or perhaps only suspected—more than he was uttering with it.

"No, of course not," Scott said sharply. "What ever gave you that idea?"

"I don't know," Tullio said. "This is the first time I ever knew you to turn down ready money."

"I'm not turning it down," Scott said. "I was just looking at both sides of the picture."

"Well, cut it out and just look at the side that shows all those great big shiny dollars," Tullio said. "You going to help me grab them off, or do I have to come up to Siena with the Cragers and do it all myself?"

Scott drew a deep breath.

"Stay down there in Rome," he said. "Of course I'll help you."

For several moments after he hung up, Scott remained like that, standing motionless at the window, looking down into the sunny square, wondering what it was about the change in plan as Tullio had outlined it that bothered him. Then, as the pain began to creep past the guards he kept posted at the doors to his consciousness, Scott realized that wondering could do him no good. He shook off the pain and looked at his watch. It showed a few minutes short of one o'clock. If he wanted to get back to Enzo's before the dealer closed his shop for the siesta, he would have to hurry. Scott took his hat and went out.

The uneasy, shapeless thought went with him, however, like a shadowy stranger dogging his footsteps but keeping carefully out of sight. It was not until he turned into the small side street of the sweeping Piazza Matteotti, and he actually saw the crowded window of Enzo's shop, that the answer came, or rather returned, to him. It came back the way it had arrived in the hotel room, along the telephone wire from Rome, in a single word that exploded in his mind and hung there, like a puff of smoke from a distant, faintly heard explosion.

"Cameos!"

Except that the explosion was hardly that. It was a girl's voice, clear, and fresh, and tinkly with the special laughter that had been so much a part of Helen Minton that Scott had never been able to think of her without hearing its very special sound. And now that he was thinking of her again, time and distance seemed to vanish in the echoes of that laughter, so that Scott was no longer standing on a sunny side street off a sweeping square in an Italian hill town on an afternoon that, according to Dr. Benatti, was one of the two or three hundred still left to him.

All at once a dozen years were gone, and there was a war on, and Scott was a twenty-two-year-old sergeant who had been hauled out of his tail gunner's blister in one of the Eighth Air Force's B-17s and sent down, under sealed orders, from his airfield base near Liverpool to the stately old mansion, about an hour out of London by train, that was known to its inmates as The Hutch.

Inmates was probably the wrong word for an American colonel, a British captain, a Welsh cook, and a WAC lieutenant, but that was the word Helen Minton had used when Scott arrived. Now, after three weeks, it was still the word she preferred. It went very well with her special laughter.

"Sergeant Scott," she said. He turned from the map he had been studying on the wall of the Common Room. Lieutenant Minton said, "You're wanted in the Chief Inmate's office right away."

"Yes, ma'am," said Scott, and then he noticed that the tinkly laughter, which always accompanied her use of the word inmate, was missing from Lieutenant Minton's voice. He looked at her hard and, very quietly, Scott said, "Is this it?"

A troubled frown washed swiftly across her lovely face, and she caught her lower lip in her teeth as she tugged nervously at a button on her khaki blouse.

"My orders were to tell you that Colonel March wants you in his office at once," Helen Minton said. "I can't say any more than that."

"Sorry," Scott said.

For almost two years, ever since he had been in the army, he had heard jokes about enlisted men and WAC officers. He had even told some of these jokes himself. It was not until these past three weeks at The Hutch, however, that Scott had learned the jokes were not funny. He moved toward the door.

"Sergeant."

Scott turned back. Lieutenant Minton was still standing in

front of the map. The troubled look had returned to her face.

"If this *should* be it, sergeant," she said, "would you stop in at my office after you're finished with Colonel March?"

"Yes, ma'am," Scott said.

He wanted to say more. For almost two weeks he'd been wanting to say a good deal more. But the words refused to come, and Scott knew that the trouble was not the difference in their rank. The trouble was that he didn't have the right to say more.

He walked out of the Common Room, down the long hall from the walls of which the Gainsboroughs had been removed when the British War Office took the house for the duration and turned it over to SHAEF. At the door to the library, which had been converted into an office for the commandant of this secret Allied operation, Scott stopped and knocked.

"Come in!"

Scott came in and closed the door. Colonel March was standing at the window, his hands locked behind him, staring out across the once formal gardens that now, because of the war and the manpower shortage, had gone back to the tangled, overgrown informality preferred by nature.

"Sergeant Scott reporting, sir."

Colonel March turned from the window. He was a tall man with a slight stoop and almost white hair who had been wounded twice at Château-Thierry.

"I suppose you know why I sent for you, sergeant?"

It was the same question Colonel March had asked three weeks ago, when Scott had arrived at The Hutch under sealed orders. The difference was that now he knew the answer.

"Yes, sir," Scott said.

Three weeks ago he had not known the army was even aware that for two years before the war broke out he had been studying art in France and living near Morlaix in Brittany.

"The orders came up from London a little while ago," Colonel March said. "You're going in tonight, sergeant."

"Yes, sir," Scott said.

The Colonel's eyes narrowed slightly, and his head tipped to one side, as though he were looking at the slender young man through a film of smoke and he wanted to get a clearer view.

"Is that all you have to say?" he said.

There was so much Scott wanted to say that his heart ached with the necessity for keeping the words bottled up. But Colonel March was not the person to whom he wanted to say them.

"Yes, sir," Scott said.

The Colonel stroked the side of his jaw with great care, as though he were probing for an elusive pain.

"Then perhaps I'd better be the one to say something, sergeant." He stepped across the room, toward the map of Europe on the wall behind his desk, and he looked up at it for several long, silent moments. "Three years ago, when France fell and the Germans overran Europe," Colonel March said, "the continent was sealed off as tight as a drum. The only way to make contact with the enemy was first the RAF and later, when our country came into the war, the Eighth Air Force. It looked as though, until we'd be ready to launch our invasion of the continent, that's the only way we'd be able to fight: by dropping high explosive out of airplanes onto the enemy's strategic targets."

Colonel March paused.

"Then somebody thought of another way," he said. "And The Hutch came into existence. Since it did, almost two years ago, we've been dropping something much more effective than high explosive on the enemy. We've been dropping men."

Colonel March paused again and he glanced up at the map.

"All kinds of men," he said. "Poles, Frenchmen, Belgians, Danes, Norwegians. One at a time they've been going in, by parachute, in the dead of night, back to their native lands, to perform secret missions designed to harass the German invader. All kinds of men," Colonel March repeated, still looking up at the map. "And they've all gone through The Hutch, learning from us here in this house the details of their missions, staying with us until we're sure they're letter perfect before the time comes for them to go in. All kinds of men," Colonel March said once more. "And yet all exactly the same, the way the knights who long ago set out on the Crusades, no matter where they came from or what they looked like, were also exactly the same, all of them, because they had one thing in common: they were all brave men."

Colonel March brought his glance down from the map and fixed it on Scott.

"In the almost two years that I have been here," he said, "you are the first American who has come to The Hutch. We both know the reason: before the war you happened to study and live in and come to understand a section of France that is strategically important to us now. This is an Allied effort, and as commandant of The Hutch I should be satisfied with that reason and let it go at that. I'm afraid I can't," Colonel March said. "Because I am also an American."

Scott, who had been listening with only half his mind, suddenly found himself looking sharply at Colonel March. The older man met his glance.

"I have made it a policy never to pry into the private lives of the men who are placed for three weeks in my care," Colonel March said. "If I seem by what I am about to tell you, Sergeant Scott, to be prying into yours, I hope you will bear in mind that I speak, not as a superior officer to a subordinate, but as an American to a fellow American. Is that clear?"

"Yes, sir," Scott said.

But it wasn't. His contacts with Colonel March during the past three weeks had been few. It was the British officer on the staff, Captain Giddings, from whom Scott, working ten and twelve hours a day until every piece was seared indelibly into his mind, had learned the details of his mission.

"According to the orders I have just received from London," Colonel March said, "your stay with us here at The Hutch is ended. You will be picked up in less than an hour and driven to the airfield from which you will be taking off for the continent some time later tonight. The risks involved in a mission such as yours were explained to you long ago. It is possible, however, that you have forgotten a crucial point." Colonel March's voice dropped just a trifle. "You may never come back," he said, and he drew a deep breath. "I therefore think that if there is anything you want to say to Lieutenant Minton," Colonel March said quietly, "you should say it now, sergeant, while you still have the opportunity."

Ten minutes later, on his way down the long hall, Scott was still aware of the sense of shock. For three weeks he had guarded not only his words, but his every glance. Not even the girl with whom he had so completely and so unexpectedly fallen in love had any way of knowing how he felt. How, then, had the Old Man learned his secret?

"Sergeant!"

Scott stopped and turned. Lieutenant Minton had appeared in the doorway of her office.

"Yes, ma'am?"

She smiled, and when she spoke, the tinkly laughter was in her voice.

"You haven't forgotten your promise to stop in at my office, sergeant?"

"No," Scott said. There were few things he was less likely to forget. "I just thought I'd go up to my room first and get the books and maps I've borrowed from the library and bring them down so you can check me out." Scott paused for a moment. "I don't want to leave any loose ends," he said.

The smile left her face, and when Lieutenant Minton spoke again, the tinkly laughter was gone from her voice.

"Then this *is* it, sergeant?"

"Yes, ma'am," Scott said.

The troubled look he had noticed earlier again washed swiftly across her face, and for a moment, as the breath caught in his throat, Scott wondered if she, too, like Colonel March, had guessed his secret. For almost three weeks, ever since—soon after his arrival at The Hutch—the emotions he had not anticipated had begun to run away with him, Scott had struggled fiercely to keep uppermost in his mind the knowledge that, no matter what happened, the one person who must never suspect how he felt about her was Helen Minton herself. From the very beginning, knowing what only he himself could know, Scott had known also that to allow her even to suspect would be unpardonable. Somehow, however, in spite of Scott's vigilance, Colonel March had guessed his secret. So why not Helen?

"Sergeant," she said quietly. "Would you come into my office for a moment?"

Lieutenant Minton held the door open and, as Scott stepped past her into the room from which it was her job to supervise the administrative details of The Hutch, he was afraid she could hear the sudden wild beating of his heart. She closed the door and turned to face him. For several long, long moments, during which they stared at each other in silence, Scott tried desperately to read the expression in her eyes.

Did she know how he felt? Was she puzzled by his failure to tell her? Could it be that, because pride forbade her asking the question with words, she was asking it now with her glance? Was she saying, without words, "I know how you feel. I want you to know I feel it, too. Please tell me you love me. Until you say it, I cannot say it, either"? Or did he think that was what she was saying because, more than anything else in the world, it was what he wanted to hear?

"Sergeant Scott."

"Yes?" he said.

"I have been stationed here for almost two years, ever since The Hutch was activated," Lieutenant Minton said. "I know that Colonel March makes it a point, before a man goes off on his mission, to remind him that he may never come back." She paused, and her slender fingers began to pick nervously at a button on her khaki blouse. "I would like to remind you of something else," Helen Minton said. "You must never forget, sergeant, there is a very good chance that you *will* come back."

"Thanks," Scott said. "I'll try to remember that."

"Would it help you to remember," she said, "if I asked you to bring something back to me?"

Her voice had been so low that it was only because he was standing in front of her, watching every flicker of movement on her face, that Scott heard the words. It seemed odd, therefore, that after a dozen years, in another country, on a sunny side street off a sweeping square in an Italian hill town on an afternoon that, according to Dr. Benatti down in Rome, was one of the two or three hundred left to him, Scott could still hear those words. He could hear them so clearly, and they evoked so vividly the image of the girl who had uttered them, that Scott forgot the ceaseless vigilance he was forced to maintain over the guards he kept posted at the doors to his consciousness, and the pain began to creep past them. He shook it off with two hard, sharp twists, one to the left and one to the right, and as the pain moved back, Scott moved down the street to Enzo's shop and opened the door.

"Signor Scott!" the dealer said in astonishment from behind the counter. "Did you not tell me less than one hour ago when you came for the Aphrodite that you were taking the two o'clock train back to Rome?"

"There's been a change in my plans," Scott said. "My partner, Mr. Pazelli, just called me on the long distance phone. We have a customer who is interested in cameos. Mr. Pazelli says you have a good selection."

"For your purposes, Signor Scott," the dealer said with a small bow, "I have the finest selection in Europe."

This, after almost two hours of going through Enzo's trays, proved to be no idle boast. By three o'clock Scott had found at least two, and possibly three items, that met the specifications Tullio had given him on the phone.

"I'll take all three," Scott said, "and return the ones we don't use."

"Si, signor," Enzo said and, with a wise smile as he followed Scott to the door, he added, "Success to your venture, sir."

By the time he got back to the hotel, Scott knew the pain was getting out of hand. Vigilance alone would no longer hold it. Not for the length of time it would take to complete this additional job with which Tullio had saddled him. Standing in the middle of his hotel room, Scott made a swift computation.

It was not quite three-thirty in the afternoon. The train Tullio had said the Cragers were taking up from Rome arrived in Siena shortly after six. Since they were coming to stay at this same hotel, it wasn't really necessary for Scott to meet them at the station. If any ruffled feelings were involved, he could explain later that the quest for the cameos had detained him. So he didn't actually have to meet the Cragers until it was time for a drink before dinner, say seven o'clock, or even seven-thirty. This gave Scott, allowing time for a shower and a change of clothes, at least three hours. Maybe even three and a half. Not long enough, really. But better than nothing. And unless he took action at once, the pain would reduce him before long to a lot worse than nothing.

"Okay," he muttered. "Let's get going."

Scott took the bottle of red pills from the suitcase on the bed and swallowed two. To take the larger blue capsule, he went into the bathroom for a glass of water. By the time he came back into the bedroom, the cutting edge of the pain had already been blunted. Scott kicked off his shoes, pulled down the knot of his tie, and dropped onto the bed. As the pain ebbed away, and sleep began to wash in, he became aware of the sounds. They were as familiar as his own name. They were the price he always had to pay for this respite from the pain.

At first it was no more than a faint hum. Then the hum grew louder and louder until it became the roar of four B-17 motors. Above the roar Scott could hear his own voice counting, as he plunged like a rock through the blackness of the night. He counted slowly, the way he had been taught in the parachute school to which he had been sent before he went to The Hutch, enunciating clearly in his mind, concentrating hard on the numbers until he reached "Ten!" Then he yanked the ripcord. His tumbling body, like a potato sack that has been kicked erect by a giant foot, was jerked upright.

Scott never knew—he certainly was never able later to trace it back accurately for Dr. Benatti in Rome—whether the pain began at that moment, when the parachute harness snapped him out of the downward spin, or whether it began when he hit the ground. Scott knew only—and this piece of knowledge, years later in Rome, he could reconstruct perfectly for Dr. Benatti— that he realized almost as soon as he touched the earth that this landing in Brittany was somehow different from all the previous landings he had made on practice jumps during his stay at the parachute school in England.

He had no time, however, to do anything more than make a mental note of the difference. There was the parachute which, according to his strict instructions, had to be gathered and buried immediately. And there was the problem of getting his bearings in the dark. Neither job was easy.

By the time he finished both, Scott knew the drop had been successful. He was in a pasture about seven kilometers south of Morlaix. According to his calculations, this put him about a half-hour's walk from his rendezvous point: the Auxerre farmhouse immediately north of the town.

He started across the pasture toward the dirt road that, during his two years in Brittany before the war, Scott had come to know as well as the street in Baltimore on which he had been born and raised. As he reached the stone wall that marked the end of the pasture Scott suddenly remembered something he had said one day soon after he came up from Paris to Morlaix, an art student with a single suitcase and a box of paints and very little money, and he settled down as a paying boarder in the Auxerre household.

"I'm getting to know this area so well I could find your father's house in the dark," Scott had said to Jeanine. Now, four years later and three years after he had last seen the Auxerre farm, Scott added to himself grimly, "This is your chance to prove it!"

He never got the chance.

A moment after the thought crossed his mind, Scott became aware of a smudge of darkness against the slightly paler darkness of the stone wall. The smudge had moved. Scott dropped in his tracks, rolled carefully into the deeper shadows at the base of the wall, and held his breath. It was a few minutes short of three o'clock in the morning, and it was bitter cold. Anything capable of movement that was outdoors on such a night should have barked. Not a sound, however, came from the shadows.

For several agonizing moments the silence was broken only by the sound of Scott carefully letting out his breath. Then, very slowly, so slowly that at first he didn't believe he had seen it, Scott saw the smudge of darkness move again. A moment after that he saw that it was moving toward him. Scott's hand, groping toward the hunting knife strapped to his boot, suddenly stopped. A faint whisper had come out of the shadows. Scott replied with a whisper of his own.

"Jeanine?"

The answer was a swift flurry of movement as the shadow came hurtling along the stone wall.

"I knew you would come back," Pierre Auxerre's young daughter whispered. "I never doubted," she said. "I knew you would come back."

Some time went by before Scott could trust himself to talk. When he did, he didn't know how to say what was in his heart.

"You're cold," he said instead. But that didn't sound right, even though it was true enough. She was shivering in his arms. He made an effort and forced his mind back to the details of his mission. He said, "What is happening at the farmhouse?"

"The instructions were that you would arrive at midnight," Jeanine said. "We turned out the lights at the regular hour, as though we were going to bed, but actually we remained in the kitchen, Papa and Mama and I, near the stove, waiting." She shivered again, and Scott held her closer. "By one o'clock we were very worried," Jeanine said. "By two o'clock Papa said there was no point in waiting up any longer, since the night of the drop must have been changed for some reason at the last moment, and we would receive instructions on what other night you would be coming, and now it was best to go to bed. So we all went to bed. But I could not sleep. I knew what Papa had said made sense, but my heart would not listen to sense. My heart told me you were coming tonight, as arranged, and that you had merely been delayed."

"We took off from England an hour late because of the weather," Scott said. "And over the Channel we had to detour all the way out to sea for almost two hours because our radar picked up an unexpected flight of Messerschmitts."

"I knew it was only a delay," Jeanine said. "So I waited until Papa and Mama were asleep, then I put on my clothes, and I stole out of the house, and I came along the road to meet you."

"We'd better get to the farmhouse," he said. "I've got to wake them up."

Jeanine stiffened in his arms.

"No," she said. "The morning is time enough."

Scott hesitated. The thin trickle of information that had been coming out of Brittany to England since the fall of France indicated clearly that, while no functioning resistance movement had yet begun to take shape, the people of the area were ready for it, and Pierre Auxerre and his family were ready to assume its active leadership. Scott was bringing a plan, complete with tables of organization, demolition programs, and communications codes, which would enable such a movement to synchronize itself with the life blood that would feed it: regular U.S. Air Force and RAF parachute drops of ammunition and supplies. His instructions were clear. He must deliver the papers to Pierre Auxerre and be gone from the farmhouse before dawn.

"The morning is too late," Scott said. "My instructions are—"

Jeanine put her hand over his lips.

"I have not seen you for three years," she whispered. "The morning is time enough."

Scott hesitated again. His instructions were clear, but his conscience was not. He had not known, when he was sent to The Hutch, that a girl named Helen Minton existed. Their meeting was an accident. But Scott was the victim of that accident. If he had not controlled the conditions that had brought about his meeting with Helen Minton, neither could he control the consequences of that meeting. He had to tell Jeanine about Helen.

"All right," Scott said. "The morning is time enough."

But he was wrong. When he woke up, the sun was streaming into the hayloft in which he had spent the night. Remembering where he was, Scott remembered also how he had got there, and his face flushed with the recollection of his cowardice. At the last moment, when he had steeled himself to tell Jeanine about Helen, the words had failed him. They must not fail him again. Scott turned toward Jeanine. But she was gone.

He sat up quickly, his hand groping at the hay that held the faint outlines of her body. The hay was still warm.

Jeanine had obviously gone across to the farmhouse to tell her parents that he had arrived, and to fetch him some breakfast. Scott wondered if it was safe to risk a stealthy trip down to the pump in the barnyard. Some cold water on his face would feel good.

He was debating with himself whether to take the risk as he rolled across the hay toward the hayloft window when, at precisely the same moment, Scott saw the gray-green car at the front door of the house, with the parachute he had buried the night before flung across the hood, and he heard the first scream.

By the time he got down out of the hayloft and across the barnyard to the kitchen window, he didn't really have to look. Scott could tell what was happening. He could tell from the screams. Nevertheless, because of the training he had received at The Hutch, Scott did look. He saw all three members of the

Auxerre family strung up by their thumbs, and he saw the four Gestapo men who were working on them, and he saw that so far as Jeanine's parents were concerned he was too late, because there was no longer anything anybody could do for them, and Scott saw that if anybody was going to do anything for Jeanine it would have to be done fast. He saw that clearly.

The fact that he could, the fact that Scott was able to look at what was happening in the Auxerre kitchen in spite of what was happening inside himself, was a tribute to the training he had received at The Hutch. But at the moment Scott was not thinking of tributes. In spite of what his heart was doing, in spite of the sickening rage that kept mounting inside him like a roaring blaze in which he knew he must in a matter of seconds be engulfed, Scott was making a calculation. Swiftly, racing desperately to keep his thoughts ahead of the consuming fury, he weighed the urgings of his heart against the inflexible clarity of his orders.

He was no match for four Gestapo men. Scott knew that. But he knew also that he could do enough damage before he was overwhelmed to stop them from doing to Jeanine what they had already done to her parents. He would probably die while doing it, but Scott knew the effort would save Jeanine's life. He knew also, however, that in making the attempt he would be dooming the plan he had been trained at The Hutch to bring into Brittany.

It was always at this agonizing moment of indecision—when once again he held in his hands the life of Jeanine Auxerre and he stood at the farmhouse window, weighing her life against his sworn duty—that Scott woke up. He always woke up the same way, soaked with perspiration, his ears ringing with Jeanine's tortured screams, his heart racing wildly, the pain that had been temporarily lulled by Dr. Benatti's drugs beginning to stir again.

This time, however, it was different. This time, when Scott woke up, something new was happening. For several dazed moments, while the pain gained ground and he tried to thrust the past back where it belonged, he wondered what it was. Then he heard the bell again and Scott realized it was the telephone. He sat up on the bed and put the instrument to his ear.

"Hello? Mr. Scott?"

The voice sounded vaguely familiar.

"Yes," Scott said. "Who is this?"

"Henry Crager," the voice said. "Tullio told me this morning down in Rome that—"

"Oh," Scott said. He made the two short, sharp movements with his head, one to the left and one to the right. "Hello, Mr. Crager," he said. "Where are you?"

"Right here in the hotel," Crager said. "Our train got to Siena half an hour ago, and we're just having a bath and a change of clothes."

"We?" Scott said.

"Why, yes, Mrs. Crager and I," Crager said. "Didn't Tullio tell you my wife was coming up from Rome with me?"

"Of course," Scott said. He pushed himself off the bed. It was always easier to handle the pain when he was on his feet. "I spent the afternoon tracking down those cameos," he said. "I was sort of pooped when I got back to the hotel a little while ago, so I took a nap. I was still asleep when the phone rang."

Mr. Crager laughed.

"Sorry to disturb you," he said. "It's just that I'm anxious to see the Aphrodite and my wife is anxious to see the cameos."

"I'm anxious to show them to you," Scott said. "Where and when can I do it?"

"How about downstairs in the bar in about, oh, say half an hour?"

"I'll be there," Scott said.

He was a few minutes early, but Mr. Crager was already waiting.

"My wife will be down in a minute," he said. "What will you drink?" Scott told him, and the bartender moved away to fill the order, and Mr. Crager said, "May I see it now?"

"Of course," Scott said.

He put the small bundle on the bar, and he undid the chamois wrapping, and he stood the small bronze Aphrodite beside Mr. Crager's highball.

"Boy!" Mr. Crager breathed. "Wait till they see this in Cleveland!"

Scott was aware of a small inner release of tension. He had never had any doubts about the sale. It was nice to know definitely, however, that his year in Switzerland was assured.

"I hope your wife likes it as well as you do," he said.

"How can I possibly help it?"

The words came from behind him, and Scott had to turn around toward them, but even in the moment of shock, before he could manage to make his body obey, before he actually saw her, Scott knew who she was and how he had recognized her. It was the tinkly laughter in her voice.

"Sergeant Scott!" she said.

She had recognized him, too, and for a long, long moment he didn't answer. He couldn't. He just stood there, staring into her lovely face, probing beneath the surface of her amazement for the answer to the question that, when he had last seen her on the night of his departure from The Hutch, Scott had not had the right to ask. His probing glance told him no more now than it had told him then.

"Lieutenant Minton," he said.

She laughed, and Scott took her hand, and then there were several confused moments during which everybody seemed to be talking at once. She was explaining to her husband about The Hutch, and Crager was explaining to Scott how he had met and married her in Cleveland soon after she got out of the WAC when the war ended, and then, all at once, the explanations were finished, and it was as though the twelve years had never happened.

All at once, in this hotel bar in Siena, it was to Scott as though they were standing face to face in Helen Minton's office at The Hutch in the late afternoon of the day the orders had come up from London saying he was going in that night. Once again, as

on that day a dozen years ago, Scott was afraid she could hear
the sudden wild beating of his heart as he found himself trying
desperately to read the expression in her eyes.

Did she know how he felt? Was she still puzzled by his failure
to tell her? Could it be that, because the presence of her husband
forbade her asking the question with words, she was asking it
now with her glance? Was she saying, without words, "I know
how you felt twelve years ago. Even though now it's too late, I
want you to know I felt it, too. Why didn't you tell me then that
you loved me? Couldn't you understand that, until you said it, I
couldn't say it, either?"

Or did he think that was what she was saying because even
now, after a dozen years and with only another one left to live, it
was still the only thing in the world he wanted to hear?

"I've often wondered what happened to you," Helen Crager
said. "I heard the drop was successful, of course, and every now
and then, checking through intelligence reports for Colonel
March, I'd run across something the underground had done in
the Morlaix sector of Brittany, so I knew you were still alive and
working in the area. But then I got transferred to the Pacific and
I sort of lost touch. Until a year or two after I got married, one
day in Cleveland I saw in the paper that the French government
wanted to award some sort of medal to an American sergeant
named Scott for work he'd done with the underground during
the war, but they couldn't locate him, and I immediately thought
of you." She paused, and she looked at him curiously. "*Was* it
you?"

"Yes," Scott said. "I've been living in Italy since the end of
the war."

"Doing what?"

"Oh," Scott said with a shrug, and he touched the Aphrodite
on the bar, "one thing and another."

"But I thought it was France you loved?" she said. "That's
where you lived and studied and painted before the war."

Scott shrugged again.

"After the war Italy suited me better," he said.

She didn't answer. For several moments they stared at each other in silence.

"The medal," she said finally. "Why didn't you go back to accept it?"

"I didn't think I deserved any medals," Scott said.

"I see," she said, but of course she didn't. Nobody could see. Not even Scott. That was the whole point. It had been the point for a dozen years, ever since that terrible morning in Brittany when he had stood outside the Auxerre farmhouse, peering into the kitchen. It would continue to be the point as long as he walked the earth, and drew breath, and had a brain capable of summoning up the past and forcing him to live it again and again and again. Helen Crager cleared her throat. "The last time we saw each other, twelve years ago, just before you went off on your mission, I asked you to do something for me," she said. "Do you remember?"

Scott put his hand into his pocket and he pulled out the package of cameos he had selected that afternoon from the crowded trays in Enzo's shop for the wife of what Tullio on the phone from Rome had called a rich American sucker. Scott undid the tissue-paper wrapping, and he placed the three cameos on the bar, beside the Aphrodite.

"You asked me to bring something back for you," he said. "Take your pick."

She gave him a funny glance, but it wasn't nearly so funny as the glance her husband gave him.

"Say!" Mr. Crager said in a puzzled voice. "What's this all about?"

"My small contribution to the war effort," his wife said. "These men we were always sending off from The Hutch, dropping them all over Europe by parachute, Poles and Frenchmen and Belgians and Danes and Norwegians, Colonel March used to say they were like the knights who went off on the Crusades, and like those knights, there was no telling if they'd make it or not. So I worked out this system of my own to help them make it. Whenever a man went off on his mission, I'd take him aside and ask him, as a personal favor, to bring me back a cameo. I've always been crazy about cameos, and I've collected them all my life, and I found during the war, when I was stationed at The Hutch, that if I believed a man was going to bring one back to me, why, I could believe he wouldn't be killed and his mission would be successful." She paused, and she looked a little embarrassed, and then she shook her head with a touch of defiance. "I suppose it sounds silly now," Helen Crager said. "But it wasn't silly at that time," she said. "It was my own private way of knocking on wood for all those brave men."

Scott was glad, as the full meaning of her words sank in, that her husband so obviously wanted to say something. Scott couldn't say anything himself. Not for a while, anyway. He just stood there, watching Mr. Crager stare at the cameos on the bar, then at his wife, and finally back at the cameos.

"But that was twelve years ago," Mr. Crager said. "These things." He touched the cameos. "I thought you rounded them up this afternoon, Mr. Scott, because your partner called you from Rome and told you a couple of customers were coming up to Siena to look at them?"

Scott drew a deep breath.

"That's right," he said. "I did."

The answer didn't seem to help Mr. Crager.

"Maybe I'm not very bright," he said. "But I don't see the connection between the promise you made to my wife twelve years ago, and these cameos you rounded up here in Siena today for a customer you thought you'd never met."

"There is no connection," Scott said. It was an accident that had brought him and Helen Minton together a dozen years ago. It was an accident that had brought him and Helen Crager together today. It was not her fault that, as a result of the first accident, since that terrible morning in Brittany his life had been a walking death. Scott said to Helen's husband, "I made a promise twelve years ago. It never occurred to me that I would ever have the chance to keep it. Now that the chance has been dropped in my lap, I'm sure you won't take it away from me."

Scott turned to Helen. "Won't you choose one of these three cameos?" he said. "As a present from me?"

Again she gave him that funny little look. But now Scott had no illusions about what it meant.

"I know enough about cameos to know that all three of these are extremely valuable," Helen Crager said. "I've done nothing to deserve such a present."

She had done more than Dr. Benatti and his medicines had been able to do in a dozen years. She had answered the question Scott had not dared ask her at The Hutch.

"I wish you would take it," Scott said, and he turned to Crager. "I hope you don't mind?"

Crager scowled for a moment or two as he chewed his lower lip. Finally, he shrugged.

"No, of course not," he said. "If you know what you're doing."

"Thanks," Scott said. For the first time in twelve years he knew exactly what he was doing. He turned back to Helen. "Won't you take one?" he said. "Please?"

"Only if you assure me that you can afford it," she said.

He could afford anything now. Paying for the cameo would take every penny he would get from Tullio for his half of the profits on the Aphrodite deal, and that in turn meant he could not have his year in Switzerland. But what he had just learned from Helen was worth more to Scott than all the money he had made on all the deals he and Tullio had been involved in since the end of the war.

"I assure you I can afford it," he said.

Very quickly, without bothering to compare or choose, Helen picked up a cameo from the bar. It was the one nearest her.

"Thank you very much," she said.

Scott didn't answer. The pain, which had been creeping up unnoticed, had slipped past the guards. He turned to the bar, took the two remaining cameos, and rewrapped them in the tissue paper. He did it slowly. He always needed a few moments, when the pain overpowered him, to get back on top of it before he could talk.

"Well, now that we've settled that," Mr. Crager said, "let's all have another drink."

"Thanks, not for me," Scott said. "I must catch a train."

"You mean you're not going to have dinner with us?" Mr. Crager couldn't seem to believe it.

"I'm afraid I can't," Scott said. "I must get back to Rome." Now that he couldn't go to Switzerland, he wanted to find out from Dr. Benatti how much time he had left.

"But that's not fair!" Helen Crager protested. "We haven't had a chance to talk!"

"I'm sorry," Scott said, and he was. He really would have liked to stay. But he was no longer his own master. The bribe of a year in Switzerland now being beyond him, from here on in he would have to obey the pain that, for the first time in twelve years, he had ceased to think about as an enemy. "I really must go."

"But there's so much I want you to tell me!" Helen Crager said. "About Brittany and the underground and what you did!"

"I'm sorry," Scott said again. "There's nothing to tell."

Not to her. Or to her husband. Or to the people in France who handed out medals. He would save it all for the one person who was entitled to hear it.

"Goodbye," Scott said.

He shook hands with Mr. Crager, and he bowed to the girl who was now Mr. Crager's wife, and then, carrying the pain carefully, as though it were a sleeping child that must not be aroused, Scott turned and started out of the bar.

"Sergeant Scott!" Helen Crager called.

He continued moving toward the door. She had done her part in setting him free from the chains that had held him for a dozen years. He could not expect her to do more. Nobody could help him with the question that had forged the chains in the first place:

On that terrible morning in Brittany, when he stole away unnoticed from the kitchen window of the Auxerre farmhouse, carrying to safety the plans he had brought from England, had

Sergeant Scott been obeying orders, or had he been obeying the dictates of his own heart?

Had he allowed the Gestapo to kill Jeanine Auxerre because it was his duty not to jeopardize the plans he carried on his person? Or had he allowed her to die because her death was an unexpected and simple solution for a troubled man who had fallen in love with an American girl in England but could do nothing about it because he was secretly married to a French girl in Brittany?

"Sergeant Scott! Please!"

He did not turn back. To do so would have been merely polite, and he was beyond politeness. For a dozen years he had lived alone, locked away with the secret agony of that unanswered question. Now, however, for the first time in those dozen years, the question no longer mattered. All that mattered now was what he had learned from Helen: that he'd never had a chance; if he had told her how he felt, he would have been no better off than all those other men for whom she had knocked on wood. She had not loved them. She had merely wanted them to live.

Only one person had ever wanted more for him than that he should merely go on living. Only one person had ever loved him. He was glad now that, on that first night of his return to Brittany, he had lacked the courage to tell her the truth. At least he had spared her that.

"Sergeant Scott!"

He moved forward lightly, through the door of the bar, toward the future, with an eagerness for what lay ahead that, since the night in Brittany when the pain began, Scott had thought he would never know again. For the first time in a dozen years there was only one thought in his mind: soon the long loneliness would be over.

Jeanine had waited three years for him to come back to her in Brittany. Now that he was free at last, she would surely wait the little time that remained before he came back to her forever.

R.S.V.P.

t was the
part of the day that Ellen liked best, but of course she couldn't
tell that to Mrs. Stehli. Nor did she want to.

"You sure, now?" Mrs. Stehli's features, ruddy, solid, and
comfortably motherly, settled into the creases of worried hesitation through which she uttered these very same words every
afternoon at three. "Because if you'd rather not be alone, Mrs.
Pierce, all you have to do is say so, and my Hiram, it won't kill
him to get his own supper just once, you know."

"I know," Ellen said. She smiled at the housekeeper her
father had insisted on giving her for a year, wages prepaid, as
one of his many and almost ridiculously lavish wedding presents.
"You go along and get Mr. Stehli his supper," Ellen said, aware
that not only was she, too, using the very same words she uttered
every afternoon at three, but that it was this very sameness
which added to her pleasure in this particular part of the day. "I
don't mind being alone one bit, Mrs. Stehli."

The housekeeper nodded, fastened the buttons of her
sensible coat, and hiked the scuffed patent leather purse up
under her sturdy forearm. She sent one last appraising glance
back across the foyer, through the handsomely furnished
drawing room, toward the beautifully equipped kitchen, which
Mrs. Stehli, who loved it even more than Ellen did, kept with
almost surgical neatness.

"Now, don't you bother yourself about anything," the housekeeper said, as though the admonition, instead of being one she
repeated every day in these precise words, were some bright,
new thought that had just crossed her mind. "The roast is in the
oven, and the potatoes are all peeled, and I'll pick up the ice
cream down at Harper's on my way back. My Hiram," she said
as she reached for the knob of the front door, "I'll have him fed
by six, so if Mr. Pierce doesn't miss his 5:18 from New
York—"

"He won't," Ellen said cheerfully. "He never does."

"That's a fact," Mrs. Stehli said and, as she eased her bulky figure out onto the portico, the creases of worried hesitation faded into the more angular but equally pleasant expression of approval that was the housekeeper's unfailing reaction to any reference, direct or otherwise, to Mr. Daniel Pierce's devotion to his bride of almost a year. "That means Mr. Pierce will be home his regular time, a little after six, so you just give him his regular cocktail and let him relax in front of the fire a little while, and I'll be back by six-thirty, in plenty of time to get supper on the table." Mrs. Stehli grinned self-consciously, as she did every day at this point in her summing up of the routine that had not varied since the newlywed Pierces had bought this house in Coopersville and she had come to work for them. "I mean dinner."

"I will do precisely that," Ellen said, which was precisely what she, too, said every day at this point in Mrs. Stehli's little farewell speech, "if you will promise to stop worrying about me."

"That's a bargain," Mrs. Stehli called across her shoulder as she set off down the hill, toward her own home at the other side of Coopersville, three quarters of a mile away. "Don't you be lonesome, now."

"All right," Ellen called after her. "I won't."

She knew, as she closed the door, that she wouldn't be. She never was. Not any more, and certainly not during this favorite part of the day. Although, since marriage had changed her whole life eleven and a half months ago, there actually were no parts of the day Ellen Pierce did not like.

The mornings were crammed with the special excitement of breakfast with Dan and getting him off to the 8:53. Midday overflowed with the hitherto unsuspected fascinations of running a household of her own, even though Ellen's role in this particular activity seemed to consist mainly of agreeing with Mrs. Stehli's suggestions or admiring the housekeeper's completed acts. And early evening, of course, was charged with the tingling anticipation of Dan's return.

But these three hours of late afternoon, after Mrs. Stehli had gone down the hill to the duties of her own household and before she came back to resume her duties in the Pierce household, were the best. Because this was the only part of the day when Ellen Pierce was alone, and therefore free to contemplate her happiness.

This contemplation was important to her. It was as necessary to her well-being as the daily nap Dr. Pritchard had prescribed and which Dan, as well as Mrs. Stehli, assumed Ellen took every afternoon from three to six. She had lived so much of her twenty-seven years in the future, waiting wistfully and with diminishing hope for what other people seemed to achieve without effort, that now when the future had miraculously become the present, she could scarcely believe it. She certainly could not take it for granted.

More than the nap which Dr. Pritchard insisted was the only cure for the strange lassitude that had plagued her all her life, Ellen Pierce needed this island of solitude in each day during which she could, by going back over and reliving in memory all the bits and pieces of the preceding hours, convince herself that they had actually happened. That she had really lived through them. That it was Ellen Bowker, and not some other and luckier girl—Maud Tennent, for example—who was now Mrs. Daniel Pierce. That it was she, the ugly and sickly duckling of the handsome, popular, and wealthy Bowker tribe, and not somebody in a dream, who had that morning poured a second cup of breakfast coffee for a husband of her own.

Peering out the window of the drawing room, to make sure that the retreating figure of Mrs. Stehli was actually moving down the hill, Ellen's body shook in a small shiver of delight. Alone, she could at last believe what, until this moment of each day, she could merely enjoy: the reality of her happiness. As Mrs. Stehli's firm strides carried her around the mailbox at the foot of the hill, and the housekeeper disappeared into the bend of Pine Road that led down to the railroad station, Ellen left the window, crossed to the chair near the fireplace, sat down, and surveyed the beautiful room in which, in a little more than three hours, she would be handing to Dan the first of the two cocktails he took every evening before dinner.

The room was no more beautiful than the many rooms to which Ellen had been accustomed all her life: in the Bowker duplex on Park Avenue; in the Bowker summer home at Southampton; in the Bowker suites at the Crillon in Paris and Claridge's in London, where Simon Bowker had taken his daughter to see the eminent doctors who proved unable to do more in Europe toward curing her mysterious and debilitating tiredness than Dr. Pritchard had been able to do back home in New York. But, because this was the room that belonged to her and Dan and to nobody else, it had for Ellen a value that transcended the very considerable sum Simon Bowker, as another of his wedding presents to his daughter, had spent on its furnishings.

It was for Ellen more than a room. It was a symbol of the still unbelievable distance she had come: from a lifetime of being alternately pitied and scorned—so painfully the poor little rich girl of tradition that not even the traditional fortune hunters had been interested in her—to the incredible moment when Dan Pierce had asked her to marry him.

Reliving that particular moment was suddenly such an unbearable delight, that Ellen could not sit still. Knowing she was tired, and knowing even more strongly how important it was for her to rest so that when Dan came home he would not suspect how tired she was, she nevertheless had to get out. If only for a moment. Ellen stood up and went to the hall closet. She took down—from the preposterous array of three brand-new fur coats her father had unexpectedly showered on her only a month ago—the reasonably simple beaver, flung it around her shoulders, and went out the front door.

On the portico steps, breathing deeply of the crisp November air, Ellen hesitated. There was really no place for her to go, since the nearest neighbor in this stretch of pleasantly rolling Connecticut countryside was more than a mile away and, between her chronic tiredness and her still somewhat unbelievable happiness, Ellen had not yet had the time, the strength, or even the inclination to call on, and make friends with, people in the area. And, of course, there was nothing for her to do since, between Dan's thoughtfulness and Mrs. Stehli's considerate efficiency, every conceivable chore, however small, was completed long before Ellen even thought of it.

The mailbox, winking brightly in the sunlight at the foot of the hill, caught her eye, and Ellen smiled. It was not much of a walk, a couple of hundred yards at most, but it would give her an objective, and it was just far enough to allow her to work off the delicious tension of contemplating her happiness without tiring her too much. Stepping down to the gravel walk, Ellen stumbled slightly. With a small gasp of remembered pleasure, she turned quickly to the left and put out her hand, as though she half expected it to be taken by Dan, the way he had taken it on that day, just a little more than a year ago, when she had stumbled on the front steps of her father's house in Southampton.

"Watch it," Dan had said through his extraordinary grin as, with a gentle but firm movement of his powerful right arm, he had set her upright in the October sunlight. "Scuffed knees are okay on little girls up to, say, the age of twelve, but on grown-up young ladies, pretty ones around the age of, say, twenty-five, scuffed knees are out."

"I'm twenty-six, or will be in January, as you know damn well," Ellen had said, furious with herself because she could feel her face growing hot. "And aren't you wandering into the wrong pew, Mr. Pierce?"

She nodded across the acre of immaculate Bowker lawn that separated her father's mansion from the small and rather seedy Tennent home at which Mr. Daniel Pierce, one of the more promising and certainly one of the most handsome young architects in New York, had been calling, with significant regularity, for several months.

"Nope," Mr. Daniel Pierce said cheerfully and it seemed to Ellen, who was so confused that she knew she had no right to trust any of her senses, that his pressure on her elbow increased just a trifle. "Not only am I in the right pew," Mr. Daniel Pierce said as, with a contemptuous wave of his free hand, he dismissed the neighboring, ramshackle Tennent home in which, as all Southampton knew, he had for so long been paying formal court to Maud Tennent, the strikingly beautiful blonde who had been, since childhood, the mousily unattractive Ellen Bowker's school chum and confidante. "As a matter of fact," Mr. Daniel Pierce added, "I have stumbled, by what I hope you will forgive me for describing as a good omen, on the very person I have just traveled two and a half hours on the Long Island Rail Road to see."

"Me?" Ellen said in amazement. Her role as Maud's confidante had done more than acquaint her with the rather obvious fact that Maud was as crazy about Dan Pierce as Dan Pierce seemed to be crazy about Maud. Her role as Maud's confidante had underscored for Ellen what, after so many years of being too tired to complete school terms or finish college or go to dances, scarcely needed further emphasis: she was destined, in spite of her father's money and efforts, to the spinsterhood that she knew in her despairing heart must be the inevitable result of the unpopularity, first with boys and then with young men, that was, in itself, the even more inevitable result of her timidity and uncertainty, which were part and parcel of the unfortunate lack of energy that had refused all her life to respond to the finest medical attention Simon Bowker could buy. Looking at this handsome young man whom she had met casually several times in the Tennent home next door, Ellen could feel her already flushed face grow even warmer. "I don't believe it," she said, making an effort to free her elbow from his grasp. "Why in the world would you travel two and a half hours on the Long Island or any other railroad to see me?"

"Very simple," Mr. Dan Pierce had replied, and a touch of
seriousness worked its way through to the surface of his extraordinary smile. "I wanted to ask you to marry me."

It was difficult now, little more than a year later, to recall
what she had said after the first stunned moment of shock. Just
as it was still difficult for Ellen—walking slowly down the
Connecticut hill, on which she and Dan now lived, toward the
mailbox in which they now received letters addressed to Mr. and
Mrs. Daniel Pierce—to believe that the whole thing had actually
happened. There were people—Maud Tennent, to take one
understandably bitter example—who had refused to believe it.
Even after Dan had explained, in an interview which must have
been far more painful than it sounded later in his report to Ellen,
that it was one of those things he could neither explain nor
attempt to justify.

He had thought for months that he was in love with Maud. He
had scarcely paid any attention to the quiet, self-effacing,
wealthy girl from next door whom he occasionally met when he
visited Maud's house. Then, one day—to be precise, it was the
Sunday preceding his astonishing call on Ellen—Dan Pierce
happened to look out the window of the Tennent living room,
and he saw Ellen crossing the Bowker lawn. It was just a casual
glance but, in the phrase Dan had borrowed from the song that
was now one of his and Ellen's favorites, his heart stood still.

Ellen's own heart, which had been so full ever since that
wonderful Sunday just over a year ago, seemed to do the same
thing now, as she reached the mailbox and turned to look up the
hill at the house her father had given Dan and herself as what
Simon Bowker called his basic wedding present. In the thin but
intensely bright November sunlight, which tinted the chimney
with a wash of pale rose and the leaves of the surrounding
maples with a searing splash of red flame, the house looked so
sturdily solid and yet so delicately lovely that it ceased, for a
moment, to be merely a house. It became a sort of castle, an
impregnable citadel in which was locked away, secure from the
world in which she had for so long been an unhappy spectator,

all the happiness Ellen had achieved when Dan Pierce had with his love made her a participant.

Turning away from the sight that caused her heart, which had been for a moment motionless with happiness, to leap in the ecstasy of realization that came to her every day during this period of solitude she enjoyed and needed so much, Ellen saw with surprise that the small metal flag on the mailbox was raised, indicating that there was mail inside.

There was only one mail delivery a day in Coopersville, at eleven-thirty in the morning. And Mrs. Stehli had, as usual, gone down the hill for that, before she had prepared Ellen's lunch at noon. Reaching up, Ellen opened the box, put her hand in, and drew out a single envelope.

It was addressed to "Mr. and Mrs. Daniel Pierce, Pine Road, Coopersville, Conn." Then Ellen saw the "Special Delivery" stamp in the corner, and the creases of puzzlement eased away from her forehead. Apparently the carrier had brought the letter along after the regular morning delivery. Ellen closed the mailbox, knocked down the small metal flag, and started back up the hill.

She paused two or three times to catch her breath. Each time, as she stared at the letter in her hand, she became increasingly aware of a sense of mounting uneasiness. This was puzzling rather than upsetting because, aside from the special delivery stamp, the letter looked innocent enough: one of those square envelopes, made of thick watermarked paper, without a printed or written return address, in which wedding invitations and announcements are sent out. By the time she got back into the house, Ellen felt so tired that she sat down beside the fire to rest for a moment, before facing the effort of removing her coat.

For some reason that seemed to go beyond the excessive, but for her normal, exhaustion she always felt after any sort of physical activity, her knees had begun to shake slightly. Staring down at the letter on her lap, Ellen had a sudden desire to hurl it, unopened, into the fire. Some instinct, as powerful as it was

obviously unreasonable, urged her not to read whatever it was
the envelope contained.

Then the clock, on the mantelpiece over the fireplace, chimed
the half hour, and the small, familiar sound brought her back to
reason. Telling herself crisply not to be silly, Ellen stood up
deliberately, put the envelope down, went to the closet, and hung
away her coat. Then she came back into the drawing room,
picked up the envelope, pried away the flap with her forefinger,
and drew out a printed announcement. It read:

THE NEW YORK MEDICAL RESEARCH INSTITUTE
REQUESTS THE PLEASURE OF YOUR ATTENDANCE
AT A DINNER IN HONOR OF

## DR. CARLETON B. TOYNBERRY

WHO HAS JUST RETURNED FROM A THREE-YEAR
FIELD SURVEY IN THE BELGIAN CONGO
WITH VALUABLE NEW DATA ON

*Encephalitis lethargica*

THE GREEN ROOM                                    NOVEMBER 16, 1950
TARLETON PLAZA HOTEL                                        8:00 P.M.

R. S. V. P.

Attached to the announcement was a smaller envelope, addressed to The New York Medical Research Institute, contain-
ing a card with the conventional blank spaces calling for the
recipient to advise whether Mr. and Mrs. Daniel Pierce "Will"
or "Will not" attend.

Staring at the printed announcement, Ellen wondered what
was bothering her. Certainly it was not indecision about what
her reply would be. Since Dan had insisted, from the moment
they settled down in Coopersville after their honeymoon, that the
first year of their married life must be a quiet, restful period,
unmarred by the distractions of social engagements in New York

or on Long Island, Ellen had written "Will not attend" on so many similar cards that she knew, after discussing it with Dan over cocktails in the evening, she would write the same thing on this one. Nor could she possibly be bothered by Dr. Toynberry's name, which meant nothing to her. Or the phrase, in what Ellen assumed was Latin, describing the subject the good doctor had been studying in the Belgian Congo, which had no interest for her. In fact, as she poked about in her strangely troubled mind for some possible clue to her even stranger discomfort, Ellen couldn't imagine why on earth The New York Medical Research Institute, whatever *that* was, should want to send her and Dan an invitation to—

Her head came up abruptly. For a terrible moment, during which it seemed to her that the suddenly violent sounds of her own beating heart filled the room, Ellen felt as though she had been struck. In a way, she had been. Exploding without warning, from the concealed depths of her consciousness to the quiveringly alive surface of her mind, like a scream in the night, came a simple, innocent, long-ago learned and long-forgotten fact. Staring at the printed words that read "The New York Medical Research Institute," Ellen's shaking knees carried her across the room to the telephone.

Wishing all at once that Mrs. Stehli were in the house, so she could call out and plead with the housekeeper to stop her, Ellen picked up the phone. In a voice she scarcely recognized as her own, she asked the long distance operator to get The New York Medical Research Institute, please. While the call was being put through, Ellen told herself fiercely, again and again, that there could be no possible connection between her sudden terror and the even more suddenly remembered fact that for years, ever since she could first recall spending her summers as a child in Southampton, The New York Medical Research Institute had been the pet hobby of Maud Tennent's father. Ellen told it to herself in vain, but the process served some useful purpose, anyway: by the time an efficient female voice came on at the other end of the wire, Ellen's voice sounded more normal. At least in her own ears.

"This is Mrs. Daniel Pierce, calling from Coopersville, Connecticut," she said. "I have just received an invitation to the dinner you are giving next week for Dr. Toynberry, and I was wondering if there is any way to find out how my husband and I happened to be included in your guest list?"

"Why, I think so," the efficient female voice said. "The guest list is quite small, because Dr. Toynberry's talk is going to be rather technical, and it had been limited to members of the Institute and the few friends each member is sponsoring personally. Did you say Mrs. Daniel Pierce?"

"Yes," Ellen said. "Could you tell me who sponsored the invitation for myself and Mr. Pierce?"

"One moment, please." There was a long pause at the other end of the wire, during which Ellen fought back an impulse to hang up, and then the female voice returned. "The invitation was sent to you at the request of our vice-president's daughter, Miss Maud Tennent. Is that what you wanted to know, Mrs. Pierce?"

"Yes," Ellen said. "Thank you."

She stared at the instrument in her hand for a long moment, suppressing a small shudder that was perilously close to hysteria, before she hung up. If it was not precisely what she had wanted to know, because Ellen could not yet in her present state of mind imagine why she had wanted to know it, there was something ominously ironical in those last words uttered by that efficient female voice at the other end of the wire in New York. Maud Tennent had used those same words just a little more than a year ago, the last time the two childhood friends had seen each other, two weeks before the wedding that had clearly been as shattering a blow to Maud as it had been an overwhelming joy to Ellen.

"Is that what you wanted to know?" Maud Tennent had said coolly. "Is that why you came waltzing over here, across your old man's diamond-plated lawn? To hear me say: no hard feelings Ellen? It was a fair fight, and the best man or, rather, the best girl won? So you could have, in addition to Dan, a clear conscience as well? Is that what you wanted to know?"

Ellen had shaken her head slowly and then, because there were really no words to express what was in her heart, she had dropped her glance from the lovely face of this girl she had known all her life, this girl who, until a few days ago, had been the only friend Ellen Bowker had ever had.

"No," Ellen said. "That isn't what I wanted to know, Maud. I came over because there was something I wanted *you* to know." She paused again, and she looked around the shabby, crowded living room in which, because ever since she was a little girl she had been received in it as an equal, she had always been more comfortable than in her own far more lavish home. Ellen knew she would never be received in this room again. And, even though that did not matter because, now that she had Dan, nothing in the world would ever again matter, she knew she would have to try to find the words with which to say what her heart told her could not be said. "I wanted you to know that I'm sorry this happened."

"Are you?" Maud said with a touch of the icy sarcasm that, because it seemed to suit her cool blond beauty so perfectly, had always been one of the many reasons why Ellen Bowker had admired her friend so passionately. "You don't look particularly sorry to me."

"I don't mean that I'm sorry about Dan," Ellen said quietly. "I'd be lying if I said that, and we've never lied to each other. I love him, Maud. And Dan loves me."

"Does he?"

Ellen stared at her friend in surprise.

"Why, yes," she said simply. "But that's not the point."

"Whatever the point is," Maud said coldly, "I wish you'd come to it, and then get out."

"The point is that I'm sorry it had to be you," Ellen said, looking down at her hands so that the film of tears, which suddenly obscured her vision, would remain unnoticed. "The point is that I came over to ask the impossible," Ellen said in a low voice. "The point is that I'm asking you to have pity, Maud." She paused again, but Maud Tennent remained silent, and Ellen did not dare look up. "You've got so much, Maud," she said, still addressing her hands. "You're beautiful. You're popular. You've had dozens of beaus, and you'll have dozens more. But I've never had anything, Maud. I'm nothing to look at. Nobody has ever done it, anyway. Nobody except Dan. He can't mean as much to you as he means to me, Maud. You'll have others, Maud. I never will. I know it's an impossible thing to ask, but I want to ask it just the same. I want your friendship, Maud, the way I've always had it."

"Why?"

"Because, until now, it's been the most precious thing in my life to me," Ellen said. "Because, even if only indirectly, you're responsible for my having Dan. And because, if you look at it realistically, it isn't really my fault, or even Dan's. It just happened, Maud. We couldn't help it. We fell in love."

"I'm looking at it realistically," Maud said, and the tone of her voice made Ellen look up quickly. She saw that Maud Tennent was regarding her with a mocking smile. "So I've had everything, and you've had nothing," Maud said. "So it isn't your fault, or even Dan's." The mocking smile etched itself deeper into her beautiful face. "Take a look around," Maud Tennent said, and she swung her hand in a short arc that took in the furnishings of the shabby little room. "Then waltz yourself over to that fur-lined skating rink you call home, and take another look around. If that doesn't do the trick, I'll show you my father's bank balance, and then you ask your father to show you his." A short, harsh laugh erupted in the quiet room. "Maybe *you* couldn't help it," Maud Tennent said. "As for Mr. Daniel Pierce, chum, I suggest you refrain from starting your married life with any romantically unrealistic notions knocking about in your innocent little noggin. In some respects, the daughter of old man Tennent may look a lot better than the daughter of old man Bowker. But when it's a struggling young architect who is doing the looking, those respects don't count for half as much as the one that gets spelled with a capital dollar sign."

Ellen could feel her face grow hot as she stood up. She gave herself a moment in which to recapture some fragment of her self-control, but her voice shook badly when she spoke.

"That's a lie," she managed to say. "I know in my heart that Dan is not marrying me for money, and you know it, too." She drew a deep breath. "I don't suppose I had the right to hope that you would accept my offer of continued friendship," Ellen said. "But one thing I did not suspect was that you would be cruel and insulting."

"Let me tell you something else you probably never suspected," Maud Tennent said as she stood up. "That I'm something of a prophet, too." She smiled contemptuously. "The first round goes to you. Or, to be more accurate, to your old man's money. But I don't give up as easily as all that. You can have Dan," Maud Tennent said. "For about, oh," she looked up at the ceiling, as though she were making a calculation, and then she brought the smile back to Ellen's face. "Shall we say for about a year? Yes, why not?" Maud Tennent said. "Since I'll have him for all the rest of my life after that, you can take him on loan, so to speak, for one year."

It had been a joke, of course. A joke so cruel and tasteless that Ellen had never even mentioned it to Dan. But now, now that the year was almost up, Maud Tennent's mocking words, spawned in the bitterness of defeat, seemed to be ringing in Ellen's ears. They rang with a note of prophecy so utterly senseless that, with a gesture of fury not unmixed with fear, she flung from herself the hateful invitation that had brought back Maud's bitter words to foul what had been for so many months the happiest part of Ellen's endlessly happy days.

The bits of pasteboard separated in the air. They dropped lazily to the rug that, according to Dan's jesting calculation, must have set Simon Bowker back a neat five thousand dollars.

The R.S.V.P. card curled lazily, like a toy glider caught in an updraft, and fell at Ellen's feet, face up. Mr. and Mrs. Daniel Pierce "Will" or "Will not" attend?

Stooping to retrieve it, Ellen's glance stopped on the invitation itself, a few inches away. For a shocked moment she stared at The New York Medical Research Institute's politely phrased request that she and Dan honor it with their presence at dinner the following week. For another moment she wished, with the desperate hopelessness of a swimmer who has struck out curiously to explore some corner of a familiar pond and finds herself unexpectedly being carried out to sea, that she had obeyed her original impulse to fling the envelope, unopened, into the fire. Then, as though the pieces of a terrifying puzzle had suddenly begun to drop into place, Ellen snatched up both pieces of pasteboard and ran back to the phone. She was panting as she gave the operator the number. Her breath came in deep, whistling gasps so loud that she did not realize, until he spoke her name again, and sharply, that Dr. Pritchard was on the wire.

"Ellen," he said. "Ellen, is that you?"

"Yes," she said, making an effort to speak calmly. "I'm sorry, Dr. Pritchard. I set the phone down for a moment to light a cigarette, after I put the call in, I mean, and I didn't hear you—"

"Ellen," Dr. Pritchard's voice, fifty miles away in New York, was as crisp and forthright as though she were sitting across the desk from him in his consulting room. "Is anything wrong?"

"Why?" Ellen said sharply. "Do you expect it to be?"

There was a pause, and then Dr. Pritchard's voice, coming back on the wire, seemed to have exchanged its crisp directness for an almost perceptible mantle of caution.

"Ellen," he said. "Why did you call me?"

"I want to know something," she said, and she lifted the invitation of The New York Medical Research Institute closer, so she could read better. The late afternoon sun was sinking, but she had forgotten to turn on the lights. "Dr. Pritchard," Ellen said. "What is *encephalitis lethargica?*"

There was another pause. It was more eloquent, at least to Ellen who had known him all her life, than any words Dr. Pritchard could have used.

"It's an ailment," he said finally. "Why do you want to know?"

"It's an ailment somebody seems to think I ought to be interested in."

"Who is this somebody, Ellen?"

"Never mind that," she said. "Is that what I've got?"

"Now, look here, Ellen."

"*You* look here," she said, and all the self-control, which she had managed to drag together into a sustaining knot, seemed to flow away in a resurgence of the terror that had struck her when the pieces of the puzzle began to fall into place. "Is that what I've got?" she demanded, her voice rising. "Is that what I've had all my life? Tell me. For God's sake, tell me!"

"I can't tell you anything while you're in that state," Dr. Pritchard's calm, measured, cautious voice said. "I don't know what's got into you, Ellen, but I would advise—"

"I don't want advice," Ellen said, making no effort now to control her voice. "I want information. Is that what's been wrong with me all my life? Is it fatal?"

"Of course not," Dr. Pritchard rapped out. "If it were, you wouldn't be alive today."

"Will I be alive two weeks from today?"

"What?"

"Answer me," Ellen said, sending the words out in a wild rush. "Did you begin to realize it was going to be fatal a year ago? Did you tell that to father? Did you tell him a year ago, or did you tell anybody else, that in twelve months I'd be dead? Is that why—?"

"Ellen!" The voice, raised to a pitch that from almost any other man would have been a shout, stabbed at her eardrums, but Ellen did not answer. She couldn't. She sat there, holding the phone, weak with exhaustion, drained utterly dry, abandoned by even the eruption of terror that had supplied the false

energy on which her frightening questions had hurled themselves at Dr. Pritchard. "Ellen!" he repeated. "Ellen, can you
hear me?" She nodded slowly, as though the small movement
could carry its soundless message across fifty miles of telephone
wire, but she could not concentrate on Dr. Pritchard's soothing
words. Like pieces of cargo that have broken loose in the hold of
a vessel during a storm, the questions rolled about drunkenly in
her head. Why had Maud Tennent arranged to have this
invitation sent to her now? Why had her mind betrayed her into
the one recollection Maud must have known the invitation would
arouse? Why should Maud, who had a whole lifetime ahead of
her, take from Ellen, not only the pitifully short eleven and a half
months that were all she had ever had, but also the even pitifully
shorter two weeks that were all she could possibly ever have?
What had driven Maud to this act of cruelty? What had driven
Ellen, even though warned by the very instinct that had betrayed
her, to impale herself on this quest for the facts that could end
only in the collapse of her world? "I don't know who has been
talking to you, or telling you things," Dr. Pritchard said in an
even, steady, but compulsive voice. "All I know is that you are in
no state to listen, or to do anything else, until I have a chance to
see you. Ellen, do you hear me? I don't want you to leave the
house. I don't want you to do anything until—"

In the sudden silence, Ellen looked down, without comprehension, at her hand. It was empty. She glanced at the phone. She
had hung up. Wearily she pushed herself away from the telephone table. She walked slowly out into the drawing room. She
stopped in front of the fireplace, which provided the only light in
the rapidly darkening room.

The gently dancing flames, which Mrs. Stehli had ignited
before she went down the hill at three o'clock, sent their impish
little shadows flickering across the magnificently furnished
room; leaping nimbly along the five-thousand-dollar rug; caress-
ing the secretary which was so beautiful that not even Dan had
dared guess how much it had cost; skipping on to the closet in
which the three preposterously expensive fur coats hung in

cedar-enclosed splendor; ticking off with delicate tongues of light the catalogue of outrageously extravagant presents which, showered down on them by Simon Bowker with increasing rather than diminishing speed and quantity as their first wedding anniversary rolled closer, had once caused Dan to say, in a jesting moment, that her father's limitless extravagance made him feel less like a husband and more like the leading actor in a gangster funeral.

Again, as when she had first associated the printed words on the invitation in her hand with the fact that Maud Tennent's father was a leading member of the Society from which the invitation had come, Ellen's whole body seemed to stiffen under the shock of a new recollection.

"Forgive me," Dan had said less than a month ago, in this very room, across the cocktail she had just handed him after showing him the fur coats which had arrived that afternoon. "I shouldn't have said that."

"Forgive you for what, darling?" Ellen had asked in a puzzled voice. "You shouldn't have said what?"

"That silly remark about a gangster's funeral," Dan had replied with a touch of uneasiness that had made her laugh at the time. "It's hardly the proper spirit for me to display in the face of your father's generosity."

Ellen Pierce did not laugh now. Nor did she wish any longer, as she had wished before she went to the phone to call The New York Medical Research Institute, that Mrs. Stehli were in the house to prevent her. The pieces of the puzzle, falling into place with disillusioning and terrifying inexorableness, exercised a compelling fascination that went beyond terror, and beyond disillusion. It was as though she were a mere spectator, watching rather than participating in the reconstruction of an edifice of deceit that represented the destruction of her happiness.

Dan had been right. He shouldn't have said that. Even though, at the time, in her glowing innocence, Ellen had not been able to imagine what on earth he had been talking about. It was hardly proper, as Dan had himself pointed out, for him to

say such things about the man who was providing him with so
much luxury. But what *was* proper? Dan's thoughtful devotion,
by which even Mrs. Stehli had been impressed? The bliss he had
given an ugly duckling named Ellen Bowker for eleven and a half
months, which had made the despair of her preceding twenty-
six years seem as nothing? The secret joy of these three
wonderful hours every afternoon which she had believed, until
now, would go on forever? Who could say what was proper?
And who could define the word forever?

"You can have him for a year," Maud Tennent had said. "On
loan."

Ellen's body shook in a bitter laugh. Maud could do more
than define the word forever. Maud, who had always been
Ellen's friend, could even afford to be honest. But Dan, who was
her husband, could not. Dan had joined with the others, with her
father, with Dr. Pritchard, in building the fool's paradise in
which she had wallowed for eleven and a half months. Why? Her
father loved her, which was reason enough. And Dr. Pritchard,
of course, received his considerable fees. But Dan? What had
there been in it for Dan?

"No," Ellen heard herself saying, "person-to-person, please,"
and she realized that she had gone back to the phone to get her
answer. "Yes, I'll hold on," she said. "I know he's there. He's
always in his office at this hour."

He was.

"Ellen?" Simon Bowker's voice sounded disturbed. "I've
been trying to get you on the phone," her father said. "But the
operator said nobody answered. Were you out?"

"No, I must have been upstairs and didn't hear the phone
ring," Ellen said. "Why were you trying to get me?"

"Dr. Pritchard just rang up," Simon Bowker said. "He said
you had called him a little while ago, and he said you
sounded—"

"That's right," Ellen said. "I did call him, and now I'm
calling you. Tell me something, Father," she said, and once
again she drew a deep breath as though, by filling her lungs to

the bursting point, she could keep out the irritating and distracting terror in which, oddly enough, she was no longer interested. She was beyond terror. As though she were in truth no more than a spectator whose casual interest had been trapped and then converted, against his will, into an absorbing passion, she wanted only to see the final pieces fall into place. "How much did you pay Dan to marry me?"

The explosive sound at the other end of the wire could have been almost anything. But Ellen, who knew her father's habits as well as the furnishings of his brokerage office overlooking lower Broadway, knew that Simon Bowker, startled and disturbed, had pushed back his chair and risen at his desk.

"What in God's name are you talking about?" he said harshly. "Who has been talking to you? Has Dan said—?"

"Nobody has been talking to me, and Dan won't be home until six-fifteen, so he hasn't had a chance to say anything, either. I asked you a question, Father. How much did you pay Dan to marry me? How much did it cost, once Dr. Pritchard told you I had only a year to live, how much did it cost to provide me with everything a girl could want or need for one perfect year of happiness, including a handsome husband? Was it expensive, Father? Did Dan come as high as the rug, or the secretary, or the three fur coats, or the house itself? Is that why Mrs. Stehli's wages were prepaid for only one year, no more, and no less? Is that why Dan has insisted we live quietly out here, and accept no invitations, for a full year? Is Dan on a weekly salary, Father? Or did you get him to do it for a flat fee? And what's he going to do with the money after I'm gone? In about two weeks? Quit his job, and set himself up as an architect with offices of his own? Or are you going to invest it for him, and have your office keep an eye on his portfolio, because he did such a good job? How did you sell him on the idea? Was Dan difficult to convince, Father? Did you tell him it was a chance that came only once in a lifetime? Did you happen, perhaps, to describe it accurately enough as a killing? Did you—?"

"Ellen!" Her father's voice, choked with emotion, cut her

short. "Ellen, have you lost your senses?" She sat there for a moment, shaken by her outburst, and she considered her father's question as though it were of the utmost importance. No, Ellen decided, she had not lost her senses. For the first time in over a year, she had found them. The fact that what she had found was so inferior to what she had lost, did not change the fact that finding it had a value all its own. Now she knew where she stood.

"Was it that damned Maud?" Simon Bowker was asking angrily. "Has she said anything to you?"

"No," Ellen said, and even though this was not strictly true, it was true enough. Because Maud had said everything there was to say a year ago. The trouble was that Ellen had not understood. Now she did. "And please don't be upset, Father," Ellen said. "Because I'm not. I just wanted to know."

"Ellen, listen to me."

"Not now," Ellen said. "I'm quite tired." She paused, and then she said, "But I did want to say one thing."

"What, Ellen?"

"Can you hear me?"

"Yes, of course."

"Thank you very much, Father," Ellen said. "It was a lovely year," she said. "Or almost a year, anyway."

"Ellen, listen to me."

"Thank you," she said again, and then Ellen added quietly, "It was worth every penny, Father."

For several moments, after she hung up, she remained at the phone, motionless, watching the shadows lengthen in the darkening room. She watched them with regret, as on other days during the past wonderful months, she had watched them with tingling anticipation, because they meant that Dan would be home soon. They still meant that, of course, so at last Ellen stood up. She sighed as she moved about the room, turning on all the lights. There was so much to do, and so little time in which to do it.

Glancing around, to see that everything was as tidy as Mrs. Stehli herself could make it, Ellen's glance stopped on the invitation from The New York Medical Research Institute. She had forgotten that she was holding it. She carried it across to the secretary, and she set the pieces of pasteboard on the other mail that was waiting for discussion over cocktails with Dan. Ellen's forefinger, moving idly across the blank spaces on the R.S.V.P. card, stopped. Mr. and Mrs. Daniel Pierce "Will" or "Will not" attend?

She shrugged. It was really too bad. Because now that Ellen knew where she stood, she knew also why Maud had sent the invitation. If their positions had been reversed, Ellen knew that she would probably have done the same. She could not have allowed Maud to die with the firm belief that Dan had really loved her. If you loved someone as much as Maud loved Dan, if you loved someone as much as Ellen had loved him, you could not let a third party believe she had ever really shared that love. It was all or nothing. For Maud, as well as for herself.

So the fault was really Dan's. He never should have told Maud. And even though Ellen could see that it had been a matter of practical necessity for Dan to tell Maud—so that Maud would wait through the year for him, until he had fulfilled his part of the bargain with Mr. Bowker—the fact remained that, by telling her, Dan had provided Maud with the opportunity to spoil it. Dan should have known better. Dan should have realized what any woman would know: that it was too much to expect Maud, or any other woman, not to take the opportunity. Even though, in a mere two weeks, Maud would have Dan forever. Plus all the money, and this house, and those three fur coats, which he had earned by having Ellen for a mere year.

"Since I'll have him for all the rest of my life after that," Maud had herself said, "You can take him on loan, so to speak, for one year."

No, Ellen decided as she opened the top drawer of the secretary, Maud should have allowed the loan to reach maturity. According to plan. Maud should have been strong enough to resist the opportunity that any woman, even Ellen, would have lacked the strength to resist. Because Maud was getting so much more than any woman, even Ellen, had ever had. Maud was getting Dan.

That was what made it too bad, Ellen thought as she pushed aside the gun Dan insisted on keeping in the drawing room so that she would feel safe at all times while he was in the city and Mrs. Stehli was away at her own house. That was what made it *really* too bad, Ellen thought as she picked up the fountain pen, uncapped it, and leaned over to fill in the space on the R.S.V.P. card. In fact, Ellen thought as the pen touched the piece of pasteboard, Maud's weakness was more than merely too bad. It was fatal.

The sound of a key in the lock of the front door brought Ellen's glance up, and the pen away from the card. She looked at the clock over the fireplace. Astonished, she saw that it showed eighteen minutes after six. It was Dan, then, at the front door.

Still aware of the regret that suffused her spent body, but moving swiftly and surely, Ellen dropped the pen, which had not completed its task, and she picked up the gun, which would.

Crossing quickly into the foyer, Ellen had a moment of doubt. She almost stumbled as a sudden thought, sharp and clear and even stronger than regret, exploded in her mind. How did she know? How could she ever be really certain? Perhaps Dan had *not* married her for a fee? Perhaps he had married her because he actually loved her? Perhaps it was all—?

The click of the lock brought Ellen back to the moment that mattered. Moving swiftly across the foyer, toward the opening door, she brushed away with an irritated shake of her head the distracting question that no longer seemed to matter at all.

How could she possibly expect to know things like that when—in this irrevocable moment, as her finger closed down on the trigger—she still did not know whether the bullet would be directed at herself, whose life was over anyway, or at Dan, whom she could not allow Maud to have?

# THE
# CITY
# OF
# LIGHT

It seemed odd
to be speaking French again. Not funny, or even fun, but odd.
Like finding, in an attic closet, a mildewed and long-forgotten
coat that had once been a cherished garment.

"*Merci*," Spalding said. He tried to remember how to say
"that will be all," but the words wouldn't come back to him, so he
said, "*Merci, beaucoup.*"

"You're quite welcome, sir," the little old man said in heavily
accented English. He was very thin, and he walked with a stoop,
and his face was deeply lined. He looked hungry, and the striped
vest with silver buttons under his green coat was shabby, and it
didn't seem possible that he could have carried Spalding's three
heavy bags all the way up from the lobby. "Will that be all,
sir?"

"Yes, that's all," Spalding said, and then he saw the little old
man staring at the hundred-franc note. "What's wrong?"
Spalding said. "Isn't it enough?"

"It is generous, sir," the little old man said. He folded the
note and slipped it into his pocket. "As for enough, sir, there is no
longer such a word in France."

"Well, look," Spalding said, and he felt annoyed with himself
as he pulled out his wallet. He disliked people who overtipped,
and he particularly disliked people who overtipped when they
were traveling on an expense account. "I'm expecting a phone
call," he said, handing the little old man another hundred-franc
note. "Would you stop at the switchboard and make sure the
operator has my name and my room number right? I don't want
to miss this call."

It was a legitimate enough expense, if you overlooked the fact
that he could have accomplished the same purpose by lifting the
receiver and talking to the switchboard operator himself, but the
franc was dirt cheap, cheaper than it had ever been, and if
Marathon Motors could afford to send him to Paris for a sales

survey, they could afford these extra few cents that might buy this little old man an extra meal, or part of an extra meal. It would go down on the swindle sheet as Miscellaneous.

"Thank you, sir," the little old man said. "I'll see that there is no delay or confusion about your call, sir."

He went out and Spalding lifted his small bag onto the canopied bed. He snapped the locks and he opened the lid. Then he noticed that the bedspread was badly frayed, and at once Spalding lost interest in unpacking. There was no reason why the bedspread shouldn't be frayed. When you considered the war, and what the country had been through, and the shortages, it was remarkable that they had bedspreads of any kind. Just the same, this was the finest hotel in the city and the rate per day, even though it was being paid by Marathon Motors, gave the frayed bedspread a special and disturbing significance. For Spalding, anyway.

He walked to the window and looked out at the Champs Elysées. It seemed curiously deserted in the late afternoon sunlight. Spalding had never seen the Champs Elysées from this angle, probably because he had never been in Paris on an expense account before, so perhaps that was why the wide thoroughfare looked deserted, but of course that was nonsense.

The Champs Elysées looked deserted because of the taxi strike, and it was even worse nonsense to feel the way he did about it, but Spalding couldn't help himself. The feeling had started on the boat train, when he sat down to the boiled carrots and powdered eggs that were called the de luxe lunch. It had become bad in the Gare St. Lazare, where he would probably still be at this moment, standing impotently over his luggage, if the black market chauffeur had not approached him. It had grown worse when he saw the emaciated little old man looking at the hundred-franc note. And it was reaching its climax now as he realized that, in this extravagantly furnished suite, his hands were cold because there was no heat in the radiators.

It was a ridiculous feeling, if you were an adult with any awareness of the grim realities of the European postwar world, but Spalding had pulled strings in the New York office for this assignment, and all the way across on the *Queen Mary* he had lived with a sense of excitement that he could scarcely control, the excitement of a man going home. He knew it was unreasonable and even stupid to feel the way he felt now, but knowing it was unreasonable and stupid did not change the way he felt. The phone rang and he turned toward it with relief. Spalding did not like his own thoughts.

"Hello."

"Spalding?" a man said. "Is that you?"

"Yes." Spalding recognized the harassed voice of the chief of Marathon's Paris office. "How are you, Adams?"

"At the end of my rope, and the end is frayed," Adams said. "Thank heaven you managed to get to your hotel. I've been worried sick about you. I'm sorry about not meeting you at the train, the way I promised in my cable, but this damned taxi strike has messed things up in a way you wouldn't believe."

"That's all right," Spalding said. It seemed odd, almost as odd as talking or trying to talk French again, to have somebody worrying about his ability to get from a railroad station to a hotel in Paris, and thanking heaven because he had succeeded. "I found one of those black market boys with a Citroën minus a meter," Spalding said. "For a mere two thousand francs it was no trick at all. How are you fixed?"

"I'm not, that's the trouble," Adams said. "I haven't been able to get in to the office all day. I'm still out here and—"

"Don't let that bother you," Spalding said. "You don't have to pick me up. I'll take the Métro."

"Look, that's what I'm calling about," Adams said, and an apologetic note worked its way to the top of his worried voice. "You can't take the Métro, because they went out at three o'clock. Sympathy strike. And even if you could get one of those black market pirates to drive you out here to Auteuil, I'm afraid we can't give you the dinner Kay and I planned."

"Oh," Spalding said. "Well—"

"We managed to get the food together, all right, which was

182)

no cinch, I can tell you, with the way things are going in this country, but the lights conked out early this afternoon, and I haven't been able to get an electrician. The stove's electric, too, which means we can't cook, and the furnace has been on the blink since last October, so we've been using space heaters, and without electricity, they're not working, either. The house is like a cave and the kids are beginning to sniffle, and Kay's scared stiff it'll be measles or something before morning." The desperation in Adams' voice gathered itself into a knot. "This damned town," he said savagely, "Honest, I can't figure out why I ever left Bronxville."

"Well, now, look," Spalding said. "Is there anything I can do?"

"If you just won't be sore at me for being such a lousy welcoming committee and host, that will be more than enough."

"Nonsense," Spalding said. "You've got your hands full. Forget about me."

"You sure?"

"Positive," Spalding said. "I'll be all right, and I'll see you at the office in the morning. If you can get to the office, that is?"

"I'll get to the office in the morning if I have to come on my oldest son's bike," Adams said grimly. "You're being damned decent about this, Spalding. Kay and I have been worrying about you all day. We hate to think of you left high and dry like this on your first night in Paris. We know how you must feel, arriving in a strange city in a foreign land and not being met."

"Nonsense," Spalding said again, and this time he wasn't merely using a word. Neither Adams nor his wife Kay had the remotest idea how he felt. "You don't have to worry about me."

They didn't, of course. To Adams and his wife, Spalding was just a visiting fireman from the home office, and visiting firemen always arrived at inconvenient times. He knew Adams only casually, and he had never met his wife, yet Spalding realized with irritation that he was disappointed. Ever since those boiled carrots and powdered eggs on the boat train, he had been uncomfortable about his memories. He hated the prospect of facing the evening alone with them. It was ridiculous, he told himself again and with anger, to feel this way. He wasn't a child and it wasn't a strange city in a foreign land. Not to him, anyway. And he should have understood, before he left New York, that there was nothing but inconvenient times in Europe these days. The phone rang again. Spalding was ashamed of the speed with which he reached it, and picked it up.

"Mr. Spalding?"

"Yes. Who is this?"

"Bill McCord."

"Who?"

"McCord. Bill McCord?"

"I'm sorry," Spalding said. "I don't think I—"

"Bill McCord," the voice said. "Philadelphia? My mother wrote that you were coming in today, and she said you planned to stop at the Crillon, so I thought I'd give you a ring."

"Oh, McCord," Spalding said. "Of course. How are you?"

It was a silly question, because he had never met Bill McCord, but it was no sillier than the eagerness with which he had answered the phone. Mrs. McCord, a woman he had never met, either, was an old school chum of Spalding's wife's mother. How Mrs. McCord, who lived in Philadelphia, had learned that her friend's daughter's husband was going to Paris on business was one of those mysteries about marriage that Spalding never bothered to think too much about. Mrs. McCord had asked Margaret's mother to ask Margaret to ask Spalding if he would look the boy up when he got there. Spalding had said sure, and he had jotted down the boy's address in his pocket notebook, and he had forgotten all about it, and now, two hours after Spalding's arrival in Paris, the boy was on the phone, and Spalding was so delighted that he was also embarrassed.

"Why, I'm swell, sir," Bill McCord said. "And you?"

"I'm fine," Spalding said. "Where are you?"

"At my place, sir," Bill McCord said. "I suppose you're all

tied up for days, but I thought I'd call and ask, if you were free one of these nights, we might have dinner or something?"

"What's the matter with now?"

"You mean tonight?"

"I mean now and tonight," Spalding said. "It's almost five o'clock."

"Why, sure. Yes, of course. That would be swell. Shall I pick you up at your hotel, sir?"

It occurred to Spalding that Bill McCord sounded just as eager to see him as he was to see Bill McCord, and he wondered about that for a moment.

"The Métro's out on a sympathy strike, I hear, and I don't want you spending a fortune on a black market taxi," Spalding said. "Let me pick you up."

"Why, that's very nice of you, sir."

"Not at all," Spalding said. "I won't be long."

"Let me give you the address, sir."

"I have the address."

"Well, then, let me tell you the best way to get here. You go down the Champs Elysées to the Pont Neuf, and then you go over to the—"

"I know how to get there," Spalding said, but Bill McCord didn't seem to believe him.

"It's sort of out of the way, sir," he said. "Perhaps you'd better let me—"

"I know the way," Spalding said. "You don't have to worry about me."

He wished he didn't have to keep saying that because it sounded as though he were one of those insufferable tourists who keeps trying to show that he knows more than the natives, and Spalding wondered, as he changed his shirt, if that was the way he had sounded to Bill McCord, but of course there was no way of knowing because he had no idea what Bill McCord was like. It was difficult to put together a picture of a man from the few facts Margaret had given him, facts to which, Spalding realized with some embarrassment, he had not listened very carefully. The boy had been in the army, Spalding recalled, or thought he recalled. Drafted very young, before he'd had a chance to enter college, or perhaps during his freshman year. Something like that, anyway. After the war, Bill McCord had felt restless, Margaret had said. He hadn't wanted to go to college, or back to college. He wanted to paint, Spalding thought Margaret had said, so Mrs. McCord had staked him to a couple of years in Paris. Or was it three? Spalding didn't remember, and he didn't really care.

All that mattered, he thought as he left the Crillon and started down the Champs Elysées in the glare of the dying sun, was that he was killing two birds with one stone. He was fulfilling his promise to Margaret and her mother that he would look up Mrs. McCord's son and, at the same time, he was avoiding the unwelcome necessity to eat his first dinner in Paris all by himself, alone with his troubling thoughts. These were interrupted at the corner of the rue de Rivoli, where the short thoroughfare came out into the Place de la Concorde.

A crowd had gathered on the corner. Spalding stopped to look. A taxi was lying on its side in the gutter, and half a dozen men were locked in what looked like a snake dance but was obviously a more serious enterprise. Fists were flailing, and some were finding their targets with dull, sickening thuds, and the spectators were screaming incoherent encouragement or discouragement. It was hard to tell which, but Spalding did not stay to find out.

He hurried on, through the gardens, and across the Seine, and past the imposing façade of the Chambre des Députés. He walked quickly, without hesitation, until he was deep into the Boulevard Raspail. Then he slowed down. He felt more comfortable here, on this side of the river.

He turned right at the Balzac statue, into the Boulevard Montparnasse, and he went up toward the railroad station. Before he reached it, he turned into the rue Littré. The crooked, dirty little cul-de-sac was deserted, and dusk was falling, but Spalding had no trouble finding the right number. He walked through a narrow, smelly hallway into a cobbled courtyard and he looked at the cards tacked on the concierge's board. One of them said "William McCord, Jr., Top, Rear." Spalding climbed the splintered wooden stairs that circled upward steeply.

"Mr. Spalding?"

The voice came down the stairwell.

"Yes," Spalding said. "Am I getting close?"

"One more, sir."

Spalding came out on the top landing, puffing hard, and the young man in the tweed coat smiled apologetically.

"You wouldn't think I'm only thirty-four, would you?" Spalding said, drawing a deep breath as he put out his hand. "Glad to meet you."

"So am I, sir," Bill McCord said. "These stairs are pretty steep. Come in, sir."

Spalding followed him into a studio room with a skylight that looked out on the roofs behind the Boulevard Montparnasse. There was a rickety bed in one corner, with a Belling stove beside it, and a small table with a scarred oilcloth top, and three straight-backed chairs long past their first youth. An easel was standing in front of the skylight and several canvases were stacked, face down, along the walls. It was a shabby room, and even with the way prices were skyrocketing it couldn't have been very expensive, but it looked surprisingly clean and neat, like Bill McCord himself.

"I'm afraid I can't offer you anything but vermouth," he said. "And that's not very good, either."

"That's all right," Spalding said. "I like vermouth, good or bad."

Bill McCord brought out a bottle from a cupboard over the table and, as he poured two glasses, Spalding examined him with interest. He seemed to be about twenty-three or four. In his gray flannels and tweed coat and bow tie, he looked more like an undergraduate entertaining a friend in a fraternity house than a young painter struggling to learn the fundamentals of his art in Paris, but Spalding knew you couldn't go by appearances.

Over the glasses of vermouth they made the uneasy conversation that was inevitable between two strangers who were ten years apart in age and had nothing in common except a mother and a mother-in-law who had gone to school together. They talked about Philadelphia, which was strange to Spalding, and about New York, which was strange to Bill McCord, and about the way in which they could very easily have met, because they had both served in the Pacific, but hadn't. Bill McCord apologized for his cramped quarters, and Spalding told him not to be silly, but Bill McCord explained that he'd come here to work and, while the allowance his mother gave him was generous enough, he disliked the feeling of being dependent, even though he had to be until he became a good enough painter to earn his own living, so the least he could do now was not live extravagantly. Besides, it seemed wiser to put the money into his lessons. Spalding agreed, and told him about his sales survey for Marathon Motors and about the conversation he'd just had with Adams on the phone, which led to a discussion of the taxi strike, and the petrol and food shortages, and the black market, and the discomforts of living in Europe these days. Then Spalding became aware that they had run out of conversation and that Bill McCord was only half listening.

The young man seemed much too awkward even for a shy person, and much too uncomfortable in the presence of a man who was not, after all, exactly an old gaffer, and then Spalding remembered that Bill McCord had called him practically as soon as he had got off the boat, and Spalding began to wonder if anything was wrong.

"We've talked about everything but your work," he said. "How is it going?"

"Pretty well," Bill McCord said. "I've got more to learn than I thought, but I think I'm moving along all right. I've got these classes in the morning, and then I put in several hours every afternoon here in my own place, and then—" He paused and looked down into his glass of vermouth. "Oh, the work's going fine, sir." He paused again, and Spalding waited for Bill Mc-Cord to tell him what it was that was not going fine, because quite obviously something wasn't, but the young man seemed to change his mind. "You must be hungry," Bill McCord said. "Shall we go out and try to find some place where we can eat?"

The place they, or rather Bill McCord, found was a small restaurant on the north side of the Gare Montparnasse. Spalding stopped in front of it.

"This doesn't look too good," he said. "I think we can do better, don't you?"

"They're all pretty much alike, sir," Bill McCord said. "Bad food and high prices. I come to this place fairly regularly, though, so they don't gyp me too badly."

"I still think we can do better," Spalding said. "You come with me."

They went back up the Boulevard Montparnasse. There was a chill in the early evening air. It was not much, but perhaps it was enough to explain why there were so few people at the little tables in front of the Dôme, and why the wide thoroughfare seemed almost empty. A street fiddler grinned at them half-heartedly and the street lamps glowed dully. The policeman at the corner looked bored and even the girls parading along the curb appeared disinterested. It seemed more like a poorly painted still life than a living scene. Spalding led the way across the Boulevard Raspail, past the row of apartment houses with iron grillework on the balconies. He found himself walking faster, almost holding his breath, and then he saw the sign painted on the green awning, *Au Cheval d'Or*, and he slowed down.

"Here," Spalding said. "How does this look?"

Bill McCord glanced at the small restaurant. The awning was torn and the six small tables out in front were covered with soot. It didn't look much different from several other places they had passed.

"I guess it's all right, sir," he said doubtfully. "I've never noticed it before."

"Most people never go beyond the Dôme," Spalding said. "Let's try it."

They went in and Spalding could feel a slight constriction in his throat as he looked around. The single room was small and dirty and poorly lighted. It seemed empty and then the proprietor came out of the back, rubbing his hands dry on his stained alpaca coat. The constriction in Spalding's throat eased away. He had never seen this man before. The proprietor didn't seem particularly interested in seeing them, but he said he would get dinner for them, and Spalding asked if they could sit outside. The proprietor shrugged and said they could sit where they chose. Spalding chose the table on the right, against the window, looking down the Boulevard Montparnasse toward the railroad station.

"Isn't it a little cold to be eating out?" Bill McCord said.

"Not really," Spalding said. "Once we get some wine into our stomachs."

The proprietor flicked the soot off the tablecloth with a soiled napkin, and he rubbed the tarnished silverware on the sleeve of his coat, and he gave them a spotted menu. Spalding merely glanced at it, noting that a glass of beer was twenty-five francs, and then he asked if there was any squid. The proprietor shook his head, and Spalding saw Bill McCord watching him.

"It used to be run by a Basque," Spalding said. "Squid was the house special. I guess we'd better take what he's got."

What the proprietor had was sardines and veal and a salad and cheese. He put down a carafe of *vin ordinaire* and two glasses and went to get the food. Spalding filled the glasses and saw that Bill McCord was still watching him. Their eyes met and the young man blushed and dropped his glance.

"Well," Spalding said. "Here's hoping it's edible." They touched glasses and drank. The wine was sour. Spalding said, "I imagine it will be. The French can't do anything wrong with veal."

"I guess not," Bill McCord said. He scowled as he looked down the street and Spalding waited for Bill McCord to tell him what was wrong, but the young man said, "Did you used to come here often?"

"Fairly often," Spalding said. "It was inexpensive and I didn't have much money."

"A long time ago?"

"Yes and no, depending on how you figure time," Spalding said, following Bill McCord's glance down the street to the lights in front of the Dôme. "Ten years," Spalding said. "Before the war."

"What was it like?" Bill McCord said.

"I've never tasted anything as good," Spalding said. "A lot of people won't touch it, because they think of squid as some sort of sea monster that squirts ink, but actually the flavor is quite wonderful."

"No, I don't mean that," Bill McCord said. He gestured with his glass down the Boulevard Montparnasse. "I mean this whole thing," he said and, for an unguarded instant, a trace of anger flashed through his polite voice. "Back there, before the war," Bill McCord said. "What was it like?"

"Why," Spalding said, and he hesitated, because he knew all at once that he did not have to wait for Bill McCord to tell him what was wrong. Spalding knew why the young man had called him so soon after he had checked into the Crillon. "Why," Spalding said again, "it's hard to say."

It was.

Not only hard, but almost impossible, because Spalding was thirty-four, and he had a wife and a son and a career in New York, and Bill McCord was only twenty-four, perhaps younger, and all that was still ahead of him. It didn't seem much of a gap when you said it aloud: ten years; but there was a whole war imbedded in those years, a whole attitude toward life that had disappeared in that war, and a whole new point of view that had been forged by that war, and perhaps it was those things that made the gap seem wider. Those things plus the fact that, as he looked at Bill McCord, it occurred to Spalding that he was looking at himself, as he had been ten years ago, when he first came to Paris. It was harder to explain things to yourself than people thought it was.

He had been twenty-three, and he had just spent a year in the New York offices of Marathon Motors, where Mr. Merritt, the Foreign Sales Manager, had taken a fancy to him. It had been surprising and it was still somewhat incredible. Mr. Merritt was a bluff, hearty, dynamic man who gave you the impression, even when he was reading a report behind his enormous desk, that he was taking part in a relay race. Spalding had been so awed by him that he used to duck into the file room when he saw Mr. Merritt coming down the corridor, like a schooner under full sail, but Mr. Merritt had an eye for what he called "the X quality." He had not achieved his own success, Mr. Merritt used to say, by riding along on the coat tails of other people's opinions. Mr. Merritt was proud of his ability to think for himself, and he had confidence in his eye for spotting the X quality. He spotted it in Spalding, to the astonishment of Spalding himself and the chagrin of the rest of the New York staff. One day Mr. Merritt had trapped Spalding in the corridor, between the water cooler and the door to the file room, and he had seized his elbow.

"You," Mr. Merritt said. "What's your name?"

"Spalding, sir."

"Just as I thought," Mr. Merritt said in a tone of thundering self-congratulation. "An excellent name. The kind of name Europeans recognize at once as American. It has the X quality. How would you like to go to Paris for us?"

"Why," Spalding said, "I never thought of it before, sir."

"Well, start thinking about it at once," Mr. Merritt said. "The *Normandie* sails on Tuesday and I promised Brophy by cable this morning I'd have an assistant on board for him. See my secretary right away about your passport, and come see me in my office at eleven-thirty. I'm busy now."

When the *Normandie* sailed on Tuesday, Spalding was on it,

and when the boat train pulled into the Gare St. Lazare, Brophy was on hand to meet him and see him through the customs. Brophy had not been like Adams, or perhaps being chief of Marathon's Paris office in those days had been less harassing than it was now. Anyway, Brophy was there, and Spalding soon learned that, wherever Brophy was, things seemed less complicated and went more smoothly. Brophy came from North Carolina, and Paris suited his temperament.

"It's important to remember that we're in the business of selling automobiles," he used to say to Spalding at lunch, "but it's also important to remember that we're in the City of Light. If old man Merritt won't let you forget that there's no business in the world like ours, don't you let his cables let you forget that there's no city in the world like this one. Have another *fin* and relax. I told Miss Picard we'd be back at three-thirty."

Brophy was dead now, killed on Okinawa, but Spalding would always remember him the way you remembered a schoolteacher who had been kind to you. Actually, there had been nothing particularly personal about Brophy's kindness. He had been a jovial, slothful, friendly man who loved laughter and food and wine and anybody who would share these things with him. In spite of his laziness, he was enough of a busybody to enjoy taking an active part in helping people. Brophy found Spalding his room in the tiny Hotel du Bac on the even tinier rue Vieux Carré, and Brophy taught him how to get more francs for his salary which was paid in American dollars, and Brophy taught him not to waste money on bottled wines when you could do just as well and better by going to the right places for *vin ordinaire*, and Brophy taught him the pleasures of eating squid and sitting at a sidewalk table for hours on end, doing absolutely nothing, and Brophy introduced him to Spike Gulliver.

"You don't want to get into a rut," Brophy said. "You take your work too seriously. The world is full of all kinds of people, not only customers for Marathon Sixes, and they're all in this town. What are you doing tonight?"

"Why," Spalding said, "nothing special."

He was ashamed to tell Brophy that he was reading, or trying to read, all through Balzac in the original French. It wasn't that he had a passion for the language or for literature. It was merely that he couldn't think of anything else to do with his evenings. He was shy and awkward and unsure of himself. Even though he had been in Paris for ten months, Brophy was the only friend he had, although Brophy didn't know that. It may have been the most wonderful city in the world, but Spalding was lonely and homesick in it. When he was not with the easygoing Southerner who was his boss, Spalding didn't know how to spend his time. Occasionally, after work, he would go to an American movie on the Champs Elysées, or do a little sightseeing, or sit at a table in front of the Dôme, watching the crowds. But the sight of other people talking animatedly, the sound of their laughter, and the echoes of their pleasure, only increased his loneliness. He wanted to join them, to become a part of their fun, but he didn't know how to go about it. His shyness and his pride got in the way. Madame Duporte, the fat, elderly woman with the dyed hair and the choker collar who sat at the desk in the lobby of the Hotel du Bac, looked at him with disapproval when he came home in the evening and went up to his room. It was plain, from her glance, that she thought it was wrong for a young man in Paris to go to bed at eight or nine o'clock. Finally, Spalding had formed the habit of having an early dinner, on his way home from the office, and staying in his room all evening, reading Balzac. He was in the middle of *Seraphita*, and having trouble following the story, when Brophy asked him what he was doing that night.

"If you haven't anything better to do, you come have dinner with me," Brophy said. "I want you to meet a friend of mine, just got into town, newspaperman. Harwood Gulliver, he signs himself, but everybody from Hitler to Shirley Temple calls him Spike."

This was an exaggeration, of course, but Spalding half believed it. Brophy's most outrageous statements were delivered with such an air of conviction, and Spike Gulliver had such an air of quiet confidence, and Spalding had never met a newspaperman. Brophy and Spalding met Gulliver and his wife at a Basque restaurant that was new to Spalding. They ate squid and drank a good deal of wine and, for once, even the garrulous Brophy was forced to remain silent. Spike Gulliver did all the talking, and Spalding could not remember when he had enjoyed listening to anybody so much, although when he tried later to remember what the newspaperman had said, Spalding could recall nothing very specific.

He remembered only that there had been something exciting about the handsome man with the broad face and the closely cropped blond hair, that Gulliver had just come from Vienna, where he had met and married his wife, that the newspaperman felt the situation in Central Europe was worse than people in Paris thought, and that he was about to write a series of articles for an American magazine that would arouse the English-speaking world to its peril. They didn't finish dinner until very late, and then they went down the street to the Dôme, where they sat and drank *armagnac* and listened to Spike Gulliver until the waiters started stacking the small iron chairs. When Spalding came into the lobby of the Hotel du Bac, Madame Duporte, knitting behind the desk, looked up, glanced at the clock on the wall, and smiled at him with approval.

Three days later, shortly after Spalding came back to the office from lunch, Miss Picard rang him and said that a friend of Mr. Brophy was on the wire. She had told Mr. Brophy's friend that Mr. Brophy was not in, and the friend had asked to speak to Mr. Brophy's assistant. Would Mr. Spalding take the call?

"Sure," Spalding said. "What's his name?"

"He would not say," Miss Picard said. "Will you still take the call?"

Spalding took the call, which proved to be from Spike Gulliver. The newspaperman explained that he was in a hurry and in a jam, and it was just like Brophy to take three hours for lunch when a friend needed him, and could Spalding meet him in front of the Dôme right away in one of the Marathon demonstrators?

"Why," Spalding said, "I guess so."

"Step on it," Gulliver said. "This is important."

Spalding stepped on it. When he reached the Dôme, he found Mr. and Mrs. Gulliver waiting at a sidewalk table. The newspaperman explained in a tense undertone that he had a hot tip on a story that required his presence at once in some suburb Spalding had never heard of. Gulliver said he couldn't go by taxi, or hire a car, because either one could be traced and, before Spalding could explain nervously that he didn't think he had the right to lend one of the company's cars to a stranger, the newspaperman had crossed the sidewalk and slipped behind the wheel.

"Don't worry about it," he said to Spalding. "I know it's okay, because Brophy has let me use your demonstrators before. I'll meet you back here at six. Buy Iliena a drink while you're waiting, will you? When I get back, I'll buy you a dinner."

The Marathon left the curb with a roar and Spalding watched it until it disappeared in the traffic. Then he turned back to the table in front of the Dôme and found Mrs. Gulliver smiling at him. Spalding blushed and walked over.

"He is, what you call, persuasive?" she said.

"Well, yes," Spalding said. "Sort of."

"It is all right," Mrs. Gulliver said. "He is quite extraordinary with machinery. He has never injured a motor. He is most careful. Please sit down."

"Thanks," Spalding said uncomfortably. "I think—I mean, I think I'd better— Will you excuse me for a minute? There's something I have to do right away."

"Of course," Mrs. Gulliver said. "You will not be long, please?"

He wasn't. When he came, she smiled again.

"Your Mr. Brophy?" she said quietly. "He said, on the telephone, it was all right?"

Spalding felt his face grow hot, and she laughed, and then he laughed, too.

"I guess that was pretty obvious," he said, sitting down. "The fact is, though, if anything happens to that car, it would take me a year's salary to pay for it. Brophy not only said it was all right. He said I didn't have to come back to the office today. What are you drinking?"

Cinzano, she said, so he ordered the same, and then he looked at her, and all at once there was a funny little feeling in his heart. It was as though he had carried a heavy trunk up several flights of stairs and, now that he had set it down, he realized that the strain had been too much and he felt faint. Mrs. Gulliver was slender and dark-haired, with lips that were surprisingly red even though they were not rouged, and her skin had a creamy pallor that reminded him of the top of a marble soda fountain that has just been scrubbed clean. She looked back at him, and the friendly smile caused her lips to tremble just a trifle. It came to Spalding with a small sense of shock, for he was not given ordinarily to stating his rather acute perceptions in such specific terms, that Mrs. Gulliver had a curious delicacy, not fragile but resilient, as though she were a long-stemmed flower swaying gently in the soft breeze of a carefully tended garden, and he remembered that Spike Gulliver had called her Iliena. It seemed a wonderfully appropriate name. Then he was struck by something his mind had recorded three nights before, when Brophy had introduced him to the Gullivers, but which until this moment had not seemed significant: Spike Gulliver seemed to be about Brophy's age, somewhere in his middle forties, but Mrs. Gulliver was young. Why, Spalding thought in surprise, she's just a kid, probably younger than I am.

"You look very much perplexed," she said. "Is it something I have done or said?"

"No, no," he said, angry with himself because he could feel his face growing warm again. "I was just thinking, we have the whole afternoon ahead of us. Would you care to go to a movie?"

"If you like," she said. "That would be highly pleasant."

She spoke English with that charming mixture of excessive precision and slight grammatical inaccuracy that came from having learned it in school, out of text books, but it seemed to suit her low voice perfectly.

"Or would you prefer to do something else?" Spalding said. "I mean, is there any special place you like?"

"It is all special to me," she said. "I have never been in Paris before."

"Oh," Spalding said, and the ten lonely months of sightseeing by himself, and reading alone in his room at night, seemed to fall away and change character. The unhappy time became a period of necessary preparation, an apprenticeship he had been forced to serve in anticipation of this moment, and he was suddenly glad he had served it. "Let's go," he said in an eager, confident voice. He put down his glass of Cinzano and he stood up. She had given him, by her simple announcement that she had never been to Paris before, all the authority and perquisites of an old settler. He said, "There are a lot better things to do in this town on an afternoon like this than going to a movie."

They did so many of them, and she enjoyed doing them so much, that he lost track of the time. He took her to the Louvre to see the "Mona Lisa," and to the Invalides to look at Napoleon's tomb, and to Montmartre to show her Sacré Coeur, and to the top of the Eiffel Tower for a glimpse of the view that had bored him so often but now, standing by her side at the parapet, brought a lump to his throat. It was almost as though he had never really looked at the city before.

"It is lovely," she said. "It is so—so—so—"

She could not seem to find the word she wanted, and the sound of her hesitant voice made him turn to look at her. He saw, with a puzzling feeling of pity, that her lips were trembling. He remembered all at once, for no reason that seemed sensible, that when he had excused himself at the Dôme, to go in and call Brophy, she had asked him please not to be long. Spalding looked away quickly, as though to give her a chance to pull herself together, and he saw the watch on his wrist.

"We're late," he said. "Mr. Gulliver said he would meet us at the Dôme at six, and it's ten after, now."

They took a taxi but, when they reached the Dôme, Spike Gulliver was not there.

"It is nothing to upset ourselves," his wife said. "He is never prompt, and he is forgetful of the time. Would it not be pleasant to sit and have a Cinzano while we wait?"

They had several, and it was extremely pleasant. For the first time since he had come to Paris, he did not envy the people at the sidewalk tables around him. For the first time in almost a year, he did not feel like a stranger, standing outside, looking in on the pleasures of others. The inexplicable atmosphere of the city, the thing that held a man like Brophy in its thrall, now held him, too. He was part of it at last. The long spring evening faded gently into night, but Spike Gulliver did not show up. By eight o'clock, Spalding was beginning to worry, not so much about Gulliver as about the car he had allowed the newspaperman to borrow, but Mrs. Gulliver, apparently understanding what was troubling him, said reassuringly that his fears were groundless. Her husband, she said, would return the automobile uninjured. At nine o'clock Spalding, becoming aware that he was hungry, realized that Mrs. Gulliver must be hungry, too. He asked her if she would care for some dinner and, even though it was obvious that the answer was yes, she seemed to hesitate. It occurred to Spalding that perhaps his innocent suggestion appeared, to a Viennese girl, not quite innocent, and he felt the peculiar discomfort of a shy person who, inadvertently, has done or said something that he would have censured in another.

"Perhaps you would rather have me take you back to your hotel?" Spalding said quickly. "So you can wait for Mr. Gulliver there, and have dinner with him when he gets back?"

"No, no, it is not that," she said, even more quickly, and again he remembered the way she had asked him, early in the afternoon when he went to the phone booth to call Brophy, not to be long. "When he is late like this," she said, "I know he is detained by his work and he will not return until many many hours."

"Then that's all the more reason why you should have dinner."

"Yes, thank you, but—" She hesitated and looked at him for a long moment and then she said, "It is not right that you should waste your money on me. Already you have spent too much."

"Nonsense," he said, blushing furiously because it occurred to him that perhaps he had been putting it on a bit thick all afternoon, and also because the word sounded so silly. "You don't know how much money I have."

"I know that, if anything should happen to the motor while it is in the care of Mr. Gulliver, it would take an entire year of your salary to pay for it."

He gave her a startled glance, and their eyes met, and he saw that she was smiling mischievously, and then they both laughed.

"Well, even if I didn't exaggerate that too much," Spalding said, "I can still afford to buy you a dinner. Where would you like to go?"

"Shall we return, as perhaps a small celebration, to the little Basque place in which we met three nights ago?" she said. "It was named, I think, Au Cheval d'Or?"

They went back to the little Basque place, and they ate squid and drank *vin ordinaire*, while he told her all about New York, and Marathon Motors, and Mr. Merritt, and how the dynamic Foreign Sales Manager had chosen him to go to Paris, and then he glanced at his watch and was startled to see that it was almost midnight.

"Holy smoke," he said. "I'd better be getting you back to your hotel, or Mr. Gulliver will think you've been kidnapped."

"He will not think that," she said. "When he is preoccupied with his work, he thinks only of it." She smiled, "Would you perhaps do a favor for me?"

"Of course."

"Would you call up on the telephone our hotel and determine if Mr. Gulliver has returned?"

Spalding thought the request rather odd, but no more so than a number of other things about Spike Gulliver's lovely young wife. He went into the restaurant and located the phone booth and called the George V, where the Gullivers were staying.

"They said he hasn't come in yet," Spalding said in a puzzled voice when he returned to the sidewalk table at which she was waiting. "Do you think anything has—?"

"No," she said. "When he is in pursuit of a story, often he does not return until early in the morning."

"Well, it's getting sort of chilly," Spalding said. "I think I'd better take you back to your hotel, anyway."

"No, please, no," she said, and he looked at her sharply. Mrs. Gulliver sounded terrified. "I do not want to return yet," she said. She hesitated and looked down the Boulevard Montparnasse toward the Dôme. There was now a sharp edge in the night air, and most of the tables were unoccupied. It was still too early in the year to sit out as late as this. Spike Gulliver's wife turned back to Spalding, and she said, "Could we not perhaps go to your place for a while?"

He could feel the astonishment spreading across his face, not because of the implication obvious in the circumstances of the suggestion, but because he knew, without knowing why or how, that in this case the obvious implication was wrong.

"All right," he said awkwardly. "If you want to."

They walked to the Hotel du Bac and Madame Duporte, after an appraising glance at Spike Gulliver's wife, gave Spalding a nod of approval before, with an expression of exaggerated indifference, she returned to her knitting. Spalding's room was tiny. It seemed to him that the cumbersome old brass bedstead had never occupied so much of the small space, but Iliena Gulliver thought the view of the rooftops behind the Gare Montparnasse was charming, and then she saw the copy of *Seraphita* on the small table beside the only chair in the room.

"Balzac," she said, her voice lifting with pleasure. "Do you read him?"

"Well, I try," Spalding said. "I'm afraid my French isn't really good enough."

"Nor is mine," she said. "Please, would you read to me?"

She sat down in the chair. He sat on the ugly old bed and, by the inadequate light of the single bulb that hung from the ceiling on a length of black wire, he began to read aloud from *Seraphita*. Before long he made a discovery that reminded him of the way he had felt when he had stood by her side at the parapet on the Eiffel Tower, and the sense of belonging to the city that had come to him when they were sitting at the sidewalk table in front of the Dôme before dinner: it was surprising, after a page or two, how much easier the words came than they had during the weeks when he was reading alone, and how much better he understood what had seemed, until then, a murky and far from comprehensible story. After an hour, he paused and looked up.

"Do not stop," Iliena Gulliver said. "Please."

"I thought I'd call the George V and find out if Mr. Gulliver has returned," Spalding said. "It's almost one o'clock."

He picked up the phone beside his bed and made the call, but Spike Gulliver had not yet come in. Spalding returned to *Seraphita*. Twice more, at intervals of a half hour or so, he called the George V. The third time he was put through to Gulliver's suite.

"Hello, there," the newspaperman said. "I just got in. Sorry not to have met you at the Dôme, the way I said I would, but this story turned out to be hotter than I thought and I had to stay on its tail. It's an important part of this magazine series I'm doing. The car is perfectly safe, by the way. I'm damned grateful to you for letting me have it."

"That's all right," Spalding said. "I'm glad to have been of some help." He hesitated, not quite knowing what to say next. "By the way," he said finally, "I've got Mrs. Gulliver here with me and—"

"Of course," Gulliver said, and the way he said it, with the intonation of a man who has been reminded on his way out of a restaurant that he has forgotten his hat, filled Spalding with sudden and unreasonable anger. "I'm sorry to have parked her on you for the evening," Gulliver said. "Would you put her in a cab?"

Spalding hung up.

"Well," he said, "I guess that's enough reading for tonight. Mr. Gulliver is waiting. I'll take you home."

"It is not necessary," Mrs. Gulliver said. "I will go in a taxi."

"No," Spalding said. "It's after three. I'll take you."

Neither of them spoke all the way across the city. When the taxi turned into the Champs Elysées, she turned with it, and he could feel her eyes on him, but Spalding continued to look straight ahead, at the back of the driver's neck. Then the cab swung into the Avenue George V and, this time, Spalding turned to look at her, but now Mrs. Gulliver was staring straight ahead, and he saw that her lips were trembling. The taxi stopped in front of the hotel and they both sat there for a while, without moving. Then Mrs. Gulliver picked up the purse from her lap and she made a small sound in her throat, as though she were clearing it.

"It has been a lovely day," she said in a low voice, without looking at him. "Nobody," she said, and she hesitated, as though she were not sure that she had at her command the proper words for what she wanted to say, and then she seemed to reach some sort of decision. "Nobody," she said again. "In my entire life, nobody has ever been so kind to me," she said. "I want to thank you very much."

"That's all right," Spalding said, scowling at the back of the driver's neck. "I—" He stopped, and he cleared his throat, too, and he tried again. "I—"

She reached across to the door and for an instant, as she moved to get out of the cab, her lovely face was close to his, and then the door opened and closed, and she was gone. He sat quite still. It was not until several moments had gone by, and the taxi driver turned to ask for instructions, that Spalding realized what had happened. She had kissed him.

"Hotel du Bac," he said slowly. "Rue Vieux Carré."

The next day, in the office, he scarcely saw the papers that Miss Picard kept bringing to, and carrying away from, his desk. He did not realize, until Brophy stopped by at noon and asked him if he was free for lunch, that he had been waiting for something all morning.

"I guess so," Spalding said. "Sure."

"What do you mean, you guess so?" Brophy said. "Don't you know if you've got a date or not?"

"I'm sorry," Spalding said. "I was thinking of something else. Yes, sure, I'm free."

They went to Fouquet's, because Brophy was going out to St. Germain-en-Laye at four o'clock to show one of the demonstrators to a prospect who was almost committed to an order for three and possibly four Marathons, and Brophy said this made him feel in an expansive as well as an expensive mood. This certainly seemed to be true, because he talked without pause from the moment they left the office and, for the first time in almost a year, Spalding was conscious of a feeling of irritation with the garrulous and jovial man from North Carolina who was his boss. It was not until the waiter had brought the *fin* that Spalding, distracted at last from his own thoughts by Brophy's ceaseless prattle, became aware that the older man's spate of words was not nearly so innocent and pointless as he had thought. Brophy was talking about Spike Gulliver.

"He's a wonderful guy, a really good egg, but I'll tell you frankly," Brophy said, "I don't exactly envy that kid he's married to, if you know what I mean."

"I don't," Spalding said, trying not to sound startled. "What do you mean?"

"Well, there are men who are built for marriage, and then there are men who just aren't," Brophy said. "I'm one of them," he said. "Spike Gulliver, now, he's another. Does that make it clearer?"

"Not much," Spalding said. "Why did he marry her, then?"

"Because he's got a heart as big as a watermelon," Brophy said. "Iliena was in trouble back there in Vienna. Her father was some kind of newspaper editor, blasting away at the Nazis. After the Anschluss, why, they just fixed it so he couldn't do any more blasting. Iliena was on her own when Spike blew into Vienna a few months ago to get the dope for this magazine series. The way the boys who had taken care of her old man were closing in on her, it looked like she wouldn't be on her own much longer. As soon as Spike got wind of it, he tried to pull strings to get her out of the country, but those things aren't as easy as they used to be, and Spike is the kind of boy who gets mad when he's crossed. He also likes to finish what he starts, so he finished this thing in a typical Spike Gulliver way: he married her." Brophy tossed off his *fin* and snapped his fingers at the waiter for a refill. "They couldn't stop an American correspondent from taking his bride out of the country and, if I know Spike Gulliver, even if this war that all these wise birds are saying is just around the corner should come, it won't stop him from continuing to take care of her and being kind to her, because she's had a pretty rough time, and she's still shaky." The waiter brought the fresh round of *fin* and Brophy, picking up his glass, said casually, "Have a good time last night?"

"What?"

"Watch your glass," Brophy said. "This stuff is too good and too expensive to spill on tablecloths. I said did you have a good time last night?"

For a long moment, even if he had been able to answer truthfully, Spalding would have been unable to say the words. In the light of what Brophy had told him, everything that had happened the day before took on a new, and infuriating, meaning. Iliena had not asked him to come back from the phone booth quickly, she had not asked him to read to her, because she wanted to be with him. It had been merely that she had been unable to face going back to the George V until she knew her husband was there. Spalding didn't matter. Anybody, even Brophy, would have served her purpose. She was afraid to be alone.

"Oh, you know," Spalding said. "It was pretty dull."

"I'm glad of that," Brophy said, and Spalding gave him a quick glance. "You see," the older man said, "Spike Gulliver is my age, forty-four, and Iliena is younger than you are, twenty-one. It's quite a gap, and gaps like that are too wide to be filled with nothing but kindness on his part and gratitude on hers. As a marriage, this one hasn't got what old man Merritt back home calls the X quality. It's the kind of situation in which a third party, say a very young third party with a very large kind heart

of his own, might get hurt. Purely out of pity, you might say."
The older man tossed off his *fin*. "I don't know why I'm wasting
your time running off at the mouth about it to you, though. Since
you say you had a dull time last night, the whole subject must be
a bore to you." Brophy stood up. "I've got to get out to St.
Germain-en-Laye now, to nail this boy who's been making
googoo eyes at those four Marathons, but I've got a couple of
Annie Oakleys for tonight's show at the Bal Tabarin. How about
meeting me at Prunier's around seven? We can put away a
couple of pounds of *langoustine* before we go look at what the
Tabarin is letting those poor girls wear these days to keep out
the spring chill."

"Swell," Spalding said. "I'll be at Prunier's at seven sharp."

He wasn't.

When he returned to the office he found a message on his
desk, in Miss Picard's angular script, asking him to call Mrs.
Gulliver at the George V. Spalding stared at the message for a
long time. Everything Brophy had said at lunch came back to
him, and he repeated the words to himself several times but,
when he finished, something else came back to him, too. He
picked up the phone and called the George V.

"Spike is consumed by work on his series," Iliena Gulliver
said. "It is such a lovely day, he has suggested perhaps we could
take a walk?"

"I'm afraid I'm pretty much tied up here at the office,"
Spalding said. "Mr. Brophy is away, and I have to—" He
stopped, and he tried once more to repeat to himself Brophy's
words, but the other thing came back to him instead: the look on
her face and the sound of her voice when they had stood side by
side at the parapet on the Eiffel Tower, and those last, confused,
but indelible moments in the taxi in front of the George V. "I'll
tell you what," Spalding said. "Give me a half hour to clean up
my desk, and then I'll pick you up. There's a little place, behind
the wine markets, where they serve snails in a special kind of
sauce. Nobody has the right to visit Paris without trying it."

After she tried it, he remembered several other things that

nobody had the right to visit Paris without trying and, since Spike Gulliver had said he would be working all evening on his series, Spalding and Mrs. Gulliver had plenty of time to try them all.

"That was quite a show at the Tabarin last night," Brophy said the next morning. "Too bad you missed it."

"I'm sorry," Spalding said. "I got tied up."

He continued to be tied up all through the late spring and early summer. It was surprisingly easy, not only because Brophy was far from a demanding boss, but mainly because Spike Gulliver seemed to approve. He was out of town a good part of the time, gathering more material for his series and, when he came back to Paris, he locked himself in the bedroom of the suite at the George V and worked. There were times when Spalding wished he could dislike the large, easygoing man with the close-cropped blond hair, but it was impossible. If, during those months, there was any one factor that kept the relationship of Spalding and Iliena from becoming what Madame Duporte, and perhaps even Brophy, thought it was, that one factor was Spike Gulliver's decency. It was obvious that he liked and trusted Spalding. And Spalding, even though he might have preferred it otherwise, could not help liking Spike Gulliver and living up to the older man's trust in him. Besides, there were other compensations.

In spite of the ominous talk of war, everybody agreed that Paris had never enjoyed such beautiful weather. As they moved about the city, in the limpid sunlight of late afternoon and in the soft air of evening, exploring and tasting, discovering and enjoying, Spalding could actually see the lines of fear wash away from Iliena's face. She became relaxed and eager and, for him, the city in which for a year he had been a puzzled and uncomfortable stranger, became a huge, complicated, but endearing toy which he, knowing and loving every hidden crevice, was showing a delighted child. He had never been so happy in his life and, one evening late in August, when they were sitting over the remains of their squid at their sidewalk table in front of Au

Cheval d'Or and Iliena, in a sudden, impulsive moment of revelation, said precisely that, he believed her so completely that he found himself staring at her in an entirely new way.

"What is it?" she said. "Have I said something wrong?"

"No," he said. "It's just that I've remembered something."

"What?"

"When I came to pick you up at the hotel this afternoon, Spike said he'd be finished with his series by the end of the week."

"Yes," Iliena said. "It has taken much time. He will be glad when it is done."

"Will you be glad?" She didn't answer. She was looking down the Boulevard Montparnasse to the place where, beyond the Balzac statue, the lights were coming on in the Dôme. Spalding said again, "Will you be glad?"

"Will you?"

"No," he said. "Spike said that, when the series is finished and sent off, he is going to London. You'll go with him."

"Yes."

"Do you want to go?"

"He is my husband," Iliena said. "He is a kind man, and a generous one. I owe him much, including my life."

"I didn't ask that."

"It is what you should have asked."

"No," Spalding said, and the sudden anger in his voice surprised him as much as it seemed to surprise her. "I don't care about Spike's kindness and Spike's generosity. I don't care about questions I should have asked. I care about something else. I'm asking you again. Do you want to go?"

"You have no right to ask it."

"Do you want to go?"

She brought her glance back from the lights of the Dôme, and she looked at him, and he saw in her face what had been there that night, months ago, in the taxi in front of the George V.

"I have no alternative."

"Yes, you have," he said. "We both have." He pushed aside

his plate, and he leaned forward across the table. "Listen," he said. "Iliena," he said. "Listen to me."

Four days later, toward the end of the afternoon, Brophy stopped at his desk.

"Busy tonight?"

"Yes," Spalding said. "I'm sorry."

"I hear the Quai D'Orsay is petrified about the news from Poland," Brophy said. "I just had a cable from old man Merritt in New York instructing me to tell this bird Hitler to cut it out because he's interfering with the sale of Marathon Sixes. Did I ever tell you that there are times when our Foreign Sales Manager doesn't exactly strike me dumb with admiration? Let's go over to Fouquet's and have a drink and listen to the gossip."

"I'd like to," Spalding said. "I don't have much time."

"This is the City of Light, son," Brophy said. "War may be just around the corner, but there's still time for a drink. Come on. It's hot and I'm thirsty and it's against my North Carolina principles to drink alone."

They went over to Fouquet's, and they ordered *vermouth cassis*, and they listened to the gossip, but it was exactly the same as it had been for months, and Spalding's mind was on other matters. All at once, something Brophy had said wrenched his mind back to the sidewalk table at which they were sitting.

"What was that?"

"A trip," Brophy said. "I asked if you planned to take a trip."

"What makes you ask that?"

"Miss Picard told me you drew four weeks' salary in advance this afternoon, and she asked me to okay the voucher." Brophy took a sip from his glass. "I did, of course, but I couldn't help wondering."

"I've had some—" Spalding paused and took a sip from his own glass. He was not accustomed to lying. "I've run into some unusual expenses."

"We all do," Brophy said. He stared thoughtfully across the Champs Elysées at the peanut vendor in front of Les Deux

Magots. "Spike Gulliver called me a little while ago," Brophy said. He paused again, as though he was waiting for Spalding to say something, but the younger man did not speak. "Spike said he's finished his magazine series and sent it off to New York," Brophy said. "He'll be leaving for London in the morning. I'll be sort of sorry to see him go, even though I've seen very little of him these last few weeks. Great guy, Spike. A little thoughtless, maybe, especially when he's working, but as decent a man as I've ever known." Brophy's interest in the peanut vendor at the other side of the street seemed to become almost overpowering. "I asked him and Iliena to come have a farewell dinner with me tonight," Brophy said with a scowl of concentration. "Spike said swell, he'd like that, but Iliena had to beg off. What with the excitement and the packing, she's got herself a terrible headache. So Spike and I will be alone. I'd sort of hoped you could join us."

"I'm sorry," Spalding said. "I can't."

"I know," Brophy said. "You told me." He pursed his lips and his eyes crinkled as he watched the man tossing the small paper sacks of peanuts to the men and women at the tables in front of Les Deux Magots. "I'm sort of glad, in a way," Brophy said. "I don't mean I'm glad you can't have dinner with me and Spike tonight. I mean I'm glad that you've developed contacts and interests and dates of your own. The first eight or ten months or so, after you got here from New York, I used to worry about you. I figured you were a little shy, and I sort of guessed you were homesick, which was natural enough, but it seemed to me it went on too long. I used to have the funniest feeling that, on nights when we weren't out together, you were sitting in your hotel room, reading or something." Brophy laughed. "I'm glad to see I was wrong. These last couple of months, you've spread your wings, all right."

"What's that?" Spalding said. "A crack?"

Brophy tore his glance from the peanut vendor. His round, bland, innocent face turned toward Spalding.

"A crack?" Brophy said casually. "Why, no," he said. "I

mean that I take my hat off to you," he said. "You're not a kid any more, the way you were, or seemed to be, when you came over here from New York a year ago. You've grown up."

"Thanks."

The sarcastic word, which Spalding regretted at once, did not seem to affect the older man.

"On the other hand, at twenty-three, you're not exactly a candidate for a pension, either," Brophy said. "You're just about right, and I'm sort of proud of you. Maybe I'm even a little conceited about thinking I may have had something to do with it, so I hope you won't mind my giving you a bit of advice?" Spalding didn't answer. Brophy picked up his *vermouth cassis* and looked at it. "Whether this war they're beating the drums about hits us in the back of the neck or not, you ought to bear a couple of things in mind," the older man said, addressing his glass with great care. "You're an American, a fact that people have a tendency to forget under certain circumstances. It imposes an obligation on you. Also, this post with Marathon here in Paris is just a way station for you, because you've really got that X quality that old man Merritt is always shooting his face off about. What I'm trying to say is that you've got what it takes, and that imposes a different type of obligation on you. Whether you do it on the Marathon Motors ladder, or whether you move on to other pastures and do it on somebody else's ladder, you're going to the top of the heap some day. What I'm trying to say is: don't be a damned fool." Brophy paused and he set his glass on the table. "Don't saddle yourself with something that will drag you down," Brophy said, and he paused again. "Don't do something that, no matter how soon the rest of the world may forget it, you never will. You've got more than that X quality. You've got a kind of fundamental decency. It's pretty rare, and it's not an easy thing to lug around through life. Don't make it harder for yourself." The older man stopped, and he picked up his glass, and then he seemed to remember that it was empty. "Don't say it," Brophy said. "Whatever it is you've got in your mind, don't say it right now," he said. He set down his empty

glass and he stood up. "We've been pretty good friends,"
Brophy said. "Give me the break of thinking it over before you
tell me to go to hell."

He walked off down the Champs Elysées. Spalding watched
him go, a burly, shapeless, shuffling figure, moving without
apparent purpose or even direction and, in spite of his anger and
his confusion, or perhaps because of them, Spalding felt a lump
in his throat. He knew that the jovial, slothful man was his
friend, and he knew that the older man was right, and he knew
that what he was about to do was wrong, a betrayal not only of
a man who had trusted him but of all he had been taught since
childhood and all he had learned by himself, but he knew also
that friendship had as little to do with it as right and wrong,
because Spalding knew what Brophy couldn't know: Spalding
knew he was helpless. He continued to watch the man who was
his friend until Brophy disappeared in the crowd near the corner
of the rue de Berri and then Spalding stood up, too. He put some
money on the table and he took a taxi to the Hotel du Bac.

It was a few minutes after six when he came into his room,
which meant he had almost a full hour. His bag was packed, and
it had been agreed that neither of them was to try to reach the
other by phone that day, so there was nothing for him to do but
wait. He had never realized how difficult that could be.

He sat down on the ugly old bed and he took out his wallet and
he counted the money Miss Picard had given him. It was all
there. Then he took out the train tickets and the *wagon-
lits* reservations. They told him what he already knew: the
Cannes Express left at nine o'clock. He unfolded the confirming
wire from the Hotel sur Mer, and he read it again, but it gave
him no new information: a double room facing the sea was
reserved for Mr. and Mrs. Spalding for a fortnight.

He looked at his watch again. It was only six-thirty. He
thought for a while about writing a letter to Brophy, an explanation that he would mail from Cannes tomorrow, and he even sat
down at the tiny desk and made a start, but the words refused to
come. More accurately, the wrong words came. No matter how

he tried to say it, the words added up to an apology and an excuse, and finally he gave it up. Then he looked at his watch once more, and he had a moment of panic. It was a quarter to seven.

Even though he had walked from the Hotel du Bac to Au Cheval d'Or dozens of times in ten minutes or less, this time he was certain he would be late. He seized his bag and left the room. He did not wait for the elevator. He ran down the six flights of stairs. It was not until he reached the corner of the rue Vieux Carré, and he turned into the Boulevard Montparnasse, that he remembered an unusual fact: Madame Duporte had been absent from her usual place behind the desk in the lobby. It was just as well. He had left a note for her, and her absence spared him one more explanation that, no matter how ingeniously phrased, remained what it basically was: a lie.

He was out of breath when he reached the restaurant. The Basque proprietor seemed preoccupied and distant, like a man who is suffering from a toothache but does not want people to know about it. Spalding sat down at the sidewalk table that he and Iliena had come to think of as theirs, and he pushed his bag against the wall.

"*Bon soir*," the Basque said. "Alone?"

"No," Spalding said. "There will be two."

The Basque nodded and turned. He looked worriedly down the Boulevard Montparnasse, glanced up at the sky as though to check the accuracy of a rumor that rain was imminent, and then he walked slowly into the restaurant. Spalding looked at his watch. It was exactly seven o'clock.

The moment agreed upon, the scheduled instant of meeting that was the culmination of their plan and his hope, seemed to trip some trigger of excitement inside him. It rose and spread, a great, surging wave of anticipation and fulfillment, wiping out the sensible words of Brophy, and the relentless pluckings of conscience, and the nagging worries about the future. All that remained was the moment, the moment for which countless others before him had discarded, and countless others ahead of

him would discard, as he was discarding now, all the sound
wisdom of friends and all the implacable whispers of conscience
and all the disturbing consequences of the future. All that
mattered was the moment, and the lovely city in which it was
imbedded. He leaned forward, looking down the shabby street
that could never be shabby for him again, straining to catch the
first glimpse of that slender figure with its curious delicacy, not
fragile but resilient, as though it were a long-stemmed flower
swaying gently in the soft breeze of a carefully tended garden.

"Monsieur Spalding?"

He turned quickly. The Basque was standing in the doorway
of the restaurant.

"Yes?"

"Telephone, monsieur."

"For me?"

"Yes," the Basque said. "It is apparently urgent."

Spalding's heart was pounding so hard that, as he squeezed
himself into the booth, he was certain the thumping sounds could
be heard at the other end of the wire.

"Hello?"

"That you, boy?"

Spalding's hammering heart seemed to miss a beat. It was
Spike Gulliver's voice.

"Yes," he said. "Hello."

"Sorry to drag you away from your dinner, but I guess
anything is excusable on a night like this. I was disappointed
when Brophy said you couldn't join us because you had another
date, so I figured the least I could do was call up."

"How did you know I was here?"

"I tried you at your hotel, but you weren't there, and Brophy
said to try you at Au Cheval d'Or, because that's where you
usually eat. I'm glad he was right, because I'd feel really bad if
I left town without speaking to you. Well, boy, this is it. We're
leaving in ten minutes and I wanted—"

"Ten minutes?" Spalding said. "I thought you were leaving
tomorrow?"

"This thing has changed our plans," Gulliver said. "As soon as I got the news, I pulled some strings and snagged the last two berths on The Golden Arrow. We're—"

"What news?"

There was a pause at the other end and then Spike Gulliver's voice, incredulous and high, came back on the wire.

"You mean you haven't heard?"

"Heard what?"

"Chamberlain just announced that the British are honoring their treaty with Poland," the newspaperman said. "It's war, boy."

"Oh," Spalding said and the single syllable—forced from him by pieces of comprehension that seemed wildly extraneous: Madame Duporte's absence from her desk in the lobby of the Hotel du Bac; the crowds at the corner of the rue de Berri into which Brophy's ambling figure had disappeared; the worried face of the Basque restaurateur—sounded ridiculously inadequate. "Oh," Spalding said again. "I've been—"

"I guess we all have," Spike Gulliver said. "And there's no telling where we'll all be from now on. That's why I was anxious to talk to you before we shoved off for London. I wanted to thank you for being so nice to Iliena all these weeks, while I've been working."

"That's all right," Spalding said. "I didn't—"

"Yes, you did," Gulliver said. "And I appreciate it. So does Iliena. Good luck, boy. We're all going to need it from here on in. Here's Iliena, now. She wants to say goodbye, too."

There was the low, roaring sound of emptiness at the other end and then, setting his heart off on a new hammering spiral of pain, Iliena was talking to him.

"It is as Spike said," she said. "It is goodbye."

The word seemed to hang in the air, over the stifling phone booth, over the weeks of slowly mounting happiness they had known together, over the city that had sheltered and shaped it, over the railroad tickets in his pocket and the money in his

wallet, over the shattered moment for which he had been willing
to discard everything he believed in, over all of his life that now
lay, like an empty, dusty, forbidding road, before him.

"Iliena."

"Yes?"

"You're not coming?"

"No."

"Iliena?"

"I am here," she said. "I—"

"Is it because—?" He paused and he shook his head, like a
fighter trying, in a neutral corner, to shake off the numbing
effect of a blow he had not expected. He said, "Is it because of
the news Spike just told me?"

"No," she said. "That has made it simpler, but it is not the
reason."

"What is the reason?"

In the sudden silence, and across the miles that separated
them, he could see her face in the moment of hesitation, because
he had seen it doing the same thing, in a taxi, late at night, a long
time ago, as though she were not sure that she had at her
command the proper words for what she wanted to say, and then
she seemed to reach some sort of decision, because the silence
changed character, and he could almost hear her words before
she spoke them.

"It would be wrong," she said. "I did not think of the
wrongness four nights ago, when I agreed, because I did not
want to think of it. I wanted only—" She paused again, and he
remembered that, wherever she was talking from, probably the
suite at the George V, Brophy and Spike Gulliver were probably
within earshot. "I wanted what you wanted," she said. "That
does not make it less wrong. Later, in a few weeks, in six
months, perhaps less, I would remember that it was wrong, and
you would remember, too, and then we would dislike each other.
I did not want that. I want to remember only—" Once more her
voice stopped, and when she spoke again, her words were so low

that he could scarcely hear her. "I want to remember only the way it has been," she said. "I do not want to remember, I do not want you to remember, the way it would become."

"Iliena."

"I cannot talk more," she said. "Spike and Mr. Brophy, they are—"

"Iliena."

"A long time ago, in a taxi, late at night," she said, "I said something to you. I said nobody, nobody in my whole life, has ever been so kind to me. It is true. I will never forget." There was a confused murmur at the other end, voices raised above hers, and then he heard her again. "God bless you," she said. "I will think always that you did not forget, either."

He hadn't, of course. He was ten years older, and he had come through a war, and he had acquired a wife and begotten a son and carved out a career in New York, but he hadn't forgotten.

"Sorry," Spalding said. He turned back to the young man, in the tweed coat and the bow tie, sitting with him at the sidewalk table in front of Au Cheval d'Or. "I didn't hear your question."

Bill McCord nodded down the street and asked it again. Spalding turned away from the young man his wife's mother had asked him to look up. Spalding, following Bill McCord's nod, looked from the table, at which so long ago he had learned to enjoy the special flavor of squid, down the Boulevard Montparnasse toward the place, beyond the Balzac statue, where the lights were coming on in the Dôme.

There was a raw bite in the air, and the paint was flaking away from the houses with iron grillework on their balconies, and the street was littered with refuse, and the few strollers looked cold and poorly fed and badly dressed. It was a dreary scene, all right, a far cry from what Brophy used to mean when he talked about the City of Light, and certainly it was different from what Bill McCord's active imagination had pictured and hoped to find. Looking at it, Spalding did not find it difficult to see what it was that troubled Bill McCord. What was extremely difficult, however, was knowing how to answer the young man's question.

"Well," Spalding said, staring hard at the shabby street. "It's sort of difficult to put it into words," he said. "It's not what you see. It's what—"

He stopped. He was leaning forward as though, at any moment, he expected to catch the first glimpse of a slender figure, coming up the shabby street, moving with a curious delicacy that was not fragile, but resilient, as though she were a long-stemmed flower swaying gently in the soft breeze of a carefully tended garden.

"What's the matter?" Bill McCord said. "See somebody you know?"

"What?" Spalding said, and then, "Oh," he said. "No, not somebody."

He had seen something, however, something that washed away, abruptly and completely, the disappointment that had begun early that day, on the boat train, when he had sat down to the powdered eggs and boiled carrots that were called the de luxe lunch. He saw, not the houses with their flaking paint or the rubbish in the street or even the poorly dressed strollers dipping their heads against the bite of the wind. Spalding saw, by looking at this street on which he had once been young, that what he had now, his wife and his son and his career, were his because an old friend, named Brophy, and a girl he had loved, named Iliena, had been right when he had been too young to know what was right.

For the first time since he had disembarked from the *Queen Mary* that morning, and perhaps for the first time in ten years, Spalding felt free. There was nothing wrong with his memories. At last he was remembering, not with regret but with gratitude, the way Iliena had said she would remember, the way she had said she hoped he would remember. He was remembering the way it had been; not the way it might have become.

"I wish you'd tell me," Bill McCord said again. "I'd like to know."

There was a touch of impatience in his well-bred, polite voice. Spalding turned away from the shabbiness and the inconveniences that were harassing Adams out in Auteuil. Spalding looked at the young man whose studio room on the rue Littré was so very much like Spalding's old room in Madame Duporte's Hotel du Bac on the rue Vieux Carré. He stared, with the discomfort of those to whom the passage of time has given an answer that they are powerless to convey to others, at the young man who would have to wait for the answer to come to him, the young man who might have been Spalding, as Spalding had been ten years ago, when he had not known the answer, either, when all he could find to do in Paris was sit in his room at night and read *Seraphita* in the original French.

"I'd really like to know," Bill McCord said in his faintly puzzled, almost angry, very young, and extremely lonely voice. "What do people see in this city, anyway?"

# TONIGHT
# WE
# ARE
# SHARP

t's a peculiar feeling. It sneaks up on you without warning. Before you know what is happening, all the things you have seen and known all your life are different. Everything stands out clear and sharp and fresh, as though you had never seen or known them before.

I sensed this all the way across town in the taxi, but I didn't really feel it until I started pushing my way through the revolving door with the little overnight bag in my hand. Then it hit me, hard, and I stepped into the onyx and silver foyer with a feeling of excitement. Ruffo's was the place. The year before it had been Seventy-Seven. And the year before that it had been the little basement on 52nd Street with the funny name that nobody remembered. But this year it was Ruffo's. I had known it, of course, without knowing I knew it. I knew all those things. But this night I saw it because this night everything was underlined in heavy ink. This night I wouldn't miss anything. I looked around me in surprise, as though this were the first instead of the two or three hundredth time I had been there, and I nodded to myself. It was nice that it was Ruffo's. It was nice to know that when the boys thought of me they thought of the place, whatever it happened to be. I felt great.

"Put this where the wind and the rain won't reach it," I said as I handed the small suitcase to the hat-check girl. "It contains everything that's left of your dream boy's worldly goods."

She laughed and put the bag up on the shelf.

"We're going to miss you, Mr. Keegan."

Not as much as I was going to miss them.

"Thanks. It's nice of you to say that. Miss Lynd here yet?"

"She's upstairs dressing. You're very early tonight, Mr. Keegan."

You had to try everything once.

"I'm practicing," I said. "Where I'm going to be beginning tomorrow morning, they tell me there's a lad with a bugle who gets sore if you're not prompt."

She laughed again. They always laughed when Keegan let it go.

"I heard Miss Lynd asking for you before she went up to dress. I think she left a message for you with Mr. Ruffo."

I looked at the hat-check girl in surprise.

"What about?" I said. "Do you know?"

"No, I'm sorry. I just heard her telling Mr. Ruffo not to let you go till she saw you."

Not to let me go? Where did she think I'd be going tonight?

"Okay," I said. "Thanks."

"I'll say goodbye now, Mr. Keegan. I'll be gone when your party breaks up. I go off at two."

"Oh, I forgot." I turned back and pulled a bill out of my pocket. "Here. Buy yourself a map and a manual of arms so you'll be able to tell the customers who ask for me where I am and what I'm doing."

"Why, Mr. Keegan! Thanks! I didn't mean to—"

If she didn't, she was slipping, and that would have been bad. I didn't want anything or anybody to slip on my last night.

"Forget it," I said. "Spend some of it on candles and tell Ruffo to keep one burning in the window for me."

I walked to the end of the foyer and stood on the top step, looking down into the large, dimly lighted room. It was earlier than I'd thought. There were only a half dozen couples at the side tables. The orchestra was idling, playing very low, and there was nobody on the dance floor. The barman leaned back against the mirrored shelves of glasses and bottles and the waiters stood around in the rear, watching and whispering, like ushers counting the house at a turkey that's going to close Saturday night.

"Danny!"

Ruffo came out of his little office next to the bar. He was puffing because of his fat and his tight tuxedo. I went down the steps to meet him.

"Hello," I said through my grin. "What's playing?"

"Look." He shook my hand and pointed proudly to a large

round table near the bandstand. It was laid out for a party, with little military favors near every napkin, tiny guns and planes and cannon. In the middle there was a large cake topped by an armored tank made of chocolate icing. "All for you, Danny."

"That's a layout for a general," I laughed. "It's only a buck private the boys are saying goodbye to."

"For you, the best," Ruffo said. He slapped me on the back. "This town's not gonna be the same without you, kid."

I didn't want it to be the same without me.

"Where's Margie?"

"Upstairs, dressing. You're early." He looked at his watch. "It's only eleven o'clock. The theatres aren't out yet."

"I hear she left a message for me?"

"Yeah. She said she had to see you. Wants to ask you something important."

"I'll go up and see her for a minute."

"Better not bother now, Danny."

Seeing a girl like Margie Lynd was no bother.

"Any idea what she wants?"

"No, except she said it was important. She'll be down in a minute." He took my arm and steered me toward the large, round table. "Come on over and have a bang of whiskey while you're waiting."

"Not for Uncle Daniel. Thanks."

He looked at me in surprise.

"No bubbly?"

I shook my head.

"I'm due at the draft board at a quarter to seven in the morning. I want to hear my name when they call it."

Ruffo laughed.

"You're sharp tonight, Danny."

Why not? I'd been on the hone for almost thirty years.

"I'm just feeling good," I said. "Hello, Jig."

The band leader stepped down from the stand with his hand outstretched.

"Sorry to see you go, Danny. We'll miss you."

I shook his hand.

"Don't say that," I said. "They didn't miss Diamond Jim Brady and he left for more than a year."

"He wasn't Keegan."

"No, but he had more cabbage."

Jig laughed and took a step or two after us to tug at my sleeve.

"Can I talk to you for a minute, Danny?"

"Sure, later. Say, Jig."

"Yeah?"

"When Margie sings, hit it hard, will you?"

He looked at me for a moment and then he nodded. I guess he knew as well as I did who she was singing to these days. When Keegan had a girl it was no secret.

"You bet, Danny. I'll see you later?"

"Sure."

He climbed back up on the bandstand. Ruffo sat down at the table and pulled out a chair for me. A waiter came over but I shook my head. Ruffo waved him away. I took a cigarette. Ruffo struck a match.

"Thanks," I said. "Where's Dave? Where's the Colonel? Where's Hoppy?"

"They'll be here. The party was set for eleven-thirty. You're early, Danny."

When you do something unusual nobody lets you forget it.

"I thought I'd get a chance to say hello to Margie before she goes on."

"She'll be down in a minute."

That long I could wait. I grinned at Ruffo.

"You don't know how much it means to me," I said. "You and Dave and the Colonel and the rest of the boys giving me this farewell party."

"Forget it. For you, the best." Ruffo hunched himself forward across the table. "Tell me something, kid. How do you feel?"

How did you answer questions like that?

"Like Dempsey before the first Tunney fight," I said. "Like Jolson on that old runway at the Winter Garden. Solid."

Happy and great and wonderful were the more accurate words. But in Ruffo's place you talked his language.

"Wind up everything all right?"

Everything except one. And I'd take care of that as soon as Margie asked it.

"Everything," I said. "Apartment cleaned out. Checking account closed. Tabs paid up all over town. I've even taken care of the bookie. All I own are the clothes I'm sitting in, a toothbrush and a pair of pajamas in an overnight bag in the check room, and my reporting orders in my pocket. I'm square with the world, Ruffo."

Except for whatever it was Margie wanted. Keegan never balked at doing something for a girl.

"How you going to stand being away from Broadway?"

How were a couple of million other guys going to stand being away from Main Street or Prairie Avenue?

"I'll manage," I said. "Keegan always eats."

"If there's anything I can do for you while you're away, kid, remember: a post card marked Ruffo care of Times Square will always reach me."

I had never given them a chance to do anything for me. I wasn't going to start now.

"Thanks, but I won't need anything. Uncle Sam is picking up all my checks from now on."

Keegan didn't have much, but he had his pride.

"It's good to hear you say that, Danny. I've been worried about you."

What did he think I'd been doing about myself all these years? Mailing out self-addressed valentines?

"Nobody has to worry about Keegan."

"I know," Ruffo said. "But your friends do."

"Why?"

The question was automatic. I didn't have to ask.

"You know what they've been saying about you, kid."

If I didn't I'd be a candidate for a Seeing Eye dog. "Sure," I said. "I know."

I was Keegan the Character. The bright boy everybody loved but nobody trusted. The lad who could have done big things but never did. I could see my biography rolling past in Ruffo's eyes, like a newsreel about the death of a big politician. There I was at nineteen, a fresh punk from the West Side writing sports for the *Globe*. Washington correspondent at twenty-one. Sports editor at twenty-four. Hollywood at twenty-six. Back to Broadway at twenty-seven, flatter than Joe Louis' waistline, and no jobs waiting. I could almost read the dialogue on Ruffo's face. You know Keegan. Great guy but irresponsible. Great talker but no staying power. Too much of the fermented stuff. A lover of the bottle. Can't be trusted on a job. A year of eating stones and then the newspaperman's graveyard, publicity for Gann & Lillett, radio advertising. Not much good as an advertising man, but you know Keegan. Pal to the world. Buddy of the universe. Everybody's friend. Knows how to wangle publicity. When he's sober. Guess he earns his yard and a half a week. But it's too bad he never lived up to the promise he showed as a kid on the *Globe*. Could have done big things. Too much of the old bubbly, though. Well, that's how life is. Going on thirty now. Wonder what's going to happen to him? They knew what was going to happen to me. They had seen it happen to plenty of guys before me. I grinned to myself, the way you do when it hurts just a little, and I drew slowly on the cigarette.

"It doesn't matter what they've been saying about me," I said. "It never has."

"That's why I'm sort of glad you're going into the army," Ruffo said. "I got a feeling Uncle Sam'll fix everything for you."

"You can say that again," I said. "Beginning tonight everything is going to be fine."

"You don't know how good it makes me feel to hear you say that, kid."

I knew. Ruffo was all right.

"Let's bury it," I said. "Neither one of us is much good on the all-pals-together act."

"Okay, Danny. But say. One thing."

The tone of his voice made me look at him quickly. It was the feeling that had been with me in the taxi, the feeling that had hit me when I was wrestling through the revolving door. The feeling that this night everything was sharper than it had ever been before.

"What?" I said.

Ruffo leaned closer. His dark, fleshy face grew darker and more fleshy as the jowls pressed down on the stiff white collar.

"I wonder if you'd do me a favor, Danny?"

"Anything."

"It's Dave," he said in a low voice. "He's been rapping the joint in the column."

"Oh." I looked down at the cigarette as I crushed it into the ash tray. I didn't mind doing a favor for him. For anybody. But I wished he hadn't asked. Not this night. "Why didn't you tell me before?"

"I thought Dave would lay off. But he hasn't. And now that you're going away, I just thought I'd sort of ask you to talk to him and—"

"Let it go," I said. "It's done."

"Thanks, Danny. You're a pal."

He had the right word. It had fitted me perfectly for eleven years, ever since I came out of the West Side at nineteen.

"Forget it."

Ruffo stood up and grinned.

"There's a bunch coming in. I better go over and take care of them. See you later."

"Right. Send someone up to the dressing room and tell Margie I'm waiting, will you?"

"You bet, kid."

I watched him cross the floor toward the group at the door. The small, tight feeling in the pit of my stomach relaxed. It was nothing to get sore about. Especially on my last night. Especially since Ruffo and the boys were giving me the farewell party. Everybody on Broadway wanted favors. That's how they lived. That's how the big street stayed in business. I couldn't get sore if I wanted to. Not the way I was seeing things this night. I grinned again as I watched Ruffo bow the newcomers to their tables. I felt a little proud. There wasn't a hotter guy in town. His joint was the place. And yet he had to come and ask Keegan to call off Dave Decker. I laughed softly to myself, the way you do when it doesn't hurt any more.

"Danny."

I looked up.

"Hello, Jig. What's playing?"

"You said before I could talk to you for a minute."

"Sure." I pulled out a chair. "Put it there."

He sat down and leaned toward me across the table, the way Ruffo had leaned toward me. Jig played nervously with his baton. I'd never liked band leaders. But tonight I could afford to be charitable.

"I guess I don't have a right to ask this, Danny."

He didn't. But that had never stopped any of them yet.

"As long as you don't want me to get you transferred to the coast artillery, just ask it," I said. "I can't do anything for you there. The army's never been on my beat before."

He grinned quickly.

"You're sharp tonight, Danny."

"I won't cut. What's on your mind?"

"I'll tell you, Danny. I think Margie's going to the Coast."

"How do you know? When?"

"Wait a minute, Danny. I'm not sure yet. But Clayborne's been—"

"The agent?"

Jig nodded.

"He's been in here three nights in a row, catching the show, and I've seen him watching her when she was singing. He came in about an hour ago and asked for Miss Lynd and then he went up to her dressing room. He's been there talking to her since—"

"I guess that's what's been keeping her."

Jig nodded again.

"What I was wondering, Danny, I was wondering if you'd put in a word for me with Margie. You know. I been doing all her arrangements and I know the way she likes the music when she sings. I was just wondering, if you'd speak to her, just drop a hint, you know, she might say something to Clayborne, and maybe I'd get out there, too. I always wanted a crack at pictures and this is—"

"Okay. Sure." I slipped out of the chair. Why the hell couldn't they have asked me some other night? Why did they have to save it for this night? "I'll talk to her."

He jumped up. I brushed him aside. Margie had come out of the little door next to the bandstand. A tall, thin man with white hair was talking to her. I recognized Clayborne. I started toward her. Jig caught my arm.

"All you have to do is tell her that I—"

I shook him off.

"I'll tell her."

"Thanks, Danny. That's—"

His voice died away as I hurried forward. Just as I reached her the boys came in, all in a bunch.

"Danny," she said. "I want you to meet—"

Then Dave and the Colonel and Hoppy were pounding me on the back. Margie smiled across their heads. I smiled back and waved my hand but the boys were pushing me and yelling in my ears. I saw Clayborne nod and bow to her and walk toward the big round table that was set for my party. Then the lights dimmed and the band hit the first bar of "Manhattan." Margie reached around the Colonel's shoulder and squeezed my hand.

"I'm sorry to be late," she whispered quickly. "I'll see you right after my song. There's something I want to ask you."

"Sure."

"It's very important," she said. "Keep the chair next to you empty."

That wasn't easy. Dave took the chair on my left and Hoppy

sat down on my right. The rest of the boys spread themselves around the table. Clayborne sat opposite me. I could see the top of his dignified white head across the large cake with the chocolate tank. Then I turned toward the bandstand to watch Margie. The blue spot was on her, the one that made her look soft and far away, as though she were coming through the mist on a windy day, the one I had insisted Ruffo get for her that night three weeks before when I had seen her for the first time. I wondered why what she had just told me should have brought that tight feeling back to the pit of my stomach. She was a girl I knew for three weeks. Long enough for her to ask me something important, whatever it was. Plenty of others had never waited three weeks before asking. She had as much right to ask something of me as Ruffo and Jig had. I couldn't help wishing, though, that she'd asked it some other night.

She finished "Manhattan" and her low, husky voice swung into "My Wonderful One." She turned and sang directly at me, across the darkened room, to where she knew I was sitting. "My wonderful one, I will always adore you." Jig hit it hard, the way he had promised. She put into the words the sort of thing that even the greatest singers of all time could never fake. It was there or it wasn't. This time it was there. I sat up straight in my chair, as though I had been punched. My stomach loosened and I could feel my face twitch in the darkness.

"That kid's got stuff." Hoppy poked me in the ribs and spoke across the applause. "The new Etting. Give her a couple more months and she'll be up there with the income tax worriers."

For a bookie, Hoppy knew something about singing. He should have. He'd been living in night clubs all his life.

"They won't be in the running," I said. I was surprised at the sound of my voice. I swallowed two or three times, fast, to clear it. "This town's never seen anything like her."

The applause died down and the blue spot found her again. The band picked up "Always." She tapped it, sweet and low.

"The Keegan luck is holding," Hoppy whispered through his grin. "You don't deserve a girl like that."

I turned to look at him in surprise. For a bookie, he knew a lot about other things besides singing.

"Shut up," I whispered back. "I want to hear her."

She finished the song and the lights went up. The applause brought her back. She sang an encore without the blue spot. Then she smiled and waved and headed across the room toward me. I stood up. Ruffo stepped out from behind the bandstand and stopped her. They talked for a moment. She shook her head and nodded toward our table. Ruffo held her hand and talked more quickly. She shrugged and walked back with him toward a large table at the other side of the room. I sat down.

"Don't let it get you," Hoppy said. "The customers that ask Ruffo to be introduced to her, it's good for her to say hello to them."

I didn't answer. I looked at my watch. It was twelve-thirty. What was the good of coming early if an hour and a half went by and you didn't get a chance to talk to your girl?

"You mean it's good for Ruffo," I said.

"Take it easy," Hoppy said. "Don't get sore."

I watched Ruffo introduce her to the people at the other table. A man stood up and pulled out a chair for her. She sat down. Around me the boys were kidding and laughing and making a lot of noise. I didn't hear them. The tight feeling was coming back to the pit of my stomach, but this time I recognized it. This time it was anger. And I didn't want to be angry. Not tonight.

"Hey, Danny! Aren't you listening?"

I turned back to the crowd. The Colonel was yelling at me across the table. I pulled my mind down to the party and the favors and the chocolate tank.

"Your voice is too loud," I said. "I've been training my ears to hear nothing higher than a bugle."

Everybody laughed, the way they always did. The way they'd been laughing for eleven years. This time it didn't make me feel good to hear them.

"I was telling the boys what you promised to bring back," the

Colonel said. "Hitler's scalp so we can give it to Ruffo to put up behind the bar for a target for the dart game."

He doubled up with laughter. Everybody laughed with him. Everybody but me.

"What do you say?" the Colonel said proudly. "Are we sharp tonight?"

"Yes," I said. "Very sharp."

The voices and the laughter wove into a pattern over my head, like an invisible blanket. I concentrated on all the little things in my mind. I brought them out into the open, like cards from a fresh deck, one at a time. I turned them over slowly to help me fight off the rising anger I didn't want.

"Danny."

I turned around to look at Hoppy. His pale, tight little face, with the slanting lip, looked exactly the way it had looked all the years I had known him. But it looked different, too, the way everything looked different this night.

"Yeah," I said. "What?"

"Kidding aside, boy, I'm going to miss you."

"Let it go," I said. "You'll have me crying."

"No, I'm leveling, kid. I hate to see you go."

My mind started to figure out what form his hatred was going to take. I shook the thought aside, fast. It wasn't any good to think that way. I would only get sore and I didn't want to get sore.

"I hate to leave you behind," I said dryly. "Why don't you try enlisting?"

He laughed, twisting his slanting lip all the way up on one side.

"You're sharp tonight, Danny."

"Try calling me Razor."

He laughed again.

"Say, Danny. One thing."

Here it came.

"What?"

"I wonder if you'd do me a favor?"

Since when had they begun wondering about it?

"Why don't you try asking me?"

His voice dropped low, under the laughter and the kidding around the table. He leaned toward me, the way Ruffo and Jig had leaned toward me earlier in the evening.

"You know how tough it is for bookies to get phones, Danny."

"I've heard tell. What about it?"

"How's chances of keeping your apartment and your phone in your name while you're gone? I'll pay the rent and the phone bill. If you keep it in your name, the phone company won't know it's me."

"I don't know," I said slowly. "I checked out of the apartment today."

"I could talk to the landlord if you said okay?"

I looked at him for a long moment. Then I shrugged. He was my friend, wasn't he? He'd come to my farewell party, hadn't he?

"Okay," I said. "I didn't do anything about the phone. I told the landlord to take care of it. Give him a ring tomorrow and tell him I said it was okay."

Hoppy's tight little face spread out in the slanting grin.

"Thanks, kid," he said. "You don't know how much I appreciate this."

That was where he was wrong. I did know.

"Let's not start a forum about it," I said. "It's done."

"You're what I call a pal, kid."

It was interesting to learn, after all these years, his definition of the word.

"I know," I said. "I'm a pal."

I stood up. Margie was coming across the room with Ruffo. She smiled at me and I went forward to meet her. I took her hand.

"I'm terribly sorry," she said. "Ruffo wanted me to sit with those people for a while and I couldn't—"

"It's all right," I said. "You look great."

She squeezed my hand.

"You always say the right things."

I'd had eleven years of practice.

"Come on over and sit down," I said. "Ruffo said there was something important you wanted to ask me."

She blushed quickly.

"Yes, there is," she said. "Danny I wanted to ask you to—"

The band struck up "Oh, how I hate to get up in the morning" and drowned her out. The whole room started to laugh. Jig jumped down from the stand. The band followed him. They formed a line and marched toward us. The boys at the table pushed their chairs back and joined the line. They grabbed me and shoved me down into my chair. Ruffo took Margie's hand and pulled her out front. They marched around the table, single file, singing and laughing and stamping their feet. I grinned and tried to look pleased. I couldn't. There were too many things pounding away in my brain. All of them were sharp and clear, the way they had never been, the way I didn't want them to be just then. The third time around Margie leaned down as the line went past.

"Don't look so glum," she whispered. "Remember I have something important to ask you when this is over."

I smiled and nodded and waved my hand. Then, as they circled the table, her words came back to me and the smile disappeared from my face. She wanted to ask me something. They had all used the same words. Ruffo and Jig and Hoppy. Even the hat-check girl. They were my friends. They had come to say goodbye to me. But they all had something to ask me. They all wanted something in exchange for saying goodbye.

" 'Some day I'm going to murder the bugler,' " the gang chanted. " 'Some day they're going to find him dead.' "

The band crashed into the end of the song. The line broke up. Everybody applauded and laughed and slapped me on the back. I stood up fast and walked toward Margie. Clayborne stepped between us. His white head bent over her and they talked. I dropped back into my chair. This wasn't a party. It was an obstacle race. I looked at my watch. It was almost two-thirty. I hadn't been able to talk to her since I had arrived, three and a half hours before.

"What do you say?" Hoppy said. "Some send-off?"

"Sure," I said. "The best."

The boys gathered round the table. The talk and the laughter started again. I didn't hear anything but the jumble of sound. I watched Margie walking toward the foyer with Clayborne. She nodded her head to his words. He bowed, the way you don't see people bow any more, but I was in no mood to appreciate a gentleman of the old school. I guess if he'd known me longer he would have wanted something, too. Margie turned to come back to the table. I started to get up. Someone put a hand on my arm and I dropped back in the chair. I turned and saw the Colonel sitting next to me. Years of sitting around little tables selling jewelry out of his side pocket to all of Broadway hadn't improved the face nature had started him off with.

"Danny boy," he said. "This is one of the saddest nights of my life."

If he expected me to cheer him up, he was a little late. Three and a half hours, to be exact.

"I have to take your word for that," I said. "That warped lilac bush you call your face always looks sad."

He shook his head sorrowfully.

"It's gonna get sadder and sadder, Danny boy. There's gonna be no fun in selling trinkets to the mob without you around to make cracks about it."

"Boost the prices a little," I said. "That'll brighten you up."

"No it won't, kid. I'm gonna miss you sitting around Ruffo's and cutting it up."

It wasn't talk that he was going to miss.

"You'll find somebody else to cut it up with," I said. "My days as a Broadway flannel mouth are over."

He slapped my back. His ugly face split into a laugh.

"We're sharp tonight, Daniel, aren't we?"

"Yes," I said. "Very sharp."

"You won't forget your old pals, Daniel boy, will you?"

They weren't giving me much chance.

"Don't get maudlin, Colonel." Margie reached the table. "It doesn't go well with what the rogues' gallery calls your face."

The Colonel laughed. Margie sat down next to me. I took her hand. Dave Decker leaned over and said something to her. They bent toward each other. The Colonel poked me.

"Do a pal a favor, Daniel boy?"

They must have held a rehearsal before they arrived. I could see them in a huddle, allotting each other a few minutes to make their requests.

"What do you want?"

He leaned toward me, the way Jig and Ruffo and Hoppy had leaned toward me. It was quite an act.

"Nothing much, Danny. Just keep your eyes open for me. Any of the boys in the army want any jewelry, tell them to get in touch with the Colonel, huh? You know me. The doorway Tiffany."

"Sure, I know you. You're what they call a pal."

He looked at me quickly. I guess I was getting a little too sharp.

"Listen, Daniel boy. You're not sore, are you?"

No, I wasn't sore. I was so happy I was going to rush right over and stand in front of the Palace handing out twenty-dollar bills.

"Don't ask foolish questions," I said. "Nobody's ever seen Keegan sore."

Nobody had ever looked before. Not even Keegan.

"That's the stuff, boy."

He slapped me on the back.

"Careful of the shoulder," I said. "Beginning tomorrow I'm going to need it for supporting a gun."

The Colonel laughed again. Margie squeezed my hand. I turned toward her. She smiled. Everybody stood up. I looked around in surprise. The place was almost empty.

"What happened?" I said. "Ruffo lose his license?"

"No, silly," Margie said. "It's late."

I glanced at my wrist watch. It was after three. In a few hours I was due at the draft board. I stood up with the others, still holding Margie's hand. We walked with the crowd to the door. They kept slapping my back and calling advice. All of them: Jig and Ruffo and the Colonel and Hoppy and the others whose names I knew but couldn't get straightened out at the moment. My stomach was tied up solid, in a tight, angry knot. In the foyer there was a scramble for the hats. The girl was gone from the check room. She didn't have to stay. She'd been smart. She'd made her request first, before the party started. I found my small suitcase on the shelf and walked out with the crowd into the quiet street. There was another round of goodbyes and best wishes and slaps on the back. I returned them as well as I could. I didn't try very hard. The feeling of happiness and excitement was all gone. The boys had done their best to kick that out of me, one at a time. All that remained of the mood with which I had come to the party was the clearness and the sharpness with which I was seeing things. Then the goodbyes and the back slapping were over and there were only three of us left. That meant only two more favors. I wouldn't be asking anything of myself.

"Where you headed for?" Dave Decker said.

For wherever it was that your friends didn't say goodbye with their palms outstretched.

"I'm taking Margie home," I said. "Then I'm going to a hotel for a shower before I report to the draft board."

"How about you and Margie going over to Seventy-Seven with me? I need a few more items for the column."

What was he doing? Slipping? Why didn't he ask me to give them to him?

"No," Margie said. "I don't want Danny to be too tired when he reports. He should get a couple of hours' sleep."

He should, but he wouldn't. Danny would be thinking.

"I'll get plenty of sleep beginning tomorrow," I said. "Uncle Sam doesn't run any night clubs."

"Guess I better say goodbye now," Dave said. He whistled

for a cab. It drew up at the curb. Margie and I walked him toward it. He climbed in and stuck out his head. "I don't suppose there's anything I can say, Danny boy. You know how much we're all going to miss you."

They'd made it pretty clear during the last few hours.

"Thanks," I said, shaking his hand. "I'll miss you."

The way I'd miss a mild case of leprosy.

"Oh, say, Margie," Dave said. "Do you mind if I talk to Danny alone for a minute?"

I guess I could stop worrying about his slipping.

"Of course," Margie said. "Go ahead."

She stepped aside. Dave leaned out of the cab. He spoke in a low voice.

"I wonder if you'd do me a favor, Danny."

The way they'd rehearsed this act, they could probably bring vaudeville back single-handed.

"Why wonder?" I said. "What do you want me to do?"

"There'll be a lot of big shots in the army," he said. "The draft is picking them off. Playwrights and Hollywood boys and gamblers. That gang. If you hear anything I can use in the column, drop me a line, will you?"

"Sure," I said. I was surprised at how steady my voice was. "I'll be glad to."

"You're a real pal, Danny boy."

I wonder how they would have treated a fake pal.

"Sure," I said. "You know me, Dave."

He slipped back into the cab and pulled the door shut. I remembered my promise to Ruffo that I would stop the rap against the joint in Dave's column. The words wouldn't have come even if I'd wanted to use them. I was full of a combination of anger and disgust for so many things and so many people that I couldn't speak. This was my night. This was the night they had arranged for me. The only trouble was they had taken it back, bit by bit.

"We were sharp tonight, weren't we, Danny?"

"Yes," I said. "Very sharp."

"Well, so long, kid," he called through the window. "Keep punching."

I waved and the cab started. I watched it round the corner into 54th Street. Margie touched my arm and I turned. She looked up at me and opened her mouth to say something. She closed her lips without speaking. I guess she figured it wasn't good politics to ask them one on top of the other. Always give the sucker time to catch his breath. She was learning fast. I took her arm and steered her down the block. We walked along in silence until we reached the street where she lived. In front of her house we stopped.

It was very quiet. There were no people and there was no traffic. It was too late. The sky was soft and blue, like the baby spot that played over her when she sang. The stars were bright. Behind the Empire State Building you could see a little slice of the moon. I grinned to myself, the way you do when it starts hurting again. It was a great night, all right. For everybody except Keegan. I set down my suitcase. We looked at each other. I waited for her to speak. She seemed to be having trouble putting it into words. Well, I wasn't going to worry about prompting her. And I had plenty of time. She was smooth and smart. She didn't want to put it as crudely as the rest had put it. She wanted to make it fancy. What she didn't know was that now it didn't matter how she put it. Straight from the shoulder or fancy, they all wanted something. They'd all been wanting something for eleven years. The only difference was that now they weren't going to get it. I was finished with doing favors for people. I was finished with being a character. I was finished with the town. Tomorrow everything was going to be different. In three hours everything was going to be changed. My job was to see to it that it stayed different for the rest of my life. They could get themselves a new errand boy. Keegan was through.

"All right, let's have it," I said finally. "What do you want."

The words came out tougher than I wanted them to sound. But I didn't care. I had a right to be tough.

"You know what I want," she said quietly. "I want you to come back."

I stared at her for a long moment, until the words sank in. They had to go quite a distance. They had to hack their way through all the junk that four hours with my pals had piled up around what I used to refer to as my brain.

"Listen," I said. "Say that again."

My voice sounded funny. She put her hand on my arm.

"I want you to come back," she said softly. "To me."

"What about—?"

She stopped me. I could tell from her face that she knew what I'd been thinking.

"Clayborne prevented me from meeting you at eleven as I promised," she said quickly. "He wants me to go to the Coast. That's what I've been trying to ask you all evening, Danny. I told Clayborne I couldn't give him my answer until I found out where the army was going to send you. If you were going to be sent out West, I told him I'd go to the Coast for pictures. If you were going to be somewhere near here, I said I'd remain in New York. That's what I've been trying to ask you all evening. But there was such a crowd, and your friends kept pulling you away from me, and I didn't get a chance to—"

I shook my head impatiently. She stopped. They weren't my friends. They were what I'd had for eleven years. Now, for the first time, I had what I wanted. I saw it clearly, sharply, the way I had been seeing everything this night. The tight feeling left my stomach. This time it went for good.

"Do me a favor," I said. "I haven't been hearing so good the last few hours. Say it once more. Please. Tell me what you want."

"You know what I want," she whispered. "I want you to come back to me."

I felt again the way I had felt when I came into Ruffo's at eleven. Like Dempsey before the first Tunney fight. Like Jolson on that old runway at the Winter Garden. Solid.

"All right," I said as I took her in my arms. "For you I'll do it."

# A
# SENSE
# OF
# ECHELON

 man in a
hurry, a man with a train to catch, would have made all the
purchases at one place, quickly, without hesitation or even
thought.

Mr. Harmer looked at the headlines of all the papers spread
on the newsstand inside the Seventh Avenue entrance to Penn
Station and, after several moments of deliberation, he chose his
regular paper: the *Times*. He walked into the concourse and, in
the drug store near the Savarin Bar, he considered but decided
against an attractively wrapped new brand and bought a package of his favorite cigarettes. He rode down the escalator, circled
the information booth leisurely, and selected his magazines and a
nickel bar of candy from the stand just inside the doors controlled by photoelectric cells that opened onto the asphalt apron
leading to the trains. Mr. Harmer, a successful architect who ran
his office with brisk efficiency, had a train to catch, but he was
not in a hurry. Far from it.

Mr. Harmer would not have confessed, certainly not to his
wife whose affection he reciprocated with the undemonstrative
fondness appropriate to a man of fifty-three who had been
happily married for a quarter of a century, but secretly he
enjoyed these business trips to his firm's Washington offices.
Every month his partner, Mr. Harmer's junior by six years,
offered to relieve him of what was considered an onerous chore;
and every month Mrs. Harmer, who felt that the monthly
overnight trip was taxing for a man past middle age whose
health could have been much better since he came back from
Europe, said worriedly that the very least he could do to spare
himself was to go by plane. Mr. Harmer always turned down his
partner's offer and disregarded his wife's suggestion. There was
no way to explain without embarrassment, even to these two
people who were so close to him, how much pleasure and
relaxation he got from a train trip, any train trip, even a short
one.

It was a boyhood passion that he had never outgrown. And since the end of the war, in which Mr. Harmer had served as a major in the Services of Supply stationed in England, these quiet little business trips had come to mean a good deal to him. There had been so much rushing about during the war, always by plane, and there had been and still was so much to do in pulling together again the neglected business from which he had been absent for almost four years, that moments of relaxation, moments when he could be really alone, were now very precious to Mr. Harmer.

For days before each monthly trip to Washington, his thoughts would run forward to the four unhurried hours on the train that lay ahead of him. When the morning of departure came, he awoke early, much too early, with the small twisting excitement in his stomach that took him back forty years, to the mornings of his youth when he was returning to school after a holiday at home, and Mr. Harmer, impatient to be on his way, would get to Penn Station long before train time. Railroad stations had as much fascination for him as the trains themselves, and the leisurely ritual he made of shopping for his newspaper, magazines, cigarettes, and candy, while a highly inefficient and time-consuming process, was an important part of the fun he got from the trip.

Mr. Harmer's body cut the beam of light and, with a pleased smile for the doors that opened as though by magic, he walked out onto the asphalt apron, crossed to the iron stairs, descended to the train level, located his Pullman, and turned his bag over to the grinning porter. Mr. Harmer was the first passenger in the car. He always was. He rolled up his coat, tucked it carefully into the rack above his head, and sat down. He settled himself comfortably, his chair turned at an angle toward the window, and put his feet up on the ledge that covered the steam pipes. He arranged his newspaper and magazines in a neat pile on his lap, reassuringly touched the pocket that contained the bar of candy he always took out and munched happily when the train reached Trenton, and he heaved the long, relaxed, preparatory sigh that ushered in his four hours of delicious loneliness.

"I say," a voice said. "Is it really old Harmer, or are these feeble eyes deceiving me?"

Harmer's feet dropped from the ledge with a thump as he swiveled around in his chair and looked up at the elderly man in British uniform who was standing over him.

"Colonel Ransome," Harmer said, so startled that he neglected to conceal the dismay in his voice, and the newspaper and magazines tumbled to the floor as he struggled to his feet. "For the love of Pete," he said. "I mean, how are you, sir?"

Colonel Ransome chuckled, that throaty British rumble of sound that had been so amusing at first and then, as the V-1s gave way to the V-2s, had become so inexplicably irritating during the days when Colonel Ransome had been the commanding officer of the small SHAEF supply station in a London suburb to which Harmer had been assigned.

"I say, this *is* a surprise," Colonel Ransome said. "My dear chap, how are you? Porter, is this my seat?" The porter nodded and Harmer's heart sank. The colonel pushed Harmer back into his chair and then dropped into the next seat. "What an extraordinary stroke of luck," Colonel Ransome said with obvious delight as the porter put his bag and coat on the rack. "You're looking remarkably fit, old boy. Tell me all."

Harmer did, with feigned enthusiasm. It didn't take long, not only because there wasn't much to tell, but mainly because Harmer had to omit what was uppermost in his mind: while it was true that, under conditions of his own choosing, he would probably have been pleased to meet his old C.O., under the present circumstances Harmer found Colonel Ransome's unexpected appearance a fairly large pain in the neck. Even if the colonel were not a garrulous old windbag, his mere presence was enough to shatter completely the four wonderful hours of relaxed solitude to which Harmer had been looking forward.

"And what about you, sir?" Harmer said politely. "What are you doing on this side of the Atlantic?"

Between dramatic tugs at his snow-white mustache, and a considerable amount of throaty chuckling, Colonel Ransome explained that several months after the Japs did their bunk, you know, he'd been assigned to the Planning Section of the Supplies Division of the Joint Chiefs in Washington, in which city he had been making his headquarters for the better part of a year. Damned interesting assignment it was, too. Involved a good bit of traveling between Ottawa and Washington, of course, and he always flew, but this trip he'd had to stop off in New York for a day, and he couldn't get a plane reservation on such short notice, so he'd had to take the train, and he'd been cursing his luck roundly, because he loathed train travel, so bloody slow and nobody to talk to, you know, when he'd spotted Harmer. Recognized him at once from the shape of the back of his head, recognized him just like that, even though it must be a year and a half or more since they'd seen each other.

"Damned close to two years," Colonel Ransome said. "Not since that party we gave for you and old Thorpe, wasn't it?"

"That's right, sir," Harmer said, wishing Colonel Ransome had not mentioned old Thorpe. It was bad enough to have his solitude destroyed without being saddled with disturbing recollections. "We haven't seen each other since that party, sir."

"Lord, what a do that was," Colonel Ransome said and, as the train got under way and the handsome but rather foolish old man stared out the window at the walls of the tunnel under the Hudson, it occurred to Harmer that perhaps Colonel Ransome was sorry, too, that he had mentioned old Thorpe. Certainly, for the moment at least, the colonel's garrulity seemed to have deserted him. "Curious old bird, wasn't he?" Colonel Ransome said as the train shot out into the light of New Jersey. "I mean to say," he said. "It's odd, the things one remembers, isn't it?"

Odd, hell, Harmer thought bitterly. It was infuriating. While other men remembered the war in terms of a vivid scene on Omaha Beach on D-Day, or some revealing chance remark Eisenhower or Churchill had dropped at a conference they had been privileged to attend, Harmer was trapped by the peculiar circumstances of his war assignment, and his unpredictably erratic memory, into recalling his own participation in the enormous conflict in terms of carrying a brand-new Sam Browne

belt that didn't belong to him up Regent Street in London on a
windy afternoon in March of 1945 while an alert was on. The
belt was not wrapped, because the shop in which Harmer had
picked it up for Mr. Thorpe was all out of wrapping paper, and
it was so new and stiff that it looked like a barrel hoop and was
just about as awkward to carry. Harmer, a shy man, was
convinced that everybody on Regent Street who was not staring
up worriedly into the sky was staring with amusement at him. A
taxi inched its way cautiously out of Vigo Street and Harmer,
who had learned during three years in the E.T.O. the futility of
whistling or waving at a London taxi during an alert, stepped
firmly into its path. The taxi stopped. Harmer came around to
the side and reached for the door. The driver seized the handle
from the inside and held it.

"Sorry, major," he said. "No more petrol. I'm going home."

"Which way is home?" Harmer said.

"Willesden," the driver said. "Out beyond Maida Vale."

"That's the way I'm going," Harmer said. "Murwash Supply
Station. Drop me in front of the Gaumont Cinema on Kilburn
High Road."

The station was half a dozen houses facing a small park, in a
middle-class London suburb called Murwash, that the British
War Office had turned over to SHAEF. Under the command, if
not precisely the supervision, of Colonel Ransome, the three
British junior officers and the one American, Major Harmer,
who made up the station's staff, had converted the park into a
supply depot and the six houses into living quarters for themselves, for the enlisted men who did the heavy work, and for the
company of ATS, the girls in the Auxiliary Territorial Service,
the British equivalent of the American WAC, who served as
housemaids, cooks, secretaries, and office clerks for the staff. It
was not a very exciting or dangerous segment of a global war,
even though there had been two deaths and several nasty head
wounds when a large corner of the supply depot and one of the
enlisted men's houses had been knocked out by a V-1 three
weeks after D-Day and most of the windows in the other houses

had been shattered by the bombs that continued to land almost every day all over Murwash, but there was no doubt about the importance of the job the station was doing and, after helping for so long to do it, Harmer had become attached to the station and the people on it. He was pleased, of course, with the instructions that had come through from SHAEF four days before, ordering him back to Washington: it would be nice to see his wife again and fun to be able to buy an ice cream soda once more. But as the taxi came up out of Maida Vale and turned into the Kilburn High Road, Harmer realized with a stab of regret that this was the last time he would be returning from London to the place he had, after three years, come to think of as home. His instructions from ATC, which he had gone down into town after lunch to get and which were neatly typed out on a sheet of flimsy in the wallet in his pocket, were to report to Croydon Aerodrome at eleven that night.

"Will this do you, sir?" the driver said.

"Yes, thanks," Harmer said. "This is fine."

He stepped out to the sidewalk in front of the Gaumont Cinema and, as he pulled a ten-shilling note from his pocket, the all clear sounded.

"Well, they didn't get us that time, did they, sir?" the driver said with a grin of relief. "It's those new ones, those V-2s, that I'm worried about. They come in so fast, they don't give the ARP lads a chance to sound the sirens, you know. Thank you, sir."

"Yes, they're a bad business," Harmer said, feeling again the tiny ache in his stomach that he knew was fear, the knot of pain that he was pretty certain everybody in London had been carrying around since the first buzz bomb came over, the ever-present terror that neither Harmer nor anybody else was willing to acknowledge. Then, with a quick wave of relief, Harmer realized that in five hours, when he climbed into the ATC plane at Croydon, he would leave that unacknowledged fear behind at last, and the wave of relief gave way to shame. He would be out

of it, all right, but this taxi driver and all Harmer's friends on
the station and the millions of others in the great city, they would
still be in it, very much in it. "Let's hope the war will be over
before these V-2s can do much damage," Harmer said, and he
pushed the change back. "You're welcome."

"Can't be over too soon for me," the driver said, putting the
coins into his pocket. "You don't wear those things with your
American uniforms, sir, do you?"

"This?" Harmer said, holding up the stiff, new Sam Browne
belt. "No, we don't. I picked this up down in town for a British
friend of mine."

As he walked across to the station from Kilburn High Road,
hurrying a little because it was almost six o'clock and he had to
finish packing before the party started at seven, Harmer wondered if Mr. William Chalmers Thorpe could be described with
strict accuracy as a friend of his. Harmer's definition of a friend,
which was probably hopelessly old-fashioned, called for complete knowledge of the person with whom you entered into the
relationship. So far as facts were concerned, Harmer supposed
he knew as much about Mr. Thorpe as he knew about Colonel
Ransome and Major Harrup and Captain Mitchell and Lieutenant Tetlow, the British officers with whom he worked and
lived on the station. And yet, even though it seemed to Harmer
that he should feel closer to Mr. Thorpe because they were both
almost exactly the same age, he did not feel that Mr. Thorpe was
as much his friend as the others were.

"Thank heaven you're back, sir," said Miss Grimes with a
giggle as Harmer came in the front door of what had once been a
modest suburban villa and was now known as the Officers' Mess.
Miss Grimes was a corporal in the ATS, and very proud of her
rank, but Harmer found it difficult to remember this somewhat
outlandish fact about the high-spirited, red-cheeked North
Country girl with the golden hair who served as cook and
downstairs maid for the officers who lived in the house. "Mr.
Thorpe is in such a state, you wouldn't believe it, sir. He's been

worried all during the raid that something had happened to you and you wouldn't get back with his Sam Browne in time for the party."

"You tell Mr. Thorpe to keep his shirt on," Harmer said. "Here it is, corporal. Do you want to take it up to him?"

"I think perhaps you'd better, sir," Corporal Grimes said, blushing prettily. "You see, sir, Mr. Thorpe is dressing."

Harmer could understand how the prospect of breaking in on Mr. William Chalmers Thorpe in the process of getting dressed would strike Miss, or Corporal, Grimes as somewhat less than irresistible. Mr. Thorpe's status in the house was unusual, and not only because he was the sole civilian employee in what, under Colonel Ransome's pompous direction, was run as an aggressively military organization. Mr. Thorpe was a fifty-three-year-old produce merchant from Wales who had spent thirty years of his life on the continent, buying cheese, bacon, butter, and eggs in job lots and selling them at a profit to English wholesalers. He had been visiting England on one of his regular selling trips when the war broke out and left him stranded, so to speak, in his native land. He couldn't get back to Berlin, where for ten years he had maintained his office and lived with his English wife and their two young daughters. His family was interned at once in a German camp for enemy aliens near Bavaria and, while the money he had happened to have on him ran out, Mr. Thorpe tried to get a commission in the British army.

The War Office turned him down because of his age, but Mr. Thorpe did not stop trying. The war had awakened all his patriotism and he worried as much about getting into uniform as he worried about the health and welfare of his wife and children interned in Germany. His persistent efforts brought him to the attention of Colonel Ransome, who was then setting up the Murwash Supply Station and needed a man with an intimate knowledge of continental transportation facilities. Officers with such knowledge were rare or needed elsewhere and, when he learned about Mr. Thorpe, Colonel Ransome asked the War

Office to hire him as a civilian. Mr. Thorpe accepted the job eagerly because he needed the money and because he felt it would bring him one step closer to the commission he wanted so desperately.

He was an odd figure in the Officers' Mess because he looked so very much what he was: a middle-aged produce merchant. Mr. Thorpe was very fat and extremely bald and so ridiculously short that he always seemed to be standing in a hole. No matter how often or recently he shaved, his jowly jaw appeared blue and his round face faintly greasy. His clothes looked as though they had been made by a tailor who had guessed at the measurements and they were invariably crumpled and spotted, as though the man wearing them had just stepped out of a warehouse refrigerator. Harmer had yet to see Mr. Thorpe in a freshly laundered shirt or using a clean handkerchief, and the American could never get over the feeling that Mr. Thorpe, no matter what or how much he was wearing, was not completely dressed because it seemed inevitable that he should be enveloped in a large white apron.

Mr. Thorpe's interests and personality were a depressing but perfect match for his appearance. He had apparently never read anything but produce lists and the stock market pages of the newspapers. He was not interested in music or the theatre. He knew nothing about politics or art. He did not play bridge or gin rummy. And his conversation consisted exclusively of tedious reminiscences about past business deals in butter and bacon, how much money he would be worth today if all his funds on deposit in continental banks had not been confiscated by the Germans, quotations from his correspondence with his family interned in Germany, and the sluggish progress he was making with the War Office toward getting the commission he lusted for. Mr. William Chalmers Thorpe was a bore and a boor and a thoroughly unappetizing creature to look at. Nevertheless, he was a popular, perhaps the most popular, member of the mess.

Colonel Ransome said often that Mr. Thorpe was a damned good man, even if he was a civilian, because he had an excellent sense of echelon. This was the colonel's highest accolade. Colonel Ransome, who had been regular army all of his stuffy life, deplored the laxity of his junior officers and frequently said, through his throaty chuckle, that Mr. Thorpe in his unpressed and frayed lounge suit was a better soldier than the lot of them. Harmer suspected strongly that Colonel Ransome liked Mr. Thorpe because Mr. Thorpe's admiration for the colonel was so embarrassingly obvious. Mr. Thorpe worshipped the old man with the white mustache, the beautifully cut uniform, and the foolish chuckle. From his discussions with Major Harrup, Captain Mitchell, and Lieutenant Tetlow, Harmer knew that their reasons for liking Mr. Thorpe were, like his own, far less personal and far more sensible. You couldn't help admiring the equanimity with which he refused to accept the rebuffs of the War Office and, after each refusal, ploddingly renewed his pathetic and somewhat comic efforts to get a commission. There was a touching quality in the devotion with which the gross, unimaginative man corresponded regularly, through the Red Cross, with his wife and children interned in Germany. And his almost inexhaustible knowledge of continental transportation facilities, acquired during his three decades as a produce merchant in Germany, Belgium, Holland, and Denmark, eased the burden of work considerably for everybody on the station. Mr. Thorpe was like an ungainly, slovenly, aging dog that spoiled the appearance of a drawing room but, because his loyalty had not diminished as his infirmities had increased with the years, he was tolerated in the house and, to everybody's surprise, he continued to do more than earn his keep.

"If he's in the middle of dressing," Harmer said to Corporal Grimes as that young lady eyed the stiff, new Sam Browne belt, "I'd better take this up to him myself."

"Would you, sir?" Corporal Grimes said, her eyes dancing. "I'm just dying to see what he looks like in it."

It occurred to Harmer that, though he would probably have chosen a more temperate way to express it, the pretty little ATS corporal had described his own feelings with accuracy. Four

days before, the day Harmer's orders from SHAEF to report
back to Washington had come through, the unmoveable British
War Office, after almost five and a half years of prodding, had
finally moved: the same dispatch rider who brought Harmer's
transfer orders to Murwash Supply Station also brought the
official notification that William Chalmers Thorpe, aged fifty-
three, had been commissioned at last a second lieutenant in a
Welsh regiment.

Mr. Thorpe must have known that the great day was
approaching, or perhaps he had never shared the pessimism of
the other members of the mess about the ultimate result of his
years of unflagging effort, because Harmer knew there was not a
tailor in wartime London who could whip up on such short notice
the uniform Mr. Thorpe promised to wear at the party, nor was
there an officers' supply shop in the battered city that could make
in four days the Sam Browne belt Harmer had picked up for Mr.
Thorpe that afternoon. Harmer suspected that the uniform and
the belt had been ordered months, perhaps years, before and
Harmer was glad he would have the chance to see Mr. Thorpe
wearing both before he went back to America.

"If you could spare a moment, sir, would you care to step into
the dining room?" Corporal Grimes said, and her cheerful face
blushed red. "It looks ever so pretty, we think. The girls, I
mean, sir. Nobody else has seen it yet, of course."

Harmer followed her trim little figure across the hall to the
dining room and, as she opened the door and he looked in, a lump
came up in Harmer's throat. The somber chamber, with walls
that had not been painted since before the war and the ceiling
that had been cracked by the blast from the V-1 that had
knocked out a corner of the supply depot and killed two enlisted
men, had been decorated bravely with faded streamers and
frayed bunting that must have been saved for years in somebody's
trunk. The huge table was dotted with colorful little islands of
iced cakes and bright candies and bowls of nuts and plates of
jellies and platters of tiny sandwiches and dishes of homemade
cookies, all neatly arranged and cleverly spaced on the enormous

expanse of gleaming wood to conceal the pathetic fact that, though so surprisingly much had somehow been gathered together, the accumulation was a skimpy approximation of what the girls who had prepared it thought was adequate.

For more than a year Miss Grimes and the other ATS on the station had talked jokingly about the parties they would give for Major Harmer, when the war was over and he was ready to go back to America, and for Mr. Thorpe, when he got his commission. None of them had taken the talk seriously because the war had been going on so long that nobody believed it would really end, and nobody really thought Mr. Thorpe would ever get his commission. The war was not over, of course, not with the Allied armies still fighting desperately across the Rhine and buzz bombs and V-2 rockets landing daily all over London, but somehow Major Harmer had been ordered home and somehow Mr. Thorpe's commission had come through.

Four days was such pitifully short notice, and two parties were more than anybody in all of wartime England could manage, but the loyal little ATS of Murwash Supply Station had risen to the occasion. Occupying the place of honor in the center of the table was a large white cake into which must have gone at least a month's sugar ration of every girl in the company. Around the sides of the cake, under the tiny crossed flags of England and America, in bright pink icing, was lettered: "Hail, Lieutenant Thorpe! Farewell, Major Harmer! Godspeed You Both!" Harmer swallowed hard and turned to Corporal Grimes.

"It's lovely," he said. "The most beautiful table I've ever seen, corporal. How in the world did you manage to put your hands on the stuff?"

"Oh, we all pooled our rations, sir," Corporal Grimes said, and she blushed again through her tinkly little laugh. "Please don't you go saying I told you so, sir," she said with a mischievous twinkle in her eyes, "but some of the girls made their boy friends toss in a coupon or two. We can always manage if we have to, you know."

"Well," Harmer said. "I'd better get this belt up to Lieutenant Thorpe before the icing on that handsome cake melts."

He walked across the hall to the stairs.

"That you, Harmer, old boy?" Lieutenant Tetlow called.

"Yes," Harmer said. He stopped in the doorway of the officers' lounge, which had once been the drawing room of the villa. "I see at least one member of this staff is all dressed and ready."

"Made it a rule when I was a lad of ten always to be the first at a party," Lieutenant Tetlow said with a grin. "And I've never broken it yet."

Lieutenant Tetlow, the youngest member of the Murwash Supply Station staff, had served in the desert with Auchinleck until a hip wound made him useless for further active service and he was assigned to Colonel Ransome. He was not quite thirty, a fact that the other members of the mess found a trifle irritating: Colonel Ransome was past sixty, Harmer and Mr. Thorpe were in the early fifties, and Captain Mitchell and Major Harrup both admitted to what they called the goodish side of forty. Lieutenant Tetlow was the gay blade of the mess. He had the largest collection of off-color stories; the size of his bar bill was a constant source of somewhat tiresome but good-natured jokes; he was usually ahead at bridge and gin rummy; he was always tuning the radio to whatever dance music was available when the older officers wanted to listen to the news; and Harmer often wondered just how much truth there was in Lieutenant Tetlow's arch references to his relations with Corporal Grimes and the other pretty girls in the company of ATS. In the late summer of the preceding year, when the Allies broke through at St. Lô, Lieutenant Tetlow had organized a pool in the mess on the end of the war, and he was now listening to the BBC six-o'clock news and marking the positions of the opposing armies on the large newspaper map he had pasted to the wall over the fireplace.

"Pop in here a moment, will you?" Lieutenant Tetlow said.

"Want to show you something interesting." He snapped off the radio and put his finger on the map as Harmer came into the room and stood beside him. "See that?" Lieutenant Tetlow said. His finger was pointing to a small black dot near the Bavarian border that was marked Kaiserslautern. "BBC just read off the SHAEF communiqué. General Patton captured this place early this morning."

"Good for Patton," Harmer said. "Maybe I'll win that pool after all." Harmer had chosen June 1, 1945 as his date for the end of the war. "Make sure you send me the money, too, you young scoundrel. I'm leaving my New York address posted on the bulletin board."

"No fear," Lieutenant Tetlow said. "You haven't a prayer, old chap. I still say this bloody show is going on for another year, and my 1946 date is going to take the money. Doesn't this mean anything to you?"

Harmer's glance followed the Lieutenant's pointing finger to the map once more.

"Aside from the fact that your fingernails need cleaning," Harmer said, "I don't see a thing. I've got to wash and finish packing before the party starts. What's on your mind, young man?"

"Kaiserslautern," Lieutenant Tetlow said and, after another pause, he grinned and explained. "Good show, what?"

"Damned good," Harmer said. "Does he know?"

"I shouldn't think so," Lieutenant Tetlow said. "It came through on the wireless just a moment ago, when I heard you out in the hall."

"Do you mind if I tell him?" Harmer said. "I was just taking this belt up to him, anyway."

"Not at all," Lieutenant Tetlow said. "Only fitting and proper that you should, old boy. I mean to say, the party's for both of you. One guest of honor to the other, so to speak. You break it to him."

Harmer went out and up the stairs. His room faced Mr. Thorpe's across the second-floor hall. Harmer stopped in his own

A SENSE OF ECHELON

room just long enough to turn on the water in his tub. Then he hurried across the hall and knocked on Mr. Thorpe's door.

"Who is it?" Mr. Thorpe said. "I'm dressing."

"Harmer," Harmer said. "I've got your Sam Browne."

The door opened quickly and Harmer, swept by one of those moments of irrelevant observation that he found so annoyingly characteristic of himself, realized that perhaps it was just as well that he was leaving Murwash Supply Station so soon after Mr. Thorpe had received his commission: Harmer knew he would never be able to remember to call him Lieutenant. The fat man in the doorway was wearing a beautifully pressed uniform. His starched shirt collar was immaculate. His khaki tie was neatly knotted. His freshly polished shoes gleamed brightly. And yet, for some curious reason that had nothing to do with his clothes, Harmer felt that Mr. Thorpe, no, Lieutenant Thorpe, had forgotten to put on his white apron. In the brand-new uniform and insignia of an officer in His Majesty's army, William Chalmers Thorpe still looked like a produce merchant.

"Thank God you've come," Thorpe said. "I've been worried sick about you."

"Here it is," Harmer said, handing over the belt. "I got caught on Regent Street during the alert and couldn't find a taxi. You look terrific, old man."

"Thanks awfully," Thorpe said, puffing as he tried to get the Sam Browne around his enormous waist. "Damned good of you to pick this up for me, old chap. Does the tunic really fit, do you think?"

"Perfectly," Harmer said. "Can I give you a hand with that?"

"Would you, old chap?" Thorpe said across his shoulder. "Just shove the door to, do you mind? That's right. I've been sitting in here waiting for you. Didn't want anybody to see me until I was dressed properly. Sam Browne and all, you know. I think if you took this end, no, the hasp, that's it, and gave it a bit of a tug. There, that does it. Thank you, old chap. Very decent of you. Damned decent."

"Never mind the belt for a moment," Harmer said as Thorpe eyed himself critically in the cracked mirror over his dresser. "I've got some wonderful news for you. Tetlow just heard it on the BBC's broadcast of the six-o'clock communiqué." Harmer paused dramatically. "Patton's Third Army took Kaiserslautern this morning." Harmer paused again, and though he did not quite know how the stolid produce merchant would react to what the American assumed would be a stunning piece of information, Harmer was surprised by what seemed to be a complete absence of any reaction at all. Thorpe continued to eye himself in the mirror, his face expressionless. "I guess I didn't make that clear," Harmer said. "Patton's taken Kaiserslautern."

"Has he?" Thorpe said. "Good show."

"That's where your family has been interned," Harmer said, annoyed by the slight edge in his own voice. "Isn't it?"

"Yes," Thorpe said, smoothing away a tiny wrinkle of khaki cloth at the place where the Sam Browne went through his shoulder flap. "Kaiserslautern. Quite."

"That means you should be getting some word about them in a day or two," Harmer said. "The first thing they do when they take a place like that is go through the internment camps and wire friends and relatives back home, don't they?"

"That's the customary procedure, yes," Thorpe said, and Harmer wondered if it was because he was watching with so much irritated concentration that he thought he saw the produce merchant's blue-jowled, impassive face crease for an instant. "That's what they usually do."

Harmer waited another moment and then, as his annoyance was replaced by the thought that, after three years of intimate association with various aspects of the British character, he still did not, and probably never would, understand it, the American shrugged.

"Well, I'd better get going," he said. "I left the water running in my tub, and I've still got some packing to do."

The packing took longer than Harmer had estimated because, during his three years in England, he had accumulated a good deal more than the fifty-five pounds that his strict instructions from ATC said he could carry with him in the plane. By seven o'clock Harmer, who would have denied the accusation of sentimentality as firmly as he concealed his secret passion for trains and railroad stations, had combed from his personal effects all the cherished but thoroughly useless items that it gave him a pang of regret to discard, and he fastened the last buckle on his bulging Val-Pak. When he came downstairs a few minutes later the party was under way, so thoroughly under way that nobody commented on the fact that the sirens, which went off as Harmer stepped into the lounge, were almost an hour early that night. As a rule there was a lull in the bombing attacks between six and eight every evening. A single glance at the crowded room, which was all he was allowed before he was surrounded by a laughing group of ATS led by Major Harrup, was enough to convince Harmer that, so far as the people then in the Officers' Mess of the Murwash Supply Station were concerned, no siren ever built was strong enough to make itself heard.

"Here he is, our American cousin!" shouted Major Harrup, who, in peacetime, was a chartered accountant with a dignified list of clients and, even in what might be described as the more normal periods of wartime, was a soft-spoken, retiring officer who did his job with quiet efficiency and seldom raised his voice. "Let's have the song again, shall we?" Major Harrup cried as he shoved a glass into Harmer's hand. "Ready, chaps?"

The whole room broke into "For he's a jolly good fellow" and Harmer, aware that he was blushing, smiled with embarrassment and pleasure as he glanced around. In addition to the station's own officers and ATS, there were a dozen enlisted men, looking very brushed and stiff and uncomfortable in the presence of so much brass. These were apparently the boy friends out of whom Corporal Grimes and her sister ATS had dragged the coupon or two that had contributed to the accumulation of cakes and nuts and fruits spread so artfully and lovingly on the dining-room table. Even Colonel Ransome, standing between Corporal

Grimes and Captain Mitchell, was singing lustily as he tugged at his white mustache and kept time by waving his glass.

"Now once more for our bright and shining new Lieutenant Thorpe!" Major Harrup yelled. "Ready?"

The group broke away from Harmer and surrounded the produce merchant, who scowled shyly into his glass and tugged at the buckle of his Sam Browne as the strains of "For he's a jolly good fellow" swirled around his bald and faintly greasy head. Harmer took the first sip from his glass and knew, before he turned to look, that Lieutenant Tetlow was in charge of the bar. It was a Tetlow Tiger, half gin and half cider, a drink invented by that ebullient young officer, whose favorite tipple was martinis, when the supplies of French vermouth ran out early in 1942 but you could get all the apple cider you could carry away from the local pub at sixpence the pint bottle. After two of these concoctions Harmer lost a good deal of his embarrassment at being one of the two persons in whose honor the party was given and, by the time Corporal Grimes shepherded the noisy group into the dining room, Harmer was feeling so well that he registered only a few mild and very unconvincing objections to posing for a picture with Mr., now Lieutenant, Thorpe beside the large white cake that bore the touching inscription in pink icing. Shortly after this a V-1 landed somewhere on the edge of Murwash and, as the plates rattled on the dining-room table and the few unbroken windows in the house shook noisily, the merrymakers became aware of the raid that had been going on for almost two hours and a number of them ran out into the street, carrying their sandwiches and Tetlow Tigers, to see what was happening.

Harmer seized on this lull in the festivities to take Captain Mitchell, in peacetime a poorly paid instructor in romance languages at a respectable but not quite top drawer public school in Surrey, up to his room to present him with the underwear and socks and pajamas that the American was leaving behind because there was no room for them in his Val-Pak. Captain

Mitchell was embarrassed but grateful, because like almost everybody else in England, he was running short on these essentials and was completely out of clothing coupons. He thanked Harmer effusively and carried his acquisitions happily up to his room on the third floor. Harmer left his own room to return to the party downstairs and stopped short in the hallway. The sound of voices raised in a quarrel came through the closed door of Mr. Thorpe's room. Harmer hesitated, turned toward the stairs, and stopped again. One of the voices belonged to Corporal Grimes.

"I can't, darling," she said. "It won't look right. You're the one to ask him, darling."

The reply, made unmistakably by a man's voice, was so low that Harmer could neither identify it nor distinguish the words but, remembering suddenly his suspicions about Lieutenant Tetlow, he crossed quickly to the door and pushed it open.

"Oh," Harmer said. "I beg your pardon." For a moment he didn't know whether he was more astonished by discovering Corporal Grimes alone with Thorpe in the latter's room or by the fact that he had just heard the pretty girl call the fat, middle-aged produce merchant darling. "I thought it was somebody else," Harmer said, backing out of the doorway. "I mean, I thought it was some sort of trouble. I didn't mean to intrude."

"Quite all right," Thorpe said. "As a matter of fact there is a bit of trouble."

"You ask him," Corporal Grimes said and, because she was taller than the man who always seemed to be standing in a hole, she looked down into Thorpe's face as she spoke. The tone of her voice and the quality of her glance left no doubt in Harmer's mind about what he had heard. "Please," she said pleadingly and she squeezed the produce merchant's large, thick hand. "Please ask him, darling."

Then she turned quickly and hurried past Harmer, out of the room. She closed the door softly behind her. Thorpe scowled down at his hand so hard that his collar disappeared completely into his blue jowls, and he stepped over to the window where he made a completely unnecessary adjustment to the blackout curtains.

"Well," Harmer said. "I think I'd better run along."

"Please don't go," Thorpe said. "There's something I want to ask you."

"Something Corporal Grimes wants you to ask me?" Harmer said.

"Well, yes," Thorpe said without turning, and there was a long, silent pause. "We're faced with a bit of a problem," he said finally. "And she thinks you're the only one who can help us solve it."

"I'll be delighted to do anything," Harmer said, trying hard to keep the surprise out of his voice. There might have been some perfectly reasonable explanation for finding the young girl and this elderly, uncouth man, thirty years her senior, alone in Thorpe's room, although Harmer wondered how Colonel Ransome's high opinion of Thorpe's sense of echelon would be affected by the explanation; there might even be some innocent explanation for her calling him darling; but there could be only one explanation for Thorpe's use of the word we, and for the way he used it. Harmer could understand the lonely, plodding middle-aged man being attracted to the fresh-cheeked, laughing North Country girl. He could even understand, although this was more difficult, that the young girl might, for a variety of reasons, respond, or pretend to respond, to the older man's advances. What Harmer found it almost impossible to understand was how the affair could have started and apparently gone on right under his nose without his suspecting it. Harmer had lived in the same house with these people for almost three years. He was a sensitive and perceptive man. But he had noticed nothing. The other members of the mess had noticed nothing, either. If they had, there would have been gossip. Lieutenant Tetlow would have made sly jokes about it. Harmer's astonishment gave way to something not very far removed from resentment. He felt he had been tricked. "I mean I'll be delighted to do anything I can," Harmer said with some sharpness. He glanced at his wrist watch. It was almost nine-thirty. "I don't have much time. The car will be calling for me in three quarters of an hour."

"I know it's a bit of a rush," Thorpe said. "But the problem has just come up, you see." He turned from the blackout curtains. "Do you think there's any chance of getting Corporal Grimes and myself over to the States?"

Harmer blinked slightly and, in a moment of revelation that was not nearly so irrelevant as was customary with him, the American understood what Thorpe had meant when he said the problem had just come up.

"That's a rather difficult thing to do in wartime," Harmer said. "Even in peacetime it's not easy because of the immigration quotas, you know." And he added drily, "Especially on such short notice."

He felt slightly annoyed with Thorpe and Miss Grimes. At least one of them was old enough not to have acted with the traditional thoughtlessness of young lovers. Even if the girl had been so swept away by her passion for this stodgy butter-and-bacon merchant that she had no time to think of practical consequences and considerations, Thorpe should have had sense enough not to put off those considerations until the last moment, until the inevitable news arrived that his interned wife and children were on the verge of being released and sent home.

"I realize it's not simple," Thorpe said. "But I wasn't thinking of immigration quotas. We could worry about that later, when the war is over. I was thinking in terms of getting us transferred officially, you know. To some mission in Washington or Canada, perhaps. Something like that. It shouldn't be too difficult, I imagine. Now that I'm no longer a civilian. Now that I'm in the army, too, I mean."

"Oh," Harmer said. Perhaps the produce merchant had not been so impractical and thoughtless, after all. "Well, I don't know," Harmer said more kindly. "I'm afraid I don't have that kind of drag. I'm just a major in the Services of Supply."

Thorpe nodded, a quick movement of his bald head that was

so inappropriate to the matter they were discussing, a gesture that might have signified the closing of a business deal for a carload of cold storage eggs, that Harmer had to fight back a sudden desire to laugh.

"That's what I thought," Thorpe said gruffly. "That's what I told her."

"But what are you going to do?" Harmer said. "I mean, when your wife and children, your family, they'll probably be back in England soon, won't they?"

"I don't know," Thorpe said and, for the first time, his dull voice and his stupid face seemed to lose their dullness and stupidity. There was suddenly so much hopeless dejection in that large, shapeless, middle-aged body, that Harmer forgot his desire to laugh and remembered a painful fact: he and Mr. Thorpe were almost exactly the same age. "I haven't any idea," Thorpe said helplessly and, for a terrified instant, Harmer thought the produce merchant was going to cry. "Something will turn up, though," Thorpe said without conviction. "It always does," he said. "Everything will be all right."

"I hope so," Harmer said, and he was not even mildly surprised by the fact that he meant it. "I don't think there's much I can do, but I'll try."

"Thanks very much," Thorpe said. "Decent of you, old man. Damned decent."

He turned back to the blackout curtains and Harmer, after another awkward pause, left the room. He went downstairs, where the party was going stronger than ever, and he drank two more Tetlow Tigers that were forced on him, but Harmer did not enjoy them. At ten o'clock one of the ATS came to tell him that the SHAEF car had arrived and, for a few minutes, there was a confused babble of bon voyages, and swapping of addresses, and footsteps rushing upstairs to get Harmer's Val-Pak, and pledges to write and visit when this bloody show was over, and manly handshakes from Colonel Ransome and Major Harrup and Captain Mitchell, and tearful goodbyes from the ATS, and bawdy advice from Lieutenant Tetlow about what to do if the plane should be forced down on the Atlantic, and then, somewhat shaken, Harmer was alone on the blacked-out street beside the SHAEF car and the GI driver was stowing his Val-Pak in the rear.

"How do we stand on time?" Harmer said.

"We've got forty minutes, sir, and I can make Croydon in twenty-five," the driver said, opening the car door. "If one of those buzzers doesn't drop on us, sir."

"Make it in thirty," Harmer said. "I haven't been home for three years and I'd like to enjoy it when I get there."

"Yes, sir," the driver said, his grin clearly visible in the moonlight. "You bet, sir."

The door of the house opened and closed and they both turned. Corporal Grimes came running down the cracked cement walk, her khaki skirt whipping around her trim legs, and the driver, after a quick glance at Harmer, slipped discreetly behind the wheel and slammed the door of the car.

"Major Harmer, sir," Corporal Grimes said breathlessly. "Please, sir." Harmer stepped toward her and caught her elbows and turned her away from the car. "He's just told me what you said, sir," she said in a low voice, talking to the middle button on Harmer's blouse. "About how you'd promised to help us, sir. And I wanted to thank you and, oh, please, sir, please, Major Harmer, do try to help us. Please."

"I'll do my best," Harmer said. He was uncomfortable because he knew there was nothing he could do and worse than uncomfortable because he sensed that, even if he could, he would probably hesitate before doing it. The combination made him feel mean and puritanical, which he wasn't, and he said irritably, "Why don't you both just forget the whole thing?" After all, they'd had their fun, if a relationship between two such incredibly disparate people could be described as fun. "I mean, why not be sensible?" Harmer said. "Why not end it now? That's really your best solution, isn't it?"

Corporal Grimes raised her head quickly, so that he could see her face in the moonlight. She looked terrified.

"Oh, we couldn't do that, sir," she said. "You see, sir, we've been married for more than a year."

Just then the driver hit the horn button, so it could have been the short blast of warning that made Harmer jump a little, and he released the girl's elbows.

"But that's impossible," he said angrily. "I mean, it's illegal. Didn't you know he has a wife and children interned in Germany? I mean, didn't you know it before today?"

"Yes, sir," Corporal Grimes said, looking down at the cement walk, and then she seemed to shiver slightly. "But the war has been going on for so long, sir, and we thought—" She shivered again, more convulsively, as though to shake off whatever it was they had thought, and she raised her head to look at Harmer. "He's such a gentleman, sir, he didn't want to do anything that would be improper for me," she said, and her small, round, quite lovely face was utterly guileless in the moonlight. "You see, sir, he and I, we—" Her face and voice broke suddenly, the way Thorpe's face and voice had broken in the produce merchant's room less than a half hour earlier. "You see, sir," she said helplessly, "I love him so, sir."

The change in the tempo of the clacking train wheels brought Harmer's mind back, from Murwash Supply Station, across the Atlantic and the two years that had gone by, to the Pullman in which he had been cheated of his solitude. All the fervent promises to write and visit when the bloody show was over had come to nothing. All the swapped addresses were still there, in his pocket notebook, unused and probably a little faded and no doubt, because they had been scribbled in such haste, more than a little undecipherable. Harmer shrugged away the pointless thought that time went too quickly, when you passed fifty, and he peered out the window as the train started to slow down.

"Yes, he was an odd bird," he said. "What ever happened to him?"

"Old Thorpe?" Colonel Ransome said as he gave his white mustache a small tug and leaned forward to follow Harmer's glance out the window. "Why, shortly after you left us, the war ended, you know, and he was among the first to be demobbed. Because of his age, you see. Then his wife and children returned to England and he went back into the produce business. Butter and eggs and bacon, that sort of thing. Not much of a business to be in these days, of course, but the last I heard he had offices somewhere in Tottenham Court Road and was doing jolly well. Poor chap, he didn't get to wear his uniform very long, five or six weeks at the outside, but he was a first-rate soldier all the same. Better than the whole lot of you, I always said," Colonel Ransome said through the throaty chuckle that had once been so irritating and, for an uncomfortable instant, Harmer felt again the old knot of fear in his stomach that had been such a never to be forgotten and never to be admitted part of his life in London under the buzz bombs. "A first-rate soldier," Colonel Ransome said. "Had a damned good sense of echelon, you know. Always went through channels and did the proper thing. Conducted himself very well, very well indeed, especially when we got our packet."

"What packet?" Harmer said.

"Hadn't you heard?" Colonel Ransome said. "The day after you left, one of those bloody V-2s hit us. Knocked out half the supply depot and a couple of the ATS houses. We lost one, that pretty little North Country girl who used to be our cook and downstairs maid at the mess, Corporal Grimes her name was, and half a dozen or more of the others had to be hospitalized. A bad business, that was. Very bad. I say, old boy, what station is this?"

The first red and gold platform sign flashed by as the air brakes began to take hold. Harmer leaned back in his chair.

"Trenton," he said and, unaware that a part of his body was moving, he put his hand into his coat pocket and held it there, waiting for the sudden ache of tiredness to ease away. He pulled his hand from his pocket and, for a long moment, Harmer stared at the nickel bar of candy he had purchased in Penn Station. His partner and his wife were right. Next month he would either let the younger man make the trip to their Washington office or, if that was impossible and Harmer had to go himself, he would fly. The plane was quicker.

"Colonel Ransome," Harmer said, holding out the bar of candy. "Would you care for a piece of this, sir?"

# A
# MOMENT'S
# NOTICE

In the mornings, during those first moments of sliding into consciousness, it was always Michigan. Dr. Newcomb did not mind that. It was only natural. At his age, it was even appropriate. What could be more appropriate, for a man who had lived through seventy-nine years, than the fact that the mornings of his eightieth should all begin in precisely the same way: with recollections of the small town overlooking Lake Huron in which his embarrassingly long life had begun?

"Just a moment," Dr. Newcomb said. He spoke with his eyes closed. "I can't hear you."

He didn't have to. He knew the words that had been directed at him from his bedroom doorway, during these first moments of coming awake, as intimately as he knew every word that would be directed at him during every moment of the interminable day that stretched ahead. They never varied. They were part of the ritual to which his life had been reduced. The ritual demanded that the recollections of Michigan, even though they were a distraction and therefore unwelcome, must be allowed to fade away, gently. They did, with a lingering sweetness that Dr. Newcomb wished he could enjoy, and then he was ready for the day's next step. He inserted it carefully, trailed his fingers back along the corded wire from his ear to the bedside table, lifted the battery compartment, dropped the neat little silver-plated box into the breast pocket of his pajamas, and turned his head on the pillow.

"Now," Dr. Newcomb said. "What did you say?"

"I said good morning," Robert said. "How are you today?"

Even though Robert's voice came through only faintly, because Dr. Newcomb's hearing device had not been serviced for some time, the old man on the bed heard every syllable. Not alone because habit had made Dr. Newcomb familiar with the meaningless words. Dr. Newcomb heard every syllable because he had never become quite accustomed to the small shock of amazement he experienced whenever he heard that voice. Even long ago, when this portly but still attractive man in this New York doorway had been a slender and strikingly handsome boy in a Michigan frame house, his voice had already possessed that curious power to evoke in every listener, as it still did now, that sense of confidence and charm, the impression of courtesy and intelligence, all those qualities of strength and integrity in which the harshly mocking years had proved the owner of the voice to be totally lacking.

"I'm fine," Dr. Newcomb said and he stared, as he did every morning, at the man who woke him up every day, at this same time, with those same meaningless words, the man to whom Dr. Newcomb knew his stubbornly irrational longevity was an acute embarrassment. "I'm sorry to disappoint you," Dr. Newcomb said to his son in the doorway. "But I'm really fine."

"I wish you wouldn't say that," Robert said, and he added the small, charming smile with which, every morning, at this same time, he modified the same remark. "It isn't really very funny, Father," Robert said cheerfully. "You know that."

"Yes, I know," Dr. Newcomb said, and of course he did. It was one of the penalties of old age. You knew everything, even the ironical fact that you were expected to pretend you knew nothing. But that was something his son could not be expected to know. Not yet, anyway. Robert was only fifty. A mere boy. Measured by the yardsticks to which his father had attained, Robert was not even that. Which raised, as it always did, the question of what Robert really was. And, as he always did during these first moments of the day, Dr. Newcomb eased that particular question gently but firmly from his mind. They both knew what Robert was. "Funny or not, it seems sensible to continue saying it," Dr. Newcomb said as he pushed himself carefully upright in the bed and, even more carefully, felt with his toes for his ragged slippers. "Or we'll find ourselves forced to the trouble of thinking up new phrases with which to begin the day."

"A little trouble might do us both good," Robert said. He crossed to the window and raised the shade. The bright sunlight, shafting in abruptly across Fifth Avenue from Central Park, seemed reluctant to perform its traditional function. It did not spread cheer. It merely underscored, with its harshly probing radiance, the dinginess of this once handsome room in which nothing had been altered, and to which nothing had been added, for a decade. "It would be a change, anyway," Robert said through a burst of the throaty chuckle that men and women, and especially women, had always, to their ultimate regret, found irresistible. "You have to admit that, Father."

Dr. Newcomb, who had been forced by the character and predilections of his only son to admissions that would have destroyed a weaker man long ago, had to admit this, too. It would be a change. But Dr. Newcomb did not want change. He wanted something that Robert might have been able to supply but which, because of their strange relationship, the father did not dare ask the son to provide.

"Let's not begin thinking about change," Dr. Newcomb said. He preferred to think, as he did every morning at this time, about the puzzling blind alley into which his long life had led him. He was like a traveler, all packed and ready to depart at a moment's notice, who does not understand why he cannot bring himself to call for the taxi that will carry him down to the train. There was no reason to linger. His work as a general practitioner, to which Dr. Newcomb had with zestful devotion given half a century of his vigorous maturity, had been for a long time now beyond his failing powers. His wife, whom he had loved and who had loved him, was gone. His money, which had never interested him enough to deflect any of his once considerable energies into the process of amassing more of it, was running out. Every road of logic led to the same conclusion: his day, like his usefulness, was done; it was pointless to stay on. Every road save one. This one road defied logic as well as the traveler's powers of comprehension. It led inexorably to the only conclusion that, even though Dr. Newcomb did not understand it, made sense: he had left something out. Somewhere along the way, somewhere between that small town overlooking Lake Huron in which he had been born and this large house overlooking Central Park in which he was prepared but unable to die, somewhere on the long journey that had taken eighty years, he had left behind a piece of unfinished business. The fact that his mind, in all other respects completely unimpaired, refused to disgorge the missing obligation, did not change the fact that, until it was wiped from the slate, the weary and impatient traveler could do no more than hold himself in readiness for instant departure. "We certainly don't want to begin thinking about change before breakfast," Dr. Newcomb said. He stood up and, with the deliberation of a brain surgeon making the initial incision of a complicated operation, he wrapped his tall but pitifully slender frame in the folds of the frayed robe. "Let's stick to what we've got."

What they had wasn't much, but it was enough. At any rate, Dr. Newcomb hoped it was enough, because it would have to last. They had the house, which he had bought when he was almost seventy, when he was already tired and long past his best work, when he and Robert, after Mrs. Newcomb's death in Cleveland, had arrived in New York ten years ago to make one more attempt at starting life all over again. And they had the income from the few thousand dollars in bonds, which was all he had been able to save from the holocaust that had driven them from Cleveland to New York. If it wasn't quite enough, at least it had become the equivalent of enough since they had rented the two upper floors to the Cartwells. Or was their name Hartwell? Dr. Newcomb couldn't remember. So long as they paid their rent, it didn't matter.

"I've got a kipper for breakfast, if you want it," Robert said, coming back across the room toward the door. "But I don't suppose you do?"

Dr. Newcomb—who might have wanted the kipper, if the question had been put differently—paused, in the act of starting for the bathroom, to watch Robert cross the room. Dr. Newcomb watched him with that oddly helpless and confused feeling, part pride and part distaste and part wonder, on which every attempt to understand his own son had always foundered.

Even at fifty, with his dark hair going gray at the temples, with his astonishing features blunted somewhat by the faint puffiness of nearly four decades of alcoholic excess, and with his powerful frame padded, although not unpleasantly so, by a lifetime of overindulgence at the table, Robert still moved with all the effortless grace that, at fifteen, had made him the best dancer in northern Michigan. Even to the father who loved him, it seemed wrong, somehow. Robert was not entitled to look like that. Not necessarily because Robert at fifty—the survivor, through his father's efforts, of a dozen scandals involving women, liquor, cards, and worse, which had driven the Newcombs from city to city at regular intervals—was as totally lacking in contrition as he had been when, at seventeen, he had stolen money for the first time. No. It seemed wrong for an entirely different reason.

At that time so long ago, when they were still living in the Michigan town where he had been born and raised and married, Dr. Newcomb had paid back out of his then meager savings the four hundred dollars of the high school Commencement Fund with which Robert, as Chairman of the Entertainment Committee, had been entrusted, and the Newcombs had moved to Chicago. Shortly after they arrived, when Dr. Newcomb was just beginning to get his new practice established and long before Robert forged the check that three years later drove him from the University and his parents from Chicago, Dr. Newcomb had been struck for the first time by the incredible fact that lay at the bottom of the problem: the shocking incident about the high school Commencement Fund had apparently left no mark on his son. Dr. Newcomb could not believe it at the time.

The simple decencies, which Dr. Newcomb's own parents had implanted in him without preaching or even obvious effort during his boyhood on the shores of Lake Huron, and which Dr. Newcomb had tried, in his turn, to pass on when he himself became a father, seemed to have made no impression at all on

Robert. It was something with which the normal mind felt powerless to deal. It was simple enough, even though it might be painful, to punish the wicked. It was more difficult perhaps, but certainly possible, to forgive the sinner. But how did one deal with the wicked who were ignorant of the meaning of wickedness, with the sinner who had no conception of sin?

The only occasions on which Robert seemed to be aware that he had done anything the world condemned came at the moments when he was caught. At such times he was, of course, suitably sorry and full of the appropriately phrased promises to turn over a new leaf. Dr. Newcomb learned soon enough that the promises meant nothing. He even grew accustomed to the sense of despair with which he and his wife, and finally he alone, faced each new proof that Robert was incorrigible.

The despair had been understandable, even if the love of a father for his son was not. That love was something you merely accepted. It was one of the unknown factors in the equation of life for which you sought no explanation. Blood was thicker than water. Acts that turned you, with resignation or contempt if not with hatred, from the criminal stranger, merely intensified the fiercely unreasonable desire to protect the criminal son.

What Dr. Newcomb could not accept, what he never grew accustomed to, what filled him even now at eighty, not so much with shame, as with an almost impersonal sense of wonder, was Robert's lack of awareness. It defied argument. It was impervious to punishment. It resisted explanation. Robert did not really *believe* that he was doing wrong. Robert had never actually *felt* that he had no right to do what he had done. He seemed to live with a sense of his own uniqueness. That, and only that, was what seemed wrong to Dr. Newcomb. That, and only that, was the father's failure.

"No, of course I don't want the kipper," he said, counting silently, as he moved toward the bathroom, to make sure he reached the door in the customary eight steps. He did. "You go ahead and have the kipper," Dr. Newcomb said, without bitterness, because the knowledge of Robert's selfishness, of the father's failure to rear a son with a sense of responsibility to the community at large, was as much a part of the day's inflexible routine as the twenty-two minutes he allowed himself for shaving and reaching the breakfast table. "I'll have the usual."

The usual consisted of six prunes, two inches of orange juice, and half a cup of black coffee, consumed in the basement dining room that, since they had rented the upper floors to the Cartwells or Hartwells, also served father and son as their sitting room. Dr. Newcomb ate slowly, taking between prunes just enough of the coffee, and just enough of the orange juice, so that the meticulously calculated sips would leave him, as the clock began to strike eleven and Robert came in from the kitchen, the final mouthful of coffee with which the first of the day's two meals always ended.

Dr. Newcomb never ate lunch, because the problem of maintaining in functioning balance the fragile mechanism of a body no longer capable of physical exercise was simplified by a sparse diet. And he always ate alone. Robert, who served as cook as well as maid for both of them, and whose hearty appetite made it impossible for him to wait until ten-thirty for his own breakfast, liked to get the bulk of the dishes done before his father was ready to eat.

Dr. Newcomb washed down the last of the sixth prune with the last of the orange juice, and then he set the spoon neatly in the plate with a small tinkle. The clock, as though it had been waiting for this signal, began to strike. And Robert came in from the kitchen, as he always did, between the seventh and eighth strokes, drying his hands on the dish towel and scanning, with that bafflingly affectionate smile, the plates he had set out for his father while the old man had been shaving.

"There," Robert said heartily. "Feel better now?"

"Much," said Dr. Newcomb, even though the reply was as meaningless as the question. He was beyond feeling better, and had been for a long time, just as he was beyond asking questions, and had been for an even longer time. The questions that were not pointless had been asked long ago, shortly after they arrived in New York and settled down in this house. They were still unanswered. "Yes," Dr. Newcomb said, "I feel much better."

"Then I guess I'll be pushing along," Robert said. He glanced at the clock as he untied the apron with which he protected, during his morning chores, his beautifully cut lounge suit. Because what they had left—the income from the few bonds, and the rent from the Cartwells or Hartwells—was at best no more than just enough, the suit represented an outrageous extravagance. But extravagance, like outrage and excess, was typical of Robert. "You'll be all right," He said. "Won't you?"

"Yes, of course," Dr. Newcomb said. He took the last sip of coffee, set down the cup, rose slowly from the table, and moved toward the leather armchair near the bow window in which he now spent his days. He reached the chair, as always, in twelve steps and, as always, Dr. Newcomb waited until he was seated before he uttered the second half of his reply. "I'll be all right."

"Grand," said Robert, taking down from the rack beside the door the Homburg and cane without which he never left the house. He set the hat on his head with care, cocking it at the rakish angle that, on any other man, would have looked preposterous. On Robert it looked far from preposterous. On Robert it looked almost terrifyingly perfect, the crowning touch to an ensemble and appearance that proclaimed the man of parts and virtue, in the prime of a usefully active life, at the peak of his considerable and admirably employed powers: everything Robert Newcomb was not, and had never been. "If there's anything you want," he said pleasantly, as he pulled open the door, "I'm sure it will keep until I get back."

"So am I," said Dr. Newcomb, without irony, stating no more than the simple fact. "There's nothing I want."

Except of course, he reflected as the door closed behind Robert, the replies to those unanswered questions. They rose now to the surface of Dr. Newcomb's mind, as they did every morning at this time, in a sort of lazy, purposeless

spiral, somewhat like dolphins rolling playfully in the wake of a
ship. Dr. Newcomb was aware that contemplating those questions again would not bring the answers, just as he knew that
fretting about the piece of unfinished business on the slate of his
life would not bring it out into the open, but the aimless
repetition was part of the day's ritual, and therefore important to
the maintenance of the fragile edifice of habit that was his life,
just as the playful rolling was probably, in some way, important
to the maintenance of a dolphin's health. Dr. Newcomb leaned
back, aware only faintly, because of the waning strength of his
hearing device, of the traffic noises from the street outside, and
he allowed the familiar questions to range about freely in his
mind.

Where did Robert go every day at this hour? What did he do
with himself, every day of the week except Saturday and Sunday, between eleven in the morning, when he had finished the
breakfast dishes, and five in the afternoon, when he came home
to prepare his father's dinner? He certainly did not go off in
pursuit of what used to be known, in Dr. Newcomb's youth, as
gainful employment. Although Robert had never had a career,
he had held, for different lengths of time, a series of unimportant
jobs in the various cities across the country in which the
Newcombs had lived. Most of these jobs had ended with the
troubles that had driven the Newcombs out of those cities.
During their first years in New York, Robert had worked as a
customers' man in several brokerage offices downtown and, as
recently as last year, as a section manager for a department store
on 34th Street. During each of these jobs Dr. Newcomb had,
almost literally, held his breath, but happily they had all
ended for no more significant reason, apparently, than Robert's
tendencies toward consuming half a dozen martinis at lunch and
holding inordinately lengthy telephone conversations with
bookies and women during business hours. There had been no
major scandal for ten years.

Nothing worse than a few bad checks, and several staggering
tailors' bills, which Dr. Newcomb had, of course, made good and

paid. No, on the whole, in view of what had happened in other cities, Dr. Newcomb had no cause for complaint about Robert's conduct in New York. Only puzzlement.

What went on in Robert's mind? How could a man, who had lived Robert's life for forty-odd years, live the life with which Robert had apparently been content for the last two or three? Had he succumbed gradually, perhaps even unconsciously, to the inflexible rule that everything in life, even the sowing of wild oats, ultimately palls? Was he, perhaps, more exhausted than he looked? Could Robert—for all his still dashing air, in spite of his still magnetic vigor—be, in his own way, finished? Was that why, during the last few months, even though the family's finances—which had deteriorated steadily since, almost five years ago, Dr. Newcomb had been forced, by his failing strength, to give up completely the practice of medicine—had reached the point where it had become necessary to rent the upper floors to the Cartwells or Hartwells, Robert had stopped even the pretense of looking for a job? Had the world become, as it had become for an entirely different reason to Dr. Newcomb, too much for Robert? Had he, like so many better as well as so many worse men before him, given up at last?

It was plain enough, from the odor of liquor on his breath when he came home at five o'clock, where Robert now spent at least part of his days. Was it possible that, trapped by the drab necessity for serving as cook, housemaid, and nurse to his aged father, Robert was reduced to stealing nothing more than the few hours from eleven to five every day for sitting in some bar on Madison or Lexington Avenue, nursing the one or two drinks that could be purchased by scrimping the already painfully scrimped family grocery fund that was entrusted to his care, lost in alcoholic reveries of the fiery, irresponsible, buccaneering days of his youth? Or was he merely marking time, like Dr. Newcomb himself, but for an entirely different reason, waiting for his father's death and the few thousand dollars that would then be his and with which he could launch one final assault on the world that Robert had never considered as anything but his legitimate prey?

The petulant rasp of the door buzzer, cutting through the unanswered questions tumbling idly through Dr. Newcomb's mind, brought the old man's nodding head erect. Surprised, he listened again. It *was* the buzzer.

For a long moment, as he listened to the persistent signal from the front door, Dr. Newcomb refused to believe it. He and Robert never had callers. Certainly not at this hour of the day. Yet the unmistakable sound, buzzing weakly in Dr. Newcomb's ear piece, making itself heard above the faint traffic noises from the street, indicated that somebody was at the door. Annoyed, and not a little concerned, because the movements involved were a deviation from his routine, Dr. Newcomb rose, made his way slowly across the room, and opened the front door.

"Good morning, sir," the man on the front step said with the brisk, cheery intimacy of the commercial caller. "I hope I haven't disturbed you?" He paused, and perhaps he realized, from the vacant expression on Dr. Newcomb's face, that he was either unwelcome or unknown. At any rate, the cheerful smile changed just a trifle, and his voice grew more hurried, as the man said, "Surely you remember me, sir? I'm Mr. Holley, of the Ear-O-Phonic Corporation? Manufacturers of your hearing aid?" Mr. Holley, as though summoning assistance, drew a batch of cards from his pocket, riffled them quickly, and extracted one. "Our records indicate that we serviced your Ear-O-Phonic Super De Luxe Senior exactly six months ago," he said, reading from the card. "According to this card, your Ear-O-Phonic is due for its semiannual checkup today." Mr. Holley's smile expanded to its former dimensions of confidence. "May I come in, sir?"

"Oh," Dr. Newcomb said and then, as the visitor's words sank in and conveyed their delayed message to his unprepared brain, he managed a smile of his own, and added, "Yes, of course. Come in. I didn't know for a moment who you—did you say Colley?"

"No, Holley," Mr. Holley said. "I can see from the fact that you didn't catch my name, sir, that your Ear-O-Phonic may need a new set of batteries, too." He lifted his small leather case from the front step and came in. "We like to keep our customers satisfied, sir. Now, if you'll just remove that little box from your pocket, and let me have a look at it, I'll have your Ear-O-Phonic working as good as new in a jiffy."

He did. Or as close to a jiffy as Dr. Newcomb's slow movements permitted. When the silver-plated box was back in Dr. Newcomb's pocket, he was not at all sure the improvement was welcome. The traffic noises from the street, a few minutes ago no more than a faintly lulling murmur, were now growling vigorously in Dr. Newcomb's ear; and Mr. Holley's briskly efficient voice, asking if Dr. Newcomb cared to pay the service charge now or would he prefer to be billed by mail, stabbed up through the corded wire to his eardrum like a handful of pebbles flung against a pane of glass.

"I'd rather pay now," Dr. Newcomb said. Since he had begun to understand that his relationship to the world in which people like Mr. Holley functioned had been reduced to that of a traveler waiting with packed bags for the signal to depart, Dr. Newcomb had developed an intense dislike for bills. His neat mind recoiled not only from the possibility that, if he did go, as he knew someday he must, at a moment's notice, he might leave an unpaid bill behind, but also from the certainty that, if he did, Robert would not bother to discharge the obligation. "If you'll wait just a moment," Dr. Newcomb said, "I'll get the cash."

He walked slowly across the sitting room, out into the kitchen, and across to the shelf, over the stove near the back door, on which was kept the empty tea canister that contained the household shopping money. Reaching up to take it down, Dr. Newcomb noticed that the back door, which led out to the rear entry and the service stairs that wound upward to the two top floors, was open. This was puzzling because, since those two top floors had been rented, the rear entry and the back stairs had been converted into a private entrance to the house for the Cartwells or Hartwells, and this kitchen door was always kept locked to insure their privacy. Robert, Dr. Newcomb reflected, must have forgotten to relock it after he opened the door to put

out the empty milk bottles that morning. Bringing the canister
down from the shelf, Dr. Newcomb stepped across to nudge the
kitchen door shut.

His elbow, touching the wood, seemed to set off an explosion
in his hearing device. Startled, and thrown off balance by the
gentle thrust of his elbow and his desire to keep the tea canister
from falling, Dr. Newcomb staggered forward, through the
open door and into the rear entry. His frail body, catching itself
against the newel post of the service stairs, seemed to set off
another explosion in his ear piece, and then Dr. Newcomb did
drop the canister.

It struck the rubber matting with a dull thud that, to the
normal ear, would have been no more than that, and the coins
and paper money escaped with a gentle tinkling and faint
slithering that, to the average listener, would have been not even
remotely disturbing. To Dr. Newcomb, however, whose hearing
device had just been tuned up and revitalized, the dull thud and
the gentle tinkling and the faint slithering were as the rattle of
musketry close at hand. The rattle was not loud enough, unfortunately, to drown out the rancorous voices hurtling down
from upstairs.

Clutching the newel post to support his trembling body, dazed
as much by the shock of what he was hearing as by the small but,
for his wasted frame, shattering exertion that had tumbled him
out here, Dr. Newcomb was aware only of a desperate desire to
escape before he learned more. Unfortunately, the pattern of
rigidly maintained small habits, of which his life had for so long
consisted, now held him in its relentless grasp. His body did not
know how to deal with something outside that routine. His body
could not deal with it swiftly, at any rate. By the time he was
able to get his muscles to respond to his terrified brain's plea for
help, Dr. Newcomb had heard it all. Or as much as he would
ever want to know.

Breathing with difficulty, his hands shaking crazily, the old
man managed to kneel down, claw the spilled money back into
the canister, make the agonizing return journey of half a dozen

steps to the kitchen, and close the back door. Shutting off the bitter voices from upstairs seemed to help. Temporarily, anyway. Dr. Newcomb gave himself a few moments during which, holding his body upright against the stove with both hands, his breath and his wildly beating heart began to settle down. When they had returned to an approximation of normalcy, he counted out the correct sum from the canister, decided against the effort involved in replacing it on the shelf, and went back into the sitting room.

"Thank you," Mr. Holley said as he took the money. "I couldn't help wondering—" His briskly efficient voice stopped, and a flicker of concern washed across the look of meaningless joviality on his face. "Are you all right, sir?"

"Yes," Dr. Newcomb managed to say. "I'm fine."

He wasn't, of course, and he was already aware, even in these first moments of shock, that he never again would be.

"I didn't mean to pry, sir, but it's just that, while you were out there, I thought I heard—" Mr. Holley's voice stopped again, and the look of meaningless joviality came back into his face. "Well, I guess I'll be running along." He picked up his small leather case and moved toward the front door. "Thank you very much," Mr. Holley said as he pulled the door open. "Goodbye for now, sir. I'm certain you'll find that your Ear-O-Phonic is now as good as new, and you won't have any trouble until I drop in again, six months from now, sir."

Dr. Newcomb, staring at the closed door, found himself wishing he could share that certainty. Then he realized that wishes were futile. Besides, his knees were still unsteady. He turned and, with the support provided by pieces of furniture along the way, he succeeded in reaching the leather chair near the bow window. Lowering himself into it, he became newly aware of the traffic noises from the street growling harshly in his head. Dr. Newcomb reached up and, with trembling fingers, drew the ivory receiving button from his ear.

At once the traffic noises went dead. So did all the sounds of

the world around him. All of them, that is, save one. The sound
of Mrs. Cartwell's voice, or perhaps it was Mrs. Hartwell, could
not be shut out. Not because the voice of Dr. Newcomb's tenant
was so strident that, from the upper floor, it could penetrate his
deafness. Or even because, of the two voices that had exploded
into his consciousness when Dr. Newcomb had stumbled out into
the rear entry a few moments ago, hers was the only one that had
been freighted with the unmistakable and unmanageable burden
of despair.

No. The sound of that voice, whether its owner was named
Cartwell or Hartwell, could not be shut out because it was more
than the voice of a human being caught in the harrowing
moment of certain knowledge that there is no hope. It was much
more than that. The despairing voice of the woman upstairs
provided the answers to those questions about Robert—how he
spent his time, what his plans were, whether the years in New
York had brought any changes in his character and way of
life—that had been circling idly through Dr. Newcomb's mind
for so long. And, strongest of all, that despairing voice from
upstairs was also an echo, the echo of another voice that Dr.
Newcomb had succeeded, for ten long years, in banishing from
his mind.

"Don't ask me," the owner of that other voice had said, ten
years ago in Cleveland, as she twisted away from him. "Please
don't ask me, Dr. Newcomb."

Dr. Newcomb, staring down at the sobbing figure of Cora
Ward, had wished with all the desperation of his then already
weary heart that he had the strength to comply with her
request.

"I've got to ask you," he had said. By hiring her as his nurse,
shortly after the Newcombs had come to Cleveland, he had
brought her into his house and thus, in effect, had placed her
within reach of the blow that he should have known, even if a
girl as simple as Cora Ward could not be expected to know,
would inevitably strike her. "I've got to ask you," Dr. Newcomb

had said again, staring down at the girl on the bed who had failed to come to work that morning and, a half hour ago, had summoned him by phone. "What is his name?"

"I can't tell you," Cora Ward had said, her voice muffled in the pillow she was gripping with both hands. "Please don't ask me, Dr. Newcomb," she said, and then the muffled voice broke in a whisper of shame. "Please help me."

"I can't help you until I know his name," Dr. Newcomb said. This was not true, of course, as Cora, who was an excellent nurse, should have been aware, but Dr. Newcomb had to know for reasons that went beyond the purely medical assistance she wanted. "Was it my son?" he said. She did not answer, but her body was suddenly stilled. "Was it Robert?" Dr. Newcomb said. There was a long moment of silence, and then the girl on the bed, her face averted, her body rigid, moved her head in a short, desperate nod. "When did it happen?" Dr. Newcomb asked. Cora did not answer, and he decided not to press her. Not on that point, anyway. His examination had revealed that she was at least three months pregnant. "Did you submit to him?" Dr. Newcomb asked. "Or did he attack you?" The eruption of sobs from the tortured girl seemed to bring Dr. Newcomb to his senses. What difference did it make? Robert's powers over women had been established long ago, in other cities, before the Newcombs came to Cleveland. "I'm sorry," Dr. Newcomb said quietly. "I shouldn't have asked that, but I must ask something else." He drew a deep breath, but the weariness that lay like a physical lump in his chest refused to be dislodged, and he said gently, "Cora, was it Robert's suggestion that you call me?"

There was another moment of silence, and then the averted head on the pillow moved again.

"He said to call you," Cora Ward said in a whisper. "He said you would take care of everything."

Robert had been right about that, Dr. Newcomb thought bitterly. He had always taken care of everything for Robert in the past. Why not now?

"I can take care of financial matters," Dr. Newcomb said in a heavy, plodding voice, as though each word had to be dredged up separately from the reservoirs of his despair. "I can see that you're properly cared for, Cora, and that the baby gets a decent start in life, but I can't do what you, or perhaps I should say Robert, want me to do. I can't perform the operation, Cora."

Her head came up, and the words escaped before she apparently understood the terrible indignity they implied.

"But he won't marry me," Cora Ward cried. "He said so, Dr. Newcomb. He said he never would. He said it was my own funeral. He said—"

Her voice stopped, and Dr. Newcomb leaned down to touch her shoulder.

"I know," he said and, of course, he did. He could imagine, at any rate, because he knew his son better and longer than Cora Ward did, what additional cruelties had issued through Robert's charming, irresistible, delicately savage smile. Robert was at his best with victims in their moments of hopeless realization of the extent to which they had been victimized. "I suppose it sounds cruel and insulting to say I'm sorry, Cora," Dr. Newcomb said. "I'm afraid, however, that it's all I can say. I'm more sorry than I've ever been in my life, but I can't perform the operation Robert assured you I would perform. No doctor in Cleveland, or in any other city, Cora, can perform that operation and remain an honorable member of his profession. You must forget what Robert said. If possible," Dr. Newcomb added with a touch of bitterness that he recognized even then was unforgivable, "I would suggest you forget Robert. Don't have anything more to do with him." Dr. Newcomb picked up his bag. "Mrs. Newcomb and I will see that you and the baby are both taken care of." He turned toward the door, so that this despairing girl would not see the despair that he knew was written clearly in his own face. "I'll talk to Mrs. Newcomb at once about making the necessary arrangements, and I'll come over to see you again in the morning." He turned back and, with an effort, he managed a reassuring smile. "Let's try to make the best of it," Dr. Newcomb said. "That's all that can be done, I'm afraid."

It wasn't, and perhaps he should have suspected it wouldn't be, but there had been nothing to warn him. Always, in the past, there had been boundaries. There was just enough of the coward in Robert to prevent him from going too far. Or perhaps, instead of cowardice, it was an instinctive knowledge of the point where the world, which could be duped with such ease, would finally turn and strike back. Whatever the reason, it had not prepared Dr. Newcomb for the call that reached him that night while he was at dinner, or for what he found when he got to Cora Ward's apartment twenty minutes later. It certainly did not prepare him for what, an hour after that, Robert said behind the locked doors of the surgery in their own house.

"So what?" Robert said. "Can you prove it?"

Of all the terrible and confused emotions that assailed the father as he stared at his only son, the one that stood out clearest seemed so irrelevant as to be almost frivolous: Dr. Newcomb was astonished. For several moments he could not speak.

"Yes," he said finally, trying with all the strength in his seventy-year-old body to control his voice, to keep it level and direct. "I think I can prove it."

"Can you?" Robert said. "How?"

"I'm a doctor," Dr. Newcomb said. "I was summoned to the bedside of a girl who, until this morning, was my office nurse and, since this afternoon, has been my patient. She told me this afternoon that you are the father of her unborn child. Do you deny it?"

"I'm not denying anything, Father," Robert said through his puzzlingly attractive smile. "I'm listening to your attempt to prove something."

"An hour ago, when I reached Cora Ward's apartment, I found that she had swallowed the contents of this bottle." Dr. Newcomb's hand shook as he held up the small vial. "She told me you had called on her this afternoon, shortly after I left her. Cora said that, when she reported I had refused to perform an abortion, you gave her this bottle." Dr. Newcomb could feel his voice begin to rise. He made one last effort to control it. He knew that, at all costs, he must keep his head. "Cora told me you said this medicine would achieve results similar to those of an abortion." The last effort at control failed. Dr. Newcomb's voice was close to hysteria. "Do you deny that?"

"I don't see that a denial is necessary," Robert said pleasantly. "And wouldn't it be wiser to lower your voice?" he added with a casual glance toward the locked door. "We don't want to drag Mother in on this, do we?"

"Don't you understand what I'm saying?" Dr. Newcomb said. "You knew what was in this bottle when you brought it to her. Cora Ward told me you poured it out for her. She told me you held the glass to her lips. Don't you understand what I'm saying?" His voice seemed to disintegrate into a whisper of revulsion and horror. "You killed her."

"I wish you'd stick to the point," Robert said with gentle mockery. "You said you can *prove* I killed her, father, but I don't see that you're doing that at all. Nobody saw me go in or come out of Cora's apartment. Even if anybody did, certainly nobody saw me give her that bottle, or pour out its contents for her. You're merely repeating the statements of a hysterical girl, uttered while she was dying from a dose of poison that she could very easily have administered to herself. I understand it's quite common for girls in her, ah, condition to do that." Robert paused, and the mocking smile etched itself more deeply into his handsome face. "You seem to be shocked, Father," he said. "I hate to shock you even more but, since you're the one who raised that ugly word, proof, I don't see how I can avoid it. The contents of that bottle cannot even be traced in the normal way, as I believe it sometimes is when poorly advised people try to make more of these unfortunate cases than is necessary. The contents of that bottle were not purchased in a drug store, or from any other source that can be readily traced. As a matter of fact, Father, I wouldn't be at all surprised to learn that the contents of that bottle came from your own shelves." Robert nodded, almost absently, toward the glass case full of medicines against the far wall. "If you don't mind my saying so, Father,"

Robert said, "I think you're flirting with a highly unprofitable activity, namely, making a mountain out of a molehill. Artificially created mountains have a nasty habit of toppling. When they do, innocent bystanders sometimes get hurt. You and I are not the only ones to be considered, you know. There's Mother." Robert paused and, for several moments, he seemed to be absorbed by the problem of whether or not his fingernails needed cutting. Then he looked up. "If I were you, Father," he said, "I would forget ugly words such as murder and proof. If I were you, Father, I would limit myself to writing that death certificate as suicide by poison, and then I'd sign it." Robert paused again. "Actually, if you can calm down long enough to consider all the implications," he said coolly, "I think you'll see that it's the most sensible thing to do, I'm sure."

In the final analysis, that was the core of the horror, the most shocking aspect of something that went beyond shock: Robert *had* been sure. Not only of himself, but of his father as well.

The blood that had been so much thicker than water that it had for years, in effect if not in principle, condoned theft and forgery had led, as inexorably as death itself, to condoning murder. No man, except Robert, of course, could live with that. No woman, either.

Dr. Newcomb did not doubt that this was why his wife, who knew so much about Robert that she no longer needed specific detail to know more, followed Cora Ward to the grave a week later. Neither did Dr. Newcomb doubt now that this was why the last ten years—since he and Robert, tied at last to each other by bonds more inflexible than blood, had fled from Cleveland and settled in New York—had been for the father, if not for the son, no more than a long, and until this moment successful, effort to forget.

Now that he knew the effort had been wasted, Dr. Newcomb regretted bitterly the success with which his mind had for so long shut out what he should have known from the very beginning would some day have to be faced. The ten-year delay had gained him nothing. On the contrary. It had lost him everything, including the one thing that could give purpose to the long agony of hoarding fragments of energy, of keeping himself alive over the protests of every fibre of his exhausted body and heart.

If he had done at the time what every instinct of decency and justice demanded, if he had turned the murderer, who happened to be his son, over to the Cleveland police, he would have been spared a decade of trying to blot out the knowledge that he was an accomplice, ten years of sitting about with packed bags, waiting for his mind to disgorge the piece of unfinished business on the slate of his life so that he could wipe it clean and, at last, go. More than that, if he had done his duty ten years ago in Cleveland, he would have been spared now in New York, when his mind had been shocked by what he had overheard in the rear entry into relinquishing its secret, the bitter knowledge that he was as far from the longed for moment of departure as he had ever been. He was powerless to wipe the slate clean. All he could do was sound a warning.

Wearily, like a laborer who gathers himself at the end of a long day, not for the welcome journey home, but for another and more difficult job that must be finished at once, Dr. Newcomb rose from the leather chair. Painfully, because each movement was a deviation from the rigid schedule by which he had for so long kept himself alive, he crossed the sitting room, went through the kitchen, opened the door into the rear entry, and started the exhausting climb up the back stairs.

When he reached the landing of the third floor, he felt dizzy and his whole body was quivering. Dr. Newcomb leaned against the jamb to rest, and he closed his eyes to thrust away the dizziness. When he opened them, a few moments later, Dr. Newcomb's glance was caught by a business card tacked to the center panel of the door. On it, in neatly engraved letters, was printed: "James C. Hartwell, Real Estate and Insurance." In the lower right-hand corner, in smaller letters, appeared the address of Mr. Hartwell's office and, in the upper left-hand corner, was printed his telephone number.

Dr. Newcomb, still breathing hard, smiled bitterly. Now that it did not matter, he knew that his tenants, whom he had never seen because Robert had arranged the details of the lease, were named Hartwell and not Cartwell. And now that it was too late, because at least one result of Dr. Newcomb's warning would be that his tenants would move, he knew what Mr. Hartwell did for a living.

Dr. Newcomb raised his hand and knocked on the door. There was no answer. He knocked again. Still no answer. Dr. Newcomb could feel his forehead crease with puzzlement. It seemed to him that no more than a few minutes had gone by since he had overheard the angry voices from behind this door while he was trying to extract from the tea canister downstairs the money with which he had paid Mr. Holley for servicing his Ear-O-Phonic. Raising his hand to knock again, Dr. Newcomb's glance stopped on his wrist watch.

He saw that it was almost three o'clock. He must have fallen asleep in the leather chair after Mr. Holley left. Aware now of a sense of urgency that could not be dismissed, struggling with the mounting fear that it might be too late for warnings, Dr. Newcomb brought his knuckles down hard on the door. The sharp blow, which stung his entire arm, made no sound. Then Dr. Newcomb saw why. The ivory receiving button of his hearing device was dangling from its corded wire on his chest. He had forgotten to replace it after he woke up.

With trembling fingers that seemed to get in their own way, he managed to set the ivory button back in his ear. At once, even though he still heard nothing, Dr. Newcomb's other senses seemed to grow more acute. A sharp, pungent odor, assailing his nostrils abruptly, caused his already hammering heart to leap with terror. He smelled gas.

"Robert!" he shouted as he clutched the door knob and twisted. "Robert, don't—!"

The door, moving inward, tumbled Dr. Newcomb forward into what had once been a spare bedroom and was now the Hartwell's living room. The air, which seemed delicately fogged, stung Dr. Newcomb's eyes and then caught in his throat.

Gasping, he staggered across the room, through the open door that led into the small kitchen the Hartwells had installed between their living room and bedroom. Holding his breath, Dr. Newcomb found the knobs of the gas range and turned them all off.

Then, as swiftly as his aged body would carry him, he moved from window to window, through the bedroom, the kitchen, and back into the living room, throwing them all open. Holding onto the sash of the last one, and leaning as far out as he dared, he sucked in deep gulps of fresh air.

After a few moments, he turned back. Not until then did he notice that Robert was not in the room, and that Mrs. Hartwell, her face hidden in the upholstery, was lying on the couch against the far wall.

Completely unaware that he was exerting himself to an extent that had for a long time been beyond the powers of his wasted body, Dr. Newcomb drove himself across the room, dropped to his knees beside the couch, and took Mrs. Hartwell's wrist. Her pulse, even though irregular, was still strong. From this, as well as from the fact that the air in the room was already almost completely cleared, Dr. Newcomb concluded that the gas had not been turned on hours ago, when he fell asleep downstairs. It must have been done a short time before he knocked on the door. Feeling, as he stood up, the twinge in his knees, and the lurch of his heart, Dr. Newcomb's brain sounded a warning automatically, but he disregarded it.

He forced himself back to the door, down the stairs, and into his own bedroom. From the closet, he drew the small bag he had not used for five years. Halfway up the stairs, dragging the bag rather than carrying it, Dr. Newcomb's brain sounded another warning. He shook his head irritably, as though he were dismissing a meddlesome bystander, and set his teeth for the balance of the long climb.

When he came back into the Hartwell living room, Dr. Newcomb saw that Mrs. Hartwell had stirred in his absence. Either that, or he had moved her, without knowing he was doing it, when he took her pulse. However it had happened, he was glad Mrs. Hartwell was now lying on her back. Dr. Newcomb doubted, as he set the bag on the floor beside the couch, opened it, and began to assemble the pieces of the hypodermic syringe, that he would have been capable now, after his three trips up and down the stairs, of turning even a body so slender as Mrs. Hartwell's. He even doubted, until the moment he withdrew the needle from the flesh of her forearm, that he would be capable of completing the injection.

Having completed it, he had no doubts at all about his ability to cross the room to a chair. That was out of the question. He was finished. The best he could do, as the emptied hypodermic dropped from his shaking fingers, was tip the small black bag over on its side, to form a crude stool, and ease himself onto it. Then, squatting beside the couch, Dr. Newcomb folded his arms on his knees, and he dropped his head forward on his folded arms.

He was beyond further thought, as he was beyond further physical movement. He was aware only, through the closeness of his own laboring heartbeats, of the overwhelming wish that he might die, now, before the terrifying process of thought could begin again. And, at the same time, he was aware of the futility of the wish. He could not die. He had not yet earned the right to do so. The slate of his life, on which his failure had been scrawled ten years ago in Cleveland, was still waiting to be wiped clean.

"What happened?"

The weakly uttered syllables brought Dr. Newcomb's head up. Mrs. Hartwell, he saw, was trying to say more. Staring at the young woman on the couch, watching her pretty face struggle with the effects of the drug that was fighting off the gas she had inhaled, Dr. Newcomb was only mildly surprised to discover that Mrs. Hartwell, whom he had never seen during the months that she and her husband had been his tenants, bore a distinct resemblance to Cora Ward. Why not, Dr. Newcomb thought dully. Robert's taste in women, as in everything else, had been established long ago. And, in a truth so searing that it was scarcely endurable, it was even just that this young woman, whom Dr. Newcomb had saved from death, should look so much like that other girl who, ten years ago, because of his carelessness, had died and, because of his cowardice, was still unavenged.

"What happened?" Mrs. Hartwell managed to say again.

"I don't know, but I can guess," Dr. Newcomb said quietly. "Unintentionally, several hours ago, I overheard an argument between you and my son Robert. I gathered, even though you have my assurance that I did not want to, that Robert had—" Dr. Newcomb paused, not so much out of delicacy as because he found it physically difficult to speak, and in the pause Mrs. Hartwell turned away, burying her face in the upholstery of the couch as, ten years ago, Cora Ward had hidden her shame in the twisted pillow of her bed. "I gathered that, some weeks or perhaps months ago, my son Robert told you he loved you and that, if you divorced your husband, he would marry you. Unless I am wrong—"

"He lied to me!" As the desperate words erupted between them, Dr. Newcomb was reminded again of Cora Ward. Like Cora Ward, Mrs. Hartwell had allowed the words to escape before she apparently understood the terrible indignity they implied. "He said he never promised. This morning, when he came up, he said he'd never promised to marry me."

"I take it, then, that I'm not wrong," Dr. Newcomb said wearily. "Mrs. Hartwell, you are pregnant?"

The slender body on the couch began to shake.

"Yes," Mrs. Hartwell said in a whisper. "When I told him, he said it was my own funeral."

"So you tried to arrange your funeral for him?" Dr. Newcomb said, nodding slowly, almost with relief, as though a piece of important evidence, in the presentation of the final case against his son, had at last been uncovered. He should have known that it was not Robert who had closed all these windows and turned on the gas. He should have known that Robert would not consider that necessary. Except for Cora Ward, who had been more simple than most, Robert's victims could usually be counted upon to complete their own destruction. "What did you think you would accomplish, aside from simplifying things for my son Robert, by turning on the gas?"

Mrs. Hartwell's face reappeared as she rolled her head weakly away from the upholstery.

"What else could I do?" she said in a hopeless whisper. "Jim would kill him."

Dr. Newcomb's first reaction was completely impersonal. As though he were examining a patient for symptoms, his mind merely recorded the odd fact that Mrs. Hartwell's hopeless whisper had sent a stab of hope through his own exhausted body. Then, when the implications of that stab of hope burst through his exhaustion, when they rose in his mind so that he could see them clearly, Dr. Newcomb had another reaction. This one was intensely personal. For the second time in his long life, Dr. Newcomb knew he was afraid. Again, as had happened ten years ago in Cleveland, Dr. Newcomb wanted only to turn and run, to flee from those implications.

"Jim is your husband?" he said carefully, making an effort to stand and face what he had once been unable to face. Mrs. Hartwell nodded. Dr. Newcomb said, even more carefully, because he knew he was beyond running, "You have not told your husband?"

"Not yet," she said. "If you hadn't come up here, if you hadn't saved my life," she added, and her voice broke in a final sob of despair and bitterness, "I never would have had to tell him."

With a sigh that caused his already spent body to tremble like a plucked violin string, Dr. Newcomb pushed himself up from his improvised stool. The lesson that should have been learned ten years ago in Cleveland could not be disregarded again. He was too old to be afraid. He had too little time left to fool himself with the vain hope that he would ever again be granted another chance. There was only one certainty: this was the last chance he would ever get.

"Perhaps it won't be necessary for you to tell your husband," Dr. Newcomb said. The flicker of hope, racing swiftly across Mrs. Hartwell's pale face only to be erased at once by the answering flicker of disbelief, reminded Dr. Newcomb that he had more than his fear to contend with. He had no certainty that his spent body, held together for so long by nothing more than a precariously balanced pattern of small habits, would hold together long enough for the last demand he would ever make on it. "At any rate," he said and he succeeded, as he had once succeeded for Cora Ward, in summoning for the despairing girl on the couch a reassuring smile, "I'll see what I can do."

This, for a younger man, would have been very little. For Dr. Newcomb, whose life had been over ten years ago, it was almost too much. Almost, but not quite. Perhaps the most difficult part was waiting, while the watch on his wrist ticked away the few fragments of time he had left, to make sure the drug he had injected to counteract the gas would continue its healing work by putting Mrs. Hartwell to sleep. By ten minutes after four, it did.

Certain at last that she was, for several hours, anyway, incapable of interference by making another attempt on her life, Dr. Newcomb moved away from the couch. At the door, where he turned for a last glance into this room he would never see again, he saw lying on the floor the small black bag and the spilled pieces of the hypodermic syringe. Eighty years of habitual neatness made him hesitate. Then he remembered that the effort involved in walking back across the room, picking up the syringe, and replacing it in the bag, would have to be deducted from the already inadequate store of energy he had left for the important things that had to be done. Besides, he would never again need that black bag or its contents.

Dr. Newcomb stepped out of the room, pulled the door shut, reached up, and tore away the business card tacked to the center panel. Holding the card firmly in one hand, as though he were afraid that, if he put it into his pocket, he might never have the strength to take it out again, and supporting himself on the bannister with his other hand, Dr. Newcomb started his last descent on the back stairs of this house in which for so long he had been prepared, but unable, to die.

In his own bedroom, which he reached with a sense of triumph that transcended the frantic beating of his heart, he went at once to the desk between the windows facing Fifth Avenue. A minute or two later, supporting himself with both hands, he paused to consider a problem he had not counted on. Getting the paper and the fountain pen and the envelope out of the desk drawer had proved so difficult, that Dr. Newcomb suddenly doubted the wisdom of sitting down. He might not be able to get up again. Since this had to be avoided, Dr. Newcomb solved the problem by carrying the paper and the pen and the envelope across to his bureau. It was an excellent solution.

By writing the letter standing up, leaning on the bureau top to steady his body as well as his pen, he not only saved the by now pitifully few, but intensely crucial, fragments of strength that would have been squandered in the effort to rise from the desk; he succeeded also in writing a more legible document.

When it was finished, Dr. Newcomb read the few sentences twice, folded the sheet carefully, inserted it in the envelope, sealed the flap, wrote "To Whom It May Concern" across the front, and put the envelope into his breast pocket. Then and only then, and still holding the card he had torn from the door upstairs, Dr. Newcomb lowered himself to the bed in a sitting posture. The numbness that spread at once through the lower half of his body proved beyond further doubt how wise he had been to avoid sitting down at the desk. Dr. Newcomb knew he would never again be able to stand up.

It was all he could do to lift the receiver from the phone on the table beside the bed and dial the number on the card in his hand. A girl answered.

"Good afternoon," she said. "James C. Hartwell, Insurance and Real Estate."

"Mr. Hartwell, please," Dr. Newcomb said. "It's very urgent."

"Who is this calling, please?"

"Dr. Newcomb. I am Mr. Hartwell's landlord."

"I'm sorry, sir," the girl said. "I don't know if I can disturb—"

"Please," Dr. Newcomb said. "It's terribly urgent."

The sound of his voice must have carried more conviction than his words.

"Oh," the girl said, in a sort of gasp, and then, "Just a moment, please."

Not much more than that could have elapsed before James Hartwell's voice replaced hers on the wire, but the gap of silence, to a man of eighty who could feel the last drops of his strength flowing away like water from a ruptured pipe, seemed an eternity.

"Dr. Newcomb?" James Hartwell said, and then, sharply, "Is anything wrong?"

The sound of his voice was reassuring. Until he heard it, Dr. Newcomb's entire plan, the whole edifice to which he had committed these last minutes of his long life, had been built on nothing more than the ray of hope that had shot through him after Mrs. Hartwell had said that, if she told her husband about Robert, Mr. Hartwell would kill him. James Hartwell sounded like the sort of man who would certainly make the attempt. For Dr. Newcomb's purpose, that would be enough. There was no time to do, or even hope for, more.

"I'm afraid something is terribly wrong," Dr. Newcomb said. "How long would it take you to get here from your office?"

"Why, if I grabbed a cab, I could get there in ten minutes, I guess," James Hartwell said, and he added, in a tone of irritability so needlessly savage that it brought a small smile of satisfaction to Dr. Newcomb's face, "What the hell is this all about?"

Before answering, Dr. Newcomb shifted the phone, moving it heavily from his ear so he could look at his wrist watch. It showed a quarter to five. Three or four minutes would be enough to explain the few facts that needed explanation. This meant that, if Robert came home, as he always did, promptly at five, and if James Hartwell's estimate about how long it would take him to get here was correct, both men would arrive at the same time, which was fine. James Hartwell might even arrive a minute or two earlier. His first instinct would be to rush upstairs, via his own private entrance, to look at his wife, and that would be, for Dr. Newcomb's purpose, better than fine. It would be perfect. Dr. Newcomb shifted the phone laboriously back to his ear.

"This is about your wife," he said. "I don't think I can talk very long, Mr. Hartwell, so will you listen carefully, please?"

He did. At any rate, by the time the phone went dead at the other end, Dr. Newcomb knew James Hartwell had heard all that was necessary.

Leaning forward, in an effort to replace the phone on the hook, Dr. Newcomb realized he would not make it. He didn't. The phone dropped from his already limp hand. As the clattering thud, amplified by the freshly tuned-up hearing device, stabbed up into his ear, Dr. Newcomb's sense of neatness gave him a moment of uneasiness. He had always hated to leave things lying about. Then he realized something else. He would never be able to speak into that phone again, anyway.

Twisting his body in one final effort, Dr. Newcomb succeeded in getting himself into position. With a sigh of relief, rather than exhaustion, he allowed himself to fall back on the bed. The effect was so immediate that, for a moment, he could scarcely believe it. He had been waiting so long, all packed and ready to depart at a moment's notice, that he found it difficult to accept the fact that he had at last been able to send for the taxi that would carry him down to the train.

Then the recollections of Michigan, which belonged to the mornings, and not to this part of the day at all, began to crowd in on him, and he knew it was all right. Because now those recollections, which were part of the time of his own innocence, long before Robert was born, were not a distraction. Now they were welcome. The ceaseless task of policing the precariously balanced pattern of small habits, to which his life had been for so long reduced, was over. There could be no more distractions. There could be only rest.

In the act of giving himself up to it, Dr. Newcomb's neat mind insisted first on a final check of all the details. He touched the breast pocket in which the police would find the hand-written letter requesting that James Hartwell's wronged wife be presented with Dr. Newcomb's few thousand dollars in bonds as well as the deed to this house. The police, or the law, might not honor that request, but nobody could fail to honor Dr. Newcomb's intention, which was to provide for Mrs. Hartwell, and Robert's illegitimate child, as well as the legal fees Mrs. Hartwell would probably want to pay to defend her husband in the trial that would be the inevitable result of what was about to happen under this roof. Holding the recollections of Michigan away for another moment, Dr. Newcomb retraced the telephone conversation in which he had just explained to her husband the criminal attack on Mrs. Hartwell and the reason why he would find her drugged. That would take care of Robert. And then, to make sure he had straight in his mind the reason for what he had just done, Dr. Newcomb allowed himself once again to relive the moment of horror, now ten years old, in which Robert had made his father an accomplice to murder. That took care of everything. The unfinished business of his embarrassingly long life was finished at last.

Reaching up to remove for the final time the ivory receiving button from his ear, Dr. Newcomb's faltering hand stopped dead. The freshly serviced hearing device had caught clearly the sound of a taxi door slamming shut in the street outside. The harsh sound stabbed up, through the corded wire, through the pervading sweetness of the recollections of Michigan, like an accusation. James Hartwell was on time. A moment later, as he heard Hartwell's heavy footsteps thundering up the back stairs, Dr. Newcomb tried to turn over on his side, as though to squirm away from the accusation. He could not move.

Stunned, as much by the complete failure of his body, which was of course expected, as by the accusation, which was totally unexpected, Dr. Newcomb did not hear Robert's key in the lock of the front door. What he did hear, however, was the series of smaller sounds that followed: Robert's footsteps, as he moved across the sitting room below, to the hat rack beside the kitchen door; the faint slap as Robert hung away his fedora; the slightly sharper rattle as Robert set his cane in the corner of the room; the creak of the kitchen floor as Robert walked out to swathe himself in the apron with which he always protected his fault-lessly cut lounge suit while preparing his father's dinner.

The tuned-up Ear-O-Phonic, which Mr. Holley had said was now capable of functioning as well as when it was new, had done better than that. In this moment of death, it had brought an abstraction to vivid life.

Those small sounds below were not being made by a criminal brought at last to the bar of justice. Those small sounds— cherished without knowledge as well as beyond reason, valued unawares as well as above justice, more beloved than any yardsticks of decency or reason or duty could assess—were the bits and pieces of a human life. And that human life, for all its dark hair going gray at the temples, in spite of its features and figure blunted by a lifetime of excess, was still Dr. Newcomb's own flesh and blood.

Dissolute and warped, heartless and despicable, that flesh and blood were still to the father what they could never be to judge and jury: an infant whose guileless eyes held no hint of crime, a child whose innocent smile gave no promise of debauchery, a boy of fifteen whose effortless grace had once made him the best dancer in northern Michigan.

What did it matter that Robert's life and Robert's character

belied his appearance? What did it matter that Robert had never
been entitled to look like that? What did anything matter in the
face of the overwhelming fact that Robert, whom Dr. Newcomb
had just delivered into the hands of vengeance and retribution,
was his own son?

Who was he to question the unknown factors in the equation
of life? By what right had he assumed the powers of executioner?
Was he not, by his failure to rear an honorable son, actually
responsible for shielding his son from, rather than committing
him to, the consequences of that failure?

There was still time. Robert was only a boy. A mere child,
really. It was never too late. Perhaps, if he had another chance, if
they *both* had another chance—

"Robert," Dr. Newcomb cried weakly, struggling to rise
from the bed, to make audible what sounded so brutally like
nothing more than a whimpering plea for forgiveness. And then,
as the heavy footsteps began their furious, purposeful descent—
down the back stairs, from the floor above, in which decency and
justice had been outraged; toward the kitchen below, where
indecency and injustice busied themselves unsuspectingly over
the preparations for a meal that would never be eaten—Dr.
Newcomb succeeded in raising himself on one elbow. "Robert!"
he cried again, sending out, on the last shreds of breath left in
his shattered body, the scream of warning that came not from
the brain, which provides the answers, but from the heart, which
asks no questions, "*Robert, watch out!*"

It seemed odd to Dr. Newcomb that, even though he had not
removed the ivory receiving button from his ear, he did not hear
his own scream.

# JEROME WEIDMAN

## by JEROME WEIDMAN

**Line of work:** Man of letters. My wife says that's an outmoded phrase, and that nobody knows what I mean, but *I* know what I mean, and in the long run, if you work with words, that's usually enough.

**But what would you really rather do?** I think I'd like to be a doctor, but I'm not sure, because all the doctors I admire either want to be writers or have become writers, so it seems silly to want to go back and spend years doing something else only to end up doing what you started doing when you were eighteen.

**Mainspring:** To avoid slipping back into the poverty of my youth, which means to me not only earning enough to buy for my family better cuts of meat than my parents were able to buy for me, but turning out enough good work so that, after I'm gone, somebody will know I've been here. The worst thing about poverty is its degrading anonymity; they don't scrawl "Kilroy Was Here" on walls that have looked down on people who never got a chance to do anything more than be cold and hungry.

**Most paradoxical quality:** I hate all competitive sports, but work hard at calisthenics every morning, even in hotel rooms far away from home, and as a result I can do forty push-ups without getting winded.

**Chinks in the armor:** A total—and to me surprising—lack of intelligence in personal relationships; I like people who like me, no matter how terrible they are, and I dislike people who dislike me, even if they spend all their money and time on putting out stale bread for birds in the winter and invent a certain cure for the common cold.

**Boiling point:** Reviewers who describe what is wrong with the book they feel you *should* have written, rather than the one you *have* written.

A SELF-PORTRAIT

**Personal panacea:** Daydreams, in which I always have a full head of thick black hair; the work of Joseph Conrad, in which I never fail after a while to recapture the feeling that if you'll only go back and try again it will work; the company of six people who shall be nameless here because at least three of them are members of my immediate family; and, when all else fails, a tot of rum.

**Persisting superstitions:** That if I lose the bronze medal I won at the age of thirteen in an oratorical contest about the Constitution sponsored by *The New York Times*—which I have carried, the medal, not the *Times*, as a good luck piece ever since—I will die before I complete the various projects I have outlined in my notebooks.

**The terrible temptation:** To write "thank-you notes" to favorable reviewers. I resist the temptation, not because this would in-inevitably lead to writing notes to unfavorable reviewers, which is of course a sure sign of certifiable insanity, but because I would not want to insult a man or woman who clearly thinks well of me by thanking him or her for having done no more than his or her duty.

**Unfounded fears:** That I will become fat. My doctor assures me that there isn't a chance of this happening, but I know better: I don't much care whether the food set before me is magnificent or just plain good, so long as there is enough of it, and there always seems to be too much, even when I am dieting, which is constantly.

**Secret satisfaction:** Now that my books are being translated into Hebrew, my mother and father, both in their eighties and both only barely on speaking and not at all on reading terms with English, are finally able to find out what their oldest son has been up to these last thirty-one years.

*First published in* Esquire *magazine*
© *1962 by Esquire, Inc.*